I dedicate this book to my son Brian,
gone so suddenly, but always in my thoughts.
Jan 4, 1983 – Mar 27, 2009

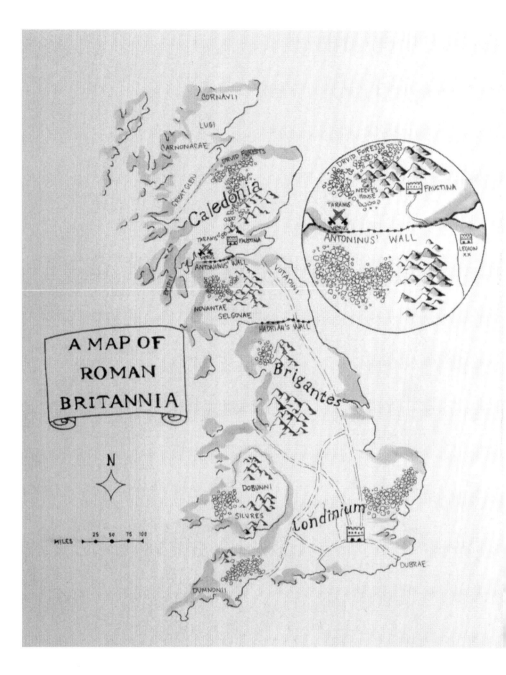

I dedicate this book to my son Brian,
gone so suddenly, but always in my thoughts.
Jan 4, 1983 – Mar 27, 2009

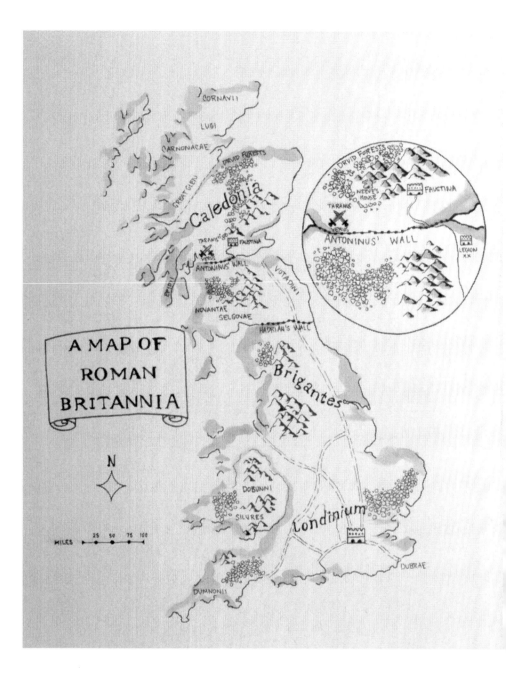

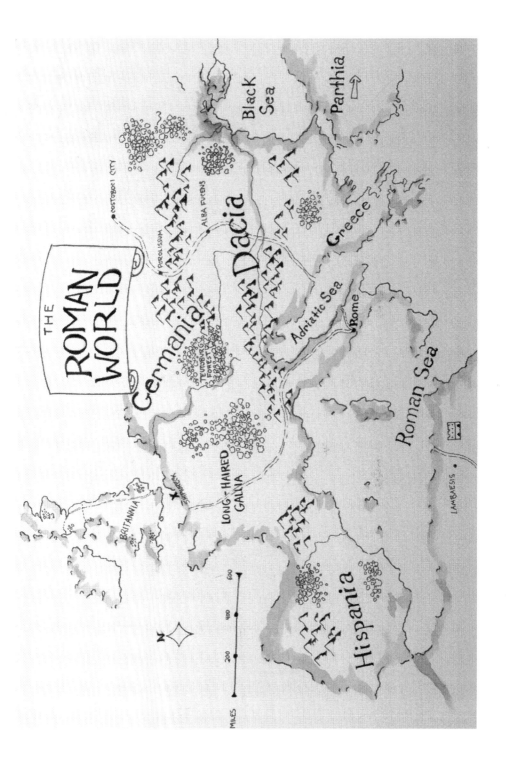

TABLE OF CONTENTS

THE BEGINNING

1

Neeve lay rigidly on her cot, listening to the night wind.

She had seen a man's face at her bedroom window, or had dreamt it, she couldn't be sure. But something had wakened her and now she was straining to hear every sound embedded in the wind.

She eyed the hole on the opposite wall, a rough-cut square that served as a window, another one of those tasks she had meant to complete, but now with no bars, it gaped open, large enough for a man to squeeze through. The night breeze came in tiny gusts from the opening, chilling her exposed arms and raising goose bumps on her skin. A woman alone, she knew, made easy prey for the increasing number of drifters and soldiers that wandered the highlands, and if someone had been looking in her window, he would certainly know that she was alone. She pulled the covers around her neck and tried desperately to calm her pounding heart.

A twig snapped outside.

Neeve bolted forward in bed, throwing off her woolen blanket.

Breathing! She could hear breathing.

Her fingers gripped the straw mattress like claws. Her face tightened. If only her brother, Taranis, were in his roundhouse, she might have cried out for help, but there would be no help tonight. Taranis had taken his warriors into the patchy forests south of the Caledonian villages in hopes of rooting out Roman stragglers that hid along the rivers. No, Taranis was far away and she was alone on the compound.

There it was again.

She cocked her head. He was outside her door now. Breathing …
no, not breathing, harsher than that, more like a wheezing sound, like
someone gasping for air. The thought that it could be a Roman soldier
terrified her.

In southern Britannia the Romans had stripped the island of
metals—minerals, timber, anything of value—ripping long gashes in
the land to get at its tin and copper deposits, which they promptly
shipped back to their Empire. Lately, they had been pushing north
into Caledonian territory, building their massive turf barrier across
the island. Antoninus' Wall, they called it, named after their emperor.
The Romans especially disliked the Caledonians because Caledonians
fought back, refusing to be Empire lackeys. Neeve had no doubt that
if a Roman were to get into her roundhouse, he would cheerfully
leave her dead on the floor.

She shifted her eyes between the door and the open window,
straining to hear beyond the sounds of the night. It was almost as if
she had imagined the harsh breathing outside her door because all she
could hear now were the incessant chirping of crickets and a lone frog
croaking in the distance. Then, abruptly, came the beating of heavy
wings. Something had startled the two gray owls behind her
roundhouse. She had seen the huge birds in a stand of red firs before
dark, and their presence gave her comfort, as if they were giant
sentries watching.

Neeve swung her legs over the cot and moved softly across the
pinewood planks toward her clothes hanging on the wall pegs—and
her large Celtic knife. The pole was still across the door. She knew it
would be, but seeing it eased her mind.

The sensible thing would be to remain in her house until the
danger passed. But that meant leaving her horse untended, a
handsome roan she dearly loved, and the only thing of value she
owned besides her house. If she cowered from protecting what was
hers, she would soon have nothing. She pulled off her sleeping tunic
and hooked it on one of the wall pegs. Then, quietly, she slipped into
her leather trousers and boots, donned her darkest tunic to blend in
with the night, and strapped on her knives, the heavier one at her hip,

the smaller secreted in her boot above her right ankle. If someone was out there, she wanted to be ready.

Neeve moved back to the door and peered out the slit, surveying the circular compound with its stone walls and low gates. No one in view. Was he behind the house? Or maybe looking in the window again? She shot a glance at the crude opening in the wall, but saw nobody. She wished she had constructed the heavy shutters she'd planned, or at least had covered the window, but with the pressures of war, window dressing was low priority. She paused before opening the door, rested her forehead on the frame, and took several breaths to calm herself.

"Nemetona," she whispered to the Celtic goddess of war, "I need you. Hear me now. Give me strength." She wrapped her hand around the two-foot hickory club she kept by the door for occasions like this, and lifted the wooden bar.

Outside, the crisp night air bit at her nostrils, astringent with the scent of pine. Thin clouds churned across the moon and seemed at odds with the gentle wind on the compound. Neeve hugged the outer wall of her roundhouse as she crept toward the back where the giant owls had been perched. More than once she heard stirrings at the base of her stone foundation, and she made a mental note to deal with the burrowing vermin the first chance she got. Before long she had reached the paddock where her horse ran free during the daylight hours. She paused and swept her eyes across the moonlit enclosure, and then inspected the red firs that crowded its far edge until she was certain no one was hiding in the shadows.

A soft shuddering caught her attention.

The barn! She squinted at the mud plastered lean-to she generously called a barn. Something, or someone, had startled her horse inside the structure, and Neeve was determined to find out what was in there. She glanced around the paddock area again, then climbed over the fence and headed for the barn. When she arrived the oversized doors stood ajar. She was certain she had secured them before dark. Her horse shuddered again and bumped the side of its stall. Neeve fingered the club, set her jaw, and started toward the doors.

Then stopped.

No, she told herself. Better not to blunder into the darkened enclosure. Thieves, even murderous Roman soldiers, could be in the shed with the roan, and a chill ran up her spine. She circled back across the compound to make certain no one else was hiding nearby. Satisfied, she crept to the side of the barn and blended into the shadows.

Neeve could hear movement inside the barn, one man, his boots shuffling on the straw-covered floor, searching for something. The saddle? she wondered. She had slung it over the central beam that stretched the width of the barn. It was high and out of the way, but visible, even in the dim light.

Clack!

Neeve jerked her head up, listening.

The man had stumbled over something on the floor. She strained to hear. Now he was picking himself up and thumping back into the stall. Only one man, she was certain of it. She could hear him making soothing sounds to the roan as he led her out. It sounded like the Roman tongue, but she couldn't be sure.

The doors opened, this time fully. Neeve stepped back and waited. A flash of tunic told her the man was a Roman officer. She swallowed hard and debated whether she should attack. He looked young and strong, more than a match for her, even with the element of surprise. He was having trouble bringing the horse through the doors, and stumbled once or twice. Neeve withdrew to the shadows again and watched. She wondered whether he might be wounded. For some reason he had slung a rope around the roan's neck, rather than using the leather reins hooked on the stall. And he hadn't taken the saddle.

He stumbled again, wincing in pain. Definitely injured.

She rubbed the smooth hickory shaft, and waited.

He led the roan a few halting steps beyond the doors.

Her body tensed.

He turned toward the horse, whispering in its ear, exposing his back.

She burst forward, the club whirling in her hand, the hickory crashing into the side of his head. He darted sideways, flinging up his arms, deflecting most of the blow. For a wounded man, he moved with incredible speed. Neeve caught her balance and struck again, this time jamming the club end into his ribs. He spun around, his outstretched hands grasping for her, but finding only air. He ripped out his sword and dropped to a crouch. She jumped back to maintain her distance.

"The gods are with me," Neeve murmured.

"A woman," he said.

She said nothing.

"Just want horse," he said in garbled Celtic. "I go now." His head twisted back and forth, as if he were looking for others on the compound.

"I'm not alone," Neeve said in the Roman tongue. "Others will be here soon."

"A good reason to leave," he said, switching to Latin, grimacing. His speech revealed an educated man of Rome. He reached behind him, feeling for the roan, then caught hold of the rope and tugged. "I'm taking the horse," he said. "Back away and you won't be hurt." His eyes blinked heavily as he stared off oddly over her shoulder.

"You seem injured," she said, studying him, but keeping her club ready.

He passed his sword through the air. "Believe me, I feel fine. Now go back to your cottage. I only want the horse."

Neeve circled softly to his right.

"I have Roman coin," he added.

She continued to circle.

He blinked and squinted his eyes in the wrong direction.

"You can't see," Neeve said.

"I only want the horse," he repeated.

"Blind."

"Not blind. Blurred vision. But I can see you well enough." He licked his lips and blinked his eyes again, trying to focus. "Think about your situation," he said. "Your first attack failed because I heard you coming." He stretched out his sword, rotating it in a threatening way. "If you try again—"

Neeve smashed the sword out of his hand. The horse reared up and bolted away. Without the animal at his back he seemed to lose his bearings. His head turned woodenly and he squinted in every direction. "Couldn't fool you," he said with a wry smile.

"Quiet! I will take no chances with you, Tribune." Neeve knew well enough not to be distracted by an enemy's pretense of affability. Blind or not, one mistake and she could be at his mercy, and then, how would he act?

He raised his open palms to indicate that he intended her no harm. Then speaking in a gentle voice he said, "Listen to me—"

"No, you listen to me," Neeve shouted. "If you want to live, you will take out your dagger with the tips of your fingers and drop it to the ground. Then you will back slowly into the barn and lie on the floor."

Without a word he did as she said.

She kept her eyes on him as she pushed straw into a brazier, still glowing faintly with the day's coals. "Not one move," she said as she gathered several lamps to the center of the barn. She lit them with stalks of straw and held a single lamp up to his face. She could see fresh burn marks around his eyes.

"Someone put a hot sword to your eyes?" she asked.

"Britannia, a fine province," he said.

"We learned it from you Romans."

"I don't doubt it."

She threw him a length of rope. "Tie your feet together," she said, "tightly."

He did so.

She threw another rope at him. "Tie one end around your wrist and lie back."

When he had finished, she approached him from behind and poked her knife into his neck. "Caledonian knives are quite sharp," she said. "If you even flinch …."

He pressed his hands together and thrust them upward, knowing what she wanted. Neeve wrapped the rope in tight loops around his wrists.

"You can sit up," she said.

"A good job," he said, pulling against the ropes. "What do you intend to do with me?"

"I haven't decided," she said.

"Celts who turn in Roman officers get rewards," he said hopefully. "Legion XX south of the Wall is less than two days' journey."

"Is that where you were heading?"

"They have a large surgery and a special eye salve made from Phrygian powder, called collyrium. Medicine from the gods, I've heard." He paused. "How did you know I was a tribune?"

"The equestrian stripe on your tunic," she said.

"A Celt who knows the Roman tongue and rankings," he said, rubbing his eyes with bound hands. "You were a non-Roman worker in a fort?"

"Faustina," she said, "before we destroyed it." Then, as an afterthought she said, "Faustina's prefect was named Vectis Trebellius. Ever heard of him?"

He shrugged. "An odd name, Vectis. What is his *Cognomen*?"

"Quadratus," she said. "His name was … is Vectis Trebellius Quadratus." She swallowed hard. She realized she had voiced her hidden fear, that Vectis was dead, killed by Celtic warriors before he could reach the southern Roman lands. "Well?" she demanded, irritated at her mistake.

"Vectis Trebellius Quadratus," he said, mulling over the name.

Neeve wished she hadn't asked. It was the first time she had used his name in a year. Even now she found it hard to believe she had married a Roman. She fingered her Roman wedding ring and tried to be patient.

"There was a man …." The tribune paused, thinking. "Yes, named *Gaius* Trebellius Quadratus. He was one of Rome's premier soldiers … emperors used him to quell uprisings in almost every province … senior Centurion of the First Cohort. He died two years ago in Rome. My family attended his funeral."

Neeve closed her eyes and asked, "Did you ever hear about the son, Vectis? If he survived the Celtic uprising?" she added to clarify her question.

Even in the lamplight Neeve could see the quizzical look on his face. He was wondering, she knew, what a Caledonian had to do with a Roman prefect. She sometimes asked herself the same question.

"You say the younger Trebellius was stationed at Outpost Faustina." He spoke slowly, as if he were processing the information. "Do you know whether he—"

Pounding hooves interrupted his question.

Neeve cracked the door and looked toward the stone gates. "Caledonian warriors," she said. "Are they searching for you?"

"For all Romans," he said flatly.

A group of Caledonian warriors were tying their horses to the entrance gate, and behind them followed several other horses, laden with the bodies of their owners. She asked: "Have you skirmished with Caledonian forces?"

He refused to answer.

"Have you killed Caledonians tonight?" she said in raised voice.

He remained mute.

Neeve glanced back at the Caledonians, who had drawn their long Celtic swords and fanned out across the compound. She recognized several of the warriors, saw their determined looks, and the bloodlust in their eyes.

She flung open the door and strode back to the tribune. She jerked him to his feet and half dragged him to the door as he struggled to maintain his balance.

"Over here!" she called, and threw the Roman to the ground.

Neeve headed back into the barn and returned with an iron lamp. The flickering yellow light cast eerie shadows on the ground, making it seem as if the whole paddock were moving. "Take your Roman," she said to the approaching Caledonian warriors. They gathered around the fallen Roman, swords drawn, as if he could harm them trussed up like a chicken.

"He tried to steal my horse," Neeve said, booting him in the stomach. "He's an important man, a military tribune in the Roman army." She kicked him again.

The men nodded their approval. They knew she was Taranis's sister, which engendered enormous respect.

"I told you he was an officer," said a warrior with a shaggy beard.

Neeve could smell his sour breath from ten feet away.

"Hard to tell when they all run like rabbits," said the man beside him.

Neeve asked, "Who is the unit commander?"

"I am." A squat man with broken teeth stepped forward.

"What's the status of this man?"

"A runaway. He escaped from our camp."

"Explain."

"We were patrolling the highlands when we came across three Romans sneaking toward the Wall. We chased them into Teuton's Notch."

"Continue."

He shrugged. "When the trail narrowed they thought they had entered a blank canyon so they turned back to fight. We killed one … and the other … well, we killed him too."

"We chopped him up," the bearded warrior hooted, "slowly so he would remember not to trespass on Caledonian land."

The men laughed, their eyes glistening in the lamplight.

"And this one?" Neeve asked, poking him with her hickory stick.

"We started to burn him, but he escaped," one of the men volunteered.

"Escaped?"

The men began to talk all at once.

"We tied him good," said one.

"Just his hands," said another.

"Yeah, just his hands," agreed the first. "But we tied him good."

The unit commander summarized. "We tied his hands to a post, and Chulainn burned his eyes so he couldn't see. Then we cooked a lamb Drogglu stole from a farm near the fork … we were bored so we thought we might have some sport, you know, make a night of it."

"But he loosed himself," Neeve said.

"Right, he loosed himself … somehow."

"You didn't remove his sword or dagger?" Neeve asked quietly.

The commander had a painful look on his face. "As I said, we burned his eyes so we thought …" He stopped, as if the silence were an explanation in itself.

Neeve gestured for him to continue.

"He killed three of our men and fled on horseback," the commander said bluntly. "We found the horse—"

Neeve stared at the commander.

He swallowed, knowing a reprimand was coming. "I thought we tied him good, but …"

Neeve put one foot forward. "Look at him!" she screamed. "He's stone blind! How could a blind man kill even one Caledonian warrior?"

The commander sucked his broken teeth.

"Taranis has given clear orders," she said, "slit the enemies' throats. No games. No delays. You slit their throats!" She scowled at them. "Three Caledonians are dead because of your stupidity. And when Taranis learns that you let this Roman pig prowl my compound …." She left the words hanging to drive home the point.

The commander mopped his brow. "This is the first time we have ever … ah … well, I'm the unit commander and I … I accept responsibility for everything that went wrong tonight." He glanced around at the other men and said in a defeated tone, "Take the Roman some distance away and dispatch him in the woods."

"No, that is far too dangerous," Neeve said sarcastically. "He might murder one of you on the way." She glanced around the compound, thinking. Her brother had asked her to find a way into Roman lands to scout troop movements. The tribune was a gift from the gods. She turned to the men and said, "I've decided. Dump him in my cart and leave. He may prove useful after all." She turned her back on them and busied herself with the lamp.

2

Gaius Balbinus arrived at the Palatine Hill dressed in his finest toga. He had instructed the fuller to bleach the expensive wool until it shone like the sun and then to rub it with chalk, to whiten it like no other. He trembled with excitement. A man of insignificant station, he had gained a private audience with Emperor Antoninus Pius at his palace on the Palatine Hill. Balbinus knew of senior senators who had yet to secure anything other than group audiences.

He descended from his carriage, the sun burning hot, perspiration dripping off his plump face. Where were the promised September winds? He glowered, cursing the priests he had paid for favorable conditions. "Might as well be stuck in the month of Augustus," he mumbled. He sucked in his stomach, tucking his right arm across his body and lifting his head to maintain an erect posture, the way the regal-looking Senator Titus Severus always did when he walked the length of the forum. But Balbinus knew that his own enormous appetite for the good things of life denied him any such pretensions. He was short and heavy, a man not given to clever repartee, and no amount of grooming and schooling would change that much. Still, Balbinus told himself, Severus and others had gained their prestige through patrician connections and family alliances, while he was a rising lion rapidly devouring the edges of their crumbling power.

Balbinus gestured to a servant who patted dry his neck and forehead, and lightly powdered his heated face. He accepted a soft cotton cloth and slipped it into his toga, and then with his best smile, he approached four scarlet-clad Praetorians that guarded the marble steps leading to the domes of the Imperial palace.

"May the gods grant good fortune to the emperor," his aide said with a flourish. Then he added, "This is Gaius Balbinus, friend of the emperor. He is scheduled at the sixth hour for an audience with Emperor Antoninus Pius."

The Praetorians were not impressed. They eyed Balbinus with his knot of servants and consulted with a further Praetorian, the centurion of the gate, who checked his name against a list on a rectangular parchment. Balbinus felt uneasy around the Guard, as the Praetorians were called. They were somber-looking men who rarely spoke and never smiled. Their sole mission was to protect the emperor. They stood a head taller than the ordinary soldier, and their bodies looked as if they had been sculpted from Egyptian granite. As the centurion of the gate approached, Balbinus smoothed the folds in his toga. He nodded toward the huge Praetorian as if the two of them shared a common understanding that everything was in order. His gesture was greeted with a stony look.

"Not them," the Praetorian said, jamming a thick finger at Balbinus's servants.

"Oh, certainly," Balbinus said agreeably. "They can wait here. That is perfectly acceptable." His voice trailed off.

"Not here," the Praetorian said. "With the other carriages at the Circus Maximus."

"Perfectly acceptable," Balbinus repeated, glancing in the direction of the chariot racing stadium. He bit his lip. How stupid he must sound! What was the matter with him? He should have known that for security reasons, the Praetorians would not want a group of men hanging about the entrance to Antoninus' palace. And his servile demeanor. Like a footman! He was a prosperous man now, he told himself. Would Senator Severus tiptoe around a common soldier, Praetorian or not? He knew the answer, and he remembered the advice of his mistress, Calpurnia: "Act like a senator, and soon you will be a senator."

Balbinus swallowed hard, turned to the Praetorian, and said in an important voice, "When I conclude my audience with the emperor, I will send down one of his aides to ready my carriage." With that, he dismissed his aides to the stables at the Circus Maximus.

Balbinus climbed the marble stairs alone. He felt naked without aides fluttering around him. They should have granted him one servant at least. One servant would hardly pose a threat to the emperor. If the Praetorians had their way, no one would ever be permitted on the Palatine Hill.

He sniffed. They obviously had no idea who he was. He was a significant man in Rome these days. A man of rising stature. How far he had come! Two years ago he occupied the humble position of a senator's aide. But now ... now he was a wealthy man. Yes, still a plebeian, but a plebeian who enjoyed the patrician's life. Yet he wanted more. He wanted respect. He longed to be granted a higher station in Rome's class-conscious society. Was that a wrongful ambition? Who in Rome had been as generous with good fortune as he?

Of course, the distinctions between patrician and plebeian had largely disappeared in the last hundred years. Anyone, plebeian or not, could rise in rank. But you could feel the patrician arrogance everywhere, the knowing nods, the turn of the eye. He ground his teeth. As if they had done anything to obtain their positions. Well, today he had an audience with Antoninus Pius, Emperor of Rome, and if he presented his case well, things might change.

Balbinus was breathing heavily when he reached the top of the stairs. The gods did not form the hills of Rome with corpulent men in mind. He mopped the rivulets of water off his face as he identified himself to another group of Praetorians. An Imperial aide appeared and bade him recline on a couch under a canopy of tangled grape vines.

Large goblets of wine, cold from cellars deep in the palace, quenched his thirst, and did much to calm his spirit. He inhaled the sweet winds that blew softly across the heights. Luminous white clouds floated lazily over the outlying countryside, and in the distance toward the east he marveled at the hazy chain of mountains that stretched endlessly along the horizon. Below, at his feet, lay the stately buildings of the Old Forum, gilded roofs, gleaming marble columns, colorful porticoes, obelisks and temples, some with incense swirling heavenward, others graced with sacred gardens. Beyond the forum lay the magnificent Capitoline Hill, home of Rome's chief deity, Jupiter the Supreme.

Balbinus swished the chilled wine in his mouth, closed his eyes, and prayed that the emperor might grant him a place in the eternal drama that was Rome.

"Forgive the intrusion," a voice said.

Balbinus turned his head dreamily, trying to focus on the person standing over him. "Oh!" he cried, and he popped to his feet when he saw Emperor Antoninus. "I was … admiring the view …."

"Ah, yes, it is truly beautiful," Antoninus said, motioning toward the skies. "Except for the Isle of Rhodes, you cannot find a more brilliant blue than here in Rome."

"Yes, yes, I quite agree," Balbinus said awkwardly. He was embarrassed to have the emperor find him sprawled on a couch. He glanced around at the Praetorians who had stationed themselves within easy reach. "I apologize for …."

"No need," he said. "I had intended for us to talk in the Imperial library, but that room is still occupied by earlier guests." He gave a patient smile. "Senators, if you must know. They undoubtedly have not yet noticed my absence."

Balbinus laughed, too loud. He reached for his goblet, then withdrew his hand, thinking it inappropriate to drink in front of the emperor.

"Would you care for something?" Antoninus asked. "Melon, perhaps? Or honeyed peacock?"

Balbinus declined as graciously as he could. He knew it was not a true offer, but the obligation of civilized conversation. "I thank you for seeing me," he said. "I know you have a demanding schedule."

"It is demanding," Antoninus agreed.

Balbinus nodded and tried to ease into his prepared remarks. "I am greatly pained in spirit," he said, "over the plight of orphans in our cities. I know your late wife, the divine Faustina—forgive me if the mentioning of her name brings you sorrow, it brings great joy to many, I readily assure you—the divine Faustina as you know had an abiding desire to assist the desolate orphans on our Roman peninsula." He paused and took a breath. "I too am grieved at the enduring sad conditions of orphan children, though not as deeply, I am sure, as was the divine Faustina. So I asked myself how I might honor her magnificent name ... and as if the gods had opened the heavens to so humble a servant as me, I knew what I must do."

The emperor seemed interested.

"With your permission, I would be honored to donate two million sesterces to the orphan treasuries, in the name of the divine Faustina, of course." He shifted on his feet and waited for the emperor to respond.

Antoninus thanked Balbinus and said, "When I was very young, my father died and I was left alone. I'm not sure if you knew that."

"No, I did not," Balbinus said, thrilled to share in such a personal conversation. "It must have been difficult."

"It was. Oh, my grandfathers saw to my education, and I wanted for nothing. But most people," he said, gesturing toward the tiny red-tiled roofs in the distance, "live in wretched conditions. They scrape for even the base things of life, and when a father dies, they starve in our so-called orphanages. I am trying to change that ... and your generosity will contribute greatly to these efforts."

Balbinus gushed his thanks for the kind words.

"Now, how may I help you?"

"Oh, please," Balbinus protested. "I have no other thought but for the orphans of our land."

"Acts of mercy should not go unrewarded."

Balbinus dropped his eyes in respect for the emperor. "I do have one small item that would be of interest to me," he said quietly and, he hoped, with the right measure of humility, "if only that I might use my new authority to support your wise policies and decisions."

"Speak it."

Balbinus hesitated, not wanting to appear self-serving or excessively bold. "I would like, if it pleased you, to be elevated to the rank of senator ... if it pleased you."

Antoninus rubbed his neatly cropped beard. "You have asked the one thing I cannot give," he said. "You must know that the Senate guards its autonomy the way the Sacred Vestals guard their virginity.

And in large measure I agree. You will remember the chaos at the close of the divine Hadrian's reign. Senators fearing for their lives, plots being hatched. It was not a healthy time for the Empire. I determined not to meddle in Senate affairs, but to give them true autonomy ... and I think it not boastful to say I have honored my conviction."

"All Rome venerates you for your wisdom," Balbinus said. "'Emperor Antoninus the Pius,' they say, with adoration on their lips, and rightly so." He paused, searching for another way to present his petition. "I was hoping ... that so beloved an emperor ... as you indisputably are ... that your person might consider interceding with the Senate on my behalf so that undecided members might know the Imperial will."

"Your concerns find a sympathetic ear," Antoninus said, "but at this time I will decline to use my influence. You might consider seeking an office on the board of magistrates. That is the standard way of moving toward the Senate."

"Under the circumstance, a prudent suggestion," Balbinus said, hiding his disappointment. "You have been extraordinarily gracious—" He stopped. A group of senators suddenly appeared under the arched walkways near the Temple of Victory. They had concluded their business in the Augustan Library and were now enjoying the breathtaking scenery afforded by the Palatine.

Emperor Antoninus was indeed beloved, but like all emperors, he was also feared. When he invited senators to meet in his Imperial library, it was not out of kindness. He was following a tradition long established by earlier emperors: encourage the Senate to meet on the Palatine Hill where they could be watched. Their very presence spoke eloquently to Balbinus about the power of the mild-mannered man he was addressing.

"A select group," Antoninus said, gesturing toward the senators in the distance. "They are discussing the Atilius Titianus affair." He was referring to the senator who had tried to overthrow the emperor two years earlier.

Balbinus flushed. He had been the senior aide to Atilius during that time, but when he perceived Atilius's plot would soon be uncovered, he warned the emperor of his master's evil. As a reward for his service to the Imperial realm Balbinus had been given a quarter of Atilius's vast holdings. He had become a rich man. But in the process he had earned the mistrust of the ever-suspicious Senator Titus Severus. Balbinus glanced toward the senators, with Severus in the center, and asked: "Have they come to any conclusions?"

"They suspect that Atilius Titianus was not alone in the plot, that other officials might have been involved."

"Indeed." Balbinus furrowed his brow. "Are they just now investigating that sordid period? It has been over two years."

"Yes, but I learned long ago to be patient. Truth will triumph. It just takes time." His face darkened. "Atilius Titianus made me look foolish in Britannia province. I have always said the Empire is large enough—in its present state it takes a year to travel from one end to the other. I wanted to avoid the adventuresome paths of my predecessors that buried us in debt." He sighed. "But I was persuaded—my vanity, you see—to authorize a small expansion in Britannia. I thought if we drove the troublemakers north of Hadrian's Wall and built another Wall, peace would follow. But that didn't happen, did it?"

Balbinus thought it wiser to remain silent.

"Everyone in the Empire began calling my turf barrier Antoninus' Wall—and I confess, I rather liked it. I was even vain enough to name Britannia's most distant outpost after my beautiful Faustina." He laughed bitterly. "And now the Celts have burned it and most of the Wall forts to ashes."

"Calamitous," Balbinus murmured. "Simply calamitous."

"Indeed. It's not enough that we have a blood-drinking cult here in Rome—the secret followers of Chrestus—now we have to deal with a crazed warrior in Britannia who calls himself the blood god. He drinks from the veins of Roman women and children … or so the rumor goes." The emperor shook his head. "It never ends!"

"Overwhelming," Balbinus cooed.

"Atilius Titianus did his work well … stirred up the Celts, spread rumors in Rome that I was incompetent … and I certainly looked the part when our soldiers scuttled south to Hadrian's Wall for protection.

But, truth will triumph. Senator Severus has found some interesting correspondence from Atilius."

"Correspondence?" Balbinus tried to remain calm.

"Yes, and he might find more," Antoninus said with satisfaction in his voice.

Balbinus's mind was flying in a hundred directions, none of them comforting. Be rational, he told himself. How likely was it Severus would find the exact letters that implicated him in the plot?

The emperor looked directly at Balbinus. "I have encouraged Severus to dig deeper." He shifted his eyes to the distant mountains. "I might be called Pius, but when I ferret out these people ...."

Beads of perspiration broke out on Balbinus's forehead, and he fumbled for the cotton cloth in his toga.

3

The sun had not yet risen when Neeve hitched her horse to the cart and headed south. She was following the old arterial road built by the bloody Roman general, Agricola, in his conquest of Britannia a century earlier. How often had she seen Roman soldiers, somber-faced, inspecting every inch of their road? But they were gone now, driven south by valiant Celtic tribes who refused to bend their knees. All that remained were the burned out ruins of what had once been their outposts above the Wall.

Neeve covered the tribune's eyes with a length of cloth, remembering how the surgeons at Outpost Faustina had wrapped injured eyes to protect them from the sun. The Roman slept mostly, waking only once to relieve himself. Neeve freed his legs and told him he could run if he wanted, but that he might do better staying with her. He seemed to agree because he returned without a word.

During the long hours Neeve thought about Vectis and wondered if he had made it safely to his Roman comrades. Hearing someone speak his name aroused deep feelings, feelings she had tried so hard to bury. The last time she saw Vectis he was riding south with his wounded soldiers, leaving behind him the ruins of his northerly outpost, Fort Faustina. Neeve had been torn between her people and the man she loved. In the end she chose her people, but not without anguish, and not without begging her brother, Taranis, to spare Vectis's life. But now she worried that with so many Celtic tribes roaming the northern territories, Vectis might never have made it to the southern Roman legions.

Neeve moved swiftly on the abandoned Roman road, stopping only to rest and water her horse. Now and then she glanced back at the sleeping tribune. She had wrapped him in a woolen blanket for warmth, hoping to prevent his feverish condition from worsening. The last thing she wanted was to arrive at a Roman checkpoint with a dead Roman officer in her cart.

When night came, Neeve removed the wrap from the tribune's eyes, bound his feet and released his hands. He blinked a few times and stared off into the distance, still unable to see. She built a fire on a rock-strewn moor and cooked porridge fortified with dried pork. Then she poured him a cup of heated Celtic beer and sat down.

"How much Roman coin do you have?" she asked.

He coughed as he sipped his hot beer. His skin had turned gray. In a scratchy voice he said, "Where are you taking me?"

"Answer my questions," she said, "or I'll leave you here. Lots of Caledonians looking for Romans in these hills."

"Everything I have is in my belt."

"Dig it out." She passed him her empty cup. When he returned it she dumped the coins into her hand and inspected them by the fire. "Five sesterces and a denarius! This is all you have?"

"Maybe I could—"

"You want me to take you to Legion XX—two days' journey—for a handful of miserable coins!"

"Is that where we're going?"

"That was my plan, but when I look at this ...." She shook her head and threw the coins back into the cup.

"I can get more," he said.

"How much more?"

"Ten, maybe twenty gold aurei."

"I want a hundred," she said.

"A hundred!" Even sick he found her brazen manner appalling. "A Praetorian in Rome receives only forty a year," he said.

Neeve swallowed several spoons of porridge, satisfied with her performance. No doubt the tribune saw her as another greedy Celt, interested only in gold. "You are from Rome itself," she said slowly, "an officer and landowner ... probably from an important family ... a hundred gold aurei or I leave you. Make your choice."

"A hundred it is."

"Swear by the gods of Rome."

"I so swear," he said.

Neeve smiled to herself. She had the perfect cover to travel into Roman territory to the feared Fort Trimontium itself, home of Legion XX. There she would be able to assess Roman strength and reinforcements, exactly what Taranis needed.

But, in truth, she had other motives for saving the tribune. He was her last enduring thread to Vectis. The tribune had lived in Rome and had known about Vectis's family. Perhaps, if she spared this Roman officer, the gods might see her compassionate spirit and spare her beloved. "Oh, make it so," she whispered to the spirits.

That night icy winds swept across the moor. Neeve used her knife to slash off the branches of a dozen heather bushes, and then laid them out for the tribune to sleep on. She did the same for herself. "It's warmer on the ground than in the cart," she said as she bound his hands to the cart wheel. She took the blanket and covered him with it, and then lay close to the open fire, wrapped in her long cloak.

"There was only one blanket in the cart," he said.

"Sleep."

"Why do you give it to me?"

"I am Caledonian," she said, "not a soft Roman."

"That's no answer."

"You are no good to me dead," she said. "Sleep."

Neeve tossed fitfully that night. Fragments of dreams came to her about her brother Taranis lying dead on the ground, or was it Vectis? She didn't know. Gusts of wind surged across the unprotected moor, chilling her to the bone and shredding her tiny fire. More than once she tucked her cloak between her knees, only to wake with it flapping behind her shivering body. She had collected as much wood as she could find, but by morning the modest fire had been reduced to ash.

She woke with a jolt. Something was wrong. She had fallen into a deep sleep and was having trouble clearing her mind of the night's imaginings. A heavy wool blanket fell off her body as she sat up. She whipped her head around. The tribune! He lay quietly on his back with the cloth still around his eyes. But no blanket! She jerked to her feet and ripped out her large Celtic knife.

"I am not dying," he said, stretching and extending his legs in front of his body. He was showing her he had no bindings.

She swept her eyes across the camp and spotted the ropes hooked neatly on a heather bush. "Stay where you are!" she ordered, and then realized how ridiculous she sounded. He could have easily killed her during the night.

"I heard your teeth chattering," he said. "Even a soft Roman can take a few hours of cold."

She slid her knife silently back into its sheath. It was enough he mocked her, but she didn't want him to know she had been standing there, knife at the ready.

"Want to bind me? I did try to steal your horse back at your compound." He proffered his wrists. Even sick he couldn't resist making a light taunt.

"We'll cross into Roman lands soon," she said, ignoring him. She wasn't about to give him satisfaction by asking how he had removed his bindings. He obviously had a skill; he had escaped his earlier captors, and now her. "I intended to cut your ropes this morning anyway. You saved me the trouble."

An hour later Neeve caught sight of Antoninus' Wall. From a distance it looked as it had since she was a girl, a huge dark barrier dominating the horizon from one side of the island to the other. It was immense—a thirteen foot turf wall topped with a heavy timber palisade, which extended another ten feet in the air. At regular intervals, the Wall had huge turf forts with imposing gates and watchtowers, and the main buildings were roofed in red tiles.

The road suddenly passed through a wooded area of spruce and tamarack, and the Wall disappeared. Neeve could see the Romans had been hard at work, clearing off fifty feet of trees from each side of the road. They were a cautious people, and did not like surprises.

The Wall appeared again, and Neeve could make out the broken gates, burnt buildings and ruined palisades. The smell of scorched timber grew stronger as they approached the derelict fort.   Once inside, Neeve stared in disbelief at the tangled mess on the center parade ground where the Romans had burned their catapults, bedding, foods, shrines, weapons, and everything else of value.   The rows of shops, from ropemakers to tanners, had been burned completely, as had the bakery, stables, and soldiers' quarters.   The Romans had left in a hurry, but they had taken time to deny their enemies any prize.

South of the Wall Neeve began to encounter Roman scouts and patrols.   The tribune's efforts during the night to remove his bonds seemed to have tired him and he lay curled under his blanket much of the way.   Neeve explained to the patrols that she was a non-Roman worker, a mapmaker from the destroyed Outpost Faustina, north of Antoninus' Wall.   She was taking the blind tribune to Fort Trimontium's surgery with hopes they might restore his sight.   At each checkpoint the patrols treated her well and she felt comfortable quizzing them about the danger from nearby Brigantes and Selgovae tribes.   She was assured that Legion XX had been augmented and was now at full strength.   She also discovered to her horror that all three legions in Britannia had been fully reinforced from the German provinces, and that Legions II and VI were only days from the Antonine Wall.

By late afternoon Neeve spotted the three jutting peaks that had given Fort Trimontium its name, Camp of the Three Hills. To the east a river flowed past the fort, twisting its way through a chaotic collection of buildings that housed the native workers, or camp followers, as they were called. On closer inspection, Neeve could see that Celtic tribes had managed to burn part of the fort, and soldiers were working feverishly to repair the damaged ramparts of the guardian of the north.

"You were a mapmaker at Outpost Faustina?" the tribune asked, pushing himself into a sitting position.

Neeve could see that he was doing better.   "I have a gift for drawing," she replied. "The fort's prefect hired me to draw maps of sectors north of the Wall."

"Prefect Vectis Trebellius," he said.

"Yes," she said, "Prefect Vectis Trebellius. Actually, I can draw most anything, people, scenery, images of the gods." She wanted to change the subject.

"Perhaps you could draw my image someday."

"I don't expect I will ever see you again," she said.

"Even if we did meet," he said, touching his fingers to the wraps covering his eyes, "you would be the only one to know it."

"I suppose that's true."

He fell silent. Neeve glanced at the wraps and felt impelled to say, "Don't worry, your eyesight will return. I sense the gods favor you."

"I am waiting for their favor," he said with a half smile.

At the fort gates, Neeve talked to the centurion, explaining her mission, and asking for a letter of safe passage for her return to the Wall. Then, with directions to the surgery, she entered the imposing bastion of the north, Fort Trimontium. When they arrived at the large rectangular building, Neeve helped the tribune out of the cart and into a reception area. Two aides placed him on a cot and assured him a surgeon would attend him shortly.

"Mapmaker," he said. "Come close so I won't be overheard."

Neeve bent down to his cot and touched his arm to let him know she was near.

"You were right," he said, "I have great wealth, and you shall receive your hundred gold aurei before you leave."

She murmured her thanks.

"I know what you're doing," he said.

Neeve swallowed.

"You demand gold, but when we arrive you ask nothing about the reward, as if you didn't expect me to keep my word. You quiz soldiers about legion strength and deployment, and then extract a safe conduct back to the rebellious tribes."

Neeve drew her hand away.

"You have nothing to fear from me," he said. "With or without your information, the Celtic tribes are doomed. The uprising of this so-called chieftain, Taranis, succeeded briefly against Rome's auxiliary troops because of surprise and ill-preparedness, but now the legions are coming." He paused. "Do you understand? These are three full legions, complete with cavalry, auxiliary and navy. Britannia has never seen the likes of it since the legions of Agricola seventy-five years ago."

The name of the bloody Agricola spoken in the same breath as her brother, Taranis, sent a shiver down Neeve's spine.

"Don't go back," he said.

She stared at his bandaged face.

"Are you still here?"

"Yes," she said.

"You want to gather information? Then listen to me. The emperor has lost his Wall, and he is determined to restore every inch of it. His best general from the German frontier, Julius Verus, will be running this campaign. Verus is brilliant, and ruthless. And now he has reinforced legions under his command. Hardened soldiers from the wars in Germania. Within three months the Celts will be decimated. Do not go back."

"Why are you telling me this?"

"You saved my life," he said.

"And now I cannot save my own. I must go back."

"Mapmaker ... you need to believe me."

She returned her hand to his arm. "Goodbye," she said.

PART ONE:
An Uncertain Trumpet

4

The wind whined along the riverbank, bowing the reeds and twisting the clumps of sedge grass that grew at the water's edge. Taranis pulled a heavy woolen cloak across his body and edged his horse to the rim of the steep valley. He turned to Cronn, his second in command, and asked, "Where exactly will they cross?"

"Farther west, where the waters are troubled," Cronn said, pointing. "It is the only passable ford for miles."

Taranis ran his eyes the length of the river and nodded. Cronn had been with him for over ten years, and had yet to fail a task. He had fought many battles and had been wounded many times, the most visible, a jagged scar, running the length of his right cheek, but always the gods had given him strength to send his adversaries to the eternal forests.

"The Romans will assume we chose this field to benefit our chariots," Cronn said, rubbing his thick fingers on his leather trousers. "The valley has no rocks and few trees, as you instructed."

"You have done well," Taranis said. He turned to study the heights beyond the valley, trying to determine where the Romans might camp.

"On that knoll?" Cronn asked, guessing his thoughts.

"Too near the valley," Taranis said. "There," he said, pointing to a rise of ground a mile from the valley. "They will build their camp on that hill. The only disadvantage for them is the easterly approach. Too many trees for their liking, but they have little choice."

Cronn patted his horse on the neck. "Preparations are going well," he said. "The commanders report we have hundreds of fighting ramps, ropes, and shelters … and river barges to transport them here."

"Plan on two, maybe three days, to position materials," Taranis said. "What about tarred arrows and torches for the cattle?"

"The carts are being filled as we speak," Cronn said.

"Remember, these are not auxiliaries," Taranis said. "Reports are few, but Legion XX is said to have been fully reinforced."

"What about the southern legions?"

Taranis grimaced. "We don't know. I am told they are remaining in the south as protection against the Brigantes and Selgovae, but Neeve might have better information." He swept his eyes north across the valley, steep at the rim but then assuming a gentle slope. "They'll like this valley. It suits their soldiers with its pitched sides and room for their cavalry to squeeze our flanks. Yes, they will meet us here."

Night had fallen. Ten thousand Caledonian warriors sat by their campfires along the foot of the great forest, thinking about wives and children, about feast days and fishing in the cold highland streams. Not long ago they had driven the arrogant Romans from the northern lands, but now the soldiers were back. The Empire always seemed to have more armies, more soldiers, more weapons. Far away in Rome a faceless emperor had decreed that everyone should fall on his knees before him, and he would not be satisfied until all tongues and tribes were his slaves.

"The sky is burning!" someone cried.

Warriors leapt from their campfires and scurried to the edge of the valley.

"The gods have rent the heavens!" warriors were shouting.

"Cry out to the gods!"

Taranis pushed his way through the warriors to the rim of the valley. He stared at the long slash in the fabric of the heavens. Fire and smoke glowed in the crack and Taranis half expected the god of thunder he had been named after to emerge from the fiery opening.

"Druids?" Cronn asked.

"They've called on the gods," Taranis said, still staring at the sky.

"Have you ever seen a god?"

Taranis shook his head. "I have seen the Druids many times, witnessed strange and awesome things, but I have never seen a god." He scanned the pandemonium as it erupted among the warriors. They all had heard stories about the Druids, their unearthly powers and their use of human sacrifices, but for many, this was the first time they had witnessed those powers. They were screaming and whooping and pointing at the tear in the night sky.

"I believe in the gods," Taranis said, "and I believe the Druids have special powers to influence the gods, but I don't believe they always use their powers to benefit the people."

Cronn glanced around. "They do know mysteries."

"Yes," Taranis said slowly, "they know mysteries—ancient mysteries."

"The gods have chosen the Druids," Cronn said.

Taranis hesitated. "I think," he said, "long ago a Druid must have stumbled across a god in the forest who was sleeping, or maybe bound by a magic charm. He captured him and forced him to reveal some secret about the gods, one that forever after has given the Druids power over these immortals."

"Do you know this to be true?"

"No," Taranis said as he watched the flaming tear fade to smoke. "The Druids do magic," he said, "sometimes dark magic, evil magic. I cannot believe the gods are pleased. Yet, when the Druids call, they appear. They always appear." He looked at Cronn. "The Druids know secrets. That I believe."

Farther down the valley, fiery globes suddenly flared low in the sky, and warriors cried out in fear. They began shouting, "The gods are burning the heavens!" and, "I see gods crouching in the fire!" Taranis had a clear view of the spheres but saw no gods crouching inside. He believed in the gods, but he often wondered how much of what he saw were Druid tricks. The Druids were intermediaries between the gods and men, and infused warriors with courage before battle, but Taranis never felt comfortable with their magic, or their human sacrifices.

One by one the fireballs shriveled and burned out. Darkness gripped the valley again, and Druid voices chanted, growing more urgent as they called on the gods. Several Druid priestesses shrieked, and fell silent. A great hush descended on the valley. No one spoke or looked around lest by some fate they be chosen as an offering to the gods, to have their head taken from them and placed in a forest shrine. More screams pierced the darkness. Suddenly, a dozen torches fell from the sky; dark-robed Druids scuttled across the ground, gathering up the sacred items. On the valley floor they danced around a solitary oak tree, chanting in ancient speech to the gods. The torches they had gathered now bobbed above a churning sea of Druid hoods. Then, with the sound of a rushing wind, the tree exploded into flame, and the priests began to screech the names of gods as they leapt into the air and circled the burning oak. When the tree sputtered and died, another fire, like the tongue of a dragon, slithered up an enormous mountain of logs, roaring into an inferno that shot angry sparks toward the heavens.

The Druids gathered in a tight circle by the fire, and threw themselves on the ground, waiting.

Warriors everywhere strained to see what was happening on the valley floor. The huge bonfire hissed and popped and flared red in the wind. Then, a door seemed to open in the heart of the fire, and the high priest Cathbad emerged from the flames, stepping as if from one world to another. The borders of his robe glowed with flame from the huge bonfire behind him, and several priests patted out the smoking remnants of fire.

Taranis took a deep breath and marveled at the magicians' ability to do the impossible. That they understood the mysteries of the gods, he had no doubt, and many times he had whispered prayers asking forgiveness for his attitude toward these mediums-on-earth. Still, when the Druids changed into animal form, as they sometimes did, or dwelt in flames, as he just saw, he suspected he was witnessing not an act of the gods, but an act of deception. He had no idea how they performed their magic, but he knew the purpose. The Druids, no different from anyone else, wanted to increase their power over the people.

Even so, like every Caledonian commander before him, Taranis did nothing to minimize the majesty of the Druids. They knew the secrets of the ancient ones, the incantations that wakened the world of shades and imparted strength to warriors preparing for battle.

Cathbad now stood with his back to the fire, almost a god, his black robe glowing with crimson light. As he stepped forward, his hood shadowing his face, he spoke with an unnaturally high voice, which made him seem all the more sinister in his power.

"The ancient ones are here," he cried, looking around, as if he expected one to appear before them. "They are not pleased. They are bitter … and angry … and craving the warm milk of men. Whose blood will they drink? Without blood there is no appeasement. No mercy. No rest. Without blood, the heavens above and the earth below cannot be balanced. The hills and rocks cry out in pain. They throb in misery, in deep despair. Oh, how the very ground you stand on aches for the pouring out of sweet libation."

He pointed a long finger toward two naked men being dragged from a heavy corpse of trees. Their bodies had been painted white to make them visible in the dim glow of the moon, and a dull red glow danced off the hollows of their bodies. Every now and then they would struggle against the ropes binding their necks, but a cohort of Druids prodded them forward with sharpened sticks, reminding them to continue their journey toward the fire.

"The evil ones will this night satisfy the thirst of Toutorix, lord of the oblation," Cathbad intoned.

The great company of Caledonians held their breath as the sacrifices were herded toward the smoking tree where Cathbad now stood. One was mumbling prayers in the Roman tongue, telling Taranis that the pair had been captured at a Roman settlement near the Wall.

"Their blood shall quench the earth, and their flesh shall make glad the birds of the air," Cathbad sang in his high voice as he slipped out his ceremonial knife.

Taranis turned his back on the dancing Druids, and pushed through the throngs of warriors.   He had seen enough Druid sacrifices.

5

Vectis Trebellius sat outside the Senate house in Rome.

He and his long time friend, Julian Quintillius, watched as the massive bronze doors slowly opened and dozens of senators poured out, still arguing with each other about the day's decision.

Julian shook his head. "I don't like it," he said. "The Senate needs a body to nail to a tree, and you are very convenient."

"At least they received the governor's report by now. That should be positive."

"I am certain of it. Governor Verus is vain, but at root an honorable man."

"Yet you fear his words will not be enough."

Julian grimaced. "Britannia is in ruins, and someone is to blame. It cannot be Governor Verus because he is a first-rate soldier and a friend of the emperor. It cannot be the Senate who ignored every letter warning them of impending disaster, and who refused to reinforce Britannia's legions, because they are the ones judging the situation."

"And that leaves me," Vectis said.

"There's always the priests," Julian said with a sympathetic smile, "but I do think it difficult to judge what is an effective sacrifice and what is not."

Vectis smiled. Julian saw humor even in the darkest situations, and his words gave Vectis cheer. Julian was a white-skinned, North African soldier from Cyrene, and he constantly complained about the leisurely life he had left behind—the afternoon baths, the theater, the women who sought his companionship. As a military aide to Vectis, his lot in life seemed to be tramping from one provincial nightmare to another ... and now to the Roman Senate where politicians were trying to figure out who to blame for the Britannia disaster.

Vectis rarely responded to Julian's laments, knowing he was not serious. Few were as loyal as Julian Quintillius. Vectis had met him twelve years earlier in Africa when they began their military careers. Many times Julian had risked his life where another would have abandoned a friend. Behind the grin and off-handed manner, Julian was rock of dependability.

Minutes later a senatorial aide signaled Vectis to follow him through the Senate chamber and into an adjacent meeting room. Julian remained behind, still mumbling about the hypocrisy of senators who denied reinforcements for Britannia, and then, when proved wrong, searched for a sacrificial goat to roast on an altar.

The senators waiting for Vectis, ten in all, sat stiffly on their ornate couches. Evidently, they had been arguing—he'd heard muted shouts as he approached the closed door.

"My name is Servius Sulpicius Tertullus," said a senator with bushy eyebrows, "Consul of Rome."

Vectis nodded to the senator. It would not be a friendly gathering. No one had invited him to be seated, and several had scowls on their faces. Two scribes sat in the corner recording every word.

"We are not here to discuss the Britannia mess," Consul Tertullus said with a poor attempt at a smile, "nor to assign blame for the loss of the emperor's Wall, though in all my years as a senator, I have never seen such incompetence in a military leader."

"Nothing but a coward, if you ask me," a senator said, curling his lip.

"A Roman abandoning his post to a collection of rabble!" someone groused.

"Reports were you had been killed in Britannia," said another. "At least death has honor!"

Murmurs filled the room.

Senator Titus Severus broke in and said, "May I ask the noble consul why he allows senators to voice opinions when we have already agreed not to assign blame for the catastrophe in Britannia?"

One or two senators grunted their agreement.

Tertullus cleared his throat.

"Or perhaps the consul wishes to appoint an impartial senator to preside over our meeting," Severus said.

"The consul can and will conduct this meeting with strict neutrality," Tertullus said, clearly irritated by Severus's comments. "But certain facts must be discussed in order for us to complete our task." He leaned forward on his couch and spoke to Vectis in a patronizing voice. "We are your friends, not your judges. We have chosen this format because there is division in the Senate, even rancor, and we feel this assembly of leading senators affords you an opportunity to explain the recent happenings in Britannia. Do you understand?"

"I do."

"State your name for the recording scribe."

"Vectis Trebellius Quadratus."

"And your assignments in Britannia?"

"Prefect of the five outposts north of the Antonine Wall."

"And after the Wall fell?"

"I served as a military tribune for Legate Julius Verus, governor of Britannia."

"And served with distinction," Severus said. "We have letters of commendation from the governor. I note for the record that these commendations cover the entire time the prefect spent in Britannia." He held up the papyrus rolls.

"Thank you, Senator Severus," Tertullus said in an overly polite tone. He turned to Vectis. "Now, if you would be good enough to remind us why the Senate appointed you as prefect of the five outposts."

"There had been significant unrest among the Celtic tribes," Vectis said, "particularly the Brigantes, Selgovae and Caledonian tribes, and the Senate feared we might lose the five outposts, and possibly the Wall."

"What was your assignment?"

"To strengthen defenses in the five outposts," Vectis said.

"And is it fair to say you failed to do so?"

"I leave it to you to judge the fairness, but I strengthened the outposts significantly."

"Evidently not enough," the consul said.

"True, not enough."

"It might be helpful," Severus said, "for this Senate commission to acknowledge its shortcomings in supporting our commanders in the field. I for one argued that we had little to fear in Britannia. Most of us in this room refused to send reinforcements from Germania because we were more concerned about German hordes beating on the gates of Rome than uprisings in Britannia." He paused. "I still fear the ferocity of the Germanic hordes and the unruly tribes in Dacia, but there is no doubt we made a mistake in Britannia."

"I think all of us would concede we underestimated the Britannia threat," the consul said.

"If I may," interrupted a younger senator named Publius Coelius. The skin on his neck crinkled in soft folds, and his pampered face reminded Vectis of the men who spent their lives soaking in the baths. He wondered how such a young patrician would be included in a group of older, leading senators. Inherited wealth, Vectis guessed.

"Tribune Trebellius," Coelius said with a puzzled look on his face. "I fear I have much to learn about the Britannia situation, and I was hoping you might help me."

"Of course." Vectis said.

"I thank you for your patience."

Vectis said nothing. Coelius's polite manner did little to hide his contempt. He might have addressed Vectis with the distinctly higher title of Prefect, customary in the current setting, but he chose the lesser ranking of Tribune to set the tone.

"I have a curiosity," Coelius was saying, "about Emperor Antoninus' Wall. Would you agree that the collapse of the five outposts contributed to the collapse of the Wall?"

"Yes, I would agree."

"So your failure," Coelius said, rolling his thick lips and scratching some irritant in his eye, "was a direct cause for the collapse of the Wall."

"I would say that once the outposts were abandoned, the Wall was in great peril."

The senator's face glowed with triumph. "Well, then, I do not see what more we need to ask. Tribune Trebellius admits his actions put Antoninus' Wall in great peril. He failed in his responsibility, and that failure caused the debacle in Britannia." He leaned back on his couch and glanced at the other senators.

Severus rose and said, "Senator Coelius wonders what more we need to ask. With the permission of the consul, I will try to satisfy his curiosity." He turned to Vectis. "What were the conditions of the five outposts when you arrived?"

"On the verge of collapse."

"We need specifics," Coelius huffed, "not self serving—"

"Prefect," Severus said, using Vectis's rank as commander of Britannia's five outposts, "Senator Coelius needs specifics."

Vectis shifted his eyes to Coelius and said, "My monthly reports to the Senate contained detailed information on the conditions of the outposts, but in short, the forts had ill-trained soldiers, poor morale, few scouts or engineers, no night patrols, hundreds of non-Roman workers that spied on operations—"

"Yes, yes," Coelius said, waving his hand dismissively. "I take it you rectified the situation."

"Largely, yes," Vectis said, growing weary of the senator's pompous attitude.

"Then perhaps you might explain how these … tribes, if that is the appropriate word, were able to overwhelm five Roman outposts so easily."

"They overwhelmed only one outpost, Senator," Vectis said.

"One?" Senator Coelius's face had a pained look, as if he were offended by having to process the additional information. "I do not understand."

"Three outposts were ordered to retreat to the Wall, stranding the two most distant outposts, Stragenia and Faustina. Stragenia's soldiers tried and largely failed to link with Faustina … so that left only Faustina, my home fort, to deal with the vast numbers—"

"Your orders," Coelius said with his finger up as a reprimand, "were to maintain the outposts at all costs. Is that not correct?"

"That is correct."

"But at the first opportunity you ran—if that is not too provocative a word—you ran to the safety of Emperor Antoninus' Wall. Or am I wrong?"

Vectis looked at Coelius and wondered whether he had ever fought in the legions. He knew the answer, of course. The man had done nothing more dangerous than pluck his eyebrows with silver tweezers.

Coelius was still talking. "You abandoned your post to save your neck!"

Consul Tertullus said, "Senator, I think it unproductive to—"

"Brave men died because of your cowardly actions!" Coelius intoned, jutting out his chin in righteous anger.

Vectis could no longer take the abuse. "Senator," he said, "even if I explained what happened, I doubt you would understand. War is conducted by men, not spineless effeminates that sit on cushions and ramble on, simply to hear themselves speak."

Senator Coelius jumped to his feet shouting in an incoherent babble. A group of senators gathered around him trying to soothe his rage, but he kept shouting and pointing at Vectis. After several minutes he managed to choke out a demand that Vectis be taken from the room in chains.

"Nonsense!" Senator Severus roared.

"Agreed!" someone growled near the back.

"Senator Coelius received just due," Severus said. "He called Vectis Trebellius a coward, a man who fought with distinction in North Africa and the Egyptian Wars, who risked his life countless times in Britannia—here are the commendations from Rome's greatest living general!" He shook Governor Verus's letters in the faces of the other senators. Then, dropping his voice, Severus went on. "Now, of course, the prefect ought not to have … ah … characterized a senator the way he did, even if provoked. He naturally apologizes for his improper remarks." Severus shot a look at Vectis.

"Yes, I do apologize," Vectis said, without sounding the least bit repentant.

"There, you see," Severus said.

An awkward silence followed. The senators returned to their couches, and the consul took Senator Coelius by the elbow and spoke quietly to him. When the consul finished, Senator Coelius looked as if he had been whipped in the public square. He accepted a cup of wine from an aide, cleared his throat and said, "I still maintain this man abandoned his post, but I may have been too harsh in my choice of words." He swallowed. "I was simply trying to elicit information for the record."

The consul thanked the senator and said, "Prefect Vectis, we were talking about your orders from Rome to protect the outposts. Please continue."

Vectis glanced around the room. The apologies had done little to reduce the tension. Coelius and several other senators were glaring at him, no doubt waiting for him to make a mistake. He fixed his eyes on Coelius to show that he would not be cowed. "Let me repeat," Vectis said, "my original orders were to maintain the outposts at all costs. In this singular fact Senator Coelius is correct. But during the hostilities, three outposts received orders to burn their forts and retreat to the Wall. That stranded my fort, Outpost Faustina and the remnants of Stragenia. Moreover—"

The consul raised his hand and said, "You need not repeat yourself, Prefect. We understand your defense that you believe someone changed the original orders and instructed three outposts to retreat to the Wall."

"That is correct."

"Then please enlighten us," Coelius said. "Who would have given these orders?"

"I don't know," Vectis said. "The former Senator Atilius Titianus, perhaps, and possibly others."

"Preposterous!" shouted a senator.

"This is outrageous," said another.

Others muttered their agreement.

Consul Tertullus glared at Vectis through his bushy eyebrows. "Do you know this to be a fact?"

Vectis replied, "The commander at Stragenia told me that a senator—"

"This is exactly what I warned about," Coelius said. "The commander at Stragenia is dead and now his voice from the grave condemns the Senate. Not only does this man use the banished Senator Titianus to cover his failings, he even suggests some in the Senate may have aided in the plot."

"Shameful," cried a senator.

"I concur!" shouted an elder senator.

Consul Tertullus rose from his couch. "Senators, please," he said, "I remind you we are not here to cast judgment, but to collect information. Prefect Vectis has a right to voice his opinion. If he says that a senator—or even a god, for that matter—issued new orders to abandon the outposts, then he has a right to say so."

"We have no record of new orders being issued," Coelius said.

"Well said," a senator agreed.

Consul Tertullus furrowed his brow and asked gravely, "Prefect Vectis, do you know with certainty that former Senator Atilius Titianus issued new orders?"

"No, but I have suspicions that—"

"The Senate does not deal in suspicions," Tertullus said. "Do you have any evidence that implicates a present senator in sending counter orders?"

"I have no written orders, if that is what you are asking," Vectis said, "but—"

"I think that answers our question," Coelius said, holding up his hand to prevent Vectis from saying more.

Consul Tertullus remained standing and said, "Everyone knows I have always supported our commanders in the field. It is no easy task to deal with barbarians and still maintain Roman honor, but ..." he surveyed the group of senators, "the Senate needs evidence. And while it is obvious the former prefect has strong opinions, he does, I am afraid, have little evidence." He paused. "Who gave the orders for the three outposts to abandon their duties? Were countermanding orders actually given? We might never know." He gestured to Senator Severus.

Severus rose and addressed Vectis. "In accordance with the agreement reached earlier in Senate chambers, you are absolved of blame for the unfortunate happenings in Britannia. You have been assigned duties as a military tribune in the provinces. You will leave in one week."

When the senators had gone, Vectis thanked Severus for his support.

The senator nodded. "I hope you understand what has happened here," Severus said. "You have accused unspecified Senate members of overruling the emperor's orders in Britannia."

"I accuse no one," Vectis said. "I only defend myself against the charge that I abandoned my post. The facts are quite the opposite."

"I have no doubts about that," Severus said. Then he asked, "Is it possible that written materials, senatorial orders, for example, might be found in Londinium's archives?"

"I suppose," Vectis said. "All papers from the outposts, burned or not, were collected and sent there."

"Would you be willing to return to Britannia?"

Vectis thought about Neeve. "Of course," he said.

"Then we will plan for your return," Severus said. "Unfortunately, at present you have been assigned duties in Dacia province."

"Dacia?" Vectis was stunned. For a moment he thought he might be given permission to return to Britannia. Somewhere in that northern province, Neeve was wondering whether he was alive or dead. But now he would be heading in the opposite direction, to the icy Dacian hills.

"Clever, sending you to Dacia, I must acknowledge," Severus was saying. "I couldn't very well argue against the logic given by Consul Tertullus and Senator Coelius that—given your innocence—you are the best military tribune to handle the problems broiling on the

German frontier. After all, I have spent the past few days extolling your frontier experience in Britannia and North Africa. The truth is, many in the Senate are eager to send you away for a while. They fear what you might know. Anyone involved in countermanding orders would also be involved in Senator Atilius Titianus's failed attempt to overthrow the emperor two years ago. At this very moment I am investigating the whole Atilius Titianus affair."

A cluster of senatorial aides passed by the open door. Severus waited until it was safe to speak. "These are treacherous paths we tread. Take great care. Enemies lie in wait like highwaymen on a road." He ran his fingers through his gray hair. "I will be leaving soon to inspect my holdings in Gallia, and believe me, I intend to retain an entire cohort of bodyguards. I take every precaution, and you should too."

"Thank you for the warning," Vectis said.

"I know you are being commissioned by the Senate and as such have been granted a contingent of soldiers for protection. All that is good," he said, leaning forward and speaking in tones much like a father. "But I believe you are in danger. Allow me to offer the additional services of a first-rate protector."

"Thank you, Senator, but—"

"No one would know he was there."

"The soldiers will suffice."

Severus sighed, then turned his attention to a papyrus sheet stamped with the great Senate seal. He handed it to Vectis. "Your duties are outlined here," he said. "Do well. Your success will go far to quell criticism, and it will give me reason to argue for your return to Rome. Then, if you are willing, we can talk about those letters in Britannia. As for Dacia, you will be under the supervision of a man named Commodus."

Vectis blanched. "Gaius Jovius Commodus?"

"Yes, I believe so."

Vectis stared at the paper.

"Is there a problem?"

"No," Vectis said, "no, of course not. Everything is fine."

6

Scouts from Legion XX crossed the ford late in the morning.

From his vantage above the valley, Taranis watched the four mounted scouts splashing across the river, their horses shuddering in the cold mountain runoff. They paused before the scorched tree where the druids had performed their rituals, cut down the two bodies and dragged them upriver, concealing them in the thick brush. Then, like seasoned soldiers, they set about their tasks. If they saw Taranis, it seemed not to matter. They were used to working in full view of the enemy.

As a warrior, Taranis couldn't help admiring their efficiency. One dismounted and walked off every conceivable angle of the valley, measuring even the slope gradations. Another plotted the rocks and studied the valley terrain. He even tested the firmness of the basin floor by galloping his horse across its breadth. They took note of the high ground in the rear, the treed land on its easterly approach, and the angle of the valley to the rising sun. They also saw the smoke rising from Caledonian fires and ventured as close as they might with reasonable safety. Satisfied, they crossed back over the river and returned to the main body of legionaries who were still marching north.

Two hours later a large group of Syrian archers appeared, riding with five officers. Again they forded the river and inspected the terrain, but mostly, they were deciding where to locate their war camp. As expected, they chose the most defensible position, the distant rise, and immediately Taranis sent riders back to ready the siege materials in the woods.

For the next five hours, the soldiers of Legion XX worked tirelessly. First, they gathered around the standard they'd planted in the ground, and gave a loud shout, then they began digging a trench that encircled the entire camp, five feet wide and three deep, throwing up the dirt as a further barrier to any attack. Next came seven-foot palisade stakes pounded into the top of the earthen barrier and tied together with thongs to form a crude defensive fence. Remarkably, by late afternoon the whole camp was ready.

Neeve arrived at the Caledonian encampment an hour before sunset. She found Taranis under the huge flap of his tent giving last minute instructions to his commanders. She positioned herself behind the commanders and looked directly at her brother. She was always surprised at his size when he stood alongside other men. He was big even by Caledonian standards, a bold-looking warrior with long yellow hair like hers, and piercing blue eyes. His shoulders were broad, his body lean, his determined face clean-shaven and surprisingly free from scars despite his many encounters with the enemy. He had a golden torc round his neck, silver bracelets on his wrists, but more striking to Neeve was the brilliant red battle tunic he always wore, something their father had done before him.

Taranis's eyes met Neeve's, and he motioned for Cronn to finish the briefing.

"Something wrong?" he asked, after kissing her forehead. Even on days like this Taranis never failed to kiss or embrace his sister.

"You have to break off the attack."

Taranis glanced back at the commanders. Then looking intently into her face, he asked quietly, "You made it into Roman territory?"

"Yes."

"And?'

"Three legions are coming," she blurted out. "Legions II, VI, and XX."

Taranis shifted his eyes away to scores of passing carts loaded with fighting ramps, ropes and drinking water. "Did you see these legions yourself?" he asked, turning back.

"I saw a fully reinforced Legion XX."

Taranis nodded and said, "They are already here. That's Legion XX and its auxiliaries camped across the valley."

Neeve instinctively glanced toward the distant fires of the Roman camp.

"Tell me about legions II and VI," he said. "Fully reinforced as well?"

"Yes, and marching north."

"Toward our positions?"

"I'm not sure," she said. "I do know they are only days away."

"Days?" He looked concerned.

She nodded.

He took her arm and asked, "How do you know about their movements?"

"A Roman tribune told me." She held his eyes and answered his next question before he asked. "He was not lying," she said. "I am certain of it."

Neeve could see Taranis struggling with the information. He was wondering how the Romans could maintain control of the province if they depleted their legions south of the first Wall. Many times her brother had told her that Roman commanders were cautious in their use of the legions. They protected their base and took few risks in pursuing the tribes. Even in individual battles they committed only two thirds of their troops to actual combat on the field; one third remained behind, guarding their circular stockade, ready to admit soldiers in the event of a disaster.

"There's more," she said.

He folded his arms, waiting.

Neeve told him about the new general from Germania province and the emperor's determination to reoccupy his Wall.

"We can't break off our attack," Taranis said. "It is too late for that. But Rome's new aggressive policy might work against them. If they are sending two other legions, expecting to support Legion XX in the coming days, they will find nothing but Roman bodies." He looked at her. "We will fight them, but not in this valley, and not in the way they expect."

"Taranis," she said, reaching for her brother, "I have dread in my heart for you."

He patted her shoulder, his large hand squeezing her as he said, "Don't despair. The gods will give us victory."

"Sometimes," she said softly, "I fear the gods are deaf."

Senator Coelius's heated rooms at his private bath smelled of perfumed oils, burned lemonwood, and the rich aroma of unbridled power.

Balbinus could not believe his good fortune. First, an audience with the emperor, and now an invitation for a morning of relaxed conversation with a key senator of Rome. Balbinus sighed as Coelius's servants applied freshly heated cloths to his sizeable body, skillfully removing the cooler ones so as not to provide any discomfort. Other servants took turns massaging his feet with rare Patavium oil and patted his face dry. On the table next to him lay Senator Coelius, his eyes half closed.

"Your invitation was most gracious," Balbinus said.

"Nothing like heat and steam," Coelius replied.

"Ah, yes."

"Tired?"

"Like the dead."

Coelius moaned his concurrence. "Often the servants carry me to my room and roll me into a heated bed."

"Nothing finer on a chilly autumn day."

"The heat ... it does wonders for the skin."

"How do barbarians survive?"

Coelius smiled lazily and said, "They know nothing beyond mud hovels." Then he added casually, turning his eyes, "I sense something more than the baths occupies your mind. Am I right?"

"Indeed, several items do concern me, if I may say."

"You may," Coelius said, signaling his personal aide. Immediately a retinue of servants helped the senator and his guest to a sitting position, then stripped off their heated cloths, rubbed their bodies with scented oil, and provided them with thick robes and slippers. Others appeared carrying silver goblets and amphorae filled with wine, cooled goats' milk, and a blend of peach and orange juice. Balbinus chose the juice and waited as Coelius dismissed his servants. The senator preferred to talk privately.

"These concerns of yours," Coelius said, "would one be a further elevation in station, perhaps to senatorial rank?"

"Your discernment has always been your strength," Balbinus said. "You have great influence—"

"I quite understand your situation, and sympathize," Coelius said, sipping his wine, "but let us agree to visit this subject another time. Tell me your other concern. It may be more pressing."

Balbinus's fingers tightened on the goblet. No one—not the emperor, not Coelius—no one took seriously his desire to ascend to the Senate. Oh, they were polite. They smiled and addressed him as a peer, sometimes even invited him to their outings, but behind their hands they whispered about him, as if he were a chamber attendant who had mistakenly entered an elegant dining room.

Balbinus gulped down more juice. He wished he had chosen wine. "My other concern," he said, suppressing his anger, "is that Senator Severus is investigating the Atilius Titianus plot against the emperor, trying to discover who else might have been involved."

"I see." He looked upset.

A burst of hope surged through Balbinus. He always wondered if Coelius had a hand in the insurrection. If so, he would have an interest in slowing the investigation.

Coelius set his goblet on the table. "May I ask how you came into this information?"

"I obtained an audience with Emperor Antoninus and discovered that Senator Severus was examining Titianus's correspondences, to find names of others involved."

Coelius wiped his lips with a linen cloth. He seemed to be deep in thought. Then his face changed, and he said slowly, "You were Senator Titianus's senior aide, were you not?"

"Yes, you know I was."

He ignored the comment and said, "Do you suppose your name might figure prominently in those letters?"

"I exposed the plot to overthrow the emperor," Balbinus said defensively, not liking the intent of the question.

"True," said Coelius, "but let us suppose the letters suggest you were as eager to overthrow the emperor as the contemptible Senator Titianus, or that you had reason to believe the plot was unraveling and warned the emperor to save your miserable hide." He smiled. "Of course, I give no credence to these scurrilous fantasies. I merely suggest that this could be the perspective of Severus."

Balbinus swallowed hard. "I exposed the plot to overthrow the emperor," he repeated. "The emperor was grateful for my actions." He pushed off the table and stared absently down the hall at the hot room where steam shimmered above the waters.

Coelius shrugged. "Simple musings," he said. Then he stopped. "One other item that lingers in my mind ... have you ever wondered whether there might be other letters, say from Vectis Trebellius while he was in Britannia, warning the emperor of Titianus's treachery?"

"I don't see how that would involve me."

"Oh, I am certain it affects you not at all ... unless, well ... it is of no import. The whole idea is fantasy, as I said before. You need not trouble yourself."

"No, please, I am quite interested." He was also boiling with rage. Coelius had turned the whole conversation around.

Coelius furrowed his brow. "I was reflecting on how Severus the investigator might view such a letter from Vectis Trebellius—if indeed one could be found. Would he not think you had reason to be worried about such letters, and in fear or desperation betrayed Titianus, again to protect yourself?"

Balbinus said nothing.

"Severus is a hard man," Coelius said. "And crafty. From the moment Vectis Trebellius returned to Rome, Severus has been trying to befriend the wretch. And why do you think that is? Clearly, Severus believes Trebellius can further his investigation. Fortunately, the Senate issued orders sending Trebellius to Dacia. But I can promise you, the moment he returns Severus will push and probe until he finds every line ever written from Britannia."

"I had nothing whatsoever to do with the insurgence," Balbinus said lamely.

"Of course, you are guiltless in this matter," Coelius said, "but that is not how Rome works." He raised a finger. "Perception … she's the goddess on the throne. If you aspire to the Senate Chamber, you must learn this."

Balbinus paced the room. "What would you suggest?" he asked, defeated.

"Begin with simple tasks," Coelius said. "Vectis Trebellius conceivably has information damaging to you. You could wait and hope that Severus finds nothing … or you could act."

Balbinus looked at the senator. "I don't understand."

"I think you do. Trebellius has been sent to Dacia province, a wild and unpredictable territory. You are now a man of means. Such men need only raise a finger and others disappear."

"I knew his family—"

Coelius gave Balbinus an encouraging pat on the arm. "You regret actions of this sort, I know, and that is commendable. It shows you have the sensitivities of a patrician. It also shows that you have the strength necessary for a senator."

"Thank you," Balbinus said, trying to smile.

"Some are born to privilege and power; others, like yourself, grow into them."

"Your words give one hope."

"You need feel no remorse for this Vectis Trebellius," Coelius said, his face darkening. "He is a simple man who presumes to instruct his betters … and in so doing he has become a threat. As with any important matter, you deal with it forcefully. I have confidence in you."

"I will not fail."

Coelius sighed. "Of course, we still have Senator Titus Severus and his investigation. There are many in the Senate who would not be upset were it to starve for want of information. But let me handle this matter." He called down the hall for the servants to return. "So you see," he said, "we both have responsibilities."

Balbinus motioned to the amphorae immersed in vats of cold water and said, "I will take that wine now."

7

Neeve twisted her hair nervously, trying to quell her feelings of uncertainty about the coming battle. The sun was almost gone. Shadows curled around the rocks, and in the distance, the line of mountain peaks stood out against the purple sky.

"Saddle your horse," a voice said. "You will accompany me on my inspections."

"I thought you'd be with Taranis," Neeve said, her eyes on the ground. She knew Cronn's voice instantly.

"I'm handling operations in the valley."

She nodded. "I suppose Taranis asked you to stay by my side." She turned to face the huge warrior whose fierce eyes always seemed to soften when he looked at her. Her brother had never hidden his desire for them to settle together. And Cronn himself had plucked up the courage more than once to escort her to the village feasts. When eager fathers displayed their daughters in suggestive dance rituals, Cronn hardly noticed them. He tried not to be rude, nodding occasionally in feigned interest at the whirling girls, but his attention was wholly devoted to her. Often he seemed to be nearby when duties might have called him elsewhere, and with safety a concern in the war-shattered northlands, she sometimes called him her "protector."

He smiled, displaying square, even teeth. "I was not sent to protect you, if that's what you are thinking. I am coordinating the valley attack."

She returned a small smile. He was a good man, with gentleness behind his severe exterior. Even with a facial scar, he was not unpleasant to look at. She had to admit she felt safe with him. No man she knew, except maybe Taranis, could stand before him. But while she liked and respected Cronn, she did not love him. Her heart was elsewhere, far away in Roman lands, and despite moments of doubt, she still had hope that Vectis was alive. And Cronn knew it.

"Taranis is worried," she said, dragging her mind back to the issues at hand.

"Your report of Legions II and VI worries all the commanders," he said. "But we have no choice. The Romans are determined to annihilate us. If we retreat into the hills and prepare for another day, we might find ourselves facing all three legions. At least this way we have surprise on our side. The Romans will not expect us to attack so soon, and we might destroy Legion XX before the other two arrive."

"Can we do it in so short a time?"

Cronn looked toward the fires of the Roman camp. "Legions II and VI cannot be within striking distance, not tonight." He sounded as if he were trying to convince himself.

"We are taking a large gamble."

"We are."

The wind changed, blowing smoke from a nearby fire in their direction. Neeve blinked away the soot and glanced around the empty camp. A handful of warriors, mostly older women who could no longer stand for battle, had been left behind to tend the hundreds of fires. They shuffled from fire to fire, some with limbs missing, some limping from battle wounds, some bent from age, but all intent on keeping the fires burning. From a distance the Romans would suppose the Caledonians were still huddled around their campfires, waiting for the morning battle.

"Taranis said we have Iceni trackers here."

"They arrived a few hours ago," Cronn said, shifting his eyes toward a group of shadowy figures all but invisible at the base of a grassy hillock. "They'll wait for dark."

Neeve peered into the gathering gloom. The Icenis squatted on the ground beside a tiny fire, their long hair falling to their shoulders, their eyes glinting in the fading light. They never carried a bow or sword—only two knives at their hips. They wore dark green tunics, leather trousers, and soft leather boots tied below the knee. They traveled in pairs, but never spoke, not even in a whisper. Always hand signals.

Neeve had seen them only once before, at the Wall, when they slipped through the elaborate Roman defenses and slit the throats of scores of sentries. The Icenis lived hundreds of miles south of the Walls in lands controlled by Romans, and it was difficult to hire them. But this was a desperate hour. For the ambush to succeed, the Caledonians needed Icenis. Soon they would crawl through the woods and along the riverbanks and in the ravines, searching for Roman scouts. Their presence struck terror in the hearts of the enemy, and it wasn't uncommon for even well trained Roman scouts to desert on hearing that Icenis were tracking them.

Minutes later all traces of the day had fled, and stars like precious gems shone down upon the preparations of desperate men.

Cronn and Neeve stopped at a succession of homesteads where hundreds of cows, sheep and goats had been squeezed into the bulging pens. The foul odor of excrement and animal sweat hit Neeve like a wall, and she moved upwind from the beasts. On the animals' horns the Caledonians had attached wooden torches, dipped in resin. Warriors were already herding the beasts to prearranged locations, readying them for the attack.

To surprise a Roman camp—even a temporary one built for a single night—was no easy task. Legionaries were expert in choosing defensible sites, and their scouts roamed the surrounding countryside through the night, searching for potential threats. Their trenches and earthen barriers, their roped wooden fences, and their alert sentries protected them well. Few enemies surprised the vigilant soldiers from Rome.

But this night would be different. Within hours the Iceni trackers had lit their signal fires. The Roman scouts were gone. Legion XX was blind.

Shortly before dawn Cronn ordered the torches lit.   An assortment of young boys emerged from the rear bringing shielded lamps to the warriors who lit the thousands of torches lashed to the animals. The pungent smell of burned resin filled the air, and a forest of torches flared in the wind, bobbing and weaving as they approached the western side of the Roman position. Warriors fought to keep the spooked cattle moving toward the Roman camp, prodding them with spears, and at times even lighting their tails on fire. As the assemblage of beasts neared the rise of ground on which the Romans had built their camp, the panicked sentries, seeing the multitude of torches approaching, blew their trumpets and shouted out warnings. Legionaries, half asleep, some still strapping on their segmented armor, some without armor at all, ran to defend their picket fence.

On the opposite side of their enclosure, to the east where Neeve could not see, she knew a dozen Icenis were already sawing through the thongs that bound the picket fence together. Soon they would slither through the fence, and like avenging spirits slit the throats of Roman sentries. Behind them hidden in the woods lay thousands of Caledonian warriors, their bodies painted blue to intensify the wrath of the gods. They had brought their carts laden with hundreds of fighting ramps, ropes and shelters, and they had a savage determination to rid their lands of the Roman menace.

Like a four-footed army of blood-crazed warriors, the cattle thundered up the incline toward the western edge of the Roman camp. At the same moment a phalanx of archers filled the air with flaming arrows to distract Roman officers from looking too closely at the cattle stampeding toward them. Many of the arrows set tents and carts aflame and struck the open stables where the cavalry had tied their mounts for the night. Startled, the horses broke free and charged through the burning camp, creating greater confusion.

Then the Caledonian warriors on the eastern side—where few Roman soldiers now remained—swarmed out of the woods and overwhelmed the broken fences. Centurions bellowed orders and soldiers scrambled to stem the flood of shrieking, blue-painted warriors. But it was too late. The Caledonians smashed their way into the Roman camp, fighting from sturdy ramps laid across the trenches. They whirled their great swords and screeched in high-pitched voices as they charged into the stunned legionaries. Shaken and confused, the Romans rushed to form a defensive perimeter inside the camp, expecting at any moment to be overwhelmed from the other side where the cattle were.

Neeve cheered when she saw Taranis and his warriors breach the fence. As the battle raged, she caught glimpses of her brother whipping his angry sword like a scythe, blasting Romans out of his way like wooden sticks in a field. She joined the archers and poured arrows into the back ranks of the Romans, creating further chaos.

By now the cattle had reached the camp, and without the constant prodding of warriors, most ran about crazily, shaking their heads, bumping into each other and trying to escape from the sputtering torches.

The Romans immediately recognized the deception. A shrill trumpet sounded, and then several more. Neeve could see them forming into lines as they marched out of the campground, shields held high to protect from the arrows still raining on their heads. They seemed to understand that only a handful of warriors and a collection of terrified cattle stood between them and the safety of open ground.

"Archers!" Cronn was waving his arms. "Over here!"

Neeve scooped up her arrow pouches and hurried with others toward a knoll that overlooked the expected route of the retreating Romans. The first rays of sun were now brightening the skies, which promised clear targets for the archers. Neeve could see that half of the legion had been decimated, leaving countless soldiers draped over their picket lines and sprawled on the ground. She could also see that the centurions had gained control of their confused soldiers. A senior centurion had picked up the fallen standard, the treasured symbol of power for all Roman legions, lifting it high, announcing to his comrades that victory was still possible.

Neeve stared at the Roman standard with its many images of their gods. At the top of the pole a golden eagle with extended wings grasped a thunderbolt in its talons. Beside it, on another pole shuddering in the wind, was a square linen vexillum with a fighting boar. This was the emblem of Legion XX. She had seen the standards many times before, and she knew their proud history. It made her uneasy. There was a myth about this legion, that it could never be defeated. It had been given the title, *Valeria Victrix*, Valiant and Victorious, because a hundred years earlier during Nero's reign, Legion XX with 10,000 soldiers had defeated the magnificent army of Boudicca, 230,000 strong. At the end of the day 80,000 Celts lay dead on the ground. The rest fled in terror.

Today the myth about Legion XX would end, Neeve told herself.

But fear nibbled at the edge of her mind.

Below, she could see the Romans gathering around the centurion who was hoisting the standard and shouting out victory slogans. Slowly the legion formed a ragged line to defend against Taranis's charging warriors. More trumpets sounded, these ones deeper and more urgent. The chaos suddenly disappeared. The battered legion formed into a hollow square with its officers and standards at the center. Except for the front rows, where soldiers kept their shields squarely in front of their bodies, the legionaries raised their shields over their heads to protect against arrows. From Neeve's vantage, the whole square looked like a metal box with legs, marching quickly toward the open valley, away from Taranis's warriors.

But the retreating legion was badly overmatched. Thousands of Caledonians flooded the grasslands and surrounded the fleeing Romans. The blue warriors whipped themselves into a frenzy, terrorizing their enemy with shrieks and whoops. Then, as if a dam broke, they surged toward the Romans. They slammed their bodies into the wall of shields, wheeling their swords like axes, a cacophony of sound rising from the grasslands.

The archers halted their shooting for fear of striking their own comrades, knowing their swordsmen would soon finish the enemy.

On the knoll the archers cheered on their warriors.

They clapped each other on the back.

Neeve shook her head in amazement at the heroic efforts of her countrymen. "The gods are truly with us," she cried.

As if sensing defeat, the Romans fought like trapped bears, jamming their shields into the crush of Caledonians and arcing their swords upward, often catching warriors by surprise. They struggled tenaciously to preserve their tight square. When a legionary fell, another stepped forward to take his place. Dust and steam rose from the battle, and it grew difficult to make out individual combatants, but it was clear the box formation had shrunk considerably.

"It won't be long now!" an archer called. His eyes glistened with excitement.

Another was spinning in a circle, laughing.

Suddenly, a large group of Caledonians broke off their attack and bolted toward the valley behind them. Neeve squinted into the rising sun and saw Cronn leading the warriors toward the valley. Something was wrong, but she couldn't see what had caused Cronn to so abruptly break for the valley. She turned to the battle raging below. Taranis was still there, his warriors still attacking the Roman box, but with fewer numbers, or maybe because the legionaries were fighting with renewed vigor, Taranis was having less success.

"Another legion!" an archer cried, thrusting his bow toward the valley.

In the morning light Neeve saw to her horror a full legion, with auxiliaries, archers and cavalry, marching briskly up the valley. Caledonian scouts must have brought news of the approaching legion, and Cronn was sent to delay them until Taranis finished with Legion XX.

The archers shouted again, this time pointing toward the river.

A third legion!

Neeve felt sick. Legions II and VI had force-marched to join Legion XX for what they must have presumed would be a morning battle. They were using XX as bait to draw out the Caledonians, but they miscalculated, never imagining Taranis would hazard a night assault. Still, the outcome would be the same: defeat for the Caledonians.

From the ranks of Legion XX a spontaneous roar filled the grasslands. They had spotted the other legions. The myth was true: *Valeria Victrix* could not be defeated.

Neeve knew Taranis had also seen both legions because his warriors broke off their attack, and were now hastening toward Cronn's more defensible position on a rocky incline at the valley's edge. Neeve, too, ran toward the valley where the Caledonians had formed into battle lines. The archers were so stunned by the turn of events that they almost trampled her in their rush to the safety of their army.

When the archers arrived at the valley's edge, they were directed to a rise of ground behind the warriors. The Caledonian position was protected by woods on its flanks and rear, and before them stretched an open plain in which to fight. But with the arrival of Legions II and VI, events had turned decisively against them.

Back on the grasslands, Legion XX's defensive hollow disintegrated and reformed into a battle line. For a moment Neeve feared they would pursue the fleeing Caledonians, but they waited patiently until the legion crossing the river arrived at their position. Then the two legions melted into each other, becoming an enormous body of soldiers. Bugles called to each other, and units of soldiers shifted forward, some back, as if they were performing marching drills on a parade ground. Then abruptly they separated into three horizontal lines, one behind the other, each eight to ten men deep. Each line was a series of separate blocks of about eighty men with an officer at its rear. Behind the first line two detached units formed. These were reserve soldiers to plug holes that might develop, or to attack should a weakness become evident.

A single trumpet pierced the air.

The front line of soldiers jerked forward all at once, as if they were attached to each other. The thud of hobnailed boots repeatedly striking the ground reverberated through the grasslands, like the dead hollow beating of a drum. But the strangest sound came from the groin protectors, the decorated leather strips that hung from their thick belts, that created a jangling noise when they walked, a sound designed to intimidate the enemy.

The second and third lines waited until they were each spaced about sixty feet from the other. Then as a unit they too pounded across the grasslands. Flanking the legionaries were auxiliary soldiers, Gallic warriors, and an enormous number of mounted archers and lancers. When they were about a hundred yards out they halted, and stood perfectly still, like stone figures in a field. Two legionary standards towered above the mass of steel, and two vexilla fluttered in the wind, the winged horse and the fighting boar. Legion II had joined Legion XX.

In the valley the soldiers of Legion VI advanced slowly up the valley floor, almost leisurely, as if they wanted the Caledonians to see them. More than a thousand German auxiliaries strode menacingly in front of this legion, their gleaming axes gripped firmly in their hands. At the rear of the legion Neeve could see the eagle, and a vexillum bearing a fearsome bull, indicating Legion VI had its origin with the vile Julius Caesar, the first Roman conqueror to set foot on Britannia's soil. And she saw something else. A Roman General. Legate Julius Verus. He was seated on a white horse guarded by a dozen Sarmatian heavy cavalry he had brought with him from the continent. One carried a standard she had never seen before. It had the head of a dragon, a gaping mouth, and a sinister ten-foot tail. The wind filled the mouth and whipped the tail around like an angry viper, hissing and crackling with every breeze.

Trumpets rang out. The legion stopped. The Germans rested their axes on the ground. Bugles played. The legionaries shifted in their block formations. The blocks slammed shut, leaving a solid row of metal shields. Then, like Legions II and XX, Legion VI stood dead still. No one moved. No one spoke.

Rome projected the image of invincibility. Emotionless soldiers. A killing machine; unafraid, because they already knew the outcome of the battle. Standing in their rows with armor glinting in the morning sun, they wanted the Caledonians to take a long look at the army that had enslaved the world. They wanted them to think, and in thinking, to grow in fear.

Above the heads of Legion VI the dragon wriggled and hissed.

Neeve had never seen so many soldiers collected in one place before. She estimated that with auxiliaries and cavalry, the three legions must have numbered twenty thousand men. And the Caledonians had less than ten thousand. She collected her arrows and shoved them all into one pouch.

Then, sipping some water from a goatskin, she murmured a prayer, and waited.

8

Balbinus scowled out the window of his covered carriage. Normally, the rich grain fields of his estate, the brown cattle sheds nestled in rolling green hills, and the smoke from a dozen fires heating his private villa filled him with joy. But today anger burned inside him, knotting his stomach. He hated being played for a fool. He had begun to notice that with his newly acquired holdings came servants eager to take advantage of his good nature. They thought their new master wouldn't notice their slothful ways, but they were so very wrong. Their new master saw everything.

His eyes roamed the wheat fields on either side of the carriage, studying the slaves as they flashed their sickles through the grain and piled armfuls of golden stalks on overloaded carts. Everywhere sun-burnt backs stooped to their tasks, everywhere but in the field directly ahead.

"Aha!" he hollered. "Stop right here!"

He bounded out of the carriage and bolted across the field, heedless of his toga catching on the prickly stubble jutting out of the black earth. The chief overseer, a freedman of Germanic extraction, galloped his horse toward his master.

"How are you tending my fields?" Balbinus demanded.

The freedman scrambled from his horse and said, "Master?"

"That slave! That slave!" Balbinus screamed. "The one lying in the grain, sleeping! Bring him to me."

The freedman signaled, and two men seized the sleeping slave by his feet and dragged him across the field to the waiting Balbinus.

"You think you are in the Greek isles?" Balbinus spat in the man's face. "I will teach you about sleeping in my fields." He turned to the freedman and said, "Lash him, ten times."

The freedman said, "Master, this man—"

"Lash him!"

The freedman unhooked the whip from his saddle and used his foot to flip the man onto his stomach.

Balbinus watched with satisfaction as the man shrieked and writhed under the whip, but he stopped the punishment after the third lash. He eyed his freedman. "You took care not to cross the lashes," he said with a questioning tone in his voice.

"Master, this man has been coughing blood and so I ordered him into the cool of the tall grain, hoping a short rest would make him more productive for you."

Balbinus glanced around awkwardly and said, "Well, I don't like him. If he's unable to work tomorrow, have him chopped for boar feed." He left the field angrier than he had arrived, embarrassed at his mistake. Ungrateful slaves, he thought. He had done so much for them and they rewarded him with their miserable ruses of sickness. If it weren't for the whip they would all be sleeping. He pulled himself into the carriage, slapping away the eager hands that tried to assist.

"What are you waiting for?" he called to his driver. "You can see I am situated in the carriage." He slouched uncomfortably against the cushioned seat as the carriage bounced along the farm road, and for the rest of his journey, his eyes scoured the fields for anything amiss.

A dozen servants filed out to meet Balbinus when his carriage stopped at the entrance to the villa. Sensing his mood, they stepped aside as he bulled his way into the atrium. He'd scarcely mumbled the obligatory word of homage toward the lararium, the shrine to the household spirits, before he smelled the smoke in his villa.

"Why are my nostrils burning from the smell of pine fires?" he hollered at the assembled slaves, his eyes sweeping across the row of bowed heads. He jammed his finger toward the open ceiling and said, "This is the atrium! If an open room stinks of smoldering ashes, I can imagine what my dining and bedrooms are like. Is it too much to ask that when you heat the floors of this villa, you keep the smoke outside?" He strode over to his housekeeper and said in a patronizing voice, "If the wind is uncooperative and swirling char manages to enter these rooms, then kindly use a fan to clear the air."

"Yes, Master."

"Or maybe a month chained to the lever at the grist mill would make you more attentive to my needs. Is that what you want? Because I would be delighted—"

"Balbinus," a voice sang out from the courtyard, "stop abusing the servants and come to me."

Balbinus swung his head toward the courtyard. "I am too upset," he called back in a pouting voice.

"The air is fresh out here in the garden," the woman said, "and I'm lonely on this large couch."

Balbinus started toward the courtyard door, and then paused. The servants might misunderstand and take advantage of his kindly ways. It was always the same. Treat them well and they become idle. For their own good he had to be consistent in his determination. He glared back at his housekeeper and mouthed, "Never again," then pushed past his cowering servants.

In the garden he found his guest draped across a pillowed couch that had been placed under a sizeable fig tree. "Calpurnia, I am so glad you're here," he gushed. "Today, I tell you, I am so agitated—"

"Nonsense. Crisp autumn afternoons are gifts from the gods," she said.

"I swear before Jupiter I could plunge a dagger into a Salian priest."

Calpurnia patted the broad couch and said, "Come here and let me soothe away the pain of this vexing day."

"I dare not," he said, plopping himself on the stone barrier that encircled a large fishpond.

Calpurnia tilted her head seductively and fastened her eyes on him. Although she wore a loose-fitting gown and had a woolen blanket warming her feet, the lines of her lean body showed through. She looked as if she could have posed for one of the many Aphrodite statues that dotted the capital, and though she was taller than he by several inches, people rarely noticed, so caught up were they in her startling beauty. Her blond Celtic hair and ice blue eyes contrasted starkly with the raven-haired beauties of Rome, as did her shrewd mind.

"No," Balbinus said to his mistress of a year. "I shall not be enticed. I must maintain my wits to deal with the day's urgent obligations."

"Do these obligations flow from Senator Publius Coelius?"

He stared at her, stunned.

"You talk in your sleep," she said.

"And I also tell you far too much," he said. "I deserve what the Fates have slated for me."

"And what is that, my love, anathema in the lower regions of Hades?" She laughed and her voice sounded like a chime tinkling in the wind. "Now that we have established the grim nature of your destiny," she teased, "there appears little reason to maintain your stolid silence on the day's happenings."

"Look around you," he said. "I am a wealthy man ... and generous."

"You are."

"But at every turn they thwart my efforts to rise any higher than a cobbler." He shook his head. "Now danger haunts my every step, pursues me like a starving animal."

"And what faces should we put on these pursuers?"

Balbinus sighed. "A soldier named Vectis Trebellius and—"

"A soldier? A common soldier?"

"Yes, but—"

"Balbinus, look at me," she said, inclining her head. "How could someone of his station pose a problem to a great man like you."

Balbinus allowed himself a smile. Calpurnia was right. He was a great man. "Modesty forbids me to repeat what Senator Coelius had to say, but he too made your same observation. He wants me to ... well, do away with the man ... hire someone, you understand."

"Sound advice."

"Yes ... it's true ... then I would have only one pursuer."

"And who might that be?"

He opened his mouth but found it hard to say the name.

She waited.

"Senator Titus Severus," he said, "is conducting an investigation that might involve me."

Calpurnia moved her body to make more room on the couch.

"No," he said, "my soul is vexed. I must—"

"Come."

Like a child he obeyed, collapsing into her open arms and pressing his head into her breast. He closed his eyes and poured out the events of the past weeks, how Emperor Antoninus and Senator Coelius had denied his petition for a Senate seat, and everything he had learned of the investigation.

"And the worst of it," he moaned, "is that I offered the emperor two million sesterces to aid the orphan brats of Italia."

"Two million," Calpurnia said, "you *are* generous."

"And now that I have spoken, I will have to render payment."

"Yes, he is the emperor."

"You would have been proud of me," he said. "I stood before the emperor himself and like a gladiator facing his own destruction, I never hesitated to offer my neck. As quick as you could imagine, I put myself into debtor prison." He laughed bitterly. "I pledged the money in the name of the divine Faustina … that dead cow."

Calpurnia stroked his hair, calming his spirit. "The emperor gave you nothing in return?" she asked.

"Nothing."

"Well, then," she murmured, "he can hardly expect you to turn over the entire amount to his special charities. You might give his orphanages one million, and donate the other million to orphanages of your own choosing."

"What orphanages—" He stopped.

She smiled.

"Yes, of course," he said. He bit his lip, thinking. "With a million sesterces added to his coffers, the emperor will have no reason to complain."

"Nor to scrutinize your other donations."

Balbinus felt a burden tumble from his shoulders. He nestled into her and inhaled the costly Spanish perfume she had dabbed on her neck. Calpurnia might be an expensive woman to maintain, but she was worth every sesterce.

"This is a season of triumph for you," she said. "The emperor has given you a personal audience, a rare gift indeed. And you responded magnificently. In the future when he hears the name of Gaius Balbinus, he will think of compassion."

"That's true," Balbinus said. "Orphanages are important to this man. And who else has been as openhanded?"

"What was it the emperor said about acts of mercy?"

"They should not go unrewarded," he said, feeling at ease. Her warmth contrasted sharply with the cool of the garden. Something about Calpurnia soothed his soul, whether her eminently sensible suggestions or her total lack of fear, he didn't know, but her strength imbued him with a confidence he had never before possessed.

"Master?" The steward had arrived flanked by four servants bearing trays piled with steaming ducks' legs wrapped in bacon and lettuce, whole quails, honeyed asparagus and artichokes, burned almonds and walnuts mixed with peach slices, tiny rolls fresh from the oven, and containers of wine.

"Finally," Balbinus said, rubbing his ample stomach. "With the pressures of the day, I have eaten less than an Athens beggar."

"Tell me about Senator Coelius," Calpurnia said as she nibbled an asparagus head.

Balbinus stuffed a roll into his mouth and said in a muffled voice, "You can be certain Coelius finds Severus's investigation intensely interesting. He thinks I know nothing, but believe me, Coelius's name occurs sufficient times in Atilius Titianus's correspondence. How deeply he involved himself in the plot," he said, gesturing with a duck leg, "I cannot say. But he has reason to fear Severus."

Calpurnia reached across and dabbed his face with a cloth. Then she said, "We will keep a close watch on events, but for now leave Coelius to deal with Severus."

"And Vectis Trebellius shall disappear in the Dacian mountains," he said, feeling a measure of peace for the first time that day.

"I think you will make a fine senator," she said.

"The gods are arrayed against me."

"You despair too soon."

"And you are a dreamer of dreams."

Calpurnia moistened her lips with wine. Then she asked softly, "What would you give this dreamer if she gave you your dream?"

He tried to answer but her hot breath was on his mouth, and her lips whispered urgently, "Whatever would you give me for such a prize?"

9

"Caledonians! Listen to me!" Taranis shouted. He had mounted a flat rock near the open plain, cupping his hands to make his voice heard. Beside him stood Cronn and several other senior commanders, their faces resolute and grim.

Neeve strained to hear. Commanders were repeating Taranis's words, but the wind shaking the leaves behind her made it difficult to hear.

"There is the mighty Roman army!" Taranis bellowed, pointing to the endless sea of metal clad soldiers. "Slaves! That's what they want. They have their carts loaded with chains to drag us to the other side of the world so, like mules, we can grind out our days serving their Empire. But there are no chains for me ... not for me."

Warriors everywhere roared their approval.

"The Romans will not leave us in peace," he continued. "I have always believed—and still believe today—that there will come a time when this land will be free from these arrogant tyrants." The warriors cheered. "They force us to work the mines and till the fields so they can sit in their hot baths and screech orders. Well," he said, raising his long sword, "we are free Caledonians, and we don't take orders! Not from them," he shouted, pointing to the Roman legions behind him. "Not from anybody!"

Neeve tilted her chin forward, proud of her brother.

"How many of you have walked across the battlefield at Mons Graupius?" he cried. "And how many of you have not wept as you remembered the bravery of Calgacus and his thirty thousand warriors? Yes, you wept. I did too. Calgacus refused to run. He refused to kneel. He refused to be remembered as a lap dog that crawled to his master. He planted his sword at Mons Graupius and he said, 'No! I will not bend!' He chose to die rather than serve foreign masters."

"We will not serve the Romans," the warriors shouted over and over again. "May the gods give us death!"

Neeve remembered her premonition. She had seen her brother lying dead on the ground and the Romans gathered like wolves around his body. Taranis too must have had a premonition about this day. Why else would he mention the fated Calgacus and his thirty thousand? He expected to die and was preparing his warriors for a perilous battle.

"Our enemies surround us," Taranis said. "Look at them! They stand in lines like tin idols at the traders. And they can stand there until they fall asleep. We will not attack. We will not leave this position. We will force them to come to us, and then we will take ten Romans for every Caledonian."

The warriors roared their approval.

"Do you understand?" he asked. He waited until all the commanders had explained the situation to the warriors, and then he repeated: "We will not leave this hillside until I give the order. You know what Roman armies do … they stand forever in their formations trying to make us lose patience. When that doesn't work—and it is useless for them to try it today—they will tempt us with their auxiliaries. But-we-will-not-move!"

Commanders everywhere urged patience.

Taranis gestured around him. "Look well upon this stony hill," he said. "Generations from now, Caledonians great and small will say, 'This is where it happened! This is where your fathers faced three legions of the Roman army, and they spit on the ground and said, "Who are these Romans that they should enslave our children?"' Yes, many of us will die today, but I tell you the truth. Many more … many thousands of Romans will fall to the ground cursing their leaders for bringing them to Caledonian land. When the Roman overlords think of sending other armies beyond the Wall, they will tremble because of this day. Look well upon this hill."

Neeve cheered again, her voice lost in the roar of deep voices.

"I pledge to you this day," Taranis shouted above the noise, "that I will fight as a true warrior of this sacred soil. And if I see you tonight in the eternal forest, I will look you in the eye and say that I did not die easily, that I took a hundred Romans with me to the grave! I will say that this sword," he raised it again, "sliced that hissing dragon off its pole!"

The Caledonians shrieked and howled. They banged their swords on their shields and cried out to the gods for power. Some cut their arms. Some cast themselves to the ground. And some ignored the cries of their commanders and burst across the grasslands toward the enemy. They threw off their clothes and ran with swords high, calling out curses. When they reached the other side of the grasslands, the wall of shields opened and closed again, swallowing its victims, and as if nothing had happened. Moments later a stern reminder came from the commanders that the Caledonians were to discipline themselves. They were to wait for the Romans to attack. Every Caledonian life must cost the Romans dearly.

Taranis stared at the legions, looking for clues. He knew it was a useless effort. They lined up the same way no matter what the plan. They were nothing like a Celtic army that overwhelmed its enemies with a sudden, bone-shattering attack. The legion had great flexibility. Even in the fever of battle, it could detach cohorts and use them to exploit weaknesses in their enemies.

Taranis turned to one of his interpreters who could read Roman signs. "Anything yet?" he asked.

"Uncertain, commander," the interpreter said, his eyes riveted on the officers near Legate Verus who were using smoldering fagots to spell out orders. In the southern Roman lands the legions used code books to prevent enemies from understanding their messages. But here in the north they assumed no Caledonian would have the skills to decipher their signals.

They may have been right. The interpreter was frowning as he stroked his wax tablet with a stylus. Clearly, he was having difficulty interpreting the Roman signs from Legion VI. Finally he turned to Taranis.

"Well?" Taranis was growing impatient.

The interpreter groaned. "They have finished signing," he said. "I'm sorry, commander. There is much I didn't understand."

"We have little time," Taranis said curtly. "If you know something, you had better say it now."

The interpreter mopped his face. "The signs were clear on one thing," he said. "Legion VI will hold a defensive position."

"A feint?"

"Yes. The orders call for VI to initiate the action, then fall back to a holding position."

"Anything else?"

The interpreter took a deep breath. "There was something about Legions II and XX holding until they received a signal from Legate Verus, but ... I can't be certain." He gave Taranis an apologetic look.

Taranis clapped him on the shoulder. "You have done well," he said.

The interpreter mumbled his thanks but left with drooping head. He had hoped to do better.

Taranis glanced at Cronn. "What do you think?"

Cronn shrugged. "It looks like Verus wants us to think the primary attack will come from his own legion."

"A natural thing," Taranis said. "Most Roman generals want the glory."

"He's crafty. He is betting you will think he is no different."

"He is no different."

"Then why would he order Legion VI to fall back and hold?"

Taranis surveyed the legions and said slowly, "He will fall back because he wants us to hit him with our full assault. Then when we are engaging him, he will signal Legions II and XX to attack our left flank, to turn us."

"A good strategy," Cronn said, but he looked puzzled.

"What troubles you?"

"The strategy reduces Verus to a defensive position. It seems strange that so vain a general would permit the lesser generals in Legions II and XX to take the glory."

"True," Taranis said, "but I think he wants to pressure us into the gap between the two legions. Then he can swing Legion VI around to trap us in the center of the grasslands. He will deliver the decisive blow."

Cronn nodded. "If this is what Verus intends, can we disrupt his plans?"

"I think so. Give orders for everyone to press together to make our army appear smaller. Then gather the senior commanders. I have a plan."

Neeve stood in the tightly packed wedge of archers that had been positioned on a hill behind the swordsmen. The blue-painted warriors were crammed together by the thousands on a rocky hillside with their backs to the woods. Many were bare-chested and wore only trousers and boots. Some had helmets with horns, or had spiked their hair with chalk to make their oversized bodies look even bigger.

The Romans always planned carefully before making war with the gigantic Celts. Even Celtic women were taller than most Roman men, and there were many women in the Caledonian army besides Neeve. The Celts prized their women warriors. Around the fires they told stories about Celtic women who chanced across Roman soldiers and came home with their ears. Women landowners fought equally with the men, though most were archers or supply train workers.

"A commander!" one of the archers said, poking Neeve.

Neeve looked to see a heavily armed man bulling his way through the crush of warriors. The commanders were easy to recognize. They wore tunics and armor, and something distinctive to make themselves visible to their men. This one wore a black and yellow tartan and a single elk's horn that pointed straight up from his helmet like a spike.

He spoke briefly to the leader of the archers, who then selected three hundred bowmen to follow the tartan-clad commander up the rocky slope into the woods where several other commanders were waiting. A thousand warriors had already slipped along a ridge that led to a steep ravine at the north end of the valley. The plan was simple. Use the events of the previous night to work against the Romans. Legion XX had been tricked once, and they might be overly vigilant in protecting their flanks. It might be possible to convince Legions II and XX that the main body of the Caledonian army was not on the rocky incline, but behind them in the woods, the way they'd been the night before. The smaller force of warriors would move quietly down the ravine until they emerged behind Legions II and XX. Then, sounding a dozen horns, they would charge out of the woods, stirring up dust and making as much noise as possible. When Legions II and XX turned to protect their flank, Taranis would fall upon them with the main body of his army, leaving a skeleton defense to hold off Legion VI.

Neeve found herself staring at the elk's horn as she listened to the commander explain the plan. A chill ran through her body as she thought about the impending battle. She moved out of the shade onto a sunny patch of ground, but it did little to calm her fears. Several archers gave her encouraging smiles, but she knew that with three legions arrayed against them, there was little hope. Her eyes drifted across the forest. She couldn't help noticing the autumn wash of colors that cheered the darker parts of the woods. White birches with yellow-stained leaves blended with the reds and oranges of oaks and hazels. Creeping lady tresses peeked over the moss carpet under old pines, and high overhead, black squirrels bent branches as they bounded from tree to tree. Neeve inhaled the crisp, sweet air, and reminded herself she was a Caledonian warrior. Every generation had to stand against tyranny, and now, like it or not, her day had come.

"Warriors first," the commander said. Already half the warriors had disappeared into the rocks and trees along the edge of the valley.

Finally, he signaled the bowmen to follow the warriors. Many of the men had hunted these woods and had great confidence they could make it behind the Roman forces without being spotted. The legions had no familiarity with the northern forests, they said, and would easily be taken by surprise. Neeve had no reason to doubt their claims, but she also had years of experience in Roman forts, and she knew what these soldiers could do. Surprise or not, the Caledonians were facing three battle-hardened legions. Even Taranis knew the Caledonian cause was lost, and Neeve remembered the blind tribune. "Don't go back," he had said. "The Celtic tribes are doomed."

A disquieting thought pushed into Neeve's consciousness, a thought so absurd and incongruent with Caledonian blood, and so much a stigma of shame that she was embarrassed to admit it even to herself. She hurried along the narrowing trees, as if she could outrun the thought that was keeping pace with her. The forests were deep, she knew, and a person could easily slip off when no one was looking. Soon the battle would begin, and in the ensuing chaos, who would notice if she lingered at the edge of the fray? One archer, more or less—what did it matter? She could lie and tell survivors she had fought till the end. But if she stayed … would she survive? Would she ever see Vectis again? Or would her life end on the forest floor with some brutal Roman driving a sword into her stomach?

She shuddered.

"Stop it!" she told herself. "Stop it now!" She had faced dangers before, many times, and never once had she shirked her duty. Why should this be any different? But of course she knew why this was different … she had too much time to think, and feared what the gods had planned for them.

She shook the loathsome thoughts from her mind. Cowards who hid in the woods were already dead on the inside. They lived lives of shame and were better off in the ground. Her brother would never run, and how could she even think about abandoning him?

The wind swirled through the trees and seemed to whisper the precious name of Nemetona, the Celtic goddess of war. Neeve ran her eyes over the darker parts of the woods wondering if Nemetona were watching her at this very moment. Surely the goddess knew every fear that pulsed with Neeve's rapidly beating heart. Yes, Nemetona knew, and she would provide a wall of protection around her servant. And if, as sometimes happened, the goddess decided to collect Neeve's spirit on this day, at least her spirit would be taken to the eternal forest in a chariot of light because she had fought bravely and not slunk off into the woods.

Neeve sighed. A measure of peace began to settle her fragmented thoughts. Everything rested securely in the hands of the gods.

"Move! Move!" a commander mouthed to the line of Caledonians that approached his position. He pointed to a half-dozen spots on the embankment where hundreds of feet had trampled the grass to mud. The warriors immediately clambered up and disappeared into the woods. Neeve followed, trying to keep her balance as she mounted the slippery embankment. When she reached the top of the ridge, more commanders were giving directions, sending warriors one way, the archers another. On the ground lay the bodies of two Roman scouts who had been inspecting the woods when the Icenis passed by.

Taranis studied the three legions stretched out before him. With his back to the woods, he had a defensible position, but not one that favored Celtic-style warfare. The Celts charged with wild abandon, blowing horns and shrieking, terrorizing the enemy with the erratic movements of their chariots. But here they had no chariots, and no room for their warriors to maneuver. They were facing a straight-ahead battle against disciplined Roman legions that rarely broke and ran. Everything depended on the Celts' ability to deceive the enemy. Taranis mumbled a prayer to the gods that his ruse would work, for without their help, he knew all would be lost.

"Julius Verus may be better than other Roman generals," Cronn said, "but I think you have unraveled his battle plan. His aggressive style will deliver to him an unpleasant surprise."

"I hope you're right," Taranis said as he squinted in the morning sun at the endless rows of soldiers that made up Legion VI. Thousands of legionaries stood dead still, legs apart, short swords at their right hips, supported by long straps slung over their shoulders. Each carried a dagger and two needle-topped spears. Their shields, which rested on the ground, were almost as tall as their stunted, olive-skinned bodies, and they wore identical segmented armor, hob-nailed boots, and helmets tied under the chin. Near the back with several mounted officers Verus sat arrogantly on his white stallion, his heavily armed bodyguard surrounding him.   One guard, a barrel-chested man with proud bearing, held the long pole on which flew the dragon vexillum. It writhed and moaned eerily in the wind.

"Don't be fooled by their lack of movement," Taranis shouted to the warriors around him. "They'll come to life soon enough."

Directly in front of the Roman legions stood hordes of German mercenaries with their legendary axes. They looked twice the size of their legionary counterparts, and although a Roman centurion had placed them in rows, and had undoubtedly ordered them to remain still, they seemed to be moving constantly, shooing away flies and shifting weight from one foot to the other. They were hired warriors looking for plunder, or for citizenship if they survived, but their swaggering attitude showed they were no lackeys. They had fought many battles, and this was just one more.   The entire legion was flanked by hundreds of other mercenaries—slingers, assorted bowmen, and Syrian cavalry whose sleek horses shuddered and pawed at the ground, impatient for the conflict to begin. In the center, the blocks of legionaries stood rock still.

"Verus marched two legions over fifty miles," Taranis said. "There is no doubt he's aggressive."

"He hasn't built the usual fenced camp," Cronn observed.

"Why fence a camp when you have three legions?"

"We had them," Cronn said, smiling grimly. "We had a whole legion on the run."

Taranis nodded.   He knew this was Cronn's way of saying goodbye. It would not be long now. In his heart he cursed the Druids for not calling down the gods properly. They loved human sacrifices but nothing ever seemed to come of it. And when the battles began, the Druids headed for the deepest parts of the forests. He snorted. Cronn was right. Had they been granted two more hours, they would have destroyed Legion XX. Then they could have regrouped in the highlands, added chariots and warriors from other Celtic tribes, and faced Legions II and VI at a place of their own choosing. Now three legions had them against a wall of trees with a sliver of land on which to fight.

Taranis turned his attention to Legions II and XX. They had banded together into three enormous lines that covered almost the entire grasslands. On their left flank, in the space between them and Legion VI, they had placed their Gallic auxiliaries to make certain the Caledonians had no escape route.

The bugles of Legion VI sounded. The Germans raised their axes. More bugles. The Germans started forward.

Taranis swung around to observe the Caledonians. They were ready. Their eyes gleamed as they screamed and banged their swords on their shields.   With commanders everywhere reminding the warriors to remain on the hillside, the entire army held its ground.

Taranis tied his yellow hair back and said to Cronn, "I am asking much of you, my friend. If you cannot hold Legion VI, you must survive."

"I will survive."

"You will not concern yourself for me."

Cronn rubbed his face and said, "Commander, you will surprise and destroy the other two legions—"

"If I fail, you will obey my wishes."

"I will obey," Cronn said.

10

Balbinus beamed at his beautiful Calpurnia as they strolled along the Portico of a Hundred Pillars in Rome's northern section. His whole life was suddenly coming together. He still had some distance to go to fulfill his dream of becoming a senator, but at least he was moving toward his goal. In the past two years he had become a wealthy man, someone who talked daily with the famed and powerful, and had even drawn to himself the most desirable woman in Rome. Calpurnia! The incredible, magnificent Calpurnia. Balbinus had met Calpurnia at a dinner party given by Saufeius Ahala, a senator known for his lavish gatherings. He had found her standing alone under a lantern on the broad pathway that led to the pools and sculpted hedges of Ahala's exquisite gardens

"A lovely party," he had said awkwardly. Even with his newfound wealth, he felt dumpy and unattractive beside so striking a woman. She turned to face him but said nothing for the longest time. Balbinus's face burned with embarrassment. He wished he hadn't been so ambitious in his choice of women. He wiped a thick paw across his jowls and was about to apologize for intruding on her privacy when suddenly she spoke, and her first words haunted him to this day.

"Is it you?" she asked.

He tried to say something, but managed only a quizzical look.

She searched his face for an answer.

He met her eyes and found it hard to keep from staring. They were so clear and so blue. It seemed as if he could peer into her soul. "I … I don't understand," he said. "Were you expecting someone?"

She looked away, as if she were pondering the situation. Then she said in a low voice, "Forgive me. I must appear foolish to you."

"No, not at all."

"Well, I appear foolish to myself." She turned to go.

"Wait."

She started down the path.

"Please," Balbinus said, trying to gain her attention. "It is I who must apologize. You were waiting for someone and I disturbed you."

"You are very kind."

"You were waiting for someone, weren't you?"

"I was," she said, a mysterious smile on her lips.

Balbinus suppressed his curiosity. What was he doing striking up a conversation with a woman of her grace and sophistication? He should leave now before he humiliated himself further. But like a seafarer encountering a siren after a long voyage, he could neither draw himself away, nor resist the impulses surging through his body. Something good would come from this chance meeting; he would make it so. Not knowing what to say, he repeated his earlier words that it was indeed a lovely night for a dinner party. She said nothing so he feigned interest in the roses and hyacinths that bordered the walkway, concluding his inspection with praise for the hothouses that produced such wonders in the off-season.

"Yes," she said, "the frost has already claimed most of the flowers even in the lowlands." She glanced around the gardens. "I love this time of the evening, when the light is fading and the lanterns are being lit along the pathways. It reminds me of childhood fables."

Balbinus was thrilled she had volunteered a pleasantry. He pulled in his stomach and tried to appear refined when he said, "My favorite tales were always about Greek adventures in faraway lands."

"I too enjoy Greek tales."

Encouraged, he said, "I remember Aeschylus talking about lanterns by the sea. He called them 'flaring torches on towered bastions.'"

"Sounds like a delightful castle to visit."

"Yes."

"You have a good mind for beautiful words."

"Thank you," he said, uncertain whether he had garbled Aeschylus. But no matter. She seemed pleased.

"Do you believe, like Diogenes the philosopher, that a pure man can be found under the light of a lantern?"

He glanced up. "You mean like this one?"

"Yes."

Balbinus swallowed. Definitely an unusual conversation. Why had she mentioned Diogenes, who taught that light could pierce the eye, laying bare the soul? In the glow of the garden lanterns her lucid eyes transfixed him, and for an instant he wondered whether she somehow might have glimpsed something of his own soul.

As if she knew the effect her eyes were having, she rescued him. "You were right," she said, turning. "I was waiting for someone … someone very special."

"And who might that be?"

"I'm not certain."

Balbinus moved slightly to gain a better view of her face. "If you are uncertain," he asked, striving for wit, "how will you know when he arrives?"

She didn't smile.

He scolded himself for his blunder. In a serious conversation with an attractive woman, you do not try to be witty. He assumed a thoughtful face and said, "If you don't mind my saying so, I find you a fascinating person."

"I'm a lonely person," she said.

So beautiful a woman, lonely? Balbinus didn't know what to say, and his emotions were running away with his thoughts. He wondered whether potential suitors might have felt inferior in this woman's presence, and as such, never dared approach her. Could it possibly be that he had a chance after all? He screwed up his courage and said, "What did you mean when you asked if it was me?"

"Why did you come to the courtyard?" she countered.

"I don't know. I suppose I was admiring Saufeius's gardens, and then I saw you, and thought it strange you were alone."

She nodded, again as if she were weighing his answer. "Do you believe that in the stars we find our destinies?" she asked.

"I do."

"Then I will give you your answer." She paused. "A year ago, on this night, a falling star directed me to a seer on the outskirts of Rome. He predicted that on the same night the following year … if I were alone under the light of a lantern … my love would come to me."

Balbinus felt his breath grow shallow.

"For an entire year," she said, "I have been alone, waiting for this night."

"So you expect the Fates will reveal someone to you?"

"Yes."

Balbinus straightened his back.

"I chose a lantern in this remote part of the garden," she said, "because I wanted to be certain there was no mistake."

Now, many months later, Balbinus found himself strolling along the crowded Portico of a Hundred Pillars with the most intriguing woman in Rome. She had lost none of her mystery, and her beauty had become almost a burden to bear. Everyone, it seemed, stared as they passed, especially the men. But under that exquisite exterior, Calpurnia possessed a keen mind, shrewd and a shade crafty, but totally dedicated to helping him succeed.

Calpurnia squeezed Balbinus's arm tightly.

She enjoyed these walks through the gardens and colonnaded streets of Rome, a wealthy man by her side, a cluster of attendants treading softly at a respectful distance, eager to indulge her every whim.

Not long ago she had arrived in Rome virtually penniless, looking for a suitable match. For months she had studied every accessible senator and high council official, their patterns, their friends, their vices, but in the end she settled on a man of humble origins and newly acquired wealth. The more she learned about Balbinus, the more certain she became that the gods had prepared this man for her. He was the plodding sort, she had to admit, and he wore his accidental wealth like an ill-fitting tunic, but he was a perfect match for her talents. He was not like those born to power that swaggered about the forum with their gaggle of women, and who, with the changing of the wind, could discard a mistress like soiled linen. No, Balbinus was different. He was at heart a simple man, a servant who had by the will of heaven risen to occupy his master's villa. Of course, he could be imperialistic and vain about his elevated status—who wouldn't be? But inside he contended with rivers of doubt that threatened to overwhelm him. He desperately needed a discreet hand to protect him as he wended his way to the top. Calpurnia was the right woman to lift this simple man to dizzying heights and to make him respected even in the vaunted circles of Rome.

But Calpurnia knew that Balbinus was vulnerable in the shifting sands of Rome's political maneuverings. Senators like Publius Coelius could easily destroy her precious benefactor, and that, in turn, threatened her own existence. This she would not allow. She decided to visit Coelius to see if she might encourage him—and in turn, Fortuna, the goddess of fate—to move in her favor. Calpurnia remembered steeling her mind as she stepped out of her carriage at the magnificent estate of Senator Coelius. She had come uninvited, a risky maneuver, but one that she thought was absolutely necessary. After speaking to three successively higher ranked servants, the senator finally appeared.

"Mistress Calpurnia!" Coelius said, obviously unsure how to address her. "I trust your health is well."

She smiled and leaned toward him, allowing him to kiss her cheek. She understood the impact of her beauty and had learned long ago that her physical presence pleasured men. "I don't mean to intrude," she said.

"Not at all." He ushered her toward his private library. "Some mutton or oysters … wine perhaps?"

"Wine would be lovely," she said. The library was furnished with low tables, luxurious couches, and the kinds of sculptures you would expect to find only in the grandest of Rome's public buildings.

Floor to ceiling bookcases bulged with old books, scrolls and documents, and at the far end a large window overlooked a marble fountain and sculptured trees, a pleasant view that seemed more like a painting than a garden. Even with the open window, the library felt cozy and warm to the feet. All the floors and walls in Coelius's villa radiated heat, something that could only be accomplished with twenty slaves working full time to maintain the fires needed to pump that much hot air through the system.

Coelius waited until she had taken a seat under a lavish wall covering of Alexander riding his horse somewhere in Parthia, and then he drew a small couch near so they could chat. "I don't think I have ever actually conversed with you," he said, smiling faintly, "not that I haven't noticed Gaius Balbinus's good fortune. You embarrass this old room with your incredible loveliness."

"And you with your generous words," she said.

They talked about the provinces, about the recent fare at the Theater Marcellus, and the cool weather that had struck Rome so suddenly. After such pleasantries and several cups of the cellar's finest wines, Coelius felt free enough to ask her how she came to be Balbinus's mistress, and then observed that the Fates might just as easily have brought her to his door. Calpurnia laughed and commented that the Fates might have shielded him from a life of misery.

Somewhere around this time Calpurnia remembered asking permission to speak her heart.

He opened his arms and said, "I am yours to command."

She thanked him for his understanding, and then said simply, "I need your help." She sensed that putting her request in personal terms was the right approach. It made her seem weaker and acknowledged his position of power as one able to grant requests. Coelius was a senator, a man of influence, and used to people trying to manipulate him. She could see he rather enjoyed the challenge before him. And he was curious. Here was a woman in distress—an attractive woman—and she needed his help.

She watched him lean back on his couch, almost toying with her when he said in a chastening voice, "Now, Calpurnia, I hope you haven't overspent your allowance given you by Balbinus. Because I must say, you have exquisite taste in clothes and jewelry." He chuckled at his own humor and added, "A woman like you could be costly for someone of modest means. You might broaden your vista when considering suitors. A person of my station, perhaps, would be more appropriate."

She allowed her eyes to linger on his face longer than would be appropriate in a purely conversational setting. "I do spend generously," she admitted with a small smile on her lips, sensing his attraction to her, "but that is not my concern today."

He gestured for her to go on.

"It's about the Vectis Trebellius situation," she said in lowered voice.

"I see." He supplied a grave face. "I am surprised Balbinus would bother you with such weighty issues. You should be indulging yourself at the baths, trying new hair styles, or scampering about the theater, but not this ..." he waved his hand, dismissively, "this sordid political business. The man in your life should assume that responsibility."

"Perhaps, as you say, if I were with someone of higher station, I would choose other interests, but I'm afraid I must handle these details alone." She drew a deep breath and played her fingers across the patterned cushions. "Balbinus is a good man," she continued, "but I'm afraid he ... well, he does not have your ability or wisdom. I must arrange everything to make certain it flows smoothly and discreetly."

Coelius took a large swallow of wine. "I'm not certain I understand," he said.

"Yes, you do." She looked him directly in the eyes.

He rolled his lips. "You're right," he said, "and I won't let you struggle alone with this Trebellius matter. As I said, a woman should not have to involve herself in such distasteful things."

"I thank you for that." She patted his arm. As a gesture, it wasn't much, but she knew the power of a simple touch on a man's arm. "I need guidance. A name of someone with a proven reputation, and a contact would be invaluable."

Coelius rose and closed the library door. She smiled inside. He was acting the great man now, as he moved slowly toward the window, making a big show of weighing his words before he spoke. He turned, hands clasp behind his back in a thoughtful pose. "There is a man," he said slowly, "a Syrian called Brutus. Not that I think Brutus is his real name, but he is by all accounts excellent and discreet—some say the best in Rome at his trade. You might send a boy to inquire at the olive oil importer across from the amphitheater."

Calpurnia nodded. She already knew about Brutus but needed some realistic pretense for meeting with the senator. She had other things on her mind. Now she would be patient, wait until the last minute before driving home the stake. "You have been overly kind with your time," she said, rising.

"Believe me, my time was well spent. Perhaps you would stay for the noon meal."

"I would be delighted another day," she said.

"Then we shall plan for it." He took her arm and escorted her through the door and down a broad passageway toward the entrance.

"You have lifted such a burden from me," she said.

"And you have graced my home like a goddess," he replied, covering her hand with his, and saying, "I would be honored if you would reconsider, and stay awhile."

Calpurnia understood the invitation, but was not about to throw away the permanence of Balbinus—plodder though he might be—to satisfy the fleeting appetites of a senator. Even if he were genuinely interested in her, it would undoubtedly end in a month. And then where would she be?

They stopped at the large walnut doors. "You are so kind," she said, offering her cheek. He leaned to kiss her, but as he did so, she turned her face slightly so they kissed in that small place at the corner of the mouth, where only intimates and cherished friends dare invade.

Encouraged, he tried again, this time with humor. "Stay, and I will dismiss every female from the entire villa so that I will attend only to you."

She laughed. "And who will attend to us?"

"You are right. I will buy hundreds of new slaves, all of them old and withered."

"Curse the Fates that they led me to another door," she said with a sigh. Then with a serious voice, she added, "You have given me strength today. Soon this unpleasant Trebellius issue will be a dim memory and our minds can turn to other things."

"I would like that," he said.

She dropped her eyes to the gleaming marble stairs that descended graciously to the paved drive and the rich fields beyond. Then she steeled her mind for what was to come. She wasn't fooled by Coelius's friendly manner. She knew all about his bullying ways, his veiled threats to Balbinus. Now that his guard was down, it was time to clarify the situation and show Coelius who ought to be feared.

"Again," she said, "I thank you. I'll find this Syrian, Brutus, and hopefully the next time we meet, Vectis Trebellius will pose no trouble for anyone." She paused. "But I'm sure you know there are many with access to troublesome correspondences besides this one soldier. Just the other day I ran across a packet of letters that linked several senators to the schemes of former Senator Atilius Titianus." She gave him an apologetic look and said, "I am sorry to say, but your name did appear more than once."

Coelius dismissed her comment with a waft of his hand. "It must have been a ploy by Titianus to spread responsibility for his treasonous acts," he said. "It's quite common for senators to do such things."

"I have little knowledge of the Senate," she said, "but I am sure that's true."

"The letters are of little import, but I do appreciate being informed of them."

He spoke smoothly, but Calpurnia noted the tension around his eyes.

"What have you done with these letters?" he asked casually.

"I burned the ones that falsely implicated you," she said with pride in her voice.

"And the others?"

"I sealed them in a pouch together with Balbinus's will and sent them to a scribal aide of the Emperor Antoninus."

"Indeed."

"Yes. In the event that Balbinus should suffer an untimely death, I gave instructions that the pouch should be opened." She narrowed her eyes and said, "I do not trust certain senators, and the sooner they learn that, the safer Balbinus will be."

"You are an enterprising woman," Coelius said.

She smiled slightly. "I believe in loyalty. You have helped Balbinus often, and I in turn burned the letters that concerned you, false though they may be. We need not fear our friends, wouldn't you agree?"

"There is no greater gift than friendship," he said.

Calpurnia left that afternoon confident that the scheming Senator Coelius would think carefully before causing Balbinus trouble. He certainly knew she would not be so foolish as to burn letters of such importance. Given the situation, he might even have reason to aid Balbinus in his bid for the Senate, but that was a matter for a later date. In any event, Calpurnia had no doubt the senator preferred his skeletons left in the ground.

When Balbinus sensed Calpurnia squeezing his arm, his heart warmed. He felt safe with her, so shrewd a judge of situations she always seemed to be. Increasingly he had found himself relying on her judgment, especially when it came to the dangers that stalked him in the halls of Roman intrigue. She had often warned him about Senator Coelius, so he was surprised to hear she had paid the senator a visit, and that the senator had again said they should consider using an assassin to remove the troublesome Vectis Trebellius. Coelius, she believed, was no friend, but his concerns about Vectis Trebellius were indisputable. Trebellius had the potential to destroy lives, including their own, with the Atilius Titianus mess. So Balbinus had given her permission to find an assassin. Not only did she hire Rome's best assassin, a Syrian named Brutus, she conducted business using several intermediaries to make certain nothing could be traced back to them.

She chose this particular assassin because of the care he took in protecting his own identity, using his own intermediaries. Although Coelius knew about their plans to hire the assassin, she was certain that neither he nor the meddlesome Senator Severus would be able to prove Balbinus had anything to do with Trebellius's death.

On the positive side, Calpurnia's choice of assassins made certain that the removal would be clean and well-planned; he had never failed an assignment. With such a reputation, Balbinus knew the negative side: the man would be expensive, but he had no idea how expensive until he was told that he would have to see his bankers personally to approve the massive outlay of gold. Calpurnia always did things well, but she bothered herself little about cost.

Balbinus knew that Calpurnia had come from great wealth, because she had told him everything about her noble family in Germania and the wars that had devastated her fortune. With nothing but her good name she set off to make a new life in Rome. Naturally, Balbinus offered to settle her debts. It was a shrewd move, he reasoned. He would pay her trivial debts and appear enormously generous in the process. After all, what could she possibly owe? Would any merchant allow a foreigner to mark up significant credit? Of course not. But as it turned out, she had accrued debts that would stagger a senator.

A lesser woman might have hidden her impoverished situation. But Calpurnia told him the startling truth with an unwavering eye. She had arrived in Rome with a carriage, a reasonable gown and a few coins. Everything else she left in Germania. But those with noble blood, she said, never fear adversity. They always rise again. Having been accustomed to wealth and privilege, she determined to continue her lifestyle once she was in the capital. She sold her carriage and used the money to hire a cluster of fawning servants. Shopkeepers simply couldn't believe someone of her bearing had few assets. She quickly acquired silk gowns from Serica, the mythical land in the east, rings of ruby and sapphire, and costly perfumes. She rented a luxurious villa on the fashionable Esquiline Hill, which Balbinus had since purchased for her, and attended the best dinner gatherings. No one questioned a woman with hair sprinkled in gold dust and shoes covered in pearls.

Yes, Calpurnia was an amazing woman.

Balbinus adjusted his cloak to fend off a sudden breeze that shook the broad-leafed plantains lining the colonnaded street. Calpurnia pressed closer to him and said, "Brutus left Rome today."

Balbinus wrenched his head around, startled by her comment. "How do you know this?" he asked in a hoarse whisper, as if other strolling couples insulated by throngs of servants would understand such a conversation.

"I receive reports," she said, her eyes roaming the pergolas adorned with twisting grape vines, now brilliant with autumn leaves. "Our army friend is already heading east by public carriage on the Valerian Way. He intends to cross the Adriatic Sea at Aternum."

"Public carriage? How uncomfortable."

"Yes, and how accessible."

"You amaze the gods," Balbinus said. "How did you—"

"I sent Senator Coelius a message, anonymous of course, but I am sure he knew it came from us, suggesting that the Senate might consider giving Trebellius a legion escort only *after* he crossed the Adriatic Sea. Brutus, I'm told, is pleased with the travel arrangements."

"So Vectis Trebellius will take a carriage to Aternum, unescorted, and then cross the Adriatic," Balbinus mused.

"Yes, but he won't make it to the Adriatic," she said, pausing momentarily to greet a man who had wished her a good day. "Brutus intends to finish it before Aternum."

Balbinus leaned over and kissed her lips. Yes, everything was flowing together.

11

The Roman cohort of German auxiliaries, axes raised, moved steadily toward the Caledonians.

Taranis had no illusions about Roman intentions. Their best general and three full legions were here to destroy the northern tribes. No Celtic army, he knew, could face Roman legions in the field. They were too organized, too disciplined, and too experienced in the art of war. For centuries they had campaigned in every theater imaginable, and like artisans working a craft, they practiced their skills daily. They knew how to fight in mountainous terrain, in forests, on the sea; they had the best weapons, the best armor, and superbly disciplined soldiers. When they faced formidable opponents, like German warriors, Balearic slingers, or Syrian archers, they soon hired them as mercenaries. Legionaries were not large men, nor particularly skilled in individual combat, but in battle formation their separate parts combined to produce an incredibly destructive machine.

Halfway across the field the Germans broke into a trot.

Their axes gleamed in the sun.

They burst up the hill toward the Caledonians.

"Hold! Hold!" Taranis shouted. All along the line commanders repeated the order to hold positions, stretching out their arms to contain the frenzied warriors. Clouds of arrows streaked through the air toward the fast-closing Germans. Dozens stumbled to the ground. Still they pounded on.

When the Germans were thirty feet out, the Caledonian attack horns sounded. The commanders stepped aside and the Caledonian hordes surged forward like a wave of water, the thunder of their feet filling the grasslands. Seconds later, the two armies crashed into each other, and the sounds of axes and swords shook the trees. Dust rose like smoke from a furnace and the acrid smell of blood burnt the nostrils. Men screamed and hollered; they slipped on the sticky, red muck that collected at their feet. Taranis shouted orders at his commanders, but his voice was lost in the tumult of battle.

The huge mass of Caledonians engulfed the smaller number of Germans. They slashed and stabbed at their equally vigorous enemy. Stunned warriors on each side fell to the ground screaming. Never could they have imagined themselves floundering at the feet of struggling men, holding their stomachs or throats as their life blood drained onto the pitiless soil. Hands, whole arms, steaming torsos met them as they tumbled into the dark place of forgotten men.

As the initial jolt of battle passed, the Caledonian wings listened to their commanders and tried to encircle the enemy. The Germans understood the strategy. They fought stubbornly against the encircling wings, charging and hacking with their giant axes. They seemed unperturbed by the growing threat on the wings as they whooped and darted at the closing pincers. Then, suddenly, the German commander turned and fled. Others around him followed. Then the whole German center collapsed. They bolted down the hill and toward the legionaries who were still standing in rows of tight boxes.

Taranis had seen the tactic before. The Germans were trying to lure the Caledonians down the hill and onto the flats where the legions waited. The Romans always trained their auxiliaries to follow the battle plan. Auxiliaries were the legion's shock troops, usually large German or Gallic warriors. They charged with uncontrolled fury and fought with such ferocity that they drained the enthusiasm for battle out of their enemy. That's when the legions would advance, often being met by a lifeless enemy, ready for defeat. Today the auxiliary's task was to lure the Caledonians onto the flats.

It didn't work.

The moment the Germans headed back toward Roman lines, Taranis signaled the horns, long, dull blasts that told the commanders to restrain their swordsmen from pursuing the enemy. The Caledonians complied, and a semblance of order returned to the ranks as the warriors found their way to their respective commanders. Then came the carts. Boys too young for battle hauled the squeaking carts through the mobs of warriors and onto the battlefield, collecting the dead and wounded. The heads of slain Germans were jammed on spikes to terrify the legionaries still waiting on the grasslands. "This will happen to you!" they shrieked in broken Latin, waving the severed heads and dancing gleefully.

Taranis mounted a large rock in front of the Caledonians, his brilliant red battle tunic contrasting sharply with the cheering blue-painted warriors. "The gods are with us!" he shouted, as he clasped his hands together to signal his pride in his warriors for not breaking ranks and chasing the Germans.

The hillside exploded in a thunderous noise.

"Be patient!" Taranis hollered through cupped hands. "We must wait again until the Romans advance. Obey your commanders." Everywhere commanders were praising their warriors and reminding them to wait for the attack horns.

Taranis ripped out his heavy, bloodstained sword and thrust it over his head. The warriors shrieked and howled. "When our horns sound ...." He paused. The ruckus subsided. "When our horns sound," he shouted, "we will stun these little Romans with the ferocity of the gods. They don't understand the rage on this hillside. They come from across the waters, bind us as slaves, kill our wives and children, and laugh as they do it." Taranis shook his fist and screamed, "They will not laugh today!" The warriors roared. "Toutorix will lap their blood from the ground!" The Caledonians pounded their shields, and commanders worked their warriors into a frenzy.

On the grasslands the mass of steel waited silently.

Taranis nodded to Cronn, who had caught his eye from the far side of the rocky incline. Cronn was busily instructing the commanders on their part in the battle, but in the brief glance he had said a lifetime of words. The Calgacus battle, as they called it, had finally come. They would not see each other again. Cronn would follow his orders, as he always did, but this time his loyalty would be tested.

Above the banging of Caledonian shields Taranis heard the Roman bugles. The legions were preparing for attack. They had concluded that the Caledonians were determined to hold the higher ground. A piercing trumpet cut through the racket on the hillside, sounding the advance. In that instant thousands of legionaries across the field lifted their shields from the ground and lurched forward.

The Caledonian commanders shouted orders to their sections. "Wait for the horns," they yelled. To keep the warriors at a fever pitch the commanders gnashed their teeth and cursed the invaders.

"Do you want the Romans to rape your mother tonight?" shouted one. "Because that's what they do."

"Romans hack children into chunks and feed their pigs," cried another.

"Do you want to be a slave of Rome?"

"Down on your knees! Worship the emperor!"

"Kill them all!" the commanders shouted. "Wait for the horns and kill every last one of these bastards!"

The warriors shrieked their war cries and smashed their swords violently on their shields.

By the time Neeve had reached the edge of the forest, the Caledonian diversion units were in place. She could see the back ranks of Legions II and XX, and with scores of other archers around her, she crawled into shooting range. Hundreds of warriors were already on their bellies, wriggling through the heather and stiff broom that dotted the grasslands. In the distance a lookout that was perched high in a tree sounded his horn. Suddenly the grasslands sprang to life. Horn blowers all over the field leapt to their feet and began blaring their horns. Warriors hidden in the grass also jumped up and banged their shields, stamped their feet, and whooped and hollered. Like everyone else, Neeve was shouting and throwing handfuls of dust into the air. Smoke fires swirled at the forest's edge and drifted across the field, further obscuring the true nature of the Caledonian attack.

The backside of the Roman ranks turned abruptly to face the new threat. Crowds of slaves that ministered to the officers in the field were scurrying to the edges of the ranks, as were the baggage handlers with their wagons. The scene was utter chaos with Roman surgeons scrambling to load wounded into carts, and centurions pushing engineers and other personnel not essential to the battle out of the way. The Caledonians were upon them. A thousand warriors were racing toward them out of the dust and smoke, screaming and battering their shields, and for all the Romans knew, this surprise attack could well be the main body of the enemy. Arrows flooded the skies. Some arced so high they fell like rain upon the startled legionaries.

Neeve herself released two-dozen arrows before the tartan-clad commander with the elk's horn signaled the archery commanders to stop the barrage. The charging warriors had reached the Roman lines.

Taranis waved the scout away. He didn't need to be told that the attack on the back ranks of Legions II and XX had begun. He could see the dust and smoke rising in the distance, and hear the screams and clash of battle.

Moments before, all three legions had been advancing slowly toward his position on the rocky slope. Then, as predicted, Legions II and XX stopped. They rested their shields on the ground, and waited. A trumpet blasted. The first line of Verus's Legion VI marched forward double time. Taranis signaled Cronn. He in turn signaled his commanders, who rushed out with a wall of warriors to meet the rapidly closing Romans. The warriors had spread themselves across the breadth of the hill, and many more warriors from the main body of Caledonians followed, but they were not part of Cronn's assigned forces. They were trying to make it appear as if the whole Caledonian army were charging down the hill toward Legion VI. When the time came they would join Taranis in his full assault on Legions II and XX.

As Taranis watched Cronn and his thin force bearing down on Legion VI, he had second thoughts.   Maybe the interpreter was wrong. Maybe Verus intended to crack the Caledonians with his own legion, in which case Cronn and his warriors would be cut down immediately. Taranis's body tensed when the legionaries hurled their needle-topped spears, striking scores of Cronn's warriors. The legion quick marched up the hill in its familiar protective formation, its front soldiers holding their shields steadily before their bodies, the rest with shields raised over their heads to provide a protective roof against falling arrows. They looked like a turtle shell approaching. When the two forces collided with each other, the Romans rammed their oversized shields into the sword-whirling Caledonians, trying to frustrate and slow the pace.

Taranis smacked his hands together.   Any thread of hope energized him. The interpreter was right. He had read the signs well. Legion VI was maintaining a defensive position, slowly falling back, acting as if the gritty Caledonians had surprised them with their aggressive charge down the hill.

That's when Legions II and XX were struck from behind.

The third line of every legion was populated with older soldiers who were experienced but nearing retirement. The first and second lines did most of the fighting, leaving the third to fight only in dire circumstances. They were reserves, mostly giving encouragement to the younger crop and, some would say, proving annoying with their endless recollections of glorious battles. Put simply, they had paid their dues. But suddenly they found themselves beset with screaming warriors and deadly missiles. The old men straightened their backs and squared up to face the nimble-footed enemy. They squinted into the growing smoke and dust and readied their spears.   Aged centurions twisted their heads, screamed orders.   Frantic buglers wailed their warnings. The mounted lancers, trying to bring order to the situation, lashed their horses toward the charging Caledonians, but with the smoke and spreading grass fires, their horses skittered from the fray.

Confusion swept over the Roman third line. Somehow the Caledonians had massed behind them! The enemy was cunning;

many Roman soldiers probably wondered if they should be this far north on an island that had nothing to offer but fog and rain. Who cared about these giants in the north? Let them paint themselves blue and run naked in the woods with their fanatical Druid priests! The legions should reinforce Emperor Antoninus' Wall, not chase after Caledonian warriors in Rome's most distant province. Twice now their wily adversary had tricked Legion XX. That in itself was omen enough for the common soldier to leave. But, of course, this was not the way of Roman officers. Already they had shifted their lines to meet the incoming threat.

On the rocky incline Taranis watched. He had been waiting for this moment. He signaled his horn blowers to sound the charge.

Neeve could see that Taranis's strategy was working better than anyone had reason to hope, and a feeling of indescribable joy filled her entire body, so much so that she found it hard to breathe. She had despaired of life for Taranis and Cronn, and for herself as well—but now Legions II and XX were in tatters. The dust and smoke had obscured the true nature of the attack, and Taranis's warriors were cutting a swath through the disorganized soldiers. With the battle now in the hands of the warriors, the elk-horned commander released the archers, and Neeve decided to climb farther up the hill, where the forest thinned into a rocky bluff, a difficult climb, but once on top she would have an unobstructed view of the battle. Several other archers had the same idea and were already nearing the summit. Neeve slipped her bow and arrow pouch over her back and climbed on all fours up the moss-covered mess of stone and broken trees.

"A good view," one said as he helped her up to the flattened top.

Neeve breathed her agreement. The panorama that stretched from one end of the grasslands to the other left her speechless. In the distant hills she could see threads of mist blowing lazily through the trees, and three sparrow hawks circling high in the sky, as if it were just another day in the Caledonian hills. She dropped her eyes to the smudge fires that still churned smoke into the dirty air. Even this far away she could taste the soot.

The battle raged in the valley below. The screams and shouts bothered her the most. Behind every cry, she knew, metal was piercing flesh. She searched for her brother's scarlet shirt amid his bare-chested warriors, but with the dust and smoke, all she could see was a brown cloud over the warriors.

Then she spotted him. Taranis was leading a spike of warriors, driving into the stubborn legionaries, trying to break through their ranks to split them in half. Neeve marked Taranis's position between two mountain peaks on the horizon, knowing how easy it would be to lose him in the thousands of milling soldiers below. Then she searched for Cronn's smaller force on the near side of the grasslands, and her mouth opened in pain. He was in trouble. The front wall of his warriors still held firm, but he was about to be surrounded.

The archers on the hillock noticed it too, and began pointing and lamenting, "What are the Romans doing?"

The entire second line of Legion VI had detached itself and was encircling Cronn's left flank. Taranis had surprised Legate Verus when he ambushed Legions II and XX from behind, but Verus swiftly corrected the situation with a bold sweep around Cronn's flank. Only a Roman legion could detach a third of its soldiers in the fever of battle and swing them around the enemy.

In minutes it was over. The mass of steel closed around Cronn's men like a metal fist and squeezed until there was no one left. Clouds of dust obscured her vision, but Neeve feared the worst. Then trumpets sounded and Legion VI squared up and marched briskly toward the backside of the main body of Taranis's warriors. The mounted lancers herded the warriors into tightly packed groups, making it impossible for them to use their long Celtic swords. Then the legionaries waded into the Caledonians, ramming them with their four-foot shields, pushing them into even tighter clusters as they arced their short swords upward in deadly underhand thrusts.

Neeve could see Taranis directing more warriors to the rear to face the oncoming Legion VI. But it was no use. Seeing the turn of events, the double legion of II and XX threw all three lines into the battle to make scores of tiny bridgeheads in the tangle of Caledonian warriors. When the bridgeheads linked, they used their shields the way Legion VI had done, and drove their swords into the bodies of the hapless warriors.

"The gods have deserted us!" cried one of the archers. He ran by Neeve and stumbled down the hillock. The others left too, their eyes wide with fear. Alone, Neeve stared at the bedlam below. Everything had changed. Whole groups of warriors fell under legionary swords as though they were being fed into a meat grinder. The clang of metal on metal died away, replaced with the dull sound of bodies being chopped, bones being shattered, groans and howls.

Suddenly, as if given a signal, the shredded remains of the Caledonian army took flight back across the valley. The Romans encircled and destroyed small clusters of the Celts, but always they left an escape route for the main body of warriors. They knew that trapped soldiers would fight to the death, but given the chance, those same men would flee to fight another day. The Romans, however, were not interested in giving their enemies another day. Hidden from view on the flanks they had stationed their cavalry to pursue and destroy the fleeing Caledonians.

Neeve knew she should leave too, but instead found herself peering through the smoky haze, hoping to glimpse her brother in the chaos below. She focused on the two distant mountain peaks and followed the line down to the grasslands, but the entire field of combat had changed.

Then she caught sight of Taranis's brilliant red tunic and his whirling sword. A cadre of commanders still flanked him, but the number had shrunk considerably. She could see him exhorting those nearby to link up with a larger pocket of Caledonians a hundred paces west of him. Then she understood. The battle was lost, but the Caledonians were not far from the woods. With the larger body they could regroup and beat back any Roman attempt to capture them. Legions functioned best in open spaces and they were unlikely to chase through the woods with a sizeable Caledonian force waiting for them. What he couldn't see, and Neeve could, was the beginning of flight in the larger group. The warriors at the edges turned and ran. Then the center, seeing no point in continuing the battle, discarded their swords and dropped to the ground. They had decided to throw themselves on the mercy of the Romans. They were choosing slavery rather than death.

Neeve turned her eyes back to Taranis and his group, who were slashing and hacking their way through the legionaries. She knew it was useless. They were now so few.

One by one the warriors around her brother disappeared into the disciplined killing machine as it ground steadily toward him. Centurions were pointing and directing their legionaries to focus on the commanders. A score of needle-topped spears held in reserve hurtled through the air. Several commanders beside Taranis fell. Then something struck Taranis in the back of the head. A sword, a spear, an arrow—Neeve didn't know. But she saw an explosion of yellow hair and a splatter of red, and her brother tumbled to the ground.

A groan escaped Neeve's lips.

She sank to the earth.

She stared mindlessly at the knot of Caledonians that had gathered around her fallen brother. They seemed as stunned as she was. Then, suddenly, the circle of warriors threw down their weapons, as if their will to fight had died with their commander. Some tried to flee the field, but the surging Romans cut them down instantly. Neeve couldn't pull her eyes away from Taranis. The whole world seemed to fade into shadows—the roiling mass of men, the stench of blood, the cries of victory. All she could see was the lifeless form of her brother. She had feared this moment, but now that it had come, she simply could not believe it. First Cronn, and now Taranis. How could it be? Where were the gods that they would let this happen? Her lips trembled as she gasped for air. It seemed so unreal. Her brother dead! He never lifted his head. Never even moved.

Across the battlefield, the efficient legionaries finished their work.

Except for the one block of seated warriors, the whole grasslands were filled with dead or dying Caledonians, and jubilant Roman soldiers. The victory shouts blended with the moaning and desolate lamentation of the fallen.

Neeve lifted her eyes. In the distance, cavalry were still pursuing scattered clusters of fleeing warriors. Small units of legionaries disengaged from the main body of soldiers, scores of the units, fanning out to eliminate any stragglers that might be hiding in the woods or along the riverbanks. For the Romans, the battle was never over until they killed or captured every enemy warrior.

She glanced around.

Everyone had gone.

She rose warily.

Not one archer remained on the hillside. Not one Caledonian anywhere. They had all fled into the wooded areas where protective spirits dwelt. She suddenly realized how visible she must be, standing at the flattened top of the bluff, silhouetted against the sky. She started down the hill, and then stopped. Coming toward her position were four Romans with swords drawn, and they were pointing up at her.

Neeve whipped her head around, looking for refuge. But there was none. The backside of the hillock was filled with jagged rocks. The only way down was the route she had taken up, and even that would be slow going. She fingered the taut string of her bow. A silly thought, she knew. Four Romans with shields? She pulled her hand off the weapon. They were nearing the hillock. One said something to the others about Celts and their use of women in battle. They laughed. Crude laughter. Neeve jerked her eyes around, trying to think, trying to find a way out of her hopeless situation. But she knew the reality. She was a Caledonian warrior. If she wanted to live, and she did, she must do everything to preserve her life.

She eyed them. Like wolves they seemed, tongues dangling, panting up the hill, bent on tearing apart her flesh. She closed her eyes, as if that would make them disappear. Better raped than murdered, she had heard some say, but the thought turned her stomach. She wanted to live—how desperately she wanted to live— but she knew she couldn't comply like a soft-eyed doe. "Nemetona," she prayed, "Can you hear me? Please … one more time, I beg you."

She swallowed and started down toward them.

PART TWO:
Dangerous Travels

12

For five days Vectis and Julian had been riding awkwardly in a mule-pulled carriage, a squeaking wagon that bounced and thudded with every pebble on the road. They called it a sleeping carriage because it was topped with an arched canopy of tooled leather to shield the rain, and because on long journeys you could stretch out on the benches. Vectis remembered the hawkers shouting at the livery gates: "Arrive refreshed!" But the carriage tossed the passengers around like dolls, threatening to dump them onto the floor or, worse, out of the carriage itself. If you valued your life, you would use the sleeping benches only when you tied yourself to the struts. Everyone knew the story of the famous wisdom teacher, Pausanias, who broke his neck when thrown from a carriage seat. People found great humor in the story: even the fool knew enough to keep awake in a Roman carriage.

"Alba Fucens ahead," the driver shouted.

Julian gave Vectis a knowing look. "Didn't he say that before?"

Vectis smiled. "I think he did, but he might be right this time. Looks like a major settlement."

"I'm telling you, this misfit has no idea where we are."

"It's difficult with the milestones under repair."

"Milestones have nothing to do with it," Julian muttered. He gestured toward the driver, whose head was tilted back. "That's his second wineskin today. Do you think he could even see the milestones if they were there?"

"He does have a sizeable stomach," Vectis admitted.

"I wish he'd get these mules moving. At this speed the baths will be locked when we crawl in the gateway."

"That will give you time to buy olive oil," Vectis said.

"Don't think I won't. My ears cannot take one more mile of this agony." He swept his eyes around the cart. "Ever seen a wagon without an oil pot? Of course not," he said, answering his own question. "Our grizzled friend sold the oil the owners gave him, and pocketed the money—"

Vectis smiled and shrugged at Julian's snort of disgust.

Minutes later, as they fell silent, Vectis thought about their situation. Normally, the Senate would have provided a soldier of Vectis's rank with horses and Praetorian Guardsmen for his journey, but Senator Coelius had argued strongly against granting them any protection while they were still in what he called the safe environs of Italia. A waste of money, he said. Once they crossed the Adriatic Sea into Dalmatia province, the senator would allow them a small contingent of legionaries for protection. But for now they had to content themselves with a hired carriage that would take them from Rome to Aternum on the Adriatic, a ten-day journey that was looking more like two weeks. It was all the Senate would appropriate for spending. Worse, it wasn't even a private carriage. Along the way, they would have to share the vehicle with paying customers. Coelius was big on preserving Rome's coffers.

More than once during the trip, it occurred to Vectis that he might have held his tongue rather than calling Coelius a "spineless effeminate." But he was glad he did. The man was a jackass.

So far, only two passengers had used the carriage. One boarded the third morning and left by noon, and the other had been with them from the beginning, a menacing-looking soldier with calculating eyes that never stopped moving. He deposited his trunk in the rear of the wagon and paid a full fare to Aternum on the Adriatic Sea without uttering a word. When Julian greeted him, he eyed him briefly and turned away. It was obvious he wanted to be left alone. In five days, he had spoken only once, privately to the driver. "Don't bother me," Vectis overheard him say when the driver sidled up to him and suggested he might find the soldier cheaper rates for crossing the Adriatic.

Vectis gave the man space and spoke only to Julian, and to the driver when it was necessary. He was wary of strangers, especially from Rome. The city was full of intrigue, with assassins eager for hire on every street. He didn't escape certain death in the wilds of Britannia to have some paid killer in the middle of the Empire plant a dagger in his back. He eyed the soldier. Vectis had the feeling that the silent passenger had been watching him, tracking his moves. At night the man often scrutinized entrances to the sleeping rooms in the inns, and repeatedly chose to sleep outside. Vectis said nothing, but he kept alert.

As a concession to the cautious Senator Severus, he and Julian had dressed as merchants, and assumed fictitious names. Hiding behind secret identities struck Vectis as cowardly, but he recognized the wisdom of such a ploy. He was not well-known in Rome, and any assassin would find it difficult to identify him. But if an assassin did find him, Vectis intended to be ready. He fingered the ten-inch Roman dagger inside his cloak, and again glanced at the mysterious soldier. Yes, let him come.

An hour before sundown on the fifth day, the cart finally entered the gates of Alba Fucens, seventy miles east of Rome. With its stout defensive walls and strategic location in the heart of central Italia, it was obvious the town had begun as a military colony. Four hundred years earlier, adventuresome Roman legionaries and their families trekked across the Italian peninsula through treacherous rocky chasms to settle in this exposed valley framed by snow-capped mountains. They had spent their lives subduing the hardy Samnites and Etruscans, and now centuries later the town boasted luxurious public baths, an aqueduct, colonnaded streets, a theater, numerous gardens, and an amphitheater for that most glorious of traditions, the gladiatorial games.

The public baths were closed, as Julian had predicted. Vectis felt responsible. He had dragged Julian through the rain and fog of Britannia and now they were headed for the bitter cold of Dacia. He pulled the driver aside and asked him if he knew of a private bath for hire. He was thinking of the dozen or so villas he had seen nestled in the mountains. They all had private baths with hot and cold pools and servants to massage their backs with oil. Julian was right. Lying in a hot pool sipping wine sounded good after days on the road. It was the one indulgence Vectis truly enjoyed.

"Not cheap hiring a bath," the driver said.

"How much?" Vectis asked.

The man scratched his scraggly beard and said, "Only one or two places for hire." His breath stunk of rotting teeth and wine.

"How much?"

"Give me a hundred," he said, "and I'll see what I can do."

"A hundred! You want a hundred sesterces for a lousy bath? Forget it!"

"I meant a hundred would cover everything, food, wine, the bath, and this would be up to a party of six," he said, keeping the bargaining alive.

"I would hope so," Vectis said, stunned. He couldn't believe the price. "You must think I'm the one who's been drinking all day," he said, irritated. He hated being cheated.

The driver shifted his eyes around, as if he were concerned that someone might overhear and demand to be included in the astounding deal he was offering Vectis. "Eighty," he said. "These are gorgeous private baths. They won't go lower than eighty."

"Forty."

"Seventy maybe."

Vectis turned away.

"All right, fifty. I will die begging on the streets, but I do it for you," he said, patting Vectis on the face. "You are a hard man."

Vectis counted out forty sesterces and said, "Take it … or not."

The driver shook his head in disgust, but plucked the coins from Vectis's hand like a vulture snatching meat.

Vectis couldn't believe he was handing over the best part of a week's wages, and all for a few hours in the baths. As it turned out the private bath was at the edge of town, not in the mountains. It was anything but gorgeous. The rooms were drafty, the water as greasy as the driver's face, and the wine as sour as vinegar. But at least the heated pool was hot and the massage deep and thorough. Julian was happy, and the two of them had opportunity to discuss the disquieting news that three additional passengers would join them the next morning when they left Alba Fucens.

At sunup the carriage continued on its journey, but not before Julian smeared olive oil on the wheels. He gave Vectis a satisfied look as he plopped down in his seat.

The driver had been mistaken about the number of additional passengers. There were not three, but six new fares, four men and two women. One woman was upper class, dark hair, dark eyes, and exceedingly handsome. The other had a plain look, a mother with two small children. The mother pushed in beside Julian. She obviously had little means, wrapped as she was in a tattered cloak with no hooks or brooches. The older child had some kind of sickness because he coughed and cried in Julian's ear most of the morning.

Julian leaned over to Vectis and whispered, "Maybe if I dumped some oil on his head … what do you think?"

At noon the carriage stopped in a meadow for the passengers to stretch their legs. As they were climbing back into the carriage, Vectis heard the driver ordering the mother off the wagon.

"You promised to take me to Maris," she said, referring to a small logging town farther up the road.

He pulled himself into the driver's seat. "I said we would likely be at Maris by noon. But with all this weight, it's taking longer."

"But you said—"

"Nothing I can do."

"Please," she said, gathering her children so they wouldn't be crushed by the wheels, "it's only a few more hours."

"You got no money," he shouted. "You're lucky I even gave you and your brats a ride." He flicked the reins and the mules jerked forward.

"Stop the carriage!" Vectis roared. He could imagine what the grubby driver had extracted from her to bring her this far. The constant crying was grating to everyone on the wagon, but he couldn't leave her to the mercy of brigands prowling the road. She would be raped, probably murdered, and the children would wind up on some auction block in the city. He reached into his purse and was about to climb from the carriage when the dark-haired woman swept past him. She said something angrily to the driver, thrust a half dozen coins into his hand and helped the children back into the carriage.

A fat merchant in the back commended her for her deed, but she waved him off, saying she was too angry to speak. Julian grimaced at Vectis, obviously feeling guilty about his earlier comment on oiling the child's head. He extracted dates from his small traveling bag and gave them to the children.

The carriage reached Maris earlier than expected, and the mother left with her children, full of thanks to her benefactors. It was only then that the dark-haired woman addressed Vectis.

"My husband bid me speak to no one," she said, "mind my business no matter what. But when I thought of that poor woman …." She dropped her head, almost in pain.

"Our driver is not the kindest man," Vectis said.

She glanced at the driver and then back at Vectis. "But you are," she said.

Vectis shrugged.

"I was nervous about making this journey alone," she said. "Quite nervous, actually."

"Worried about thieves?"

"I had heard stories about bands of robbers."

"The Valerian Way is well patrolled."

"Then you have traveled this road before."

"Many times," Vectis said. "My friend and I are barrel merchants. We purchase the milled barrel staves in Dalmatia and ship them to Rome." He told her his fictitious name and went on about the merits of Dalmatian timberlands, and although she pretended otherwise, he knew his conversation was boring her.

She glanced toward the brooding soldier and said in a lower tone, "Do you know anything about that passenger?"

Vectis shook his head.

"He has a fearful presence about him," she said.

"I wouldn't worry about him," Vectis said.

"I am so pleased you are traveling today."

Vectis nodded, but looked away. For some reason Neeve's face flashed before his eyes. Maybe because this woman was attractive or because he hadn't seen Neeve for so long. Whatever the reason, he tried to be rational. The woman had mentioned her husband to establish a baseline. She wanted to be friendly, but she also wanted him to know she was being no more than that. Still, something about her demeanor troubled him. She was a strange mixture of vulnerability and strength, and behind her black eyes were oceans of mystery. "Is your husband a tradesman?" Vectis asked, making conversation.

"A Praetorian captain," she said.

"Impressive."

"You will meet him," she said. "He and several other Praetorians will join us before we reach Aternum on the sea."

In that moment, Vectis realized what troubled him, but he said nothing. She had claimed to be married to a Praetorian Guardsman but wore no ring. If he challenged her, she would surely say the ring was being repaired, or some such story. The truth was obvious. She was afraid. She had concocted the Praetorian tale and made flattering remarks to encourage him to defend her in the event of an attack. After all, if the elite Praetorian Guard were about to appear at any moment, a man should have little fear to step up and do the right thing. It was a wise move on her part. There was nothing wrong with a woman trying to protect herself.

Later that day, however, Vectis was shocked to see the woman calmly sit beside the soldier. Without being forward, she smiled once or twice and made casual conversation. She seemed to sense when to be quiet, and sometimes allowed long minutes of silence to pass before speaking. But she definitely had determined to exchange pleasantries. What was she doing? An attractive woman can have a surprising effect on a man, any man, but Vectis worried that this might be the wrong man. The soldier's brooding face remained unchanged, but Vectis noticed small differences in his manner. He was having trouble keeping to himself, and sometimes even responded to her when she spoke. He seemed to be not entirely adverse to her company, but Vectis knew that if she gave him the Praetorian story, he would spot her vulnerability in an eye blink.

The carriage discharged three more passengers: the fat merchant and two miners. That left the original three, the woman, and what turned out to be a Thessalian magician. The temperature had dropped radically in the days since they had left Rome. The road wandered upward through increasingly mountainous territory, the way growing ever more treacherous. Slick patches of frost appeared on the cobblestones, and more than once they had to climb out and walk the steeper sections. Vectis kept away from the canyon rims and never allowed the striding soldier to move behind him. He had no desire to be bumped accidentally over the edge. On one of those occasions, the magician plucked a handful of stones from the roadside and stunned everyone with his juggling ability. Standing on one foot at the edge of a precipice, he kept a dozen stones whirling in the air. Then, he closed his eyes and hummed a tune, the stones still whirling. Even the soldier seemed impressed.

They arrived at the mountain settlement of Corfinium as the rain began to fall. Vectis pulled out his oil slicker and draped it over his shoulders. The weather had a threatening look as clouds darkened the afternoon skies and violent winds bowed the stands of conifer along the roadway. Thunderclaps shook the mountain peaks, heavy rain hammered on the leather canopy, and water gushed down the road as if from a broken cistern. The carriage plowed through the water on the main street and stopped at an inn where they would stay the night. Icicles hung from the slate roof, telling Vectis that, as cold as it was, recent temperatures had been significantly colder. To cheer his fellow passengers, and to garner a few coins for himself, the magician promised an evening of amusement.

After a brief stint in the public baths, Vectis and Julian returned to the inn where they ate and consumed more than a few cups of wine. They were in good spirits. Even a dark, windowless inn was better than the biting cold outside. The locals seemed to agree because the inn was crammed with patrons, both men and women, who were drinking and singing and waiting for the entertainment to begin.

It was an excellent day for the innkeeper. With overnight guests, a magician, and a roomful of paying customers, he scuttled about making sure that everyone sampled the house specialty, salted pork rinds. He shooed the bargirls through the crowd with their trays of wine. It was an old trick. Salt to encourage thirsty customers.

"No charge for the pork rinds!" he cried, a broad smile filling his brutish face.

The room smelled of damp bodies, smoke, and stale wine. Torches flickered along the walls, creating banks of swaying shadows, and at the front, two charcoal braziers glowed with yellow heat, warming the crowds. Some were seated on wooden stools, others were standing, but all were enthusiastic about the day's fare. Word had spread that they would see magic tricks.

"I hope this Thessalian does well," Julian said as he glanced around the smoky room.

Vectis understood immediately. The mountain men were a rough-looking bunch who would not take kindly to being cheated. They had paid their coins, and they expected something for their money. They also had strong superstitions. Already Vectis had heard a dozen conversations about the secret arts, sorcerers, and demons that lurked in the deeper shadows of the night. The idea of magic intrigued the crowd, but under the veneer of curiosity lay a sea of anxiety, and even outright fear. Magicians, especially ones from foreign lands, were thought to be in league with the darker spirits.

The innkeeper, aware that a practitioner of the magic arts might create unease in his patrons, began with a glowing tribute to the emperor's favorite entertainer, as he called him, saying that the magician had astounded the crowds at the Theater Marcellus in Rome. Vectis smiled to himself. Emperor Antoninus' favorite entertainer? He would bet a year's wages that even these backward mountain men knew the magician had never been within a hundred paces of the emperor, never mind performing for him at the Theater Marcellus. But it seemed to settle the crowd, and that was in everyone's interest.

"Those pork rinds made me thirsty," the performer said as he began. "Would someone bring me a cup of wine?" He took a small sip and then said he should save the wine for later. He removed a scarf from his tunic, made a pocket, and poured the wine into the scarf, then turned the cup upside down on a pedestal. He asked for more wine. He emptied the cup into the same scarf and turned that cup over. Six more cups of wine went into the same scarf and six more were turned over. He showed everyone the scarf bulging with wine. "Where should I keep it?" he asked, and then tripped, spilling the scarf over the heads of his audience. The men near the front jumped back, then gaped in stunned silence as a single goose feather floated to the floor.

The scarf was empty.

Everyone cheered.

Some looked nervous. "Could a spirit be helping the magician?" they whispered.

They gulped more wine to fortify their courage.

"I like to keep my wine close at hand," he said as he wrapped the scarf around his wrist, "just in case I get thirsty later." For the next hour he juggled burning rocks, made coins disappear and a marble head speak. (The last also produced an explosion of talk among the patrons.) The magician used a sling to hurl an invisible rock at a colorful vase. The vase exploded into a thousand pieces. Then, claiming he had grown thirsty with all his work, he removed the scarf, shaped it into a pouch, and used it to refill the overturned cups.

Vectis was frankly amazed at his ability to do magic. The man reminded him of the crafty Druids he had seen in Britannia, only this man did things without help from the gods, or so he continually said.

No one in the room had any complaints about the tricks being second rate, even when the magician made their hard-earned coins disappear. They poured down the wine and stamped their feet after every trick. The only person in the room not cheering was the soldier with the watchful eyes. He stood with his back against the wall and in a clear line of vision to where Vectis sat. More than once Vectis reached for the leather grip of his dagger. He enjoyed the show, drank some wine, but he kept alert to the people around him, especially the somber soldier.

"For my last act, I need a volunteer," the magician was saying. "A beautiful woman is always best." He stretched out his hand to the dark haired woman and with a flourish intoned, "Come."

She said nothing, but shook her head in such a way that the magician felt impelled to move elsewhere. He covered his discomfort by saying that he had licked her neck before the show and she was afraid he would do it again. The crowd laughed. "A small lick," he added, "nothing for her to be upset with." They cheered even louder. Bawdy humor they understood.

"You … merchant," he said, pointing at Vectis.

"Choose a local," Vectis said, ignoring the whistles and jeers. He had been in the legions long enough to know never to volunteer for anything. Besides, if Senator Severus was right, determined enemies might be stalking him at this very moment. He was glad Julian was watching his back.

The magician swept his eyes across the spellbound faces. "This is your opportunity," he said. "Years from now the whole town will still remember you … because of this special night. Who will volunteer?"

Vectis shifted his eyes to the soldier. He was gone! He whipped his head around. He saw the carriage driver and the woman, but no soldier. He cursed. He should have kept his eyes on the man.

A volunteer went forward.

Vectis rose from his stool, inspecting the crowd behind him. Julian motioned toward the center of the room.

Vectis nodded. The soldier was much closer than he had expected, but he breathed easier. The man had simply wanted a better look at the feat of skill, as the magician called it. Vectis turned back to the performance. Several men were binding the volunteer to pegs on the wall. The magician opened a leather case stuffed with throwing knives. The man immediately protested, saying that he no longer wanted to volunteer. The crowd laughed.

"Wait!" the magician shouted. "Let me show you how good I am with these knives." He took a lump of white chalk, outlined on the adjacent wall the approximate shape of the man, and then hurled all six knives at it. The crowd gasped. The knives followed perfectly the shape of the body. He retrieved the knives and said, "I wonder how I would do blindfolded?" He pulled a brown sack over his head and made a big show of aiming carefully at the outline. He whirled the knife. The thud was followed by absolute silence. The knife had struck the throat.

By now everyone was standing.

"How did I do?" the magician asked, pulling the sack off his head.

"Untie me!" the man shouted. "Untie me *now*!" Even in the smoke filled room, it was obvious his face had lost all color.

The magician retrieved his knife from the wall. "I thought I would do better," he said, shaking his head.

"Let me loose!"

"Be very still," the magician said, collecting all six knives into his left hand.

The man's face glistened with perspiration.

The magician again slipped the sack over his head.

The crowd pressed forward.

"Wait!" the man wailed.

"Very still."

No one in the room moved or even breathed. The magician steadied the first knife. The man closed his eyes. Six thuds followed in rapid succession as the knives drove deep into the wood surrounding the man. The room exploded. Men were shouting and pounding their feet. They clapped each other's backs and sloshed wine everywhere. Throwing knives had nothing to do with the black arts, as the talking head might have been. This was pure skill, something they admired greatly.

Screams!

Screams replaced the cheering. A half dozen women at the back of the crowd were shrieking and waving their arms. They formed a circle around a man who was lying on the floor. Vectis pushed closer. It was the soldier who had been watching him. He was lying on his back, eyes wide-open, mouth twisted in pain.

"What happened?" Julian was beside him.

Vectis shook his head. "I think he's dead," he replied.

The innkeeper asked if anyone saw what had happened.

"I was right beside him when he fell," a bargirl said. "He just toppled over."

Everyone in the inn had now circled the man, staring. Vectis called for a torch to be held over the body. He bent down and put an ear to the man's chest. No sound. Vectis unbuckled the victim's legionary belt and pushed up his heavy woolen tunic. His inner tunic was stained with blood. Vectis exposed his chest. What he saw troubled him deeply. A tiny hole under the ribs. Nothing else. Just a hole that led to the heart. Someone with incredible skill had thrust a needle-like knife under his ribs and into his heart.

"What kind of weapon would do that?" a voice in the crowd asked.

"A very special one," Vectis answered. "Maybe a filed down legionary dagger, I don't know."

The innkeeper bulled his way to the door and bolted it. "I sent a boy for the Vigiles," he said, referring to the watchmen who policed the streets and put out fires. He turned to face the crowd, his voice shaking as he shouted, "This is my inn! I won't have it taken away because of some murderer. I want everyone searched." He selected two men, patted them down, and stepped forward himself to be searched. Then the three searched every man in the inn. When they came to the magician, the men found he had a tunic unlike any other, with slits and neatly tailored pockets everywhere. He had lengths of twine, sticky resin, hollow reeds and coins of every sort. But no knife. Nearly everyone else in the inn did carry a knife, but no one had the needle type.

"He has to be here," the keeper spat. "No one could have left that quickly."

"Or killed a man without anyone noticing," someone added.

The crowd muttered its agreement.

"There's only one person here capable of deceiving everyone," the keeper said, "and we all know who that is."

Accusing eyes turned toward the magician.

"He's innocent," Vectis said. "Not even a magician could be in two places at one time."

The magician was nodding his agreement.

"He destroyed a vase from across the room," said a gruff voice near the back.

"A trick," Vectis said.

"He's in league with the dark spirits!" someone cried. "He summoned one to speak from the severed head!"

Several in the crowd mumbled a prayer.

"Maybe he has an invisible knife," another said.

"I sense a devilish spirit about him," a barmaid said.

The crowd murmured again.

"I think it would be good if you explained how you did that one trick," Vectis said to the magician, "the invisible rock trick."

He shook his head. "I never tell an audience how I—"

"Look again," Julian said. "This is no longer an audience."

"It's a mob," Vectis said, glancing around at the drunken mountain men. "I think this would be a good time to make an exception."

The magician eyed the men. "Yes," he said, "well, actually, I ..." he raised his voice, "I ... ah ... pull a string with my foot that swings a small iron ball at the vase. I use the sling to distract you so you won't notice what I am doing with my foot. It's really quite simple."

"There, you see?" Vectis said. "Just tricks." He glanced around and asked, "What about the women?" He was trying to take the focus off the magician.

"Don't be ridiculous," the innkeeper snapped. "Whoever killed this soldier has killed many men before."

The woman from the carriage stepped forward, her black eyes showing a studied calm. "I say search everyone," she said. "It's the only way to be certain." Then she smiled and added, "But if you don't mind, we women will search each other."

Despite the situation, the men laughed nervously.

The Vigiles arrived, a unit of six men. The innkeeper sketched out the situation and said he ran a respectable inn, and that he had done everything possible to help the Vigiles in their investigation.

The centurion of the Vigiles squatted down beside the man. "A legionary," he muttered. "Complicates things." One of his men handed him a torch. He examined the wound, scrunched up his face, and examined it more closely. He whistled. "Never seen anything like this before." He turned to the bargirl. "Just toppled over, you say. Did you see—"

"Nothing, Master," the girl said.

The centurion ordered everyone searched again, and the room scoured for places a needle knife might be hidden. He found nothing.

"I run a respectable inn," the keeper said for the third time.

"I find you blameless," the centurion said. "My report will read: Murder by an unknown assailant who managed to flee the inn."

The innkeeper bubbled his thanks.

"Now, I would like to see his equipment trunk."

The keeper nodded and hurried off to retrieve the trunk. Vectis couldn't help noticing the relief on the keeper's face when he heard the centurion's judgment. Roman inns were notorious for their shady dealings, and it was common for innkeepers to be at the center of misdeeds.

"He's a legionary," the keeper said, breaking open the lock, "so if his identity papers are not in his purse, they must be in the trunk." It was an obvious point, but the keeper seemed unable to resist making it. Inside they found a handful of legionary tunics, cold weather gear and assorted toiletries, but no papers.

"A legionary with no papers," the centurion mused. "And, of course, no one knows his name or legion."

"I know his name," the carriage driver volunteered. "It's under the trunk handle."

The centurion pulled up the leather handle and read, "Vectis Trebellius Quadratus."

"Well, well," Julian said quietly in Vectis's ear.

Vectis stared down at the man who had been watching him ever since Rome, who had been checking the windows in the inns, who had slipped in behind him in crowded places, and suddenly he realized who he was. He worked for Senator Titus Severus. He was the bodyguard. The senator had sent him anyway.

A chilling thought swept over Vectis, like a shiver on a wet day. Someone was stalking him. Someone with incredible skill. He had inspected the trunks for names, and he had killed a soldier he thought was Vectis Trebellius Quadratus.

Vectis glanced around the room at the faces mostly hidden in shadow. The centurion was wrong. He was here. The assassin with the needle-thin dagger had not escaped. He was here in this room.

13

Neeve descended the ridge toward the waiting soldiers, the odor of dust and blood clotting her nostrils. It was as if she had wandered into a sheep-slaughtering yard. But as much as the smell and the distant hum of choking, writhing bodies sickened her, she knew she had to focus on the danger at hand. The four Romans were signaling each other now to fan out, as if they were hunters cornering a rabbit. In a way, they were. The battle was over and the chase had begun.

"No harm!" one of them called up to her in broken Celtic. "You are safe." He sheathed his sword and laid his shield aside. He signaled the others to put away their swords. "See, no harm." He patted his armored chest. "My name … Lucian."

Neeve moved haltingly down the hill, picking her way through the slippery rocks. The four had spread across the base of the hill, from the bog to the steep incline on the opposite side. Lucian was thirty feet below her and beckoning with his hand, the way one would to a child. He was indicating he would help her down the steep part near the bottom. "You are safe … no harm," he kept saying. "Lucian … friend."

She continued down.

He pulled off his helmet and let it drop to the ground. His matted hair dripped with sweat, making crooked streaks on his blood-spattered face. He forced his mouth into a smile and tried to look pleasant, but all Neeve saw were his cold dark eyes and his thick fingers that continually tugged at the side of his dirty knee-length breeches.

"You are safe … yes, no harm."

"The gods are here," she murmured. "The gods will protect me." But the awful truth obliterated even the slightest hope she may have had. The Celtic gods were not here, and she knew it. They had fled from the powerful Roman deities and were now hiding in the highland forests with the Druids. She was alone. Truly alone. And a horrific fate awaited her.

She tried to push the images out of her mind, but they persisted. How could this be happening to her? Raped? Beaten? Is that what this day held? Would she die like Cronn and Taranis? Before the sun set … would her wretched body be thrown behind a bush to be torn apart by hungry wolves? The soldiers had spent the better part of this day in battle, killing, and perhaps seeing their friends killed. Rage boiled just below the surface. They would think nothing of sticking a sword in her neck if anything set them off. And even if she did comply with their every demand, they might easily kill her anyway … for the added sport. Death thrilled some men. They liked to watch things die … see the struggle for life, the last desperate clutching at impossible threads of hope, the dimming light in the eyes as the inner essence was snatched off to its final abode. She scanned the four soldiers. Yes, death thrilled these men.

Every fiber of her being screamed for survival. But what to do? She thought about speaking in Latin, telling them she had worked as a mapmaker for Outpost Faustina, and that she had married a Roman. No … that would be the worst thing to do. Faustina had been destroyed. They would assume she was lying, or worse, a spy, and both merited death. Her mind raced. Think! Maybe pick up some rocks … or run straight through them. Maybe—

"I get her after Lucian," one of them said in Latin, thinking she wouldn't understand.

"No! You always hit them too hard."

"Some of them like it."

"Well, I don't. There's nothing left when you finish."

"Shut up!" Lucian hissed, his mouth twisting in anger. He seemed to be the leader of the group, and determined to keep his quarry from running. His pleasant face returned when he looked up at her and again said in Celtic, "No harm to you."

The others continued their vigil at the bottom of the hillock, cutting off any avenue of escape. They removed their helmets. Their eyes glistened. Their faces burned with desire.

Neeve took a few more hesitant steps. She tasted bile in the back of her mouth and felt her stomach beginning to turn. She licked her lips incessantly. Her eyes darted around uselessly. What could she do?

Even as she tried to focus, the same alternatives cycled through her ragged mind. If she ran, they would catch her and kill her for sure … or beat her into a broken mess. If she submitted, the outcome was the same. She knew that others had been strong enough to disconnect their minds from their disgusting ordeals, and they survived. But she couldn't do it. She could never imagine herself looking up with pleading eyes at her tormenters, begging for mercy. And that's what would happen if she went down to them. They intended to beat her until, what did one of them say, until there was nothing left? How brave would she be then? After that, they would drag her down to the cages headed for the slave markets. She knew what happened to women in an army pen on their way to the markets. Oh, she could get lucky and be given to the officers—she was not unaware of her physical beauty—but even a minor beating by these four could flatten her nose or knock her teeth out, and then all would be lost. She would service the common soldiers until they reached the markets in the south. And how many in the army pens ever made it to the markets?

Her heart pounded. She needed to do something—and soon. That's what her inner voice kept telling her. Quit thinking and do something! Time was running out. She was nearing the moss-covered rocks at the bottom.

She took a deep calming breath.

And another.

Lucian was still crooning in his hushed tone, as if he were soothing a skittish horse.

Neeve swept her eyes over the grasslands one last desperate time, a futile exercise. The Caledonian warriors were dead, or running through the woods, and not a few sat cross-legged in the distant battlefield. She glanced quickly at the bog field below, then longingly at the sharp drop off into the ravine, and the forest beyond. She imagined herself racing along the ravine and into the protective woods. Wasted thoughts, she knew. She eyed the bog again. The soldiers had steered clear of the sphagnum moss that had spread itself innocently over the bog like a colorful patchwork carpet. And with good reason. Under the emerald surface lay a quagmire of dead, waterlogged moss, piled up through the centuries, layer by stringy layer, a dangerous place for the unwary.

She had crossed bogs before—they were everywhere in Caledonia—but always she had roped herself to others for fear of holes. That was the problem with bogs. You could walk its spongy surface for fifty feet before hitting a gap, but in that moment, you sank in the tangled remains of ancient, saturated moss, sucked down into the dark wetness, never to rise again.

Neeve licked her lips. She was lean and tall, a fast runner, and at this moment appallingly short on options. She might not be able to outrun an athletic man, but on a bog, against stumpy-legged Romans, she bet she would fare well, especially since the legionaries wore hob-nailed boots and heavy field equipment.

But she had to get there, and there was no path down other than the one the Romans were now blocking. The sharp incline of loose rocks falling away below her was impossible, dropping as it did, almost straight down in places. She looked back at the Romans, her eye catching their discarded shields by the ridge's edge. Suddenly she knew what she would do.

Her breath grew shallow as she stepped over a rotting tree and moved closer to the abrupt drop that separated her from Lucian. He was now directly below her, so close that Neeve could see the large veins in his neck. She took a quick look at the legionary closest to the edge. He was the heaviest of the four, with a chest like a tree trunk, and legs to match. A tiny hope pried its way into her mind.

"Roman!" Neeve called out.

Lucian's head jerked up.

"No harm to me?" she asked. She used the Celtic words he obviously knew. At the same time she moved as quickly as she dared on the treacherous slope. Another ten steps and she would be at the ledge.

"Yes, no harm," he said, returning to his theme. He gave her what he thought would be a reassuring grin, but it looked predatory on his dirty, blood spattered face.

She neared the ledge. She looked down at Lucian, who waited eagerly with fingers rubbing on his leggings. Neeve could smell his stale sweat in the gusts of wind. With arms widespread, balancing herself, she picked her way through the last jumble of rocks above the ledge. If Lucian were taller he might have reached up and grabbed her ankle.

"Go!" shrieked a voice inside her. "Go now!"

Neeve pivoted and sprinted along the ledge toward the slope escarpment. In a single motion she leapt from the stone outcropping and threw herself onto one of the discarded shields with a crash. Then, desperately, she clawed at the gravely surface, tipped her weight forward, and slid down the loose rocks of the cliff's edge.

An avalanche of dust exploded around her as the shield skidded and bounced down the cliff face, and her speed increased almost proportionately to the growing roar of rocks pouring down the hillside. Then, suddenly, she felt the shield torn from her hands as she flipped into the air and tumbled to a stop, the wind knocked from her chest. She lay on her stomach, breathing slowly, stunned, but alive.

Neeve pushed herself up onto her knees and tasted the metallic tang of blood in her mouth. She was at the base of the ridge, only a few hundred feet from the edge of the bog. She looked back up the cliffs. The Romans were quickly descending the path they had taken up. It would not be long before they had climbed down.

She staggered to her feet and began to limp across the grassy soil toward the bog.

"After her!" Lucian shouted.

"I got her. I got her," the heavy legionary hollered. He sounded irritated, like someone who had performed the same task a thousand times and didn't want instructions. He lumbered after her onto the spongy bog, seemingly fearless as he moved across its surface. Neeve stepped onto the soft tangle of green and instantly thought about all the hunters who had been taken by bogs. The smooth growing moss had the sweet smell of cut flowers, but she knew the placid surface concealed dangerous gaps that could easily swallow a full stag.

But what was once a perilous trap, was now her salvation.

The legionary fixed his eyes on Neeve, and laughed hoarsely, shouting triumphantly in uncultured Latin, "Where you think you're going, little girl?" His words were more for his comrades than for her, since he undoubtedly assumed she was a babbler, as the Romans called them, barbarians who spoke no Latin.

Neeve backed away from the brute legionary in front of her, surprised he had ventured onto an open bog. The wind was unusually strong out in the open, and she could feel the sticky wetness of blood on her arms and legs, causing a chill to sweep through her body. She unhooked her bow from her back and drew an arrow. The soldier was wearing strip armor on his shoulders and torso, but had no helmet or shield. She felt reasonably certain she could hit him with an arrow, injure him at least. But she hoped it wouldn't come to that. She kept her eyes on him, as he moved doggedly with her every step, keeping pace with her, but she could see his feet were sinking well above his ankles. The sucking feeling on the feet must be disquieting, she reasoned. She stopped and called across to him in Latin. "You will die here," she said, "and your friends won't be able to help you."

"You speak the language," he snorted, surprised.

"Lucian sent you onto the bog because he knows you are a fool," she said.

He kept moving toward her.

"You're too heavy," she said. "Look at your feet! Soon you will hit a hole and sink. The bog will swallow you."

"You're mine, little girl," he said, but he seemed less certain than moments before.

"You made a mistake coming out here."

He wiped his mouth.

"Why are you the only one on the bog? I'll tell you why. Because they fear being sucked under the moss."

He looked over his shoulder at the other legionaries a hundred yards away. They were moving along the edge of the marsh, gesturing with their arms and shouting encouragement.

"You're the fool of the group," she repeated. "Someone your size trying to walk on a moss bog?" She pointed to the three legionaries. "Why aren't they out here?"

He glanced down at his feet, and then around at the vast patchwork of green. The absurdity of his position suddenly hit him. "This is horseshit," he mumbled. Then, turning toward the others, he shouted: "The bog's too soft. I'm getting off." He started toward them, moving more gingerly than he had before. His face showed anger rather than fear. He didn't like it that Neeve had gotten to him with her comments about the dangers of the bog. "I'm not finished with you," he spat as he left.

Neeve felt a great relief as she watched his armored back retreating toward the distant rocks. He looked like an old man, unsteady on his feet as he hunched over and hesitated with every step he took. She ran her eyes over the expanse of green. Any relief she felt promptly vanished. She had to get off the bog herself, and she had to move quickly because the soldiers would circle to the opposite side. She could see them talking at the edge of the marsh, trying to anticipate the direction she would go, and it wouldn't be long before they discovered she had only one real escape route—the ravine and woods beyond.

Her eyes stopped on a granite tower that protruded from the ravine on the far side of the bog. She knew the area well. She remembered climbing the tower as a child with her brothers and little sister, Nes, and how Nes had fallen and split her forehead on a jagged rock. When Neeve saw the rocks stained with blood, she threw herself on Nes's still form and cried out to the spirits for pity. And the spirits listened. They protected Nes from what surely would have been an ill fate, leaving her with only a thin white scar. Kindly spirits inhabited that whole area … and if she crossed into that ground they might follow and protect her too. Yes, she would head for the great stone with its kindly spirits, and from there slip into the woods.

She started at a trot, but it wasn't long before she was running. As fast as she could, she sprinted toward the rock. She ignored the old wisdom of staying on the darker patches of moss, and just ran. Dimly, as if she perceived it from afar, there came the padding sound of her feet and squishing moss, the wind burning her eyes, and tears filling the corners. It took her five minutes to reach the shimmering mass of stone. Even from a distance she could see gorse and cranberry bushes sprouting from every crevice in the ragged chunks of granite, a sure sign of life and energy from the spirits. As she neared the edge of the bog, the moss seemed softer and a brighter green, and although she sensed a difference in the surface, she continued straight for the rock.

"*Ahiii!*" Neeve gasped.

A hole!

The moss suddenly gave way, and she catapulted forward, striking the soupy turf with her shoulder. She had no idea how large the gap might be, but as she fell, she twisted and rolled, flapping her arms like a duck as she propelled herself away. She never stopped rolling and flapping until she had put twenty feet between herself and the spot where she had fallen.

She picked herself up, a sodden mess, strings of moss in her teeth. She tested the surface— firm thankfully—and then instinctively looked behind her. No one was there, of course. The broad expanse of moss lay empty as it had before, but she felt better checking. In the distance the heavy legionary was approaching the bank and solid ground. He was alone. The others had set off toward the woods and were now out of sight. Neeve calculated the distance around the bog and guessed she had ten minutes before the soldiers reached the outcropping of rock. She looked back at the place where she had fallen, but the surface appeared even and stable. If she had to point to the exact spot she doubted she could do it. The only evidence of her fall was a dozen arrows scattered in a ragged trail where she had rolled. She checked her arrow pouch. Three left. Even with the danger that lay ahead, she felt no temptation to go back and retrieve arrows.

She started toward the rock again, and stopped.

Movement! Someone was hiding in the gorse that grew in clumps at the edge of the marsh. It was not her imagination. She had seen movement—a flash of hair, a hand, she didn't know—but someone had definitely been watching her. She wiped the water from her face and squinted her eyes. Nothing. Neeve frowned. Could the wind have tricked her? Swirling leaves could transform themselves into a thousand menacing images, if you were looking for them. A startled rabbit or a retreating badger could seem like a wood demon if you had just finished talking about the lower spirits. A frightening thought crossed her mind. Another Roman unit might have spotted her and was now waiting near the rock. She scolded herself. Stop the nonsense! Be reasonable. The outcropping of rock was a refuge, a place of kindly spirits. Only the fiercest of foreign spirits, in overwhelming numbers, could drive them out. A whole camp of Romans, maybe, but not a passing search party. She would be safe near the rock, at least for a short while.

She continued along the edge of the bog toward the trees bordering the rock, trotting as swiftly as she could, but this time choosing the darker patches. Minutes later, when she stepped into the trees, she paused to thank the spirits.

But not for long. The local spirits could only be expected to influence events, not control them. She cocked her head, listening for intruders, for any rustling of leaves, or the flight of startled birds, but heard nothing. She ran her eyes over the rock-strewn land that fed into the ravine, and the hollows sprinkled with cranberry bushes where men might hide, but she saw no one. Neeve sighed, relieved. She was glad to be off the spongy surface of the bog, glad to be hidden from probing eyes, and especially glad to be near the rocks with favorable spirits. She slipped quietly through the trees to the mass of granite bulging out of the forest floor. Then, bending her body over the swell of stone, and pressing her cheek into its rough surface, Neeve listened to the throb of spirits hidden deep in the rock. When they grew silent and she sensed they were telling her to leave, she again thanked them for their benevolence, and begged for protection on this day. Abruptly she rose and headed for the ravine.

Neeve followed the ravine north, treading carefully around the moss-covered stones and protruding roots. This would not be a good time to twist an ankle. She was heading toward a swath of forest that rose and fell, a tangle of rocks and trees where she could hide until the Romans left. If she remembered correctly, the thicker woods should be no more than a mile up the winding streambed.

Minutes later she paused, concerned. The woods had grown thicker as she had expected, but something didn't feel right. She glanced around at the brush-thickets growing along the ravine, brush that prevented her from seeing clearly into the forest. Jagged rocks poked out of the ground everywhere and towering pines obscured much of the light, as if the sun had already set. She swept her eyes across the woods in front of her. Everything seemed normal. Thicker, more tangled woods, but that's what she wanted. She swept the area again, this time more carefully. There was nothing out there, not that she could see. But inside, she felt a growing unease, though she wasn't sure why, as if a spirit were cautioning her about something in the woods. She sniffed the air. A faint odor of burning pine. She jerked her head back, looking up, straining to see clear sky between the pines. What she saw sent a bolt of fear through her body, the unmistakable smudges of blue smoke drifting through the upper reaches of the trees.

Neeve dropped low, her heart pounding.

Cooking fires! Someone was cooking meat—she could smell it now—and not too far away. She rose warily, her body crouched as she picked her way through the rocks, her eyes fixed on the bend in the stream fifty feet away where she could see a column of smoke rising from a fire. Could it be Caledonian warriors, she wondered, or a wandering group of hunters? It was a slim hope, but one she had to hang on to.

As she neared the bend she crouched even more, pushing up against the rocky bank and peering over. Her mouth went dry.

Romans! A whole group of them.

Five soldiers were standing under a tree at the top of a ridge, roasting what looked like a skinned rabbit on a spit. Every few seconds one would lift his head and glance around sharply. They had obviously been stationed along the edge of the deeper woods hours before the battle, and their singular purpose was to turn escapees back toward the patrols. With nothing better to do, they had probably set snares and were now cooking for themselves a late afternoon snack.

Neeve ran her eyes along the ridge line, and in the distance she could see other smoke fires and more huddled soldiers. They were using the fires not only to cook, but also to alert the Caledonians to their presence. They wanted to be noticed. They probably had set up scores of camps in a line that extended from the far edge of the bog, across the ravine, and for miles along the thick edge of the woods. They were determined to prevent Celtic warriors from escaping into the almost impenetrable forests of Caledonia. Neeve studied the line of camps with increasingly worried eyes. Nowhere to go.

She thought about trying to slip between the Roman camps. There were plenty of large rocks and dips in the land where she could hide, and with the swirling winds, the trees were alive with sound, certainly adequate to cover any crunching of leaves she might make. She puckered her lips. It might be possible. If she could cross the barrier she would be free. She studied the line once more … and the vigilant sentries. The Romans had spaced their camps just wide enough to make it look as if you could sneak through without raising an alarm. But every fire was built in sight of the other, and although the soldiers seemed relaxed, they were constantly watching. No, she thought, a fool's choice. Only an Iceni tracker could slip through.

Neeve turned away. Better to risk the search parties than try to breach the line. She hurried back down the ravine, her mind churning with images of the four soldiers that were pursuing her. She knew other Romans were scouring the woods for stragglers, but the thought of Lucian and his friends created in her a deep anxiety.

She had decided to make her way back to the rock tower with its friendly spirits. The four had likely searched that area by now, and it might be a good place to hide until dark. She glanced up at the sun, already in its downward arc. Two hours, she guessed. Under cover of dark she could head through the thin stands of trees east of the ravine. Traveling at night wasn't the best of plans, not on treacherous landscape where even talented goats would have trouble keeping their footing, but it was her only option.

That's when she saw them. Lucian and two of the Romans she had escaped. The heavy soldier was not with them—probably catching up.

Neeve froze, not even moving her eyes.

Too late.

She could hear Lucian yelling. She scrambled up the side of the ravine, jerking her head around, looking for a place to run. She spotted a rugged section of woods and bolted straight for it. The ground was littered with enormous slabs of stone, abrupt drops and clusters of conifers that hid treacherous surprises. Neeve didn't care. She fixed her eyes firmly on the terrain in front of her and ran flat out. What did it matter if she fractured a leg? To be caught meant rape and certain death. She veered around a jumble of giant rocks and into a gully rimmed with larch trees, hoping her erratic movements would confuse her pursuers.

Behind her she could hear the thud of hob-nailed boots, heavy breathing and curses. She tried to move faster, but was getting tired. Her muscles ached. She was losing control. She stumbled on a root, twisted side-ways, trying to catch her balance before taking several more steps and tripping again, this time plunging over a six-foot ledge. She flung her arms out as she fell, but smashed her forearm on something hard, a sharp rock buried in the mud, she didn't know. She staggered to her feet in the shadowy gully, grasping at her elbow. Her whole arm ached with a shredding pain, and warm blood dribbled out of her tunic and off the ends of her fingers.

She whipped her head around, knowing she had to keep moving.

Somebody shouted, cursed loudly, then moaned.

Neeve turned toward the sound. Through the trees she saw a man, a huge man leaping from the rocks she had just passed. A knife flashed through the air in a sweeping arc, and two Romans slumped to the ground. A third lay sprawled on the rocks several feet away, a long Celtic sword buried deep in his chest.

Cronn wiped his knife calmly on the soldier's tunic. He slipped it into its case and went back to retrieve his sword. Bending over a silent Lucian, he tugged his sword out of the body and wiped it clean. Lucian, it appeared, had been the first to die. Cronn took the coins from their purses and dragged their bodies into nearby bushes as Neeve emerged from the gully.

"Are you hurt?" he asked. His eyes fastened onto her right hand. It was sticky with blood.

She shrugged, still having difficulty comprehending the situation.

"I saw you on the bog," he said in explanation. He placed two enormous hands on her tunic sleeve and ripped it open.

She winced.

"I couldn't follow you," he said, tilting her arm toward the fading light, "because I had to clear out several patrols."

"I don't think it's broken," she said, inspecting her arm.

"A lot of dirt in the wound," he said, "and it's deep. We will need to wash it somewhere."

"I thought you were ...." She stopped short of saying the word, dead.

His face flushed. Caledonian commanders took pride in staying with their fallen men. When a battle went poorly, the commanders were the last to flee. It was the price of leadership.

"I survived," he said.

"I am glad you were spared," she said, grasping his hand, trying to cover his embarrassment. She remembered the Romans closing in on his tiny force, and the dust, and she wondered how he could have possibly escaped.

He saw the question in her face. "When Legion VI discovered our deception," he said in answer, "they shifted from a defensive posture and attacked us with their full force. An entire legion against so few men." He shook his head. "We couldn't hold ... everything was lost, so I released the warriors. Every man survived as best he could. I managed to cut through to the woods."

She nodded. Then she said, "I saw Taranis fall," and her voice couldn't hide her anguish.

"Taranis lives."

"He lives?"

"Taken captive by the Romans."

Her heart jumped. "How do you know this?"

"I watched him bound and taken away in a cart."

"You watched?" She was stunned.

"From the woods," he said without explanation.

"Taranis is like a brother to you," she said, and her voice carried an accusation. She thought she detected hurt in his eyes, but she didn't care. How could someone as brave as Cronn hide in the woods and watch the cursed Romans drag Taranis away?

"There will be other patrols," he said. "We have to leave."

She followed Cronn as he trekked through the rugged terrain, but all she could think about was Taranis. It didn't make sense. Even if Cronn had no chance to rescue him, she couldn't imagine him leaving Taranis. She stopped. Suddenly it all came clear to her, why Cronn had fought so hard to survive, why he hadn't expended himself trying to save Taranis, and why he had risked his life tramping through the woods looking for her.

Taranis had bound him to an oath. If all was lost, Cronn must survive. Whether she acknowledged it or not, Cronn had always been her protector.

Neeve hurried to Cronn's side. "Thank you," she said. She gazed into his fierce eyes, and they softened when he looked at her.

14

The carriage rolled along Corfinium's city streets loaded with four passengers eager to be heading out of town. Vectis, Julian, the magician, and the dark haired woman had taken less than ten minutes to collect their trunks, hitch up the mules, and throw their drunken driver in the back.

Darkness had fallen and it was difficult to see on the city's cobbled streets, lit as they were by only the occasional torch flaring in the night breeze. The rain had stopped hours before, but the chilly mountain air had a ruthless wetness to it that penetrated to the bone and seemed to haunt the mind with past memories of steaming baths.

They needed to get out of Corfinium before the locals had second thoughts. Julian's recent oiling of the axles had washed off in the rain, and once again, the wheels squealed like a melancholic pig, alerting the few people on the street that the strangers were leaving town. Vectis sat up front hunched under his slicker, lashing the mules. He had decided to take the reins until the driver sobered up, which would probably be morning, judging by how much he had consumed in the tavern.

"I thank you for rescuing me," the magician said to Vectis as they passed through Corfinium's stone gates. He seemed to be waiting until they had actually put the city behind them before he allowed himself to believe all was well. Ahead lay the ancient Valerian Way that led to Aternum on the Adriatic Sea.

"Mountain people have an incredible mistrust of strangers," Vectis said. "Even with the Vigiles there, they could have easily slit our throats."

"I'm just glad to be leaving," said the woman with the dark eyes. "I have never been so afraid."

"Well, I don't want to be the lone dissenter," Julian said, smiling, "but I would have preferred sleeping in a soft bed to being out here on the road with you complainers."

"You and your soft bed might have ended up at the bottom of a gorge," the magician said.

The others laughed, then cheered as Julian hopped from the cart to oil the wheels.

That night Vectis kept one eye on the road and the other on the passengers. For all the seeming comradery, he knew they were involved in serious business, and he and Julian had agreed to take turns being awake. Somebody had killed the soldier, and while the odds favored the killer being in the tavern crowd, that "somebody" might just as easily be in the carriage.

As Vectis stared at the silken ribbon of road in front of him and listened to the clopping of the mules, he thought about the drunken driver and whether he might be other than he appeared. It was an impossible task. Vectis simply could not imagine the man with rotting teeth and shaky hands being a trained assassin. The magician was another story. He was genuinely skilled in deception and with the knife. But even with unsurpassed trickery, Vectis still believed what he had said in the tavern: a man cannot be in two places at one time. Even if somehow he managed to throw a knife undetected, there was still the matter of a hole in the soldier's stomach. Vectis had seen the hole. It was not the result of a knife flung from a distance. Someone up close had skillfully and precisely driven the needle-like weapon under his ribcage. He would watch the magician, but from what he had seen, the magician was exactly as he appeared, a skilled artist whose sole interest was gaining employment to survive.

The woman bothered him. She was beautiful, almost flawless. She acted the part of a lady alone in the hostile world rather well, if it was an act. He couldn't be certain. Yet, even as she professed fear on every side, something about her exuded strength. He remembered when he was prefect of the five outposts in Britannia, how Neeve had appeared so naïve and uncomplicated, and all the while she was spying for the Caledonians. He grimaced at the thought.

Was that behind his suspicions of the dark eyed woman? He felt like the man in the tale of the bee, stung only once, but forever after jumping at the buzz of an insect on a warm summer day. Is that what he was doing, allowing his experience with one woman to color his judgment of all?

Vectis frowned. Who ever heard of a woman assassin? Could she have slipped in beside the soldier, a robust and careful man, a man who never let anyone within striking distance, and then pierced his heart with a needle-like weapon? And would she have offered to be searched if she were hiding a weapon? The whole scenario begged sanity. He would watch her, but the assassin, Vectis reasoned, had probably waited for the carriage to arrive, checked the baggage, and then attacked at the most opportune moment.

Yes, he thought, that was the most likely possibility.

For hours Vectis gazed at the ghostly outline of the mountains, and the stunted, twisted trees that spiked up like mute statues along the road. He stopped the carriage. The driver needed to urinate. Vectis waited as the grizzled old man relieved himself on the road. He mumbled something about being ready to take over the reins, but then staggered back to the carriage, crawled to his blanket and instantly fell asleep.

The woman's eyes were open. Vectis noticed it the moment the cart stopped. Evidently, she was a light sleeper. The roads were remarkably free from ruts and potholes, but with any change of speed, or turn in the road, or movement of the other men, she opened her eyes. Maybe women were just naturally cautious when traveling with strangers, always watching for fear of their safety, but it struck Vectis as odd.

The mules lurched forward. The woman stretched, the way one would upon waking, then sat up, drawing her cloak around her body. Was she pretending she had just wakened? Vectis chided himself for his continual suspicions. Being overly watchful could get himself killed. He was spending so much time thinking about a low probability that when the true assassin showed himself, would he be ready?

The woman was now fully awake. She pulled back the tarp briefly to check outside and then glanced around at the three men who were fast asleep. "Are you a skilled driver?" she asked, looking at Vectis.

"I'm sober," Vectis replied.

"Then you have my vote," she said.

"Tomorrow our driver is in for a rude surprise."

"Oh?"

"We left in such a hurry he had no time to fill his skins."

She smiled and crawled past the men to the seat beside Vectis. "Mind company?" she asked.

"No objection."

"I like the crisp look of the night," she said, allowing her eyes to sweep the vast heavens. "The moon like frozen candlelight, stars like shards of ice."

"That sounds like someone who's cold," Vectis said, pulling off his oil slicker and handing it to her.

"No, no," she said. "I'm fine. Besides, my cloak is quite serviceable. I cannot take your coat."

"Of course you can. It makes me feel gallant to give it to you. Would you deny me that pleasure?"

"Really, I couldn't—"

"The truth is, it's a ratty old coat, but worth keeping because no one ever steals it, and on certain occasions, like tonight, it transforms itself into a wonderful conversation piece."

She took the slicker, smiled her thanks, and wrapped it around her legs.

"You seem relaxed and happy," Vectis said. "The sleep must have agreed with you."

"It was wonderful."

"One time when I was in North Africa, I had no sleep for three days. I was stumbling, falling down, seeing things—imagined them, dreamed them, I don't know—but my mind conjured up weird things when I was fully awake."

"What things?"

"Well," he snorted, "one time I thought I saw geese flapping through clouds of burning hail, some catching on fire … and there was this bronze statue that talked to me when I passed, it kept asking if I could hear its voice." He laughed. "You know you're in trouble when bronze statues start talking."

"Yes, one step away from the lunatics begging at city gates."

"Don't worry. Sleep cured me. I remember when I finally flopped onto a cot, and they wrapped me in blankets, I giggled like a fool. That's how wonderful it felt." He corrected the mules. They were approaching too close to the edge. "Anyway, I know the value of sleep."

"You like confessions?" she asked.

"If they're interesting, like my story."

"I think this would qualify."

"Let me guess, you're the murderer?" Vectis said, grinning.

She laughed, a pleasurable sound that reminded him he had been too long without a woman's company. "You flatter me," she said.

"By calling you a murderer?"

"Well," she said, shrugging, "men in Rome often underestimate women. They treat them like Greek wives who have no understanding of the world."

"And you do?"

"What? Have a worldly understanding?"

"Yes."

She snorted. "I know embarrassingly little. I think it's obvious to you I'm afraid to travel a hundred feet down this road unaccompanied."

"That's not obvious to me."

"Oh?"

"You don't strike me as a nervous Greek wife. Maybe not even a wife at all."

"There's no point in even confessing," she said with a twinkle in her eye. "You already know my Praetorian husband doesn't exist.

Right? No burly swordsman to dispatch evildoers who dare touch my sacred person."

"It's a nice image," he said.

"Yes, I use it all the time when I travel. It makes the timid aggressive, and the aggressive timid."

"I understand."

She looked at him. "You understand a great deal, don't you?"

"I used to think so," he said.

"And what changed your mind?"

He frowned, surprised by the abruptness of the question.

"A *woman* changed your mind," she said dramatically, her eyes opening wide. "Yes, a tale of betrayed love. How tragic!"

"You make my dreary life sound interesting."

"If you tell me about it," she said, tilting her head like a conspirator, "I won't repeat a word. It will be our secret."

"Are you good at keeping secrets?" he asked.

"You would be amazed. Now stop stalling and begin your tale."

"Unfortunately, I have nothing exciting to satisfy your curious mind, certainly no tale of betrayed love."

"But there was someone special."

He shook his head, not intending to speak of the past, but found himself saying, "Now and then I think about a Celtic woman …."

"Continue."

He shrugged. "She was likely killed in the Britannic wars. My friend there says, I should thank the gods for the good days, and move on."

Her face was entirely serious when she said, "That's not reckless advice."

He didn't reply.

"Life is a precious thing," she said, "but it can evaporate like a morning vapor. Sometimes we need to turn our faces to the living lest we waste our days thinking about a past forever gone."

Vectis took a long look at the woman beside him, her attractive dark eyes glowing in the faint light, her sculptured lips, the confident turn of her face. Not since Neeve had he met anyone so self-possessed. "What prompts you to travel?" he asked, changing the subject. Then he added, "I don't even know your name."

"My name is Tiberia Baebius Merula, a purveyor of dyes," she said. "I have business associates, but they cannot always travel with me. So that's how I find myself alone."

"Traveling alone can be dangerous."

"I'm exceedingly careful," she replied, "and tell fantastic tales of my gallant Praetorian husband."

He smiled. "Men sometimes see through that," he said.

"Yes, that's true. I do watch and take particular care when we stop for the night. I don't trust inns, and especially innkeepers."

Vectis nodded.

"Take tonight," she said, obviously wanting to pursue the conversation, "the innkeeper continually saying that he runs a respectable inn." She snorted her disbelief. "In my mind he's the most likely suspect, and yet the Vigiles hardly questioned the man. In fact, he controlled the investigation from beginning to end."

"He allowed himself to be searched," Vectis said.

"Hah! Who were the people he chose to do the searching? Do you know who they were?"

Vectis shook his head.

"And even if they were trustworthy townsfolk," she said with a mocking tone, "the keeper could have easily hidden the knife in some nook or corner. It was his inn, after all."

"So you think he murdered the soldier."

She waved her hand dismissively. "I don't know, but innkeepers are nasty people, and not a few have been hired to eliminate travelers. For all I know he may have used one of those icicles hanging on the side of the inn and then threw it into a vat of his overpriced mulled wine, where it melted."

"I saw the hole the weapon made," Vectis said, "and I can tell you, it was no icicle."

"I'm sure it wasn't," she said quietly. "It was my feeble attempt at humor."

"Actually," Vectis said "I've seen a similar wound before."

"Truly."

"In Egypt four years ago."

She waited.

"A prince of the royal court … unreachable, they said, surrounded as he was by a veritable cohort of bodyguards. There had been many attempts on his life, but none succeeded … until that night."

"Dare I ask what happened?"   Her voice had a touch of amusement in it.

"He died at a festival with dancing women swirling around him."

"Pleasant atmosphere, at least."

"Yes, so some have remarked.   Anyway, at first the company thought he was jesting, a pretended swoon in the presence of so many beautiful women.   But then it became clear he was not jesting.   A Roman tribune showed me his body later that night.   Someone had driven a needle knife under his ribcage into his heart … and did it with a flotilla of women surrounding him."

"Interesting."

"Isn't it?"

"Don't stop now," she said.   "You must have a conclusion to this fascinating tale."

"I do."

"And?" she said, leaning closer, so close Vectis smelled the faint scent of her perfume.

"I think the assassin in Egypt was a woman, one of those dancers."

"What did the Egyptian authorities think?"

"They assumed it was a man, someone skilled with a dissolving blow dart, or some such thing."

"But you disagree."

Vectis looked at her but made no reply.

She shifted against the wooden rails until she found a more comfortable position, her coal-black eyes revealing nothing. Then she laughed softly. "You certainly have an imagination," she said. "A woman! So who killed the soldier tonight? One of the miner's wives? A barmaid?" She paused, her eyes still amused. Then slowly her face changed and her smile diminished. "Oh, I see," she said, lifting her brow. "You think it's me."

"No, I don't—"

"Yes ... you do," she said, nodding, as if processing the information. "You think I tramp about the provinces with a trunk full of dyes and cloth samples, pretending to sell my wares, but in reality, I'm a dashing Empire assassin of princes and soldiers. I secure invitations to gala festivities at the royal court of Egypt, but I cannot manage to bribe the owner of this wretched carriage to have a sober driver on board. Do you know how ridiculous all this sounds?"

Vectis shrugged. "Of course it's ridiculous. I know that. But you can relax. I'm not saying you are the killer, or any other woman in the tavern. I'm just saying that we should not discount the possibility of a woman assassin."

She smiled wanly. "This creates an awkwardness, doesn't it?"

"How so?"

"Well," she said, as she teased a finger across his chest, "if a woman like me were attracted to a man like you, how could she ever approach him, knowing that he feared being murdered in his sleep?"

Vectis eyed her. Her directness was as shocking as it was flattering.

She moved closer and encircled his middle with her arms. "How could she even warm herself against such a man on a cold night," she asked, turning her ebony eyes up toward his, "when he would always be watching ...?"

"Vigilant people are difficult to deal with," Vectis acknowledged.

"You feel so warm to me," she said, squeezing tighter.

"We've definitely changed subjects, haven't we?"

"Are you objecting?" Her hands caressed his chest and back lightly, and her face moved dangerously close to his.

Vectis started to say something but instead turned his head abruptly toward the mules plodding down the center of the cobblestone road, as if he were worried about them drifting toward the edge. He could feel his heart rate increase as she moved her body slowly against his, and nibbled softly at the bottom of his ear. He turned, and found himself staring directly into eyes hungry with desire. "Yes," she murmured as she leaned forward, and her eyes locked on his, and her lips brushed across his cheek until she reached his mouth. Vectis pulled the oil slicker off her legs and pressed into her, returning her kiss. His better judgment told him to stop, not only because he believed Neeve was still alive, but because he really had no idea who this stranger might be. He slipped his hand into her cloak and under her tunic. He had forgotten how good it felt to be with a woman, and the possibility that this dark-eyed seller of dyes could be the killer seemed almost laughable now. Julian was right. He ought to get on with his life. He stroked the silky skin of her inner thighs. She opened her legs, inviting his hand further. He paused to take a breath. Deep in his mind an urgent voice whispered warnings, but he was having trouble listening. He needed to focus. What was he doing?

He stared down through the floorboards of the carriage at the moonlit cobblestones passing by, and tried to dampen the urgency he felt. An assassin was hunting him, and like a fool he was ignoring the lethal business swirling around him. He remembered the ashen faces of the dead soldier and Egyptian prince, supremely confident men who couldn't imagine their lives ending with one thrust of a needle-knife under the ribs. Yet each in his turn tumbled lifeless to the floor. And now it was his moment. An assassin with relentless zeal was stalking him. Surely it wasn't this woman, but the thought sobered his mind.

He pulled away.

The woman looked shocked, but quickly regained her composure. "Are the ghosts in Britannia more real to you than the flesh and bones in your arms?" she asked.

"Perhaps," Vectis said, but he knew his mind had not been on Neeve, and a twinge of guilt passed through him. He realized he ought to say something to soften the embarrassment they both felt. "You are uncommonly attractive," he said, "but we would both be sorry if the mules wandered—"

"Sympathetic words …." She sighed. "Is there anything more deadly?"

Vectis gazed at the road in silence.

The woman leaned back on the rails. "You are a good man," she said finally. "I know … because I rarely meet good men."

"In your line of work as a purveyor of dyes," he said. It was a leading comment but he decided to say it anyway.

Her eyes narrowed as she studied him, almost as if she were uncertain how to proceed. Then, smiling, she said, "Yes, as a seller of dyes I rarely meet good men because most of my contacts are with other dye merchants, and most of them are assassins, especially the female dye merchants." She smoothed her tunic. "But of course you know all this."

Vectis laughed. She was mocking him.

"My melancholy has lifted," she announced, straightening her back. "See the joyful countenance on my face?" Her hands encircled her head to make the point.

"Truly joyful," Vectis agreed.

"I admit it was humbling to think a man might prefer tattered memories to an enchanting me! But now I understand. You weren't even thinking about that other woman … were you?"

Vectis didn't answer.

"You had deeper more disquieting thoughts. Hmmm? And what possibility had my charms against the anxiety you were experiencing?"

"I was experiencing anxiety?"

"Yes, I'm beginning to understand how you think. You are bothered that an assassin has worked his evil and now roams the emperor's roads free to murder again."

"I cannot deny it. You know everything about me."

She laughed, a throaty laugh. "Not everything," she said, "but I do know some things."

Vectis glanced at the road and back to her again.

"I know you still wonder whether I might be the slayer?"

Vectis shook his head. "I never said that."

"But you do wonder, don't you?"

"I wonder about a lot of things."

She ignored his evasion and said, "That's why you can never fully relax around me. You are like a Praetorian, always watching."

Vectis snorted. "So you've said. What am I watching for?"

Her hands were now deep in the folds of her tunic, as if she were warming them, and her dead calm eyes locked onto Vectis. "Maybe," she said quietly, "you are watching for a moment ... like *this!*" A hand flashed out of her tunic, so fast he hardly saw it move. He felt stiffened fingers jab him sharply under his ribs.

Vectis swept his arm down and caught her hand, twisting it away roughly. Then, realizing what he had done, he released her. "I'm ... I'm sorry," he said.

She took the pain with barely a twitch on her upper lip, and without once turning her eyes from his. "Too late," she whispered. "If I were the assassin, it would have been too late."

Vectis stared at her.

She turned her head slightly, studying him, amusement again on her lips. "But I am not the assassin," she said, gesturing with open hands, breaking the spell. 'Proof is, I had opportunity and took no advantage." She showed him a knife secured under a fold of her tunic. "So you have no reason to fear me," she said as she inclined her face toward his and gently kissed his lips.

"An interesting demonstration," Vectis said, surprised at how much he enjoyed the kiss.

"I thought it was effective," she said with an airy tone. Then, dropping her eyes, she said softly, "I want you to believe me. Is that too much to ask?" She looked up. "I don't know why—maybe because I've been alone for so long ... always on the road. Can you not set aside your suspicions, even for one night?"

"I'm not suspicious—"

"The Valerian Way has an inn less than two miles distant," she said, interrupting him. "Perhaps we might stop to rest the mules, and you and I can take a moment to discuss our lack of trust. A reasonable request, is it not?"

"Entirely reasonable," Vectis said, reaching for the hand that had jabbed him under the ribs, the one he had twisted so brutally. She was in considerable pain. He could see that now, and he wished he hadn't acted so instinctively. "Don't mind my earlier comments," he said, enfolding her hand in his. "When I'm traveling I tend to be overly cautious. I even watch the mules to make certain they don't turn on me."

The corners of her mouth crinkled in a small smile. His attempt at humor seemed to have genuinely pleased her.

He kissed her hand gently.

She stroked his hair and said, "Let's agree to speak no more of assassins. I know little about them, but regular people like us, I would think, have nothing to fear. After all, our assassin tonight did not kill indiscriminately. He ... or she ... was after this Vectis Trebellius fellow, and being skilled at his grisly occupation, he sent poor old Trebellius to the River of Styx. And that is the end of the story."

"It would be," Vectis said, still holding her hand, "except the assassin made a mistake."

Her eyes held steady.

Vectis watched carefully, not entirely sure of the gamble he was making. But he needed to see her reaction.

She waited patiently.

"The truth is," Vectis continued, "I am this poor old Trebellius fellow, still alive and healthy. The soldier was a bodyguard sent to protect me."

"I see," she said, removing her hand and brushing her fingers lightly across her chin. Her dark eyes studied him briefly, then turned away to wander the mountain scenery. She said something about Fortune protecting him and how relieved she was that the assassin had missed his mark. Their conversation moved from one topic to another, she chatting pleasantly, he nodding agreeably, almost as if they were at a dinner party. If Vectis expected her face to reveal something, he was disappointed. And never once did she suggest that the mules looked tired.

15

The Teutisci River was a meandering waterway no different from a hundred others in the highland mountains. But it did have one asset found rarely in northern extremities: it had fishing villages, and fishing villages meant boats. If Neeve and Cronn were to escape the relentless Roman patrols, they could most easily do it by boat.

They slipped quietly through the trees along the river valley, squinting into the dark for boats berthed along the shore. The moon hung low in the sky, an enormous golden globe that gave the river's surface a sheen of burnished copper.

"There," Cronn whispered as he pointed to what looked like a series of black lines etched on the river's edge.

Neeve nodded. Her eyes darted everywhere, looking for legionaries. One thing about the Romans—they were consistent. They never concealed themselves in the brush, lying in wait for the enemy, the way the Caledonians might; they preferred frontal assaults. Their method was to tramp through the woods, as if they were scaring up game, and when their startled quarry scuttled into the open, they tracked them down and destroyed them. "It looks clear," she said, stepping out of the trees, but staying low as she moved down toward the river.

Five minutes later they arrived at the boats, which had been stored bottom up to shed the rain. Neeve ran her eyes down the row, and her heart sank. In the center of every boat, someone had chopped a huge hole. She swept her eyes along the riverbank, hoping to spot one they might have missed. It was futile, she knew. The Romans were thorough. If they had destroyed one boat, they had destroyed them all. Still, she went through the motions of checking every bottom.

"There is another village two miles downstream," Cronn said, "but …."

He didn't need to finish. Neeve understood. In a full moon, with Roman search parties everywhere, it was questionable whether they could make it two miles downstream.

"We'll have to cross the river," she said. "Most of the patrols are on this side."

Cronn eyed the swift moving waters, thinking. "The only ford I know is upstream a mile or so, and I don't think we want to go back that way."

Neeve felt his eyes on her in the muddy light. She knew his question. "I can do it," she said.

He hesitated. "This water has a bite to it. We could get pulled under."

"I can do it," she repeated, with a strain in her voice. She hated when he became overprotective. She had swum plenty of rivers far more dangerous than this, and practically every day of her life she bathed in swift moving rivers all over the northlands.

"Give me your right hand," he said.

"There is nothing wrong with—"

He took her hand, ignoring her protests, and gently opened her fingers.

A shaft of pain shot down her arm, and she sucked in a quick breath to keep from crying out.

"And you think you can swim?"

Neeve jerked her hand away, suppressing a wince. Cronn was right, but it still angered her. "Well, if we're not going to swim the river," she said with an edge in her voice, "I'd like to hear your plan." Her words sounded too much like a challenge, but they were out of her mouth before she could stop them.

"I don't have one."

His stark admission made her wish she had been more respectful. Cronn didn't deserve her ridicule. She took a large breath and said quietly, "Cronn, you know as well as I do, we either cross the river or try to hide in these woods for three or four days until the Romans leave. And when light comes, they'll find us. Sooner or later … they will find us in these woods."

"We risk much if we stay here," Cronn agreed.

"The Romans have swept the area once," Neeve said, gesturing toward the boats, "but they'll be back."

"It might be worse than that," he said. "When the Romans discover how many soldiers they've lost in these woods, they will flood the area." He made a sound of exasperation. "We have few choices. If we intend to cross the river, we have to do it now. We need to get to the next village before they find and destroy those boats."

Once the decision had been made, Cronn was a flurry of action, flipping over boats, scouring for rope, and then lashing several lengths into a lifeline that stretched ten feet between him and Neeve.

Neeve followed Cronn into the freezing river, her arms out for balance, her body pitched against the current as she waded into the deeper waters. Suddenly, the bottom gave way, and the river carried her off in an instant, the rope jerking in her good arm, and pulling her under the swirling surface. Her tunic filled with water and acted like a weight dragging her deeper. She kicked frantically, propelling herself upward. Coughing and gasping for air, she turned her head downriver and spewed out a mouthful of water. Then, flipping over, she tried to sidestroke with her injured arm, but the constant tug of the rope upset her balance and dragged her onto her back. Better not to fight it, she realized, and she remained on her back, paddling and kicking toward the opposite shore.

Over her shoulder she saw Cronn slicing through the water in powerful strokes, hauling her toward shore with every downward thrust. She might have made it by herself, but with only one arm, Neeve had to confess, it would have been difficult. She grasped the rope to steady herself as she inched out of the water, and while still knee-deep at the shore she threw the rope aside and walked out alone. It was a foolish gesture, she knew, and Taranis often chided her for being too independent, but it satisfied an inner need. She appreciated

Cronn's help, and down deep knew she could not have survived without him—especially in the woods—but she still had an urging to show that she could take care of herself. Survival did not always depend on physical strength, and men often forgot that.

With water pouring out of their clothing and squishing in their leather boots, Neeve and Cronn climbed the riverbank to the flats above. Gusts of wind moaned in the rock crevices and shook the scrub bracken that crouched in shadows on the fields of dead grass, gleaming now like golden threads under the cold yellow moon. Neeve shivered. The flats smelled of frozen earth. She dropped her bow and arrow pouch, pulled off her heavy tunic, wrung it out in spite of her arm, and threw it on a clump of bracken. Next came her belt and knives, and her boots that wrenched free with a slosh of water. She wriggled out of her leather trousers, and twisted them into a tight knot, extracting every drop of water she could. Even with her exertion Neeve's lips trembled, and tiny goose bumps pricked up on her bare skin. The cold made her teeth ache.

She glanced over at Cronn, who had discreetly turned his back to her while he dried his own clothing. The gesture was so thoughtful, it made her hurt inside. The giant Caledonian, feared by all who crossed his path, wanted her to feel comfortable as they undressed. Could there be anyone like Cronn, she wondered? So gentle. So protective. She slipped off her inner tunic, wrung it out, and dressed herself again.

Neeve and Cronn set off at a quick pace for the fishing village, but not before stuffing their boots, trousers and tunics with dry grass. The highland grass was itchy, but it had magical powers. For as long as anyone could remember, Celts had used the grass to soak up water from their clothing after crossing steams. Before they were halfway to the fishing village, Neeve and Cronn stopped, shook out the damp grass, and continued on their way, warm and dry.

They heard the Romans before they saw them.

They recognized the sound—heavy axes thudding into the bottom of boats.

"No archers," Neeve whispered as they peered out from the tree line above the river.

"A mistake," Cronn said, shielding his voice behind his hand. "I count twenty Romans ... maybe more."

"Those ones by the bend in the river are not important," Cronn said. "Too far." He was referring to the bulk of soldiers readying a large boat to return to the other side. They had already scouted the surrounding area and left two soldiers to chop holes in the small fishing boats. Two other legionaries stood guard.

"We can handle four," Cronn said, "if you can draw your bow."

"I can draw with my left hand," she replied, "but I doubt if I can hit anything."

"A distraction is all I need." He checked his sword and knives instinctively, and then collected a rock the size of his large palm.

"They still have three boats to chop," Neeve said.

"We'll wait until there is one left," he said. "Their troop boat will be useless to them in a chase. Too slow." He pointed toward an oak overlooking the river valley, its base partially exposed by the spring floods, its gnarled roots like fingers clutching at the river below. "That's as close as we can get," he said.

They moved down to the oak and watched as the soldiers hacked holes in a boat that had been patched too many times, their blades slicing through the squares of black pitch like paper. Then, a gift from the gods. One of the guards started back toward the main body of soldiers.

The axmen mopped the sweat off their foreheads and said something to the departing soldier that made him laugh.

Now one boat remained, and three Romans.

Neeve drew an arrow.

Cronn placed his hand gently on her arm. He wanted to wait until the last second, until the axmen returned to their task and the departing soldier was as far away as possible.

The axmen ambled toward the final boat, their gleaming blades on their shoulders.

"Move in a crouch," Cronn said as he leapt out from behind the oak.

Neeve understood. Not only would they gain a few precious steps before being noticed, they also had to keep their footing on the muddy slope.

Like a giant cat, sword in one hand, stone in the other, Cronn bounded down the riverbank toward the two axmen. Twenty paces out the men started to shout and point toward Cronn, and in the distance the main body of soldiers turned back toward the boats. Cronn ignored everything except the two axmen who were rooted to the ground, staring at the giant warrior bearing down on them.

Neeve angled toward the guard, her bow in her opposite hand, as she tried to draw the man toward her. He was the only soldier with a shield, and as Cronn had guessed, he raised his shield and paired off with the oncoming archer. Neeve slowed. Now that the guard had started in her direction, she had no interest in engaging him. Even with two good arms, she was a poor match for a shielded legionary.

Neeve's eyes shifted toward Cronn, trying to gauge how long it would be before he could give her help. Relief swept over her when she saw him hurl the rock at one of the axmen, step toward the other, and fell him with a single sweep of his sword.

Then everything went wrong.

The second axman turned and ran. He had no chance against the huge Caledonian, and he knew it. Cronn chased after him for a few steps, not wanting to leave an enemy alive so near the boat they would be launching. This prompted the legionary to move rapidly toward Neeve. He intended to finish her and then delay Cronn until the other soldiers arrived. Neeve backed up hastily. Her right arm throbbed, but she managed to keep her bow leveled at the soldier. Even that small gesture, she knew, prevented him from charging recklessly toward her. He closed the gap to five paces. She could see his dark eyes above his shield and the point of his sword glistening in the moonlight. She continued moving backwards. He lurched toward her. She loosed the arrow. It careened off his curved shield and sailed harmlessly over his shoulder, but it was enough to break his attack. She turned and sprinted toward Cronn, who was already moving on her position.

"Get to the boat!" Cronn hollered as he rushed toward the legionary to head him off. "Hurry! Hurry!"

Neeve suddenly realized what had so shaken Cronn. A half-dozen soldiers, probably a returning search party, were racing toward them along the riverbank. Neeve spun on the balls of her feet and darted toward the boat. Seconds later Cronn flew past her, his long Celtic sword clutched in both hands. Then came the ear-splitting crash and a groan. Cronn had blasted the shield from the legionary's hand, and dispatched him in one ferocious movement.

Neeve flipped the boat over, threw her bow and the paddles inside, and tried to drag it toward the water, but with limited use of her right arm, she managed only a few feet.

A flash of light.

Neeve jerked sideways.

A heavy ax passed through the space where her head had been, and crashed into the prow of the boat, shattering the decorative railing.

The soldier cursed. He ripped his ax out of the gash and hefted it over his shoulder, poised to swing. Neeve scurried around to the opposite end of the boat. She pulled out her knife and watched him carefully, tying to see which way he would go. He took several steps toward her, then doubled back with incredible speed, trying to catch her on the reverse side. She bolted back the way she had come, but anticipating the move, he dropped his ax and sprang into the shell of the boat, lunging at her with outstretched, clutching hands.

Neeve swung her knife at the man's arms, hoping to strike something. He never reached her. Cronn's sword shimmered a ghostly blue as it swooped through the night air, slicing into the soldier's back, and toppling his body out of the boat.

"When we hit the water," Cronn shouted, "you get in and start paddling." He had already sheathed his sword and was dragging the boat toward the river, almost at a run. Neeve kept to the side of the boat and when the water reached her knees, she flipped over the rail, grabbed a paddle, and stroked in quick, rapid movements.

Cronn was pushing the boat out when two legionaries came splashing into the water behind him, pulling out their swords. Cronn

kept pushing, one hand on the craft, trying to launch it into the
current, the other hand holding a knife, jabbing it at the soldiers. But
swords against a knife will always win, and Cronn knew it. Abruptly,
he stopped pushing. His next movements were a blur. He whirled
around, shrieking in full voice as he dropped his knife into the water
and ripped out his long Caledonian sword. For an instant the soldiers
froze, stunned by his sudden aggression. Cronn lunged at them, his
sword sweeping down toward their legs, striking the water with a
huge splash. They screamed. The water darkened and they crumpled
like melted wax.

"Cronn!" Neeve shouted. "Hurry!" The current had caught the
boat, and it was picking up speed. More soldiers were running into
the water, some helping their fallen comrades, most making straight
for Cronn.

"Cronn!" Neeve shouted again. She was getting concerned.
Already the river was up to his waist. She tried to slow her speed
with the paddle.

"No," he cried as he struggled toward her. "I'll catch up."

But the boat was moving too fast, and the distance between them
growing. And both of them knew it.

She jammed her paddle into the water, steering the boat back
toward shore.

"Neeve! No! Keep going," he yelled as he glanced over his
shoulder at the pursuing soldiers.

She ignored him. The boat angled closer to shore.

"Neeve … don't …." His voice sounded defeated.

"I am not leaving you," she hollered back.

He struggled toward her, and as the water deepened, he half ran,
half swam. Seconds later he grasped hold of the rear railing, threw his
sword over the edge and started to pull himself up.

But Cronn was not the only one to take advantage of Neeve's
return toward shore. Legionaries streamed behind him, eager to
strike down their enemy.

Neeve snatched up her bow and spread her legs for balance. She
had only two arrows. In the brief moment that Cronn was hanging
onto the rail, the boat had stopped in the water, so significant was the

drag. The soldiers lunged at Cronn's exposed back as he hoisted himself over the rail. Neeve released her arrow at the leader. It struck him in the shoulder, but his momentum carried him forward, and he plunged his sword down toward Cronn's back.

Cronn yanked himself over the rail and collapsed on the bottom. The boat lurched forward in the current, and Neeve dropped down beside him. "Cronn?" she cried. "Are you all right?"

Suddenly the boat wobbled, then stopped.

Neeve turned.

A large hand curled around the rail. Then a man started to pull himself into the boat. It was the heavy legionary from the bog.

"Remember me, little girl?" he growled.

Neeve's breath caught in her throat. She clawed for her bow without taking her eyes off the brutish soldier. Then, rising, she took a breath and steadied her arms. Even at ten feet she knew she could miss with her left hand, especially if she grew excited. She aimed at his fat face. He cursed. She released the arrow. It caught him in the neck. His eyes widened. His mouth opened and tongue flopped. He probably never imagined she would be able to stop him. He gurgled, and fell backwards into the river.

The boat surged forward again, into the swift-flowing waters. They were safe. Safe? She looked down at Cronn. Her hand flew to her mouth. He was lying in a puddle of blood. She knelt beside him and cradled his head.

"Cronn?"

His eyes stared up at her. He was so very still. "You'll be fine," she said. "Just fine ... I can stop the bleeding ...."

"It's bad, Neeve," he said weakly.

"No," she said. "Don't say that. I'll find help ... upriver ... remember Finchoom? She can heal anyone. You saw Cochar after his fall. Remember how broken he was?" Neeve pulled off her winter tunic and placed it under his head. "Is that better?"

He nodded.

"Are you cold?"

"Thirsty," he said.

She wet her fingers and dribbled water onto his lips.

He coughed, and blood trickled out the corners of his mouth.

"No, please, no," she murmured as she tore a swath off her inner tunic to clean his face. She knew what blood in the mouth meant.

"We did well," he said, trying to smile, "the two of us. Almost made it."

"Oh, Cronn, I am so sorry. This is my fault. I had a chance at the Roman ... the one that ... but I missed. I tried, but I ... I am so sorry." The tears ran down her face, and she couldn't stop them.

"You were magnificent," he wheezed.

"Hold on to life, Cronn. You can do it. Hold on."

"I'm trying." His voice was down to a whisper.

She wiped the beads of perspiration from his forehead. Then she said, "You were always my protector, always there when I needed you."

"I liked being near you ... I never told you ...." His breath was coming hard now. "I should have told you ... I ... I love you, Neeve."

"I know, I know," she said, kissing him, "but I still need you, Cronn. I need you now. Stay with me." She kissed him again and brushed away the hair from his eyes. "Please, stay with me, Cronn."

His face had the gray color of death, and she could barely hear him when he asked, "Is this ... a marriage offer?"

She smiled through her tears. "Anything you want," she said, caressing his cheek. "Just get well."

"If your Roman heard this ...." He gasped, trying to smile back.

"Oh, Cronn."

"I'm tired," he said, closing his eyes.

"No! Cronn! Don't sleep!"

"... tired."

"Wake up!" she yelled angrily, shaking him, and mopping the tears off her face.

His eyes remained closed.

"Cronn?" She bent down and kissed him again. "Cronn, listen to me," she whispered urgently. "Can you hear me, Cronn? If you love me you will wake up right now."

"I ... I'm sorry."

"Please, Cronn."

With his eyes closed, he clutched her arm. "Find your Roman, Neeve … find him."

16

Taranis woke up on a packed mud floor in a Roman detention tent. His hands and feet were bound with chains, his body shackled to a wooden stake driven deep into the ground, and despite the intense cold that seeped under the edges of the tent, his face was slick with sweat. He squinted, trying to focus. The room was spinning in giant circles around him.

He lifted his head. A bolt of pain flashed down his neck and seemed to strike into his heart. There was a heavy feeling at the back of his head, as if something had been attached to it. What had they done to him? Instinctively, he reached for the wound, but the chain jerked his hand short. He took several breaths, trying to clear his mind. Then he remembered. Something had struck him. A rock from a Roman slinger, he guessed.

He had to sit up. Lying down made his head throb. He could bear the pain if he could upright himself. He pushed his aching body to a sitting position and waited for the nausea to pass, then licked his dry lips and tried to swallow. It was as if he were swallowing sand. He jerked at the chain, checking the wooden stake, but it held fast. So many proud Caledonians now bent under the Roman whip, he thought. So many mothers weeping in their roundhouses.

He closed his eyes. It was all flooding back into his mind.

He had failed his warriors.

The shame of being alive overwhelmed him. Captured by the Romans! He remembered the dragon vexillum of General Verus's legion, how it had writhed and moaned eerily in the wind, and how he had promised the Caledonians he would slice the hissing dragon off its pole. He had failed. Worse, they had him chained to a post like an animal. He should be in the eternal forest with the bravest of his warriors.

He thought about Cronn and his impossible assignment of holding off Legion VI. Was he staked to the ground as well? No, not with orders to protect Neeve. He had survived the battle, and escaped. Taranis could feel it. Whatever the odds, Cronn would never leave Neeve to the mercy of the enemy.

The tent flap opened.

Twenty fully armed Roman soldiers filed in and stationed themselves shoulder to shoulder around the walls of the tent. A centurion approached with a crop in his hand. He signaled, and two legionaries unlocked the chain that shackled Taranis to the stake. They jerked him to his feet, but with his hands secured to his legs by a short chain, he remained in a crouched position half his normal height. His long yellow hair hung down, covering his face.

Another soldier stepped inside the tent, and the legionaries grew quiet. Taranis could see only to the man's waist, but by the stripe in his tunic, he knew him to be a tribune. The tribune spoke in a crisp voice. "Legate Gnaeus Julius Verus," he announced, and moved to the side.

The legate entered the tent, and stopped. "What is this?" he said, hardly above a whisper.

Taranis could feel the tension as a pair of meticulously tooled leather sandals approached him. "Is this Taranis?" Legate Verus asked.

"Taranis, my Lord," replied the centurion.

"Who did this?" Verus asked, his voice still barely audible. He turned, looking around the room. "Who did this?" he shouted through clenched teeth. "Who bound the chief of the Caledonian nation like a dog in a stable?"

The centurion shifted on his feet and said, "My, Lord, I sought only to—"

"Tribune," Verus said, "strip this man of his rank, and have him staked to the ground for three days, without food or clothing—water only. He will learn not to treat my property as carelessly as he would his wife."

He turned back to Taranis. "Take those chains off him."

Two guards immediately produced keys and unshackled Taranis.

Taranis straightened his back and saw a hawk-faced man in his forties, with narrow shoulders, aggressive black eyes, and easy movements that spoke of power.

"Are you the one they call the blood god?" Verus asked, with a hint of amusement in his voice.

Taranis knew enough of the Roman tongue to understand almost every word that had been spoken, but he remained silent, rubbing the welts where the chains had cut deep into his wrists. Only now did he realize that someone had removed his silver bracelets and golden torc from his neck. It didn't bother him. Victors always plundered the defeated. He glanced around at the soldiers. Their swords remained sheathed, but like wolves circling prey, their eyes gleamed. An interpreter behind him translated, but Taranis refused to answer. He would not provide them entertainment.

"Yes," Verus said, tilting his head back to survey his huge captive. "I can see why you inspired such fear in our troops." He turned to the tribune. "Have him cleaned, fed, and arrange for a surgeon to tend his wounds." With that he left.

They used Julius Verus's silver plated bathtub to bathe him with steaming lemon water, and to gently cleanse his wound with soft sea sponges. In the surgery, they sheared the hair from the back of his head and drained the blood from the injury. That done, they applied compresses to stop the bleeding, covered it with salve, and bound it with strips of cloth. On Verus's orders, they increased the twenty guards to more than fifty, but Taranis remained free of chains and was given an open-faced tent with a cot and a bench. There they served him honeyed quail, antelope livers, finely ground wheat bread with goat cheese, and goblets of spiced wine. Taranis had the impression they were fattening a bull for the slaughter.

That evening they marched him back to the headquarters of Legate Julius Verus. On the way, Taranis searched the camp for traces of other Caledonian prisoners. He saw no one.

The phalanx of soldiers remained outside as Taranis entered the commander's tent. Julius Verus was sitting on a couch in the center of the main room, reading a letter. Behind him stood the military tribune, a translator, several other officers and aides, and more soldiers—evidently the legate's private guard. Taranis ran his eyes down the wall of guards and gave the officers behind Verus a smile of derision. He was mocking their excessive caution. It was the only weapon he had left.

Legate Verus continued reading his letter, as if he hadn't noticed Taranis enter the room. Taranis crossed his arms and waited. He understood. Verus had treated him as a great chieftain, threatening to discipline anyone who acted otherwise, because he wanted to enhance the value of his victory. Now he was showing that even a chieftain of Taranis's stature mattered little in the world of an important Roman general.

After a long silence, and with his eyes still on the papyrus sheet, Verus said, "Two hundred years ago, the world trembled at the name of Vercingetorix. Vercingetorix the Invincible, they called him. He lived in Gallia. A Celt ... big, strong ... like you." He folded the paper and handed it to an aide. "When the divine Julius Caesar defeated Vercingetorix and his Gauls, he held festivities for an entire month, the month Rome now calls Julius to honor his magnificent achievement." He looked at Taranis and said, "Is there any Celt more famous than Vercingetorix?"

When the translator had finished and Taranis was about to respond, the legate lifted a finger to forestall a reply, and turned to an aide. "Was that the last of them?" he asked.

"The last from the Senate," the aide replied.

"Good. See that my replies are sent quickly ... overwhelming odds, extreme bravery of the legionaries, etc., and the savagery of warriors who ... ah ... would butcher their children before allowing them to pass into the Empire. Underscore the cunning nature of Taranis, who had all but destroyed Legion XX before I arrived. I worship Father Mars who guided me to victory, and so forth. And, of course, praise Emperor Antoninus Pius and the usual senators for their wisdom and courage in choosing me to execute the will of Rome. I am humbled by their calls for a Triumph, etc."

Verus had been speaking rapidly, but Taranis understood enough to know he was sending political letters designed to glorify himself. That's what Roman generals did.

"Now, where were we?"

"You were discussing Vercingetorix," an aide said.

"Ah, yes, Vercingetorix the Invincible. No doubt you have heard about him."

Taranis shook his head. He would not give Verus the satisfaction. From a child he had heard the bards sing about Vercingetorix and how valiantly he had fought to keep the Gauls free. When all was lost Vercingetorix gave his people a choice: put him to death, or use his living body as a sacrifice to appease Caesar. They chose the latter, and Vercingetorix rejoiced that at least he had gained better terms for his defeated people. Caesar rewarded Vercingetorix's courage by chaining him in a hole for six years and then strangling and beheading him before the howling mobs of Rome.

Taranis expected no better from Julius Verus.

The legate was sipping tea now and saying that Taranis and Vercingetorix had much in common. "I respect you," Verus said. "Like Vercingetorix, you are a great chieftain."

"And you are a little man with a powerful army," Taranis replied. "Where are my warriors?"

A number of Verus's officers seemed to understand Celtic, because they shifted awkwardly on their feet and glanced at each other. The translator cleared his throat and assumed a posture that apologized for the words he was about to speak.

Verus leaned forward to hear Taranis's first words. When his translator finished, Verus's mouth opened slightly but he said nothing. He sat in silence. His black eyes darted to Taranis, to the translator as if to confirm the words, and back to Taranis again. Then Verus said to the translator: "He wants to know where his warriors are? Tell him his military skills have led them to their deaths."

"And those that survived?" Taranis asked, ignoring the taunt.

"The leaders will be hanged in Rome, the rest sold in Londinium."

Taranis listened without emotion.

Verus continued. "I have decided to send you to Rome for my Triumph in the month of Augustus." He fixed his eyes on Taranis. "This is a great honor for you," he said. "I hope you know that."

"And what if I refuse to participate in this great honor?" Taranis asked.

Verus smiled coldly. "You have little choice," he said.

"A warrior always has a choice," Taranis said.

"You are no longer a warrior. You are a prisoner of Rome."

"I am what I choose to be," Taranis said, "and I do not choose to be a prisoner of Rome."

Verus snorted. "What are you saying … that you will take your life before reaching Rome?"

Taranis waited.

"Only a coward takes his life while his warriors still live." Verus's voice grew in volume.

Taranis remained silent.

"You will not thwart my plans!" The veins popped out in Verus's neck as he glared at Taranis. "I will bind you hand and foot. My guards will sleep with you, eat with you—"

"I will not eat," Taranis said.

Verus slammed his fist into the arm of his couch. "You'll eat what I give you," he shouted, "or I will have it stuffed down your throat."

Taranis gave him a blank stare.

The legate took a breath to compose himself. He began again, this time in a reasonable manner. "Do you understand what I am offering? Immortality! You will be like the great Vercingetorix. A thousand years from now they will sing about Taranis, the blood god of Britannia, the warrior who never bowed to the Romans, who fought them to the end."

"They will also sing about the Roman general that bound him in chains," Taranis said.

"Yes, I acknowledge that," Verus said. "They will sing about us both."

"And I will be thrown into a hole like Vercingetorix until you are ready to trot me out to the mobs."

"You ... you know about Vercingetorix?"

"I know."

"I would never ... I will treat you as the great chieftain you are ... not the way they treated Vercingetorix." He shook his head almost in contrition. "No, no, not like Vercingetorix. This I promise before the gods and these officers. I will take you to the Capitoline Hill, and there before the celebrated and mighty of this age, I will administer a simple sword thrust with my own hand. My own hand!"

"I have two conditions."

"Name them."

"I want the common warriors released."

Verus blanched. "I cannot do that," he said. "Arrangements have been agreed to, promises made."

"You are a general. Unmake them."

Anger flashed in Verus's eyes. He was not used to being challenged. Then, almost instantly his face changed and his eyes shifted around the tent as if he were searching for a solution. A pragmatic man, Taranis thought. "You are the general that defeated us in battle," Taranis prodded quietly. "Who would dare question you?"

Verus sighed, almost in defeat. "I will keep a thousand for the Triumph," he said. "The rest will return to their homes."

"After your Triumph, the thousand will not be sold, but conscripted into your auxiliary forces as free warriors."

"Agreed. Your second condition?"

"I alone will die. My commanders—the leaders as you called them—will be released."

"You go too far," Verus said, and something in his voice told Taranis he had asked the impossible. "The leaders must be hanged. Even the emperor will demand it."

"Released."

"I cannot. I will not."

"We all make our choices," Taranis said.

The military tribune whispered something to Legate Verus, a solution. Verus nodded. He was desperate for his Triumph. "When the procession is over I will put your commanders on the block," he said, "but no more demands."

Taranis understood the concession, but still he pushed for more. He did not want his fellow commanders pounding rocks in the mines. Mining slaves rarely lasted more than a few years. "You will assign them as personal slaves to your officers," he said.

Verus began shaking his head.

"They are men of pride and responsibility," Taranis said. "It is worthy of their status."

Verus eyed his captive.

"It is my last request," Taranis said.

A month later Taranis and twenty of his commanders crossed the channel between Britannia and Gallia. None of them had ever been on a seagoing vessel, and having heard the tales of winter storms at sea, they were prepared to die. As it turned out, the crossing was smooth and uneventful.

Not eager to make the winter crossing, Legate Julius Verus remained in Londinium. He planned to set out for Rome at the earliest possible moment, once the warm weather calmed the seas. But it was certain he would arrive in the capital with plenty of time to organize a Triumph worthy of his noble victory.

17

Neeve stared at Cronn's face until dawn, wondering how she might have prevented his death. She wished she had told him she loved him in those last moments, a small thing, but it would have made Cronn happy. She left her coat under his head. With only her inner tunic to fight off the biting cold, she shivered violently most of the night, but preferred that to letting his head wobble on the hard, ribbed bottom of the boat.

Not once did she have to correct her course, so strong was the current. At first light she stopped at a village of Vacomagi tribesmen. They willingly built a funeral pyre, but were happy for the Roman coins Neeve offered.

She left at the height of the blaze and returned to Caledonian territory where she heard from tribal elders about Taranis and other Caledonians who had been sent to Rome for Julius Verus's Triumph. For weeks she wandered the highlands, sleeping by a fire under the stars, washing in the freezing mountain streams, hunting, setting snares. She thought about Cronn, about Taranis, and about Vectis, wondering if he was alive somewhere in the vast Roman Empire.

And then one day the gods told her what she should do.

Winter was approaching; several snows had come and gone. For days her traps had been empty, and Neeve was growing concerned. She had used up her supply of food. She was trundling through the woods, checking her snares, her eyes alert for game, when she heard a faint scratching behind a yew tree where she had set a trap. She chose the yew because the Druids held it sacred, and the gods, she reasoned, might favor her with a catch. As she crept closer she saw a rabbit with its leg caught in the snare. Her first emotion was joy. She was so hungry. Then she noticed a second rabbit, scampering about, pawing uselessly at the snare, as if trying to help. She stared at the scene for long moments and couldn't help thinking about her brother, Taranis, tied to a post somewhere like this rabbit. Then, as if the kind spirits were speaking directly to her, demanding a sacrifice that bequeathed life, she rose and cut the rabbit free.

After the sign, Neeve knew what she should do. She would search for Vectis, and find a way to free Taranis, and although the spirits from the island might not be as powerful in the heart of Roman lands, she believed they would still help. One thing was for certain, the blind tribune had given her sufficient coin for the journey to Rome—a hundred golden aurei buried in the Caledonian forest.

A week later she located her hiding spot. She could squeeze no more than fifty of the coins into the leather purse on her belt, so she left the rest in the ground for a later time. She was satisfied. Fifty aurei was a vast sum—more than enough to buy a carriage and horse on the other side of the channel and to provide funds for her stay in Rome.

She also had to worry about thieves. They had sharp eyes and would quickly notice someone who was constantly opening a belt stuffed full of gold aurei. At a village moneychanger, she exchanged an aureus for a hundred brass sesterces, minus one, the price for the exchange. The sesterces she carried in a separate pouch, obvious to interested eyes. If someone were to rob her, she would rather it be the sesterces.

Neeve's journey down the length of the island, from Caledonian territory to the southern tip of Britannia, went smoothly. The Roman patrols along the roads seemed relaxed, now that the Caledonian threat had been subdued. She traveled on farm wagons mostly, bouncing with three or four others on the rough-hewn planks. For a tiny bronze coin, farmers readily took weary travelers to the next town.

When she passed through Londinium, she stopped at Britannia's provincial headquarters and trudged from one military office to another, inquiring about Vectis. Eventually, she found herself in the records office talking to a gray-haired officer with nervous eyes who acted as if every request were a burden.

"I cannot search for anything now," he said, his eyes darting around the tiny room. "They give me no help, and everyone expects me to drop what I'm doing ...." He waved his hand at a table covered with unopened dispatches. "It's too much, simply too much for one man."

"I traveled all the way from—"

"Yes, yes, I hear it all the time."

Neeve turned her back as if to go, and slipped her fingers in her belt. "This is important to me," she said, holding up a golden aureus. It was an absurd amount of money to offer as a bribe, but she was desperate.

His eyes stopped moving. "What was the name of the fort?" he asked, snatching the aureus from her hand and holding it up for inspection.

"Outpost Faustina," she said.

"Outpost Faustina!" He shook his head and made a whistling noise.

She said, "The officer's name—"

"Doesn't matter the name ... Faustina's gone with everybody in it."

"I know that but—"

"Dead. They are all dead. Killed by the Caledonians."

"But I know some escaped."

"If they did, they would have reported in at one of the legionary posts, and we would have record of it."

"But—"

"If some escaped as you say, they never made it south through the tribes. Sorry."

"I would like you to check his name against your records," she said firmly.

He breathed heavily and marched back to his shelves. "Outpost Faustina," he said, pulling out a roll from a wooden box. "Every name here … dead. What was his name?"

"Vectis Trebellius Quadratus."

"Ah, yes, the prefect." He pushed the list toward her. "There, you can see. Dead. They're all dead. I told you."

"These records must be wrong."

"They are not wrong, but if they were, they would know in Rome. That's where the complete records are kept."

Neeve left the office in stunned silence. The records had to be wrong. Vectis was clever, enterprising. She was certain he had made it south.

For the rest of the journey Neeve thought about Vectis. In the last year, her whole life had changed. Cronn, Taranis, and her beloved Vectis—all gone. Their faces passed in front of her and she couldn't help pitying herself. She knew it was selfish. She knew others had suffered as much as she after the Romans had come. Many had lost their homes, their families, everything. But she couldn't control the deep sorrow welling up in her throat. Her thoughts spilled over to distant memories of her father and brother, Eston, killed by the Romans.

Four children, that's what her parents had. Now only she and Taranis were left. Her mother was probably dead … and her little sister, Nes, so sweet, so bright, and so young when the Romans dragged her away to the slave markets. Whatever became of her, Neeve could not imagine.

She swallowed hard. She could barely remember what Nes looked like. When she closed her eyes, she could see pieces only, her sister's flaxen hair, her attentive blue eyes—but not the whole. She did remember the kitchen hearth on their homestead where she had scooped out a glowing coal and laid it in front of Taranis, Eston and little Nes. They all stood barefooted on the fiery ember and declared they would never separate. Neeve remembered the smell of burning flesh, and the pain, but more than that, she remembered the pledge to protect each other always. How things had changed from those naïve days of childhood.

Nes and Eston were forever lost to her now, but not Taranis. Despite the discouraging news in Londinium, Neeve's plan remained the same. She would find Vectis—if the gods had spared him—and together they would somehow free her brother. With the plan firmly in her mind, Neeve arrived at the seaport town of Dubrae resolute in her spirit. Once she crossed the channel, she believed good things would happen.

Across the water lay Gallia, long-haired Gallia, as the Romans called it. Neeve never quite understood the reference. As far as she knew, everyone had long hair except the Romans. Of course, she had lived her whole life on the island—Rome's outpost—and she knew nothing about Empire peoples who occupied the mainland.

But now she was leaving. The excitement of boarding a ship for Gallia set her heart pounding. And then it would be on to Rome where she would enter the gates of the eternal city, walk its streets and meet its people. She would behold their gilded palaces, enormous amphitheaters, and magnificent chariots that rolled through the streets and across the paved forums, but she would never forget how these people, with the might of their swords, had taken away everything she loved in this world.

She still dressed in her well-worn highland clothing—wool tunic, leather trousers and high boots, and she still carried her bow and two Celtic knives. On her journey she had kept to herself, but made certain she was never alone. She was a woman and therefore a target, but with so many people traveling on the Roman roads, thieves could afford to be selective. By her rough garb, they knew she was an outlying Celt, with probable experience in the frontier wars. And she looked poor. Only one small traveling bag. Who could imagine such an unadorned traveler carried gold aurei in her belt? Her task was to convince them they should choose a more sensible target, one with less risk and more profit.

Whether from chance or good planning, Neeve had made it to Dubrae by the sea without so much as a sideways glance by the shiftless men who congregated outside the city limits of every town.

The farther south in Roman territory she journeyed, the more secure she felt. Roman soldiers were everywhere, some in tight columns marching energetically to an appointed destination, most wandering about, on leave, or with their Britannic born wives and families. A Caledonian could never have imagined such a picture.

The wharf was silent, except for the lapping of the sea. It was a good sign. Tomorrow would be a fair day.

Neeve stopped at the stalls along the dock and bought bread, strips of salted duck and a skin of Celtic beer for the journey across the channel. These she stuffed in her bag and set about to find a ship headed for Gallia. A dozen large ones with tall masts bobbed in the harbor, but none was crossing the channel. The captains hauled only coastal freight during the storm season because, as they said, their lives were worth more than the bonus paid for winter shipping. Her best hope was a ship arriving in two days from the central part of the island. It was said to be a slave-driven ship that would stop briefly in Dubrae before it set sail for Gallia.

Neeve had never paid much attention to the drab merchant ships that rode the waves along the coastline as they ferried goods from one port to another. Occasionally, she saw a Roman warship and it never failed to chill her heart. They were wind-driven, sleek and fast, and they had a large crew to man the oars once they were called into battle. The naval crews were in every respect legionaries on water, never slaves as with the freighters, but professional soldiers of the Empire.

Neeve asked several captains about the incoming ship, and she received the same answer. It was a grain freighter carrying dried spelt for the legionaries on the German frontier. The crew was sound and kept their passengers safe from brigands, but it was made up entirely of slaves, including the captain. Every winter season the ship's owner made an enormous amount of money hauling grain across the channel, and with over fifty crossings to the ship's credit, no one could deny that Felicitas, goddess of good luck, inhabited the very timber of the vessel. The ship had good omens about it. After nearly succumbing to a storm on her maiden voyage, the crew hired a craftsman to carve the lithe figure of Felicitas into the bow, and since that day, the ship had never encountered a major storm.

Two days later, Neeve arrived at the dock before the sun rose, and was surprised to see crowds of people eager to deposit their coins into the outstretched hand of Felicitas's owner. The ship was nothing special, fifty feet long and twenty wide, with a towering mast that soared above the ship. It had a small cabin toward the stern for the captain, a pointed prow, a lead sheathed bottom, dual rudder oars, and a cypress hull. Along both sides ran two oak timbers, rubbing wales, fastened by heavy iron bolts. These reinforced the hull to protect against pounding seas.

"No more than sixty passengers!" Felicitas's owner kept shouting as he stuffed the coins into his large purse. "Ship leaves at dawn."

Neeve joined the crowd but made little headway. She found herself squeezed out as determined men elbowed their way to the front. Some even clutched at her hair to gain a few steps. Her anger grew. Abruptly, she pushed in front of a balding man with a round face and a short pig nose. She tilted her composite bow so the end poked into his chest. Every time he shoved forward, she applied pressure backwards. He hollered a few times, and she immediately apologized, all the while advancing until she reached the owner seated on his raised chair. She dumped the ten sesterces in his hand, jammed her bow one last time into the pig's ribs, and boarded the ship. She felt fortunate to be included in the first sixty, but soon realized that in the face of paying customers, the owner had changed his mind, and crammed more than a hundred onto the deck. He had also filled the entire hold below with grain because the overflow crates were strapped to the deck at the stern, as were a number of wooden racks containing amphorae of olive oil.

She sat with her back against the inner hull of the ship, dropped her carrying bag and bow between her legs, and waited. Passengers filled in the open spots, a woman of about fifteen on her right, the man with the pig's face on her left. He gave Neeve what resembled a smile; she turned away.

A few minutes before sunrise, the captain ambled slowly down the gangplank and along the wharf, ostensibly to inspect his craft one last time. She watched without much interest until she saw the captain talking to the owner, an agitated look on the captain's face. He was a slave, but Neeve could tell he was not happy with his owner. He kept pointing toward the ship, and it was obvious the nature of his complaint. Too many passengers. He wanted some removed to lighten the load. Neeve knew little about sea vessels, but even to her untrained eye, the ship's crowded deck seemed overburdened. She glanced at the skiff tethered behind the ship and wondered how it could be of any help with all the people on board. When the captain returned with a satisfied look on his face, Neeve assumed he had been bribed.

For a fleeting moment she thought about leaving, finding another ship, but like everyone else, she stayed. The seas were calm, the skies clear, and besides, Felicitas protected the ship. Who knew but the next vessel might be destined for the bottom?

The sun rose, a brilliant red ball, rapidly transforming itself into a golden yellow orb, warm on the face. Tiny boats bristling with rowers towed the Felicitas out of the harbor, and by the time they had cleared the shoals, the helmsman had hoisted the huge square sail, one side of it popping as it caught the wind. Everyone on board felt the sudden tug, and visibly relaxed. They were on their way.

The captain came out on deck and greeted the passengers. "We've a fair wind with favorable currents," he said, glancing off toward the horizon. "I fully expect to land in Gallia by late afternoon." He pointed at a long wooden barrel of fresh water. "Enjoy it, but don't waste it," he said.

He turned to go, then stopped, glaring at several people in turn. His face darkened. "One other item," he said. "Thieves and troublemakers … I deal with them harshly. My crew and I are the sole arbitrators of disputes. If a passenger becomes unruly, steals someone else's goods, or in any other way disrupts the voyage, he will be thrown overboard. Be assured," he said, "the Roman administrators in Britannia and Gallia prefer definitive action at sea to prolonged negotiations in their courts." Then with a wry smile, he said, "I enjoy throwing troublemakers over the side, because as captain, I legally gain possession of their goods. Have a pleasant voyage."

For two hours the ship traveled northeast on the tail of the high tide, hugging the coastline, and waiting for the tides to change before launching across the channel. Ship captains knew the channel tides reversed direction every six hours, and they had to get it right. The captain did. Neeve heard him shouting instructions, and the helmsman and his mates were again tugging on the sail. The sharp nose of the vessel made a hard turn toward open sea, and the land quickly receded behind them.

With nothing to do but watch the roll and pitch of the waves, passengers formed clusters where they talked and sometimes exchanged food. Many had set up small v-shaped tents for protection from the rain that commonly hit the channel. The pig face beside her tried to strike up a conversation, but Neeve gave him one-word answers, hoping he would get the message: she wasn't interested.

Suddenly, the pig face thrust his thick fingers into her hair and said, "I like tribal women."

Neeve slapped his hand away. "Do you like the sea?" she said in a steady voice. "Because that's where the captain will throw you if you don't leave me alone."

He shrugged and said something about stupid outlanders. He picked at his teeth awhile, and then fiddled with his sack of clothes before eventually joining a group on the other side of the deck. Neeve smiled at the woman beside her and received one in return. A sweet smile, she thought. She glanced across at the pig. Better that she had been forced to deal with this vulgar man than a girl tender of years. She seemed truly vulnerable. They talked briefly before falling into silence. In her heart Neeve was thankful for the solitude. She wanted to be alone with her thoughts, painful though they were. Her mind flooded with memories of Vectis and Taranis, and of course, Cronn. If Cronn had not been killed, he would be sitting beside her on this very boat, ready for whatever lay ahead. But he was gone, and she was alone.

They were within sight of land when the wind changed.

It blew hard against the tide, frothing up the surface and creating a short sea, as the sailors called it.

"Keep calm," the captain said, glancing toward the sky. "Normal for this time of the year."

The helmsman was busy adjusting his sail again. The captain started two torches and placed them in their shielded holders on either side of his open-walled cabin. Everyone stared at the dark clouds in the distance, lit now and then by silent flashes of lightning.

"It might pass," one of the passengers said hopefully.

But the wind increased, and within ten minutes the clouds were no longer distant. The temperature dropped rapidly, and the heavens had an evil look about them. Clear skies turned into a dismal gray, and the green water to black churning ink. Thunderclaps shook the tiny vessel as it rose on the swell, and plummeted into the trough, and rose again. Hard, pelting rain slashed the passengers' faces and flung their tents into the sea.

They began to vomit. Some over the side, some flat on the deck.

One, bending over the oak rail, lost his balance as the ship nosed into the sea. He flipped completely over, a summersault into the trough. As the rising sea lifted him high above the ship, he waved his hands pathetically before being carried away. Neeve was close enough to see the terror in his eyes

"Don't hang over the edge!" a sailor yelled. "Spill your guts on the deck. It'll wash."

Most of the sailors were busy at the stern, hauling in the skiff. With the increasing size of the waves, it proved more of a challenge than they anticipated. They conscripted a dozen big men to haul on the rope, and soon the skiff was lashed to the stern.

As the wind grew stronger, Neeve wrapped her arms around the inner rail that ran the length of the ship, bending her face into the hollow of her shoulder, protecting it from the stinging rain, though by now she couldn't tell the difference between the rain and the blast of the sea. The sailor was right. The deck had washed clean.

"It's just a little blow," the captain shouted to the passengers from his cabin. "Find something to hang onto. It's going to pick up some."

Pick up some? Neeve frowned, shielding her eyes as she strained to see the captain and helmsman, trying to draw reassurance from them, but their faces had unreadable looks as they spat out orders for lowering the yardarm on the main mast. They left it at half-mast and placed two sailors on either side to direct the sail. At the stern, three sailors struggled with each of the rudder oars, trying to keep the vessel pointed into the wind. But it was the faces of the common sailors that concerned Neeve. Their eyes never rested, darting nervously across the gathering sea, then to each other, to the captain and helmsman, looking vainly for encouragement. They had been through rough seas before, but this one clearly alarmed them.

Darkness descended. The wind grew fiercer. The helmsman sent a sailor scrambling up the mast to the crossarm, hoping for better visibility. He hollered down to the helmsman a steady stream of sightings, but Neeve couldn't be certain what he said. His voice was swallowed by the squall.

She squinted into the storm. On each flash of lightning, she thought she could make out a murky ribbon of rock stretching along the horizon. They were nearing the shore. She looked back at the helmsman clinging to the mast handles and the captain who stood wide-legged in the open cabin. He and the helmsman were cursing and pointing in different directions, as if they were arguing about something. Neeve swallowed hard, suddenly realizing that the captain was lost. He was maneuvering closer to shore because he needed to establish a familiar landmark before the storm increased and darkness enveloped them completely. Without a landmark, they would never find the harbor at Gesoriacum.

The wave troughs deepened, and the walls of water coming at them steepened. Already the wind was at gale force, howling across the deck, ripping at the flattened sail, twisting it, despite six sailors now straining on the spar.

"Down the mainsail," the captain roared, motioning with his arms. The sailors laid hold of the brails and guided the immense yardarm down crossways into slots on the oak rails. They bound the rigging and linen sail and left the small sheet on the bowsprit for stability.

With the mainsail gone, the waves pounded the nose and turned her toward the trough.

"Oarsmen!" the helmsman screamed. "Damn you to Hades! Hold those rudders firm."

But the sailors straining on the rudder oars could not hold the ship into the wind.

"Frapping cables!" the captain cried, and for the first time Neeve saw anxiety on his face. "Gird her up."

For the next hour, as the darkness deepened, the sailors struggled with the frapping cables they used to undergird the ship. Some lost their footing in the wash as the ship rolled and dipped, and one got lifted overboard by a torrent of water flooding across the deck, but they strapped the timbers. Starting at the bow, they passed heavy ropes under the hull and secured them fore and aftships. The whole time Neeve could hear the sailors calling on Felicitas to save them. There was no hiding it now. The sailors had the haunted look of men about to die. Even the captain was worried. Frapping cables were used only in extreme danger to hold the vessel's timbers together against the pounding sea.

With the ship's nose no longer heading into the wind, the sea took control, trapping her in the trough. She rolled in a sickening motion, first putting one rail to the sea, and then the other. Huge drafts of seawater flowed onto the deck, and with each roll of the ship, the bubbling line of foam sucked at the passengers, threatening to feed them to the hungry sea.

The torches fizzled and died.

Neeve called on the gods, though she doubted they could hear her above the shrieking storm. Sailors cast the crates of grain into the sea. The gale tore at their oilskins, and not a few grabbed hold of their mates to steady themselves on the shifting deck. They dumped the amphorae of oil over the side, opened the raised hold and emptied it, except for what they needed as ballast. With the sea flooding the deck on every roll, even Neeve knew the ship had to be lightened, or it would founder.

The Felicitas continued in the trough of the sea, the giant combers battering the timbers. Under the watchful eye of the helmsman, the sailors strained on the rudder oars, but the vessel refused to turn its nose even a degree into the wind.

The waves grew in size, and with every roll, more water filled the deck. Neeve wondered how the ship stayed afloat. She clung to the rails, her hands gripping the pipe like frozen claws.

"Men on the deck! Women if you can," the captain called. He had gathered all available sailors at the huge yardarm, but he needed more to heft the impossibly heavy beam into the sea.

Neeve released her grip and rose on shaky legs. Other women were inching their way along the rail toward the center of the ship. When the vessel dipped, Neeve braced herself for the incoming wave. It thundered by, clutching at her legs like determined fingers. The woman ahead of her, the one with the sweet smile, flew off the rail like a leaf in the wind, her slender arms thrashing as she disappeared over the side. Neeve took a deep breath, squinted into the biting rain, and continued forward.

The sailors had already unhooked the winches and tackles from the yardarm by the time everyone had gathered on both sides of it. It took nearly every soul on board Felicitas to lift the enormous spar from the slots to a lengthways angle. Neeve felt better doing something than simply clinging to the railing. Surprisingly, the yardarm was longer than the entire ship.

"Slowly … slowly," the captain intoned, standing on the bow with his oil slicker beating at his knees. "Bear your weight … easy. Hold that end!"

With one end balanced on the edge of the exterior rail, the long line of recruits tramped the other around toward the sea.

"Heave to," the captain shouted, and the yardarm rolled off the rail into the rising waters of the next wave.

But the tempest struck back like a demon. The yardarm hit the water stern end first and twisted in the swell like a straw, smashing into the men standing on the bow, flinging their broken bodies into the sea. Then, having done its worst, it slid silently into the deep, leaving another five or six screaming on the deck. The next wave came and licked them off into the sea, into silence.

The captain was gone.

Cries to Felicitas rose from the ship, and to Neptune, the ancient sea god. But the storm increased in ferocity, and the helmsman had the sailors cut the forestay that roped the top of the mast to the bow to hold the mast firm. Then they slit the smaller aft rope and axed down the swaying mast. It tumbled straight into the sea, a sign to everyone that Felicitas had turned her eyes on her desperate servants.

The helmsman thought he could hear the breakers so he ordered soundings taken. Neeve could hear the sailors shouting to each other: "Ten fathoms."

"Drop anchors!" the helmsman cried, alarmed. They were almost on top of the rocks. The sailors waited for the lightning, trying to locate the breakers.

Neeve was back on the rail, her body shaking from the bitter cold, her hands frozen like stone. But still she clung to the bar as wave after wave pounded the ship and burst across the deck. Her composite bow and bag of clothes had long ago disappeared, but she didn't care. Her only thought was reaching port.

Suddenly, a loud cracking sound, more like a snap, pierced the air. Every head on deck whipped around to see what had happened, but the ship looked the same. The sailors scrambled across the deck, opening the hold and climbing down to inspect the hull. Even without a torch, they could tell what had happened. The timbers had split near the stern. Felicitas was taking water.

"Slip anchors!" the helmsman shouted. "Foremast ... rudders, bring us in." He didn't say anything more, not to the passengers, nor to the sailors. Everyone knew the ship would founder soon, and the bleak hope was to bring the vessel closer to shore.

A struggle broke out on the stern, men fighting over the skiff. But the moment it hit the water it swamped and was swept away by the surf.

Neeve stared over the rail at the growing line of rocks jutting out of the sea. Each wave drove them toward the breakers, and the sound grew louder, like the tramping of a thousand horses. She tightened the thongs on her money belt, but threw the bag of sesterces over the side. She didn't need the extra weight.

They drew closer to the crashing waves. Her breath came in short gasps. She braced herself for the explosion of timbers that would surely come as the ship dashed itself on the spines of the black rock.

The Felicitas was sitting low in the water, its stern no longer hindering the waves that surged over it. Still, they drifted toward the rocks. The crew and passengers crowded the bow, their bodies stooped in fear, their hands clutching each other, not so much to steady their feet, as to calm their horror saturated minds.

The ship shuddered.

It started down. It would never reach the breakers.

Neeve jumped with everyone else. The swell dropped away and she hit the bottom of the wave trough, feeling as though she had hit the ground. Colors flashed around her. The waves rolled over her. She gasped for air. Something pawed at her shoulder. A hand! She twisted around. The pig face. He was splashing and trying to keep his head above water, almost as if he couldn't swim. He grabbed her hair and dragged her under. She wrenched away, struggling to breathe.

The next wave crashed over her, covering her with twenty feet of water. She kicked frantically with her legs, pulling with her arms. When her head broke the surface, she was a ship length from the sinking Felicitas. She filled her lungs in an effort to stay on top of the surf, and all around her she could see men rising and falling with the sea.

And she heard screaming, as the sea hurled them against the black teeth of the rocks.

Neeve thought she saw an opening in the breakers and tried to swim toward it, but she was caught by the next swell and surged forward. Again and again the water rose and fell, and Neeve fought for air, exhausting herself against the inexorable power of the sea. Her lungs burned from salt water, and her arms and legs flopped uselessly. When she no longer had strength left to protest, she let the sea take her. An enormous wave picked her up and flung her at the hungry rocks. She felt her body rising, being thrust forward, curling downward toward the breakers, and a heavy wallop in her stomach.

Her mind darkened. Her capacity to think drifted away. She tried to tighten her grip on the rail, not realizing she had left the ship long ago. Waves crashed down on her and she squeezed harder on the rail. Her face ground into the sand and something told her she was no longer in the ship. She was on the other side of the breakers, being carried by the waves, in and out. She coughed out a lungful of water. Her nose and throat ached. Her stomach throbbed. She felt the surge carry her in again, and she clawed the stony bottom toward the shore. A receding wave sucked her back into the sea. Another wave swept her forward, flattened and lost its power. She tried to crawl, but it gathered strength and dragged her back again. She let herself float, like a dead fish. The sea brought her in again. With a last burst of energy, she jerked to her feet and staggered toward the beach.

Expended, her legs crumbled under her.

Neeve woke hours later in the grizzled light of dawn, the storm still sputtering. She was lying on her stomach, her body feeling as if it had been smashed into the ground. Her eyes focused. In the sand beside her were three bodies, washed up by the sea. And other victims, farther along the shore.

Two men were bending over them, pulling at their clothes.

Scavengers.

She closed her eyes.

They were coming for her.

18

Balbinus handed the message back to Calpurnia, his eyes darting about nervously. "What does it mean?" he asked.

Calpurnia padded across the mosaic flooring of the library and deposited the roll on a shelf partitioned for scrolls. "I don't know," she said. "The plan was for Brutus to eliminate Trebellius before he made it to the Adriatic Sea."

Balbinus glanced toward the doors to see if any servants were lounging near the entrances. He didn't trust the best of them. They would peddle secrets of the noble Socrates, if they thought it would bring a coin. He lowered his voice and wiped the sweat building on his upper lip. "Trebellius must have reached the Adriatic by now," he said, "and once across he will be escorted by legionaries. Legionaries!" He laughed at the ridiculous state of affairs. "Then what will I do? The traveling coach was my only real opportunity." He opened his mouth to call for wine, thought better of it, and poured a cup without assistance.

"I don't think you should worry—"

"Worry! You don't think I should worry?"

Calpurnia motioned toward the scroll. "The message said, 'All is well, proceeding as planned.'"

"But the plan was—"

"Plans alter," she said in a soothing voice. "Be assured, Brutus has events well in hand. Remember, there is no finer ... ah ... professional in Rome. That's why we hired him."

Balbinus gulped down his wine and poured another. "All this will be tied to me. I know it will. I can hear Atilius Titianus laughing. And I deserve to be mocked. I supported Titianus against the emperor, and then betrayed him, and now the Fates are weighing me in the balance."

"No, no, the Fates are working out their mysteries in your favor."

"I want to believe you," Balbinus said, looking at his cup. It was empty again. "But I fear Senator Severus will learn that I hired an assassin. Then he will talk to the emperor, and they will wonder what I am hiding."

"Remember what the note said. All is well." She rose and took his cup from his trembling fingers. Then drawing him toward the couch, she said, "We will receive another note soon saying that Trebellius drowned in the Adriatic, or was burned in a tragic fire, or that some barbarian took his life."

She brushed her lips lightly across his cheek, and encircled his mouth with tiny kisses, and he felt his fears melt like autumn snow.

Brutus sat alone in the dining room of her villa, sipping a goblet of wine. The servants were in the process of preparing dinner so she wandered out to the colonnaded portico and sat down beside a table. She needed to think. In her hand she held a long thin blade, which she mindlessly massaged on a sharpening stone, thinning its length to within a hair of tolerance. She had many such blades and knew exactly where the tolerance lay, where it would snap if inadvertently it struck a bone. For years she had experimented with different widths and thicknesses, practiced on animal carcasses, until she arrived at the perfect needle-shaped blade.

It wasn't always so. In the beginning, after her husband died and left her with ruinous debts at the bankers, she used an ordinary soldier's dagger. But she was a young girl with no experience. She remembered crying for a week over her heartrending loss and her desperate condition. The bankers were about to auction off her only home, a modest sized villa on the outskirts of Rome, and she had no funds to prevent the sale. She begged one of the bankers for more time, and he responded by thrusting his hand under her tunic with promises of an extra month. When she pushed him off, he laughed and said that before the winter came, she would be selling her body at the brothels for crumbs of bread.

By chance, as she walked the streets in utter despair, she heard two men arguing in a carriage. One was blackmailing the other for a sexual indiscretion. When the blackmailer left, she gritted her teeth and approached the man. "I know someone who could make this problem disappear," she said, as calmly as her wildly beating hear would allow.

The man jerked his head around, startled.

"Don't worry," she said, "your secret life is no concern of mine … but the blackmailer will never stop. You know that."

"I have no idea what you are babbling about. Be off!"

"Perhaps I was mistaken." She turned to leave.

"Wait. Who is your friend?"

"You don't want to know," she replied. "But you may have heard of him—Brutus. He goes by the name of Brutus, a Syrian." She could think of nothing else to say. Brutus was the Syrian worker who cleaned the streets outside her Greek tutor's apartment.

"I have never heard of anyone named Brutus," he said.

"Few have," she said, "and only at a whisper."

His brow furrowed, as if he were thinking.

"Brutus is said to be Rome's top assassin. No one has ever seen his face, not even me. But I know someone who can contact him."

The man fiddled with his walking stick. "How much to solve my problem?" he asked finally.

She eyed his richly appointed carriage, trying to think. She owed two hundred and forty-six aurei on her villa, and so she looked him straight in the eye and said," Two hundred and forty-six aurei."

He was more stunned by the large amount than the odd number. "That is outrageous!" he said.

"Fine," she said, glancing away. "But you will pay far more than that to your blood-sucking blackmailer, I promise you. And in the end your secret will be shouted from the rooftops. Blackmailers always tell their secrets."

He sighed. "I don't even know who you are. What guarantee do I have that this Brutus fellow will follow through?"

"You pay nothing until the job is done," she said.

He pursed his lips, rubbed his thick jowls, and then nodded.

She took the blackmailer's address, dressed in expensive clothing and waited outside his villa. She followed him to a jeweler's shop where he purchased a silver bracelet and several rings. She could see he had a taste for the good life. When he reappeared she passed him on the concourse, paused, and asked if he were a Senator. Flattered, he said he was not, but that he might be able to help her. She led him to one side, to an empty lane, and there she stepped in close and shoved her dagger into his stomach. He doubled over cursing and grasping at her, ripping her cloak off as he fell. She dropped down, pulled the knife out of his writhing body, and jabbed it into him again. He squealed like a pig in the slaughter yard. She stuck him again, and again. Ten times she stabbed him, and still he wouldn't die. She had no idea how hard it would be to kill someone. Then she thrust up toward the heart, and he jerked once, and fell silent.

She left him in the lane, minus his silver bracelet, rings and a purse stuffed with coins.

Two days later she met with the wealthy man who had hired her, and he refused to render full payment. She told him Brutus always kept his bargain, but since he had trouble keeping his word, the fee had now doubled. When the man sputtered his objections, she informed him that within one week he would suffer the same fate as the victim if he did not render double payment. She received double payment the next day.

That was her first contract. It wasn't long before her reputation soared, along with her fee, and after her first experience, she demanded full payment before setting out. Fewer complications. Her dagger gradually changed to a slender, razor-sharp needle of steel, and her skill increased until she could dispatch a man with one quick thrust. No one in Rome would have guessed Brutus was a woman, and that lessened the odds of discovery. Men, especially the kind she had to deal with, enjoyed having a mysterious woman press up close to them. They had few loyalties and no scruples, and when they crumpled onto the floor, they almost certainly were receiving just recompense for a life of excess.

That's how she lived with her conscience. Most of her partners — that's what she called them, partners, she would say she was meeting a business partner in Egypt or Gallia—most of her partners were a blight on civilization and best cleared off the stage. If perchance a decent sort or two was sprinkled among them, well, she would never know, because she spent little time with her partners.

And that was why the Vectis Trebellius affair bothered her.

Not only had she made a mistake, disastrous in her line of work, but she had also spent hours in conversation with her partner. Worse, she liked this Vectis Trebellius. He seemed to be a good man. On the journey, when the woman was forced out of the carriage, she, Brutus, had protested, as did Trebellius. The difference was that Brutus was acting, playing the part of a kindly merchant. But Vectis Trebellius— he was genuinely troubled by the woman's distress.

She thought about her message to her client. "All is well," she had written, "proceeding as planned." But all was not well. It could hardly have been worse. Trebellius knew her real name. That would have been of little consequence since she always used her real name when traveling, Tiberia Baebius Merula, a purveyor of dyes. And so she was. But Trebellius had hinted, whether in jest or not, that she might be the assassin.

The linkage concerned her.

She was astounded he would consider her a suspect, given the presence of a milling crowd, a slick magician and a vile innkeeper. Besides, the partner himself was anything but an easy target, with his guarded manner and watchful eyes. How could Trebellius even begin to suspect a woman would be capable of taking down such a robust man?

Brutus thought she knew the answer. The Egyptian prince. It was a proud moment for her. She had completed an assignment that no other assassin would have dared, and she did it with style. But Vectis Trebellius was there. He had also spent time in Britannia where Celtic women fought alongside their men. He knew what a trained woman could do in the right circumstances.

She ran an expert eye along the length of her blade. Pleased, she slipped it back into its sheath. She thought she had taken every precaution. In a public place she always made certain the Vigiles had many suspects to choose from. She even submitted herself to a search, not that a barmaid would have found the slim dagger strapped in the center of her back.

Still, Trebellius had lingering suspicions. She knew his type. He would check to see if she were truly a dye merchant and if she had given him a fictitious name. Anything false about her and he would wonder why, and his suspicions would grow. He would think about the assassination in Egypt, and he would conclude that she was one of the dancers. Eventually he would attach a name to the female assassin: Brutus. As it was, she had rolled a die and given him her real name. It was the right decision. Now when he checked, he would find her exactly as she claimed to be: a simple merchant. She had made many business trips and was well known along the trade routes. Even when she was traveling to meet with a partner, she conducted business. She always conducted business. It was tedious, time consuming, and enhanced her income precious little, but it was a necessary precaution.

What other reason could she offer for her frequent travels?

Brutus rose and walked to the end of the portico and wrapped one arm around a marble column. It chilled her skin. The fields were brown now, and her workers were tilling the soil that ran down to the Adriatic Sea, preparing it for spring seeding. This was the smallest of her six villas. Even so, she had over four hundred workers on the compound ... and she suddenly realized that she didn't know any of them. In fact, she barely knew even the servants of authority who managed her holdings, and it was the same at her other villas. She sighed, and comforted herself with the thought that in the end the villas paid for themselves, rather handsomely, if the truth were known.

Why was she doing this? she wondered. Still traveling the world after ten years, sleeping in dirty inns, meeting with partners, covering her tracks. Was it the thrill of the hunt? Pride in her reputation? Or maybe she had lost herself somewhere along the way. How else could she explain why she would follow through on her Vectis Trebellius contract?

She liked his smile. He was the kind of man she had always hoped to find, but never did. And yet she continued to make plans. She closed her eyes. It was too late for her, now. Already she had a strategy for this partner. It was quite simple. His soldiers would be of no help. He would come to her, and like so many others, she would end his life.

She took a full breath. In the distance she could see the azure blue of the Adriatic, empty except for a lonely freighter moving slowly out to sea. She returned to her ornate dining room and ate her dinner alone.

19

Through the wind and falling rain, Neeve could hear the scavengers chuckling when they found something of value on the bodies. She opened her eyes a crack and saw two men stuffing booty into a sack.

And then she saw something that made her shudder. One passenger from the ship was still alive and trying to crawl away from the scavengers. The older of the two stepped toward him, raised a club, and smashed it down with a sickening thud onto his head.

She closed her eyes again and tried to still her confused mind. She wanted to run, but wasn't sure if she could even walk. Her body felt like it had been beaten with a wooden mallet, especially her face and stomach. She groped with her fingers for her knife. Gone. Not even a belt. She had lost everything—her knife, her belt, her gold aurei. No wonder her hipbones were bruised and sore. She had hit the rocks on her stomach. The belt filled with gold had saved her life, but now it was gone, ripped away by the impact with the barrier rocks. She thought about her second knife, strapped on her leg, and was about to slip her hand down when one of the men spoke. He was within fifteen feet of her.

"What are you doing?" a gravelly voice asked, annoyed.

"Trying to get this ring off," replied a younger voice.

"What's the matter with you? Cut the finger off and throw it in the bag."

The words hit Neeve with the force of a crashing wave. Her Roman ring! She couldn't tell which direction they were looking but she had to chance it. She lifted her hips slightly and curled her hands under until they met. Then she pulled and twisted the ring. It wouldn't budge. Her hands had swollen in the water. She tried again. Still stuck. She dug her fingers under the pebbles until she felt a slimy stone. She smeared her fingers with it and tried again. The ring pulled off. She pressed it under the rocks and lay still.

Neeve heard muffled noises, then the gravelly voice again. "There ... you see? Simple. Now dump the finger in the bag."

She heard them approach, heard the bag drag across the sand. "This one?" the younger voice asked.

"Look for jewelry."

The feet stopped. Neeve's hands were yanked from under her body and checked for rings. Then she felt a hand poking around her clothes, searching.

"It's a woman!" he cried.

"Don't get excited."

"No worry about that," the younger man said. "She's beaten up." He flipped her over and rummaged around her tunic. "Nothing here," he said.

"Get the coat and boots."

Despite the steady splatter of rain on her face, Neeve lay like the dead, eyes closed. One twitch, and she had no doubt she would be dead.

Neeve felt her body scream in pain as the man grabbed her winter tunic and started yanking it over her head, half dragging her across the stones on the beach. When it pulled loose she slumped back onto the sand without a sound. He was tugging at her boots now, twisting them until she thought her ankle would snap.

"Hey!" the younger one yelled. "A knife! A good one too." He had found the knife on her leg. He was energized now, thrusting his hands everywhere, looking for hidden treasures. "Nothing," he said.

"Might as well take the trousers," the other said. "They'll fetch something. Be quick about it. I want to check the cove for wash-ups before someone else gets there."

She felt herself being dragged the opposite way along the rocky sand as her trousers pulled off inside out, leaving her with nothing but linen underpants and a thin tunic.

For five minutes Neeve lay as still as the stones on the beach. The freezing rain poured down upon her, and she clenched her teeth, but she never moved. When she finally turned her head slightly to see if the scavengers had gone, she saw nothing but a rocky coastline and scattered bodies, some floating in and out with the waves.

She rose with some difficulty, brushing the grit off her skin, her body aching all over. Then, remembering her ring, she scrubbed around the rocks, trying to find it. Everything looked the same. She dropped to her knees and began gouging holes in the stony sand. Nothing. "Think!" she told herself, as she cast her eyes around, trying to remember where she had been lying before the scavenger dragged her across the rocks. Wait! She moved some distance away, and studied the sand and rocks. There it was! A faint body outline. The hours lying on the beach had gathered sand and dirt around the edges of where her body had been. She trudged back and began digging where she guessed her hips had been. Her fingers felt a tiny circle of metal. Carefully, she pulled out her ring and shoved it on her finger. She would take no chances washing it in the ocean, not until it was securely on her hand.

A chill swept over her. The wind coming off the ocean was brisk and cold, making her teeth chatter as she stood hunched in the rain, wearing almost nothing at all. Neeve clasped her arms around her body to stop shaking. Nothing seemed broken, but it hurt even to breathe.

She glanced around. She needed clothes. The scavengers had left the trousers on several of the Celtic men but no outer coats. She stooped over the first man, and froze. It was the pig face, but she hardly recognized him. He had no eyes. She went to the next man, loosened his waist thongs, and wrenched the trousers off his body. She shook out the sand, wrung them as best she could, and pulled them on. They were ridiculously large, and the legs were in tatters. She could see why the scavengers had left them behind. She wandered down the line of victims, shocked by the sight of smashed bodies, and ashamed of participating in their violation. But the gods had spared her, and she was determined to survive. One contributed thongs to draw in her fluttering trouser legs, another a girding belt, and another a light tunic to put on over her own. She tried to find shoes, but the scavengers or the sea had taken them.

Something moved.

She whirled around.

A man was thumping down the seashore toward her. At first she thought it might be a survivor from the ship, but in the same instant she knew better. It was another scavenger. He was cursing and shouting something at her, but Neeve didn't wait to learn what he wanted. She started toward the tall grass that bordered the sea but soon realized the sedge lands were filled with spiny plants and jagged rocks, no place for bare feet.

She picked up a rock and turned to face him.

"Give me what you found!" he shouted, breathing hard from his run up the shore. He waved a seven-inch knife in her face to make his point.

"I don't have anything," she said, covering her ring hand.

"I saw you stripping bodies!"

"I was on the ship, you imbecile!" In spite of the knife, she couldn't control her rage. Her rational mind told her to be wary of a strange man with a knife, but she was cold, beaten up, and in no mood for another problem … especially from a man half her size who looked almost as dirty as she did. He was a runt of a man, about up to her shoulder, with black hair too low on his forehead, a huge nose, and shifty, rat-like eyes. And he was holding the knife all wrong, much too high.

"Give me what you found!" he repeated.

"All right," she said, extending her arm. "I found this ring."

His eyes dropped greedily to her hand.

She leapt forward, lifting his knife with one hand, and swinging the rock with the other. It caught him on the side of the head, and his stubby legs buckled. She picked up his knife and stepped back.

He groaned and looked up at her.

"I want your shoes and tunic," she said.

He rubbed his head. "Not giving you anything," he groused. He staggered to his feet and jutted out his chin in defiance.

"Unlike you, I know how to use this knife," she said, jabbing the point toward his groin. "What do you want me to cut off first? Your tongue or your testicles?"

"Wait. Let me explain—"

She drove the point into his arm, not deep, but quick and hard.

He screamed.

"Now!" she said fiercely.

He pulled off his thick tunic, and then his sandals.

She looked him over. He was wearing wool socks, and knee-length trousers, the close-fitting kind that Roman soldiers wore under their tunics. The days were getting colder, and the tight trousers under the larger ones would keep her warm until she found something better. "The trousers and socks too," she said.

"No!" he shouted.

She jabbed him in the other arm, this time with depth.

He screamed again and dropped to a crouch as if he were about to charge. Neeve thrust the point of her knife directly at his face. He jerked his head back, shocked by the suddenness of her attack, then took several large steps backwards in the sand, trying to regain his balance. She darted forward, grasping him by the shoulder, and sweeping his legs from under him. He tumbled to the ground, cursing as he crashed into a collection of rocks.

Like a cat Neeve was on him, her fingers grasping his hair, her knife jammed into the skin at the base of his throat.

"Wait!" he cried, throwing up his hands. "Please … please, spare me!"

"Why? Why should I spare you?" She twisted his head farther back, exposing his neck.

"I will be forever in your debt …."

"Pfft!" Neeve said, tightening her grip. "When I was helpless on the beach you were ready to rob and kill me."

"No–please, I'm … I'm not a thief," he said. "I would never have harmed you! I haven't eaten for days, just what I've found on the beach from the shipwreck."

Neeve felt herself hesitate.

"Please," he said again, "I meant no harm."

She pushed off him and sprang to her feet. "Trousers and socks," she said, "and be quick about it."

"I will freeze to death!"

"If you're so sure," she said, fingering the blade of her knife, "I can save you the trouble."

Still seated on the sand, he peeled off his trousers and socks, which left him wearing nothing but a short, dirty inner tunic. Neeve noticed he was clutching his front to cover his privates, and she couldn't help grinning. "You need not fear. I won't take advantage of you ... this time."

Before she left, she relieved him of his purse, two sesterces, and a tiny roll of pork mixed with dried apples, all of it soaked in seawater.

Neeve trudged through the ocean marshlands toward the rolling hills in the south. It took hours to find a road, but luckily it turned out to be a main Roman artery with milestones to the next town. She thought hard about her situation. Her body ached in every single spot, her arms, legs, hips—all were swollen purple and black. She could only imagine what her face looked like. At least she was not seriously injured.

But she was worried. Winter was coming, and she had no means. All her plans of heading for Rome before the winter snows had been dashed to pieces on Gallia's cruel barrier rocks. She had no money to buy a carriage or rent a room, and little to buy food. She was alone and in need of Roman coin. Two sesterces would be gone in a week. She thought of hiring out as a farm maid or kitchen servant where she could get free food and lodging, but she knew masters were wary of strangers, especially of those that looked as disheveled as she did. Stealing was out of the question. She didn't want to end up like thieves caught in Britannia, whose bodies were jammed on stakes outside the city walls as a warning.

Neeve was left with two distasteful possibilities—selling her body, or begging. She chose begging.

As she neared the city gates, she knew she was in trouble. Scores of beggars lined the approach to the city, holding out their cups, looking for tiny coins or scraps of food. This was a small town, but prosperous enough to have a detachment of urban soldiers to police the streets. They tolerated no begging within the city limits, and if Neeve wanted to beg, she would have to join the throng of beggars waving their cups.

The drone of voices swelled as she drew closer. Now she could hear individual cries.

"Look at me!" a legless man said. "I once was like you. Help me!"

"I have nobody," a blind girl murmured.

"My mother is sick," a ten year-old boy said over and over. "She has nothing to eat."

"Please, oh please, have mercy," a toothless woman whispered.

Others sobbed, staring at the ground, holding out their cups. One, lying on a mat, must have been carried to his spot by family members. He had no arms or legs and never said a word, just stared at the faces making their way through the city gates. Over it all, the same refrains tumbled from everyone's lips: "The gods are watching!" And, "The gods bless the merciful!"

As urgent as the cries were, not one beggar stepped over the curb onto the paved road as the merchants, dealers and shopkeepers flowed in and out. Neeve could see why. Six well-armed urban soldiers stood at the stone gate to make certain nothing impeded the city's commerce. Tucked in their belts, Neeve could see whips dangling with shards of metal and pottery. The beggars were allowed to talk, but not touch or impede traffic. Neeve had little doubt violators would receive a sound thrashing for their misadventures.

She entered the gates, located a fountain, and drank an enormous amount of water. Then, returning to the lines of beggars, she pushed beside an old man who smelled of stale wine and urine. For three hours she held out her hand and said, "Shipwrecked. I have nothing." But with all the competing appeals of desperate people who had greater needs, she received nothing save a tiny bronze quadrans, a coin she had never seen before. When she asked the old man what it was worth, he told her it was an ancient coin no longer used. It would take sixteen of them to make one sesterce, but she would not be able to buy anything with it. Her generous benefactor had given her a useless coin.

That night Neeve scrubbed herself and her oversized clothes in a creek that wound its way past town, and then slept on the grassy bank. She gobbled down half the pork and most of the dried apples, knowing that she should be more disciplined, but after not eating all day, it was difficult. Besides, she felt dizzy, as if she were coming down with a fever. At first she attributed her sore throat and dizziness to all the seawater she had swallowed, but it grew worse. She awoke the next morning, shivering and coughing, her eyes aching with every movement.

But a slender hope brightened her mind.

A thought about how she might solve her predicament.

No more begging, she told herself, as she headed for the market. There she used her two sesterces to buy a reed pen, an inkpot and a dozen small squares of papyrus paper. She would not beg; her sketching talent would raise the necessary funds for traveling to Rome. Excited at the possibilities, Neeve hurried toward the center of town, looking for carriages. She found them across from the law courts building where the important men of the town conducted business.

Neeve waited until she saw a wealthy man approach the building, and then she sketched furiously, recording every significant detail about his face and body. While he was inside, she filled in the scenery around him, the glistening marble columns, the stately roofs, the phalanx of statues that lined the walkways. Seven times she sketched an important man before one of them reappeared.

"Master!" She raised her drawing over her head and tried to catch his eye.

"Move aside you filthy scum!" a servant roared.

Neeve felt strong fingers grab her roughly by the neck. Another man, a serious-looking bodyguard, knocked the papyrus out of her hand and shoved her away from the carriage. Then with his sandal, he kicked the sketch into the street's center gutter. Neeve watched it sink into the soupy muck and disappear.

Three others left the law buildings, and every time their guards thwarted her efforts to show her drawing. Neeve despaired. She had spent all her money and had nothing left to buy more materials. She tried a new approach. When the door opened she selected the appropriate drawing and wedged it into the entrance pillars. Then she stood across the street and waited.

"What is this?" the man chortled. He took the drawing in his hand and snorted again. He liked it and was looking around to determine its creator.

Neeve raised her hand to gain his attention.

He stared at her in disbelief, and Neeve realized how wretched she must have looked with her tattered clothes and beaten face. She held up her inkpot and remaining papyrus sheets.

"A beggar," he mused, finding the whole situation incredible. He glanced around at his servants, showed them the drawing, and shook his head, amazed. "Give her some coins," the man said, and stepped into his carriage still clutching the picture.

In the following days, Neeve's skills brought her a handful of sesterces and one denarius, and she had hopes that after a month or so, she might be able to pay the carriage fare across Gallia, and maybe even to Rome. She used her money sparingly, but wisely, renting a room in public housing, buying her drawing materials at a reduced rate, and eating one meal a day. She also bought two new pairs of leather trousers, boots, several tunics, and a winter coat. It was money well spent. The urban soldiers were quick with the whip if they spied anyone shuffling around like a beggar. Now Neeve looked the part of an artisan or merchant, not a vagabond wandering the streets.

Two additional items Neeve had bought without hesitation. Knives. As a Caledonian, she carried one knife on her hip and another strapped to her lower leg. Quality knives were costly but Neeve used all the coin she had gathered to that point for a large knife and a wickedly sharp dagger, which she buried in the top of her boot. A

sleek dagger cleverly concealed, Taranis had often said, was a
Caledonian's best friend.

The disastrous effects of the shipwreck still lingered. For some
reason, she couldn't rid herself of the fever that burned like an unruly
fire inside her chest. It was difficult to swallow even the thin
asparagus soup peddled by the street vendors, and her dizzy spells
increased. She found it harder to concentrate on her drawings. Even
at night when she was exhausted, she could not sleep, shivering in her
cot one moment, throwing off her blanket the next, sweating.

One morning she couldn't lift her aching body from her cot. She
hadn't changed her clothes or bathed in the creek for three days, and
she felt wretched inside and out. She tried to sit up. Hot fingers of
pain flashed across her chest. She flopped back, breathing in a
shallow rhythm, trying to calm her throbbing head. Her eyes ached.
Her throat felt like raw meat. She was so thirsty.

Outside her window she could smell charcoal burning and the
rich odor of cooked lamb's meat. It sickened her. She wrenched
herself sideways and rolled off the cot, hitting the wood floor face
down, her body trembling in pain. For over an hour she lay hunched
on the floor, unable to move. Her body simply would not obey her
mind when she told it to stand. Then she just did it. In one sudden
move, she jerked to her feet, and steadied herself on the plaster walls
of her tiny room. Somehow, she made her way outside and to the
public toilets where she splashed water on her face and neck. Warm
tea and honey purchased from a vendor soothed her throat.

Then, at her lowest moment, the gods smiled on her.

As she was heading toward the town center, about fifty soldiers
strutted down the street, swords drawn, clearing all traffic to the side.
They were shouting, "Make way for Senator Titus Equitius Severus,
friend of the emperor." They slapped the flats of their swords on the
bodies of anyone who moved too slowly. Behind them marched a
detachment of two hundred soldiers, then lancers riding huge horses,
a score of Scythian archers, and then another two hundred soldiers. In
the center of it all, six magnificent grays pulled a long sleeping
carriage with drawn curtains.

Neeve followed the procession through the streets until it stopped across from a Greek temple dedicated to Asclepios, the god of healing. She opened her case and pulled out a large parchment square made of treated goatskin. She had several of these expensive sheets and used them only when she had a potentially profitable customer. The senator was her kind of customer.

The carriage door opened. A distinguished man of about sixty stepped onto the pavement. He wore a cloak of purple, hooded, and fastened with a golden brooch that was inset with sapphire and ruby. He glanced around at the crowd that had gathered. They cheered. He waved his hand and smiled, a genuine smile that told Neeve this might be her moment. He had shrewd eyes, but a kind face. She prayed that he might also be generous, and then swept her hand across the parchment in smooth clean strokes. She tried to catch his warmth and noble bearing, the crinkles around his eyes and patrician nose. Then with a final wave to the crowd he was gone. Neeve strolled over to the granite fencing that surrounded the entire complex of temple buildings. None of the soldiers attempted to stop her, and she supposed it was because the senator was now safely inside. She drew the walkway leading to the marble entrance arch, the fountains, the statues, the votive shields barely visible on the doorway. She ran her eyes over the drawing. It was quite good, but would be more impressive if she added color, something she had never done before.

"Will the senator be inside the Asclepion temple long?" Neeve asked a nearby soldier, who was young and looked approachable.

"Hours," he said, "maybe even till nightfall."

Neeve thanked him and hurried off to the dealers in the town forum. There she bought several vegetable dyes and a special purple dye made from shellfish. She cleaned her reed in water, dried it, and began applying the dyes to the drawing, reproducing the many colors of the Asclepion temple. When the drawing had dried, she rolled it and tied it with two red thongs. Then she ran to the public baths, ignoring the nausea growing in her stomach. She paid a brass dupondius entrance fee and another for a servant to attend her as she cleaned herself. The baths were filled with men during the morning, and few women other than prostitutes dared enter. An attendant assured her privacy and safety.

In less than an hour, Neeve was outside the Asclepian temple again, hair scrubbed and toweled dry, her face flushed from the hot water, and her rolled drawing under her arm. She was determined not to frighten the senator with a sickly appearance. He would surely flee if he thought she had the fever. She glanced around. The crowds had disappeared, and so not to be noticed, she waited on the street opposite where the soldiers had gathered.

Late that afternoon the senator emerged from the temple, walking with a cane. As he approached the massive marble arch that led to the paved roadway, Neeve marched brazenly toward him, the way she would if she were the emissary of the most important official in town. For that is precisely what she professed to be.

"A gift from City Praetor, Marcus Hortensius Balearicus," she cried, holding up the roll tied with the colored thongs. The soldiers hesitated as she strode toward the senator. She had gambled they would not remember the name of a small town praetor, and she was right. One of them, the captain of the guard, she supposed, stepped forward and took the roll from her hands. He untied the thongs and looked inside.

Neeve puffed up her chest and said with indignation, "The City Praetor, Marcus Hortensius Balearicus, will be greatly offended if his gift is not taken immediately to Senator Titus Severus."

By now the disturbance had caught the senator's attention. He signaled the captain who brought him the roll. The senator opened it, glanced in her direction, and then talked briefly to his captain.

"Bring the emissary," the captain said.

Neeve bowed politely before the senator.

"So, you bear a gift from the city praetor," he said, his brow furrowed, curious. His eyes were probing, making her feel uncomfortable.

Neeve fought a sudden dizziness as she started to speak. The last thing she wanted was to collapse at his feet.

"I know Decumius Paullus quite well," he continued. "He's the city praetor, you know, not Marcus … whatever you were spouting."

"Forgive me, Senator," Neeve said, bowing again, "I only wanted to honor your great personage with—"

"You were lying."

Neeve dropped her eyes.

"Speak," the senator said. "Let me hear your defense."

"I have no defense," Neeve said. She shrugged. "I simply wanted to honor you by drawing your likeness. I hoped you would find favor in it."

"My captain thinks I should turn you over to the urban soldiers."

Neeve kept her eyes on the paved roadway.

"Do you know the penalty for impersonating a Roman official?"

"No, Lord, but I'm certain it's harsh."

"Harsh ... yes," he said. "Penalties for this sort of thing are always harsh. And with good reason. How could we ever operate a government if people ran around pretending to be officials they were not?" He turned his head slightly to better see her face. "That's why we have a stern penalty, though I confess I have no idea what it is."

Neeve said nothing.

"Is this what you do, draw images of patricians and scrub for coin?" he asked.

"Yes, Lord, for the present."

"Go on."

"I suffered shipwreck crossing the channel from Britannia," she said. "I lost everything, Lord, but my skill to draw. I save my earned coins with a banker." She glanced toward the Asclepion temple and added, "If the great god Asclepios wills it so I shall one day arrive in Rome."

"I see." The senator paused and said reverently, "May he will it so."

"Thank you," Neeve said quietly. She continued to stare at the pavement.

The senator rubbed his chin thoughtfully. "You must have expected your little deception to be uncovered. Yes, I'm sure you did," he said, answering his own query. "So, I suppose in that sense you were not really impersonating a Roman official. You were merely using a clever ruse to gain my attention, were you not?"

"Yes, Lord."

"You see, Captain," he said, turning. "It's all a simple misunderstanding." He opened the drawing. "You say you drew this?"

"I did, Lord, to honor you."

"You've colored it ... three or four different dyes ... remarkable."

"Five dyes, Lord," Neeve said in spite of herself. "Mixed, the dyes yield nine colors. Your Excellency will see that in better light." She was proud of her work.

The senator stared at the drawing for long seconds, marveling at her skill. Then, turning toward her, he said, "Look at me."

She raised her eyes.

"Have no fear. I am pleased. What is your name?"

"Neeve mapmaker," she said, pushing the hair off her face and straightening her aching body.

He studied her. "Your eyes are like none I have ever seen," he said. "You're a Celt, I take it."

"Yes, my Lord. From Britannia."

"Well, Neeve mapmaker, no goddess matches your beauty, and probably your talent as well."

She flushed.

"Don't worry, I have no thoughts for myself. But my son—ah, yes, would that he had Fortuna's favor to discover someone like you." He chuckled to himself and looked back at the drawing. "This is excellent," he said, "simply excellent. But you overly favor me. I am not this distinguished."

"The truth, my Lord, is that my miserable reed captures only your outer image, and not the quality of your inner soul."

"My inner soul might not be so attractive," he said.

"Others will judge that, my Lord."

"Yes, and that frightens me. But no matter. I like your drawing, and you shall be rewarded." He gestured with his cane to an aide who handed him a large purse. "No, no, the other," Severus said. The aide bobbed his head and snapped his fingers to another aide who reached into the carriage and brought out a smaller purse. The senator opened it and extracted two gold aurei, paused as if he were thinking, and added two more.

"My Lord!" Neeve exclaimed in genuine surprise as she accepted the coins. She would have been pleased with a brass coin or two from the larger purse.

He smiled. "There is something about you I like," he said, patting her arm. "You bow, but somehow you are not subservient. You beg for coins, but hold inside the wealth of Egypt. Speak to me," he said, leaning closer to study her face. "I am right in my judgments about you, am I not?"

"How can I, your servant, dispute your judgments, Lord?" she said.

"Yes," he said, "there is more to you than I see. If you make it to Rome—and I pray you do—visit me at my estate. I would enjoy learning about you. Tell the servants you drew my likeness and that I requested to see you." Then he asked, "Do you know who I am?"

"Lord Titus Severus," she said, "a Senator of Rome."

"Remember the name," he said, and stepped in the open door of his carriage.

Neeve glanced around the empty streets as the soldiers marched away. A light rain had begun to fall, chilling the air. The day's intoxication had passed, as had her strength, and now her body began to shake from the cold. She felt both sick and elated. In her purse she had enough coin for her travels to Rome, but she needed to take them to the bankers. Thieves were everywhere, and any number of people might have seen the senator give her the four gold aurei.

She put one aureus in her purse and hid the other three in the band of her trousers. She started down the road, but stopped almost immediately, steadying her swaying body against a stone building.

The rain turned to ice, stinging her face.

Then the dizziness returned, and her world went dark.

20

"You tell me this now?" Julian pulled his horse to a stop.

"If I had told you earlier," Vectis replied, "you wouldn't have come."

Julian gave him a reproving look. "I followed you to the incredibly bleak Isle of Britannia, didn't I? That should prove my loyalty … or stupidity, I'm not sure which."

"It would be hard to determine," Vectis agreed.

"But now you tell me we will serve under Gaius Commodus!"

"I had little choice," Vectis said. "It was either Commodus or defy the will of the Senate."

Julian mumbled something better not heard.

"I won't hide it from you, we're being sent to clean up a mess. Senator Severus told me that Commodus is the prefect in charge of the siege, and is in over his head. He has laid siege to the city for more than a year and everything he's tried has failed."

"Am I supposed to be surprised? The man is a fool."

"Yes, and now our superior." He held Julian's eyes. "We cannot allow personal feelings to detract from our responsibility. It could be dangerous. Besides, we are soldiers, we have our orders, and will follow them without fail. I hope you understand that."

"Of course I do," Julian said, irritated for the reprimand. "But Commodus deserves a dagger in his throat, and you know it. He stranded us in Britannia and he ought to be held accountable."

Vectis glanced around at the legionary escort and nudged his horse forward

"The man is a coward," Julian said in a lowered voice, sensing Vectis's concern that a common soldier might overhear.

"He *is* a coward," Vectis agreed.

"We both know that Commodus aided Senator Atilius Titianus in his rebellion against the emperor, and that he got paid to abandon his post, expecting the Caledonians to kill you, me, and everyone else."

Vectis nodded.

"That worm wanted us dead so he could claim you ordered a retreat to the Wall."

"All true," Vectis said. "Senator Coelius and others blame me for the loss of the outposts and Antoninus' Wall."

Julian frowned. "Commodus must think the Caledonians killed you."

"That's what worries me," Vectis replied. "He has power now, and might be tempted to get rid of us so we don't cause him trouble."

"Well, now," Julian said wryly, "I suppose this is not the best assignment."

"Want to leave?"

"You mean return to the women I left behind, the hot baths, the dinner parties, the theater—don't be absurd!"

Vectis smiled.

The two rode in silence till nightfall. They had traveled for weeks across Dalmatia province and were now in Dacia on the great northern road above the Alps. Occasional snow blew in drifts across the road, but they donned thick woolen cloaks and warm breeches, built larger fires at night, and kept pressing on.

Vectis had much to think about. The assassin stalking him on the journey across Italia would no doubt be looking for other opportunities. For a moment he had entertained the possibility that the woman on the carriage, Tiberia Baebius Merula, might have been that assassin, but the whole idea seemed ludicrous in the light of day. He was glad he hadn't mentioned his suspicions to Julian. He would have been scorned. Still, he couldn't get the murder in Egypt out of his mind. The assassin there had to have been a woman—a strange conclusion, but he believed it was true nonetheless. At the inn the assassin used the same weapon, a needle-like dagger. Could it be just a coincidence? He didn't know, but before he crossed the Adriatic at Aternum, he sent a dispatch to Rome inquiring about Tiberia Baebius Merula to see if she were a dye merchant as she said.

They stopped for the night in the heart of Dacia province, at a military town called Apulum. It was the sprawling home of Dacia's protector, Legion XIII, *Gemina*.   There they talked to the fort's commander, Legate Statius Rutilius, a clear-eyed soldier who spoke bluntly about the difficulties in Dacia.

"This is the most demanding province in the Empire," Rutilius said. "Not only do we have to contend with the rebellious Dacians, but we have the blood-drinking German hordes crowding our frontiers. Every month some German tribe north of the barrier attacks an outpost looking for food or weapons." He snorted. "Rome has no idea. These Germans are the boldest thieves you've ever seen. They bring their carts and steal everything not bolted down. And they are growing bolder."

"What about Porolissum? How are they handling the situation?"

"That's on the edge of the Empire," Rutilius said, "a hundred and twenty miles farther north." He shrugged. "They have a decent wall across the valley, I'm told, but a political appointee named Tiberius is running the show up there. He's competent, but he can't always make the right decisions. Too much pressure."

"Pressure? From where?" Vectis asked.

"Senators," he said. "It's always meddling senators. I know only two names. One is Tertullus and the other Coelius, but there might be more."

"I know them," Vectis said. "Tertullus is consul this year."

He eyed Vectis and Julian. "Look, I know you are career soldiers with experience in North Africa and Britannia, otherwise I wouldn't speak the way I have. I received a report weeks ago from Senator Titus Severus—someone I have always respected—and he detailed your service record and your present assignment."

"Severus is a fine man," Vectis said.

"He is. But from one soldier to another, I feel I ought to give you fair warning about affairs farther north."

"Go on."

"It's chaos up there. Beyond the frontier barrier there are scores of tribes—most of them German—eager to test our resolve. We don't want to stir up the Germans, so we thought if we destroyed a rebellious Costoboci city north of the barrier—"

"Slavs?"

"The Costoboci are Slavs, right, and troublesome of late. The beauty of the plan is that we avoid offending the Germans, but still provide them with a powerful example of what happens when you insult the Roman Empire."

"A decent plan. Whose idea was it?"

"Mine, actually," Rutilius said, waving away the compliment. "The problem—and now *you* will have to deal with it—is that the man laying siege to the Costoboci city has as much military training as my mother."

"You're talking about Gaius Commodus?" Julian asked.

Rutilius's brow furrowed. "Do you know him?"

"Oh, yes," Vectis said. "We are old friends." The words flowed easily off his tongue, and the sarcasm was evident. He wished he had been more guarded, and immediately set about to cover himself by saying in a matter of fact voice that he and Commodus had been posted in Britannia together.

Rutilius wasn't fooled. He noted the sarcasm and welcomed it. "I have no love for Commodus," he said. "The man is blundering his way to a war with the Germans, and when it comes, he will be in Rome and Legion XIII will have to clean up his mess."

"Who appointed him to his post?" Vectis asked.

"Tiberius, the commander at Porolissum ... but I think he received pressure from those two senators."

"And now Commodus is up there with no idea how to lay siege," Vectis said.

"Exactly. I asked Tiberius to remove him, but he's afraid of offending Senators Tertullus and Coelius."

Vectis said nothing, but he was seeing a pattern in the activities of Tertullus and Coelius. They were rewarding Commodus for something, and Vectis knew what it was. They must have been aware that Atilius Titianus had bribed Commodus to abandon his fort, causing the eventual collapse of the Antonine Wall. That would mean the pair were in collusion with Titianus against Emperor Antoninus Pius, and guilty of sedition. The right to plunder the Costoboci city was Commodus's reward for his silence about their involvement in the plot against the emperor.

"Commodus has been playing soldier for over a year," Rutilius said. "A year! With no end in sight. So the quick, decisive victory designed to frighten the Germanic menace has only served to embolden them."

"I see my task," Vectis said.

"You need to wind this siege up before the heavy snows," Rutilius said. "If you don't, the Germans will smell weakness and be after us like wolves in winter, ransacking our borders before the year is out." He spread a map on the table. "Many of our frontier auxiliaries are being used in this ridiculous siege. The borders are depleted. Beyond the auxiliaries we have no other help. Legion IV, *Flavia,* used to be here to help control the province," he said, stabbing a finger at the map, "but in the infinite wisdom of Rome, they have been reassigned to a more strategically needy area. Now Legion XIII has to do everything."

Vectis nodded. He suddenly realized why Senator Severus had put up little fight when Tertullus and Coelius proposed he should be sent to the German frontier. With Commodus running the siege, the frontier could be in serious trouble. Tertullus and Coelius no doubt reasoned that sending Vectis to Dacia not only removed him from Rome, but helped the Empire. There was genuine danger fomenting beyond the Dacian barrier.

"I'm not certain what you can do with this Commodus fellow," Rutilius said. "He has powerful friends in the Senate and ignores most of the advice given him. You will be replacing one of my best soldiers as military tribune, and from the dispatches I received, he might as well have stayed here at Apulum. Commodus continually restricts his duties, and he has been largely confined to his tent the whole time."

Vectis thanked Rutilius for his candid assessment and promised he would conclude the siege as quickly as possible, though he had no idea how Commodus would react when he saw him. Julian was right. The man was a coward, and responsible for the deaths of thousands of soldiers in Britannia, good reasons to fear seeing Vectis again. Commodus might be a weak officer, but like a spooked animal, he could be dangerous.

21

The thieves took everything.

Neeve blinked her eyes, trying to melt the ice fused to her eyelashes, her confused mind straining to piece together what had happened. She remembered passing out and waking hours later in the dark to find thieves, like rabid dogs, tearing at her clothes, scrapping over anything of value. Her world swirled violently around her as she tried to claw her way to the surface. One thief was emptying her purse while another was leaning over her, ready to stick her with her own knife.

She remembered jamming her hand into her boot and feeling the weight of the dagger in her palm. When she slashed one man across the leg, they all scattered like rats in a barn. She hollered for them to come back, that she wasn't finished, but they disappeared into the shadows.

And she was certain the shifty-eyed man from the beach was there. Neeve pushed herself up on her elbows and tried to clear her head. Yes, he had been there. He had probably followed her, watching patiently the whole time while she was drawing her sketches. She cursed herself for not having killed him on the beach. She crawled to the side of a building, and propped her back against a stone wall. Her purse was gone, her heavy coat, her knife, even her drawing tools. Worst of all, her wedding ring from Vectis was gone. They had taken everything except her tunic, her boots and the dagger hidden in them.

For hours she sat in the freezing rain with her back against the limestone wall, dagger in hand, willing herself to remain alert. She tried to sort through her hazy thoughts, especially about the dark-haired man with the big nose and stubby legs, standing over her.

As the night deepened, the winds grew worse and shrieked along the broad road, pelting her exposed skin with sleet. At times the cries of the wind sounded like Esus, god of the underworld, calling out her name. She sensed the god was near, eager to claim her spirit. She didn't mind. The thought of drifting away with the wind was inviting, almost seductive. Eventually, as the storm died and large flakes of snow descended softly on the city, she fell into a deep sleep. Her mind was far away; she could feel the sun warming her skin, a soft summer breeze in her hair, but somewhere inside she knew the snow was encasing her like a shroud.

Neeve woke as the first rays of light glinted off the snow-covered rooftops. She was surprised to be alive. The snow had filled the street like a glistening river of white and covered her body up to her chest, but her arms and legs felt strangely warm, and she wondered if the snow had protected her from the cold. She tried to pull herself out of the drifts, but a fit of coughing sent bolts of pain through her chest and back. It seemed as if she were blistering on the inside. For over an hour she sat there, unmoving, her back pressed against the rough stone, her eyes on the soaring, central arch of the Asclepion temple across the street. Already people were tramping their way through the snow to the mills and shops bunched at the end of the broad road. No one stopped to help. She could hear the squishing of their boots and see the gaping, black cavities left behind as they marched past.

But no one stopped.

Why should they? She was just another beggar cluttering the street's edge. Soon the urban soldiers would take the whip to her, teach her a lesson, and she would move along. In the distance she could see knots of human refuse huddled on the lower part of the hill where a conduit of warm water issued from the temple into the sewer. It would be better there, she knew—warmer, less wind—but only the strong could claim a spot near the temple drainage culverts.

She was growing tired again. The feet still tramped by, more now that the sun had risen. The brown trail in the center of the road continually gobbled more snow, as if it were alive and bent on destroying the lovely white expanse. She cocked her head. The scrapers were coming. She could hear the muted sounds of their wooden scoops as they cleared the cobblestone road. Neeve knew she would have to move, or be buried in the avalanche of snow they heaped along the walls and arches of the street. But she couldn't move. She could hardly lift her hands. The shafts of pain seemed to bind her to the ground, like a goat shackled at offering time.

Minutes passed.

The scrapers were almost upon her.

Maybe they would take pity and not dump their shovels on a sick woman.

A blast of snow slammed Neeve's head against the stone wall. The snow was heavy, and wet, and cold, and had a musty limestone smell from the mortar in the road. She shuddered as the icy water dribbled down her chest, soaking her inner garments. A spasm of coughs possessed her. A second shovelful hit her, then another, and another, until only her head protruded from the mounds of dirty snow. The men on the scraping detail laughed as she coughed and spit the gritty snow from her mouth. How quickly they had brought the dead to life, they said. A small boy following the scrapers threw a clump of snow at her, and then hurried on past, as if afraid that somehow the pathetic creature might rise from the snow seeking its revenge.

A man was approaching, an older man with a cane, and a luxuriant cloak of purple fastened with a golden brooch. He stepped into the sloppy mess of piled snow with his sandals and began scooping the snow away from her face. Neeve closed her eyes. She felt his fingers wiping her forehead and cleaning the slush off her cheeks. Then she heard him speaking in crisp sentences and men scurrying to obey his orders. Two soldiers lifted her gently and carried her across the street toward the Asclepion temple. She moaned, and the dizziness took her consciousness.

Neeve spent three weeks in the Greek healing temple of Asclepios. At first, the priests carried her everywhere. They bathed her in warm water and wrapped her in huge towels. They massaged every part of her body. They made her nibble bits of fruit, nuts and vegetables, drink huge quantities of diluted wine mixed with herbs, and they made her sleep. Plenty of sleep. Day and night she slept. Every time she returned to her sleeping room they burned a bowl of opium incense—the scent of the gods, they said—and immediately she fell into a deep sleep. Sometimes she thought she saw a tall man moving about her room, whispering sacred words, but in her confused state, she could make little sense of it.

As time passed, Neeve grew strong enough to bathe and feed herself. She still needed the nightly opium lamps to fall asleep, but gradually she was able to walk the meandering footpaths without losing breath, and even participate in the morning exercises to strengthen her body.

Then one day an old priest in a crimson robe visited her. He introduced himself as an elder equal among brethren, but Neeve knew he was the high priest of the temple. He had an unruly shock of hair and bushy eyebrows that seemed too large for his thin face. His eyes were blue like hers, but warm and sympathetic, and Neeve felt she could tell him her darkest secret and he would understand. He sat on the single chair in her room, and she on her cot, and he asked for her name, though Neeve suspected he already knew it. He invited her to call him by his Roman name, Mucia, and then inquired about her health, her eating and sleeping habits, and her choice of exercise rooms. After every answer he would nod approvingly. Then he said, "You were quite sick when you arrived. Do you know how you were made well?"

"I obeyed the priests," she said. "I ate good food, slept well, exercised, and kept my body clean."

He smiled pleasantly. "You heard the truth and you obeyed."

"Yes."

"And you are grateful to the priests, are you not?"

"Very grateful."

"Because they made your body whole again."

"Yes."

He clasped his hands together. "What would you say if I told you the priests did little to heal you?"

"I know the gods healed me," Neeve said, anticipating his conversation, "but without the priests, I would have died."

"You are right to say the priests became the hands of the gods … but which gods? There are many gods and many lords."

Neeve furrowed her brow.

"For us there is only one lord, one god. He is greater than all the kings of earth. Greater than the Caesars of Rome. Greater than the gods of the pantheon. He is lord of heaven, and he has given us his name."

"Asclepios," Neeve said in a low voice, uncertain whether she was allowed to use the divine name of the god.

"You have spoken the truth. Asclepios, the most high god, has had mercy on you."

"I am grateful."

"You know this is an Asclepion temple?"

"Yes," Neeve said. "I have seen his likeness carved in the marble arches of the buildings."

"And you have heard the priests blessing the name of Asclepios?"

"I have, and singing his songs."

"You have seen much," Mucia said, "but I will tell you a secret." He leaned closer. "The great god knows *your* name."

"My name?"

"I have heard him in the sacred temple, calling your name."

Neeve stared at him. The thought of a god calling her name did nothing to put her at ease.

"Don't be afraid," the priest said, "Asclepios cares about you. He watches you in love."

"He watches me?"

"His eyes are upon you, yes."

"Is he always watching?"

"No, he sleeps like every living thing, but we never know when he's sleeping and when he is awake … because he comes in the night and whispers words of truth."

Neeve swallowed. "I have seen someone … in my room at night. He whispers to me."

"Is he tall?"

"Yes," Neeve said, stunned. "Very tall, with large hands that cover my face, and he wears a shining white robe."

"Asclepios is the tallest of the gods."

Neeve took a deep breath. Could the god Asclepios have been visiting her in her room as she slept?

"He knows who you are, Neeve mapmaker."

She looked at the old priest.

He paused and smiled again. "Would you like to meet him?" he asked.

"I don't understand."

"Come with me," Mucia said, rising.

Neeve resisted. "I would rather not," she said politely. She was not terribly interested in meeting a god. Her mother had always taught her that the less a god knew about you, the better.

"Come," he repeated.

Neeve followed him out of the sleeping quarters, past the consecrated pools, and along the sacred way with its many carvings of the gods. This time she noticed that in every grouping of the gods, one was very tall, double the size of the others.

At the end of the sacred way they stopped before the great wooden doors of the temple, forty feet high and half again as wide, each door with an enormous relief of a snake coiled around a knotted wooden staff. Neeve had seen the doors before and was told the snake symbolized healing. Even a venomous snake must bend to the will of Asclepios, the priests had said, and in the hands of the healing god, the most deadly of things were harmless. Mucia nodded to the priests guarding the temple. They took hold of the large circular handles and swung open the doors. The sweet smell of incense flowed over Neeve as she stepped inside the smoky temple. It was long and narrow, and gleaming in yellow candlelight, and everywhere golden incense bowls burned brightly. At the far end of the temple stood an enormous statue of the bearded Asclepios, his left hand holding a knotted wooden staff with a snake coiled around it.

The doors closed behind them.

Neeve glanced around nervously.

Mucia raised his large eyebrows enquiringly.

"Can I speak?" she asked in a whisper.

"Asclepios is not like other gods," he said. "He does not engender fear and never exacts punishment. He merely wants to reveal himself to you that you might worship him in love." The priest took her hand and asked, "What frightens you?"

"Snakes," she said. "I was told the temple was filled with snakes."

He chuckled softly. "You must have talked to a novice priest. Only on ceremonial days are there ever snakes in the temple, and then only a handful of harmless garden snakes."

As they neared the front of the temple, Neeve could see scores of votive tablets with writing carved in the stone.

"Can you read the tablets?" the priest asked.

In spite of what the priest had said, Neeve felt awkward speaking in the temple, especially with the enormous statue of Asclepios looming above her. The Druids demanded absolute silence when performing certain of their rites, and the Druid gods were known to punish those who acted improperly in their presence. She squinted in the dim light at the writing, but it was Greek. "I cannot read the words," she said.

"These are testimonials of others who have come before you. Some were scoffers, some unbelievers, some doubters. But all discovered the truth." He lifted his eyes to the massive statue of Asclepios. "Can you feel his presence?" he asked. "Asclepios is watching you as we speak. He is a compassionate god, and he longs for you to know him as he knows you. Look into his face and tell me what you see."

Neeve took a breath. She had never been this close to a god. In Roman lands the streets and buildings were filled with statues of the gods, and in Britannia's forests the spirits manifested themselves as protectors of the ground they controlled. Many times she had felt their presence. But standing before the watchful statue of Asclepios seemed different. She was troubled and unsure what to say or do. Could the old priest be right? Was this god the most powerful of all?

She raised her eyes to his face and dropped them instantly to the marble floor. "I am unworthy to stand in his presence," she said, choosing not to speak directly to the god, lest he become even more interested in her. "I pledge half of all I have to the mighty and merciful one, Asclepios, highest god of the heavens." She backed away with her head bowed to show respect, and dearly hoped she had uttered the right words. Most gods were pleased when you praised and recognized their awesome power ... and gifts, they all liked gifts. She determined to work hard, drawing her sketches, and the first time she made a significant amount, she would bring half to the shrine.

"Asclepios is in his temple," the priest intoned. "Sacred is his name."

Neeve mumbled more words of praise, trying to appease the god. She wanted no ill will from so powerful a god.

"Ask your questions," Mucia said. "Honest minds please Asclepios."

Neeve turned to the priest and asked, "Does Asclepios dwell only in this temple?" She had never seen an Asclepion temple in Britannia and wondered if he were a local deity of enormous power, or whether he might be found elsewhere.

"The hand of Asclepios stretches from one corner of the earth to the other," Mucia said, "and the sun never sets on the temples that honor his name."

"He is beautiful," Neeve said, not knowing what else to say.

"Ah, yes, but you confuse the molded representation of Asclepios with the god himself. You cannot see Asclepios, as if he were stone or metal. The priests spent many months creating this beautiful bronze statue so that mortals might gaze upon its countenance and be assisted in their worship. But the statue is no more than melted metals pressed into a particular shape. The metal figure is not alive. We could melt it down and reform it again, and it would have no effect on Asclepios. Do you understand? The statue is *not* Asclepios." He laughed triumphantly. "Asclepios is not a piece of metal. He is a god! He is *the* god! The highest of all gods! All others are like dust sprinkled at his feet. But once we set up this likeness of Asclepios, he was pleased and came to dwell in his temple, in the statue itself. So now when we look into his face, he looks back at us. He looks at you, Neeve mapmaker. Yes, he looks at you!"

Neeve stared at Asclepios's face. "The statue is not Asclepios," she murmured. "Asclepios is a spirit, and he dwells in this statue as one dwells in a house."

"Yes, and that is why you can go into Asclepion temples the world over, find different statues, but the same god. Would you like me to read some of the testimonials?"

Neeve nodded.

Mucia walked over to a long bronze shield. "It was night," he began, "when every living thing except for those in pain was asleep. An exceedingly hot fever burned me, and I convulsed in agony because of the constant coughing and choking." He turned to Neeve. "Sounds like you, doesn't it?"

"Yes," she said.

He turned back to the tablet and continued reading. "I was groggy from suffering, half-asleep and half-awake when a terrifying vision came upon me. Someone of superhuman size, clothed in shining linen and carrying a snake in his left hand suddenly appeared before me."

"I too was groggy," Neeve said, surprised, "not knowing whether I was dreaming ... when a man appeared to me dressed in a shining robe."

Mucia nodded and turned back to the tablet. "He examined me from head to foot and then vanished. I quaked with fear, and sweat poured off my body like fiery rain. I sat up, my mind became as clear as light, my fever left, and the pain in my side disappeared. Asclepios in his mercy had healed me! I ran from my sick room shouting for joy, and now I spend my days proclaiming the goodness of Asclepios."

The priest was staring at her, waiting for a response.

"I ... don't know what to say," Neeve said awkwardly.

"There are thousands of such stories," he said. "Men and women everywhere have found Asclepios to be the god above all other gods. He is the divine healer who makes bodies whole."

"I praise Asclepios for his mercy," she said, thankful that the god had spared her from sinking into the grave.

Still, she had questions. Roman doctors, she remembered, had used similar methods as the priests to heal the sick. They kept sick or wounded soldiers clean and warm, and encouraged them to rest and eat good foods. She didn't deny Asclepios his glory in raising her up, but she couldn't help thinking a large part of her healing might have come from the priests and their use of warm baths, massages and fresh foods.

"You are struggling in your spirit?" the old priest asked.

"I want to believe," she said.

"In time you will find the truth," he said, "in time." He turned to another tablet and read: "An unbeliever with a crippled hand was taken to Asclepios for healing. The unbeliever read the tablets in the temple and doubted the inscriptions that described miraculous healings. Then while sleeping he saw a vision. He was in a crypt under the temple when Asclepios appeared and seized his hand and stretched out his fingers one by one. When he had straightened all of them, Asclepios asked if he still disbelieved the inscriptions in the temple. 'Lord, I now believe,' the man cried. Asclepios said, 'Because you refused to believe those things that are believable, henceforth you will be named, Unbeliever.' When day broke, he came out chastened but healthy."

The priest read from several other tablets, and after lighting a bowl of incense, they left the darkened temple to sit in the courtyard's brilliant sunlight. In spite of the cool air, the sun felt warm on Neeve's back and did much to melt the growing tension in her shoulders. Something about standing before the giant statue of Asclepios had unnerved her, and although she was thankful for her healing, she was glad to be out of the sacred temple. Being so close to a powerful god like Asclepios was disquieting.

She glanced around at the courtyard's sculptured trees, at the impressive twin fountains that dominated either end, but her mind still swirled with images of the temple. The god knew her name, that's what the priest had said. She never wanted any god to know her name, especially one that wielded the power of life and death. Gods too easily became angry, and it was simply better to be hidden from their eyes.

Neeve found herself watching a group of priests busily sifting the earth for rocks as they prepared the next season's flowerbeds. Several of the priests gave her small nods of recognition, though she could recall only one of them, vaguely, a tall man with large hands.

"Has anyone here demanded Roman coin from you?" Mucia asked, breaking into her thoughts.

Neeve's heart sank. She had not yet focused on how much three weeks' food and lodging might cost in a complex as magnificent as the Asclepion temple. The priests had devoted themselves day and night to her recovery and would reasonably expect a donation. What was the matter with her? she wondered. She had seen others giving sheep, pigs, and coins when they left. She couldn't believe she had been so dull. Naturally they expected payment. She twisted her hair around her fingers, as if an answer could be found in her nervous behavior. She had no way to pay for her costly stay at the temple. She grimaced and said, "I have not been asked for Roman coin."

"You are a beautiful woman," he said. "What about sexual favors?"

Neeve eyed him. Up to this point, she was certain he was the kindest man in Gallia, totally unselfish, and dedicated to the cult of Asclepios. But she had learned long ago that men were driven by sexual appetites and could not be trusted. Besides, she knew little about the Asclepion religion and how priests might satisfy their needs. She had seen women about the complex, but never noticed whether they were servicing the priests. Many cults had a sacred rite of prostitution, and for all she knew, there were additional rooms and buildings set aside for that purpose. Could Mucia be suggesting she repay the temple by becoming a sacred prostitute? She looked him squarely in the face and said, "No one has approached me."

"Have you been made to feel uncomfortable in any way?" he asked.

"I have been treated with the utmost respect," Neeve said, still wary from his last question.

His face showed satisfaction. "We are not like the world here," he said. "We are not slaves to gold or sex or power, and if you expected us to be grasping for anything, you were mistaken. For indeed we are slaves ... slaves of the most high god, Asclepios, blessed be his name."

"I have seen the gifts given to the temple and —"

"Yes, we accept donations," he said. "This temple would soon disappear without the support of supplicants."

"I'll work hard and return your generosity."

"I could not accept your offerings even if I wanted to," the priest said.

Neeve looked at him, puzzled.

"The senator has paid for everything."

"Senator Severus?"

"A devoted servant of Asclepios. Whenever he is in Gallia he pays homage in our temple, and we are honored to count him a friend. He has funded many projects including the fountains in this courtyard." The pleasant smile returned to his face. "Not only has he paid a hundredfold for your stay, but he has left a considerable sum for your use. If you wish to return to Britannia, or buy a carriage for travel, you have ample funds."

Neeve combed her long hair with her fingers, trying to process the information. She had lost everything, and a stranger, a senator from Rome, had rescued her from certain death in the street. "Did he say why he helped?" she asked.

"He has brought many through our gates," the priest said. "He is a splendid man."

"Splendid men offer small coins to the destitute," she said. "They don't buy them carriages."

"Yes, yes," is all he said.

"Has Senator Severus ever been this generous before?" she persisted. She was genuinely puzzled why a Roman senator would bother with her.

"With you it was different," Mucia said. "He gave us an enormous gift and told me to take extraordinary care of you. And so I have."

Neeve had no words.

Mucia ran his eyes over the flowing water in the fountain and said quietly, "Without violating the senator's confidence … he is in the sunset of his years, as am I. When a man is young, he thinks nothing of his youth, but as time passes, he sees it as a lost treasure. His mind dwells more and more on those times, on the good as well as the ill." He took a breath. "The senator came with his family to this part of Gallia when he was a boy—spent his summers here, as I recall. He had a fondness for a servant girl who died of a fever in her sixteenth year … in the winter months while he was in Rome."

"A sad story."

Mucia returned his eyes to Neeve. "She died on the streets of this very city," he said. "So I suppose that while the senator took a liking to you, he also has other things buried in his heart. He had no opportunity to help the girl, but not so with you."

Neeve sat quietly listening to the trickling of the fountain.

"A glorious day Asclepios has given us," Mucia said, breaking into her thoughts.

Neeve agreed. She glanced at the priests again who were scraping and digging on the other side of the courtyard. They were working hard, but not so hard that they didn't have time to glance up when they thought she wasn't looking. She studied the tall priest with the large hands and tried to gather the scattered images that dangled just tantalizingly out of reach. Something about him …. She furrowed her brow and asked, "Have I ever met the tall priest carrying the hoe?"

"I think not," Mucia said, and then changing the subject, he said, "We do have someone here that you should know about."

Neeve pulled her mind away from the tall priest.

"Are you familiar with the name Sammonicus Cervidius, the younger?"

Neeve shook her head.

"He claims to be your servant."

"I have no servant."

"As I suspected," Mucia said. A man arrived three days ago—unkempt—saying he was your servant, wanting money."

"Who is this man?"

Mucia signaled a priest who disappeared down one of the walkways. Minutes later he returned with two temple guards and a stubby legged man with shifty eyes and a big nose. They had placed a rope around his neck and hands, and he seemed to be having a difficult time breathing.

"We have already alerted the urban soldiers," Mucia said. "They will nail him to the execution posts outside the city gates. At least he will serve as a deterrent to others who would steal from sacred places. We wanted to first make certain, however, that he was not your servant."

Sammonicus's eyes darted around nervously. "I serve the great god, Asclepios," he said, and his words sounded ridiculous.

Neeve rose and looked at the man who had accosted her by the sea and said, "He is not my servant. He is a thief. I granted him mercy, and he returned later to rob and kill me."

Mucia nodded to the guards, who began to drag him away. Sammonicus squealed in terror: "No! I brought your ring here—"

"Wait," Neeve motioned to the guards. "My wedding ring?"

"Yes, yes, that's why I searched for you," he said with renewed hope.

"We did find a gold ring on him," Mucia said. He motioned to a priest, who handed Neeve the ring.

Neeve stared at the ring Vectis had given her, and her heart filled with joy. "Thank you," she said to the priest.

She turned to Sammonicus. "Why would you steal this from me, and then return it? Answer me."

"I did not steal it, Mistress," Sammonicus gushed. "I drove off the thieves, chased them down, and recovered it. Before the gods, I do not lie …." He glanced at the high priest and then added, "Before the god of all gods, Asclepios the merciful, may he take my children's eyes if I came for any other reason than to return this treasured ring."

"Silence!" Mucia said.

Sammonicus cried all the louder, "May the gods slay me if I am not telling the truth! Mistress, when I saw you on the beach, I thought *you* to be a thief. I was merely collecting items that I might sell. I meant you no ill—"

His words were cut short by a temple guard who thrust the butt end of his spear into Sammonicus's stomach.

Neeve took another look at the man whose sad eyes had now latched onto hers, a most unsavory fellow, of that she had no doubt. She let her eyelids drift closed and tried to remember him in the street, as he was standing there, hovering over her. Was it possible? Her memory of the event was vague at best, but as she struggled to recall, she became more and more certain he was telling the truth. He had not set out to rob her. And now here he was with her ring.

"Take him away," the old priest said.

She watched him as he was dragged down the corridor, twisting and pleading. But he wasn't a murderer, probably just a hungry wretch trying to survive as he said, and she knew what that was like. The way he held a knife told her that he had little experience beyond threatening people. The Romans loved making examples of thieves, whipping them, beheading them, nailing them to posts. She had seen condemned men wriggling on Roman torture racks before, with seven-inch spikes smashed through their wrists and ankles. The dogs chewed at their feet and birds pecked out their eyes. Their shoulders pulled out of joint, their excretions dribbled down their legs, and they constantly begged for water. The image sickened her.

"Wait," Neeve said. She remembered that Asclepios had shown her mercy; it was fitting that she should pass along a small measure of what had been granted to her.

The guards stopped.

The man rolled his dark eyes toward her like a dog hoping for a bone. He swept the dirty hair off his face and maintained his pathetic look as he glanced back down the hallway at Neeve and the old priest.

"He's not my servant," she said, "but he serves a distant cousin."

"You want him released?" the priest asked, knowing she was lying.

"I do."

"Are you certain?"

"I'm certain," she said.

22

The Roman warships carrying Taranis and his warriors crossed the channel without incident and landed at Gallia's largest westerly port, Coriallum. The Romans had chained the thousand Caledonian prisoners in clusters of ten on the decks of the two war ships. Only Taranis and eight other chieftains had freedom to move. Their hands and feet were chained, but loosely, so they could shuffle from one part of the ship to the other, to aid warriors who were thirsty or sick from the rolling seas. If the ship had foundered in a storm, Taranis had no doubt that every Caledonian, including the commanders, would have drowned.

Taranis was finding it difficult to look the common warrior in the eye, knowing that he had promised them victory, and now they sat in chains. Word had spread that Taranis had won a concession from the Roman legate, Verus, that the warriors would not be executed or sold as slaves, but conscripted into the legionary auxiliary forces as free men. After five years' service, they would be free to marry or even make their way back to Britannia if they chose. More than once a warrior had thanked him, which made his shame more difficult to bear. And bear it he did. Such was the price of the concession from General Verus. If he were to die before Verus displayed him to the Roman mobs at the Triumph, his warriors would die in his place.

As they neared the harbor, a fleet of tugboats rowed out to meet the two warships. They secured ropes to the prows of the ships, and with hundreds of slaves straining on the oars, they pulled the warships slowly into their docks. Immediately, the commanders were taken separately to a four-wheeled wagon with an iron pen bolted on the wooden frame. From long experience, the Romans had learned it was safer to separate warriors from their leaders.

Hours later the wagon with its eight prisoners stopped in a forested area. Taranis thought the guards might be resting the horses or taking the opportunity to relieve themselves in the woods. He was wrong on both counts.

The officer in charge had spotted a large bees' nest and apparently wanted the honey. The soldiers built a ring of six smoke fires and then constructed a crude scaffolding from a stand of poplars. Then they climbed gingerly up the scaffolding toward the branch with the bees. One of the soldiers began sawing carefully through the limb ten feet back of the nest, and the others atop the scaffold supported the branch, to minimize any vibration that might stir up the bees.

The whole operation took less than an hour and although a few bees buzzed around, for the most part they seemed not to notice their new circumstances.

As the soldiers carried the branch toward the smoke fires, Taranis knew it was extremely unlikely that any of the captives would get a taste of the honey. The thought of the sweet liquid melting on his tongue made his mouth water, and it brought memories of happier days in the Caledonian forests. More than once he had covered a hive in animal skins and built smoke fires to drive away the angry bees. His sister Neeve would stand at a safe distance, laughing and berating him as a coward because he wrapped himself in thick hides when he approached the hive. But no matter how careful he was, he never escaped unscathed from his encounters with the bees. And just as well. He was after all a thief, stealing what he hadn't worked for.

The soldiers moved toward the smoke fires where Taranis expected they would break open the nest. They didn't, but continued on past toward the wagon where the officer in charge waited for his prize. His soft belly jiggled as he reached out tentatively for the end of the branch. "Thank you," he said politely, as two soldiers waved oil torches over the officer's head to ward away the growing number of disoriented bees.

Inside the iron cage Taranis and the other chieftains watched with curiosity.

The officer shifted his hands gently on the branch, trying to find a better grip. Satisfied, he moved toward Taranis and smiled. Then, coiling his body like a twist of rope, he whipped the branch toward the cage, so hard that it rocked the wagon on its wheels. The beehive burst into a thousand fragments that sprayed across the cage, covering Taranis and the other chieftains' bare bodies with enraged bees. The Caledonians jerked and screamed and swatted at the swirling bees, but no amount of gyrations prevented the insects from venting their full anger. Before it was over Taranis guessed he had been stung more than a hundred times, and the only part of his body without welts was the bottom of his feet. One man fell to the floor, gasping for air, his body rigid. He died minutes later.

The Romans stood in their ring of smoke fires and watched. When the bees had exhausted their rage, the soldiers returned waving their torches to clear the air. The second in command stepped up to the cage. He knew the Celtic tongue and served as translator. "The senior officer has a message for you," he said, shifting his eyes to the man who had smashed the bees' nest.

"I didn't know bees could kill," the senior officer said, still smiling.

Taranis fought to stand up straight, but waves of nausea swept over him and bent him in two. He wretched again and again until nothing more would come. The others in the cage were equally sick, hunched over, vomit dribbling from their mouths, bodies trembling with pain.

The senior officer had the soldiers open the cage and throw the body into the woods. That done, he ambled back to the cage, and said something that Taranis didn't understand. The other officer translated: "The commander says, 'Be happy for the wolves. They rarely get a good meal.'"

The senior officer sat on a log and pulled out a wine skin. He took long, slow drafts of the liquid and wiped his mouth on his tunic. All the while he kept his eyes fixed on Taranis. After ten minutes he rose abruptly and strutted around the wagon several times. He stopped beside Taranis and shoved his face toward the bars. "Do you know who I am?" he asked.

Taranis was too sick to answer.

"No, of course not." His face twisted. "My name is Manius Nepos Falco. Does the name Nepos mean anything to you?" The translator stood close, speaking the words as if they were coming from the senior officer's mouth.

Taranis said nothing.

The officer ground his teeth. "Answer me!"

The translator took a breath and repeated the order. "The senior officer wants an answer," he said. "Do you know who he is?"

"No."

"No, you wouldn't," the senior officer said. "You are the mighty blood god who kills for sport. You and your warriors destroyed Outpost Faustina in northern Britannia, and you butchered the finest officer ever to march for Rome. His name was Mamercus Nepos Falco, my older brother."

"People die in wars," Taranis said.

"He surrendered and you slaughtered him!"

"If he was in Caledonia, he deserved to die," Taranis said. The nausea welled up in his throat but he forced it down.

"I would kill you now," Nepos said, shaking with rage, "but I have orders from Legate Julius Verus to deliver you to Rome alive. I always obey orders. But I will promise you this, by the time you arrive in Rome, you will wish I had taken my tree saw and ripped it through your neck."

23

After leaving the Asclepion temple, Neeve strode along the main road, a raised sidewalk of sorts about eighteen inches wide in a street that itself couldn't have been more than ten feet wide. It was called the main road because it meandered through a canyon of tall buildings in the business district, and because it was the first true thoroughfare in the ancient village that eventually became a Roman town. It was difficult to navigate because of the many shopkeepers who opened their shutters onto the sidewalk and displayed their wares under the canopy. The road itself was paved with heavy lava rocks, rutted from cartwheels, and often became clogged when cart owners refused to give way to one another. Shouts from vegetable sellers, sandal makers and a hundred other merchants blended into a dull hum that made voices indistinguishable. Only when a hawker shouted and waved his wares inches from a potential customer's face did he attract any attention.

Neeve pushed through the crowds, ignoring the merchants who called to her as if she were an old friend. She had many things on her mind.

She had bid farewell to the Asclepion priests. They had been good to her, but had confused her with their talk of the one true god, as if the others were insignificant. That might be fine inside the Asclepion walls where the healing god reigned unchallenged, but what would happen outside when the other gods saw you ignoring them? Better to appease all the gods, she reasoned, minor or not, than to risk the wrath of a tyrannical spirit. She would honor Asclepios as her highest god, but still render homage to others as the need arose. It was the sensible thing to do.

At her elbow, having trouble keeping up, was Sammonicus, the shifty-eyed scavenger who had returned her ring. He had waited for her by the temple gates for two days, and immediately began babbling his thanks for her part in preserving his miserable life. He followed her to the fishmonger when she bought salted fish, to the baker, to the armory, even to the public toilets where he sat next to her and rinsed out a wet sponge for her to use in cleaning herself. She ignored him. When she went to the bankers to prepare for her trip to Rome, he waited outside like a faithful dog in the street.

"Go away," she said for the fifth time. "I want nothing to do with you."

"The gods delight in you, I can see that. Saved from the sea! Saved from the streets! Saved from deadly pestilence! Yes, they delight in you."

She walked faster.

"Jupiter, Asclepios, Apollo—they all crave your attention. How can they not but shower gifts of love on you?"

"How can the gods not punish you?" she countered. "You risk your children's eyes with your lies to an Asclepion priest."

"I have no children," he said, opening his hands. "And I was not lying, because I intended to return the ring—"

"A ring you stole from me."

"That is not true! I only happened on the men, saw them robbing you, and shielded you from harm. I then chased them down—at great risk to myself—took back the ring, and returned it to you."

"Thinking you might squeeze money out of the priests," she said.

"Is it evil to desire a small compensation, Mistress? But as for the street … I risked myself to help you, without any thought of reward--"

"Well," Neeve said, gesturing with the back of her hand, "even if you did help me, as you say, then our scales are even. Leave me be."

She crossed to the other side of the road.

He ran after her, dodging a cart bulging with turnips. "I am your servant," he declared, "and very useful. If you are traveling to Rome,

I can arrange passage on a ship from Gesoriacum by the sea. I have many relatives there and can get the best price." His face beamed with anticipation.

"I'm not traveling by water," she said. She wouldn't board another ship in the cold months if they burned incense on the town altar and gave her free passage.

"A public carriage, then," he said, nodding. "Very expensive, but I can—"

"I don't need you," she said, exasperated with his continual chatter. "I have a carriage waiting for me at the Antistius Livery."

"The Antistius Livery! You are *buying* a carriage?"

"A horse and carriage, yes."

"A horse! Not a mule?"

Neeve veered to the side to avoid a pampered looking matron surrounded by a cluster of body slaves. Her painted face and piled wig could not hide her course features and cheerless disposition. She scowled at Sammonicus for daring to cross her intended path.

"A thousand pardons," he mumbled as he scuttled away, pumping his stubby legs to catch up to Neeve. "A horse," he repeated.

Neeve could see he was impressed. Few people could afford a horse, and it encouraged him even more. He hurried alongside, prattling on about the various roads one could take to Italia, and how often he had traveled those same roads. He knew places to eat, inns to stay at, and areas to avoid. Neeve ran her eyes over the grimy little man. She knew what was in his head. He was thinking if she had money to buy a horse and carriage, what else might she have? He was not a dullard. One day she was lying on the street and the next she was heading for a livery to assume possession of a carriage. Surely, he had concluded, she had found a benefactor. He definitely saw her as a free meal, and maybe more. He might be planning another of his robberies.

She whirled around and grabbed him by the throat.

"Mistress?" he choked, his eyes wide.

"How foolish do you think I am?" Neeve shouted, inches from his oversized nose. "I know what you want, and if you even think a wrong thought, I will slit your throat like a spring lamb." She shoved him back and patted the large Celtic style knife at her hip to remind him of their encounter on the seashore. It was the first item she had purchased at the armory.

"You misunderstand," he said in a wounded voice. "Before the gods, I only want to thank you for saving my life."

"You've thanked me, now go away."

"But Mistress, I—"

"Go away!" She jammed a finger into his chest.

"If I may," he said, tilting his head in submission, "you have no servants, and I wish to offer my services."

"I have no need of a servant."

"Oh, but my lady, you do. Who will tend your horse, clean your carriage, go to market?"

"I am a Caledonian," she said. "Caledonians fend for themselves."

"Ah, yes," he said, bobbing his head, "you are truly an independent woman, and that is commendable. But you are journeying to the heart of the Empire, and it would be quite unseemly for a lady to be driving her own carriage."

"I'm not some painted matron who needs a driver to take her to the theater."

"There are dangers along the way," he said in lowered voice to lend gravity to his words.

"And you will be my protector?"

"Your servant, your protector, whatever you require."

She gave him a smile dripping with scorn. "I have had protectors," she said. "They stand twice as tall as you and their arms are thicker than your middle. Anyway, you look like someone I need protection against."

"Yes … yes," he said slowly, pushing a slab of greasy hair off his face, "I do have a certain … soiled look, I suppose, but that is what your situation requires at this time." He smiled, showing surprisingly white teeth. "The presence of a man like me could be useful to you, if only to deter unsavory characters like myself from targeting you."

"They will learn soon enough their mistake," she said.

"Undoubtedly, but do you want to bother teaching them?"

Neeve didn't reply.

"You wish to go to Rome, a long journey with many pitfalls. Opportunists crouch at every bend in the road. Lone travelers, like lone sheep, are soon eaten. True, you have a quick-moving carriage, but why encourage them? They will only slow your journey. But with me as your servant—"

"I grew up in Londinium," she said, "and had plenty of servants attending me in those days, and if I needed a servant now, believe me, it wouldn't be you."

He opened his mouth to protest.

"Someone with a knowledge of languages and customs, not you."

"Oh, Mistress, I speak Latin and Greek, as well as several native tongues. I know Roman customs as well as anyone—better actually—because for many years I worked as a servant in Rome."

"You? A servant in Rome?"

"A body servant, Mistress, at a very fine household."

"And why would you leave such a good situation?" Neeve asked, dubious.

"My master died of a fever," he said, "and I had nowhere to go but my birthplace. An uncle gave me works as a tanner, but I never much liked scraping fat off animal skins."

"Honorable work, better than stealing."

"True, but the stench, Mistress ... you could scrub all afternoon at the baths and still the cats pursued you in the marketplace."

Neeve realized her face was puckered in disgust.

He nodded his understanding. "I was looking for servant work when I fell on hard times. But I certainly know customs and can be very discreet."

"Let me speak plainly," she said, fixing her eyes on him. "I don't trust you."

He looked hurt, a face she had seen before.

"Do you think I should?"

His eyebrows knit together, not understanding.

"Trust you," she said. "Do you think I should trust you?"

"Yes," he said in righteous indignation. Then he shrugged and said, "Well, maybe I wouldn't trust someone like me either. But you have nothing to fear. You are one of those warrior women from the Isle of Britannia. I know that now. You are strong, skilled with a knife, and clearly the gods favor you."

"The gods have no interest in me," she said sharply.

"Oh, but they do. I sense it."

"Enough talk," she said. "Be on your way!"

"But Mistress—"

She glanced away and found herself watching an ox drink from the street drainage channel. She disliked talking about the gods. In her desperate hours she had sometimes called out to them for help, but when the crisis passed, she avoided them. They grew angry too easily and demanded too much. She looked back at the man. He was still beside her, making movements as if he were about to leave. He was truly a vile man, but looking at him, she felt nothing especially negative, maybe a slight irritation with his extraordinary persistence. She also knew the presence of a male driver would do much to discourage potential assailants.

"Let me prove my worth to you," he said, interrupting her thoughts. He was making one last attempt. "I couldn't help overhearing through the shutters the armory worker say he would have two Scythian style bows ready for you by this afternoon."

Neeve nodded but made no eye contact. His ear must have been directly under the window.

"Will you also pick up your bread and fish at the same time?"

"That was my plan."

"There is no need for you to run the errands, Mistress. I will take your chits and meet you at the Antistius Livery."

She drew a long breath and looked at him.

"Do not fear," he said, noting her suspicions. "I will prove myself."

Neeve hesitated. Did she even want to consider using such a man? He was like a stain she could not remove.

His eyes lit with hope. He licked his lips and said, "You will be satisfied, I promise. Besides, this is a small town. If I don't return, you can easily find me and cut my ears off."

"And your tongue as well," she said, smacking the chits into his hand. "Be at the livery in two hours."

Neeve watched him rush off to complete his errands and felt mildly uncomfortable allowing this man to perform services for her. About the only virtue she could see in him was that he sometimes returned the items he had stolen. He was almost out of sight when a thought struck her—she would follow him. Spy on him was more accurate. She would see what he did when he thought he was completely alone and accountable to no one. If she seriously intended to use him as a servant for the journey to Rome, it was the only way.

She hurried after him, keeping the top of his head in view as she pushed through the busy streets. He wasn't moving overly fast but with the smoke from vendors cooking sausages, the plodding carts and the swaying crowds, she soon lost him.

Twenty minutes later Neeve found him at the fishmonger. He had already been to the baker because he had her bread in a rope bag, and another bag with assorted biscuits. She maneuvered closer to the fish stall and heard the fishmonger protesting that he had already been generous by adding a jar of pickled fish.

"I want two more salted cod, good pieces," Sammonicus said calmly, "or my mistress will never shop here again."

She could hear the fishmonger grumbling as he added the extra fish.

Minutes later Sammonicus was at the armory. This time instead of threats he told the craftsmen his mistress might be interested in purchasing twenty additional bows for her relatives in Britannia. He thought if they included ten or twelve additional arrows, it might encourage her to buy from them. They gladly did so, and he walked out of the armory with two bows, a sack filled with arrows, and a smile on his face. Shortly thereafter, he traded six of the arrows for goat cheese, hazel nuts mixed with dates, and a large tin of grain. He poured out a measure of grain into a rag and tied the top. Then he stuffed his goods into a cloth bag along with the cod, pickled fish and selected biscuits.

Neeve kept her distance as Sammonicus moved quickly through the narrow streets until he reached a dirty section of town lined with unpainted three and four story tenements. The streets smelled of animal excrement and rotting cabbage. Children and dogs and old people peered from open doorways, and the rattle of dice boxes rose from huddled men in the side streets, betting what little they had on the whims of Fortuna.

Sammonicus disappeared in a doorway and clomped up the wooden stairs to an attic tenement above the fourth stage. Neeve knew the kind of building it was. Every floor was crammed with tiny vermin-infested sleeping pockets, cold in the winter, sweltering in the summer. She waited fifteen minutes before starting toward the tenement, and then promptly ducked behind a broken door that hung uselessly from one hinge. She could hear feet, and then Sammonicus's voice as he descended the stairs. She waited, watching through the splintered boards, breathing softly and trying not to move. She had hunted enough to know that movement, not proximity, startled game. He emerged from the doorway, minus the cloth bag. Behind him was an old woman with her hand grasping his shoulder to steady herself. Neeve noted the squat frame and wide nose under a heavy brow. Sammonicus's mother.

Neeve couldn't hear distinct words, but she understood the conversation well enough. The old woman was insisting on saying goodbye to him in the street, and brushing off concerns she would have trouble with the stairs. Her wrinkled hands constantly adjusted his tunic as she expressed pride in his new job as a servant and said something about another son who would take care of her while Sammonicus journeyed to Rome.

She thanked him for the food.

He kissed her goodbye. "The gods have turned their eyes on our family again," he proclaimed loudly as he started down the street. His mother smiled and waved a faded orange scarf to her retreating son. When he had gone she returned to the darkened stairs, stopping every third or fourth step to rest.

Neeve was about to leave when suddenly Sammonicus returned. He waited and listened at the doorway until he was certain his mother had made it into her room. Then, with a sniff from his large nose, he headed down the street at a trot.

"Mistress, I was worried when you were not here," Sammonicus said, his face showing curiosity about where she might have been. He stood at the gates of the Antistius Livery, his arms loaded with bags.

"Let me see my bows," she said brusquely.

He gave her the bows, which she inspected with a skilled eye.

"Arrows."

He untied a string and handed her the arrows one by one.

"Good workmanship," she said. "But more than I ordered."

"Yes, Mistress. I thought they overcharged you and demanded six additional arrows."

She looked at the bread.

"Fresh from the oven as you requested ... still warm," he said.

"And biscuits I didn't order."

He beamed. "I also have an extra piece of salted cod and a measure of grain for the horse."

"Well, well," she said, putting an amazed look on her face. "Your ability to bargain will more than make up for your meals."

"I can do better," he said, an earnest look in his eyes. "I know all about the Antistius Livery. They have the best carriages, yes, but the highest prices. If you permit me—"

"The carriage and horse have already been paid for. The priests at the temple—"

"The priests arranged the price?"

"They arranged everything."

"Oh, Mistress, silver will change hands. I will tell the livery—"

"No," Neeve said.

"But Mistress, these priests are notorious for—"

"I said, no! And do not speak of the Asclepion priests in that foul manner. If they receive money, I am happy for them. Do you understand? They deserve to be paid for their efforts."

"Yes, Mistress."

"Now," she said as she started into the livery, "your name is Sammonicus?"

He collected her goods. "Sammonicus Cervidius, the younger," he said.

"There are more like you?"

My father died on the Germania Prima frontier, fighting in the auxiliary."

"Mother? Brothers? Sisters?"

"All taken by fevers long ago. My people come from the Isle of Sicilia at the southern tip of Italia, and ..." he drew a breath, "before that from somewhere in Macedonia. So I guess that makes me Greek, which I am very proud to be."

Neeve said nothing. People often lied about their families. It made life simpler. She motioned for him to wait while she talked to the livery owners. Despite misgivings, she knew she had already decided to take him on as a servant. It wasn't pity, or that he had come back secretly to check on his mother, or anything else she could name with words. It was more like an intuition. She simply felt that Sammonicus, the younger, was the right choice for her journey to Rome. Not that she had illusions about him. The man was a thief and a scoundrel, and would require careful supervision, but she had always believed that in quiet whispers, not the shouts of men, the gods spoke.

Her eyes drifted down to the ring she wore, and she wondered about Vectis, if in the end she would ever find him. She was trying very hard to listen to the gods, but sometimes she felt as if they were punishing her. She wished she knew what good deed she could do to please them.

24

Brutus liked the night.

She liked the star filled sky and the nether gloom before the dawn, the crisp air and the hush when shadows fell, but mostly she liked the solitude of darkness. When the light faded, wary travelers sought refuge in caves or inns, knowing that predators ruled the night. But for Brutus, darkness was a friend.

In all her travels, never once had she felt threatened in the night. Not that she hadn't encountered thieves and murderous villains. She had, many times. But she kept a second horse in tow and could easily outrun them. She knew the roads and the places where thieves gathered. When she couldn't skirt an area, she used stealth.

From the beginning Brutus had used Fell Ponies, hardy, sure-footed animals with great stamina, even in cold provinces like Dacia. They were comfortable on Roman cobblestones and open fields alike, a favorite of smugglers because Fell Ponies never objected to sacks on their feet. Over the years Brutus had developed her own method, slender bags with soft leather pads to mute the sound of her ponies' feet. In the darkness she had little difficulty slipping past the thieves before they realized it.

Brutus arrived at the frontier town of Porolissum as the sun was rising. It was the perfect town for her business. It had clean streets, beautiful baths, expensive theaters, and it had hordes of Germans sharpening their knives on its northern border. Yes, it was a good town for her, a busy town, a place where people hardly noticed strangers. They had more pressing concerns.

She pulled out her water skin and swallowed a mouthful of diluted wine. Already soldiers were preparing for the day's work. They hardly glanced up as she rode by, dressed as she was in heavy, winter clothes. Centurions barked their orders and soldiers marched out to their duties, undoubtedly where they had left off the day before. It was serious work. They were replacing the turf walls of their camp with heavy stone, cleaning out defensive ditches, and constructing double walls to protect the town from assault.

Brutus took her ponies to the livery, hired a boy to feed and exercise them during the coming weeks, and found a room in a part of town where people kept to themselves. Porolissum was a good-sized frontier settlement with over twenty thousand civilians and five thousand soldiers. She had been in many towns like it all over the Empire. Soldiers transferred in and out; merchants came and went; prostitutes, thieves, charlatans, they all set up tents or rented cheap rooms, and then disappeared when prospects elsewhere beckoned them. She would have little trouble melting into a busy and transient populace.

Her body ached. She had been traveling for weeks, mostly at night, along the great northern road that cut through Dalmatia and Dacia, and the cold had taken its toll. She longed for a hot meal, a bath, and hours of uninterrupted sleep, but she knew survival favored the disciplined. She paid the innkeeper three copper coins for a ten-day stay and headed up to her room on the second floor, a narrow space with a straw-filled cot against the wall, a single couch pushed alongside a low table, and a basin of water. The room smelled of smoke, probably from the cooking fires at the side of the inn, and slender shafts of light filtered through the tiny window at the far end, making the room seem smaller than it was. With her back to the door, she closed her eyes, visualizing the picture as she had entered the room, opened them to make certain she had an exact image, and then surveyed the entire room, every log and cross-beam, every mud-plastered corner, every protruding nail. Satisfied, she went down to the eating room and had a surprisingly tasty leg of lamb covered in mushrooms and asparagus.

Brutus bathed in the heated tubs outside the inn and returned to her room ready for sleep. Already the sun was fast receding into the hills and her room was banked with purple shadows. She closed her door and surveyed the space. The haze of sleep dissolved in an instant. Something was wrong. The image wasn't right. Her body tensed. She slipped her hand inside the pile of clothes she carried and felt for the bone handle of her needle knife as she gently set the clothes on the floor. Her eyes raked every shape and shadow of the room, but there was nothing. She stepped out of her sandals, bent her knees, and moved soundlessly toward the center of the room, directly under the main crossbeam. She tilted her head upwards. She took two more steps. Her breath grew shallow as she ran her eyes along the beam. She turned slightly. Suddenly, her hand flashed upwards and she snatched a rat off the crossbeam.

"I'm faster than you thought?" she asked, thrusting her face into the rat's face, her eyes level with its yellow glistening eyes. "People make that mistake all the time, but I thought you would be shrewder because you live by your wits." The rat squirmed in Brutus's tight grasp. "Nothing to say? Hmm? Then listen to me. This is *my* room and I don't want you here." She raised her needle knife slowly until the gleaming point stroked the side of the rat's cheek. "If you don't leave, I will kill you. Do you understand? I will kill you and your mother, your friends, and anyone else that comes into my room. I will kill every one of you." Brutus pricked the skin under the rat's eye with the tip of her needle so that the animal twisted its head away. She removed the needle knife and stared intently into its eyes. "Go away," she said, "or you will die." She lifted the rat back onto the crossbeam and released it. For a long minute the rat looked down at Brutus as if assessing the situation, and then abruptly it turned, darted the length of the beam, squeezed under the side supports and disappeared.

Brutus smiled to herself and prepared for bed.

The next morning she was up with the sun. She scrubbed her face in a basin of heated water, rinsed her mouth and lightly powdered her face. She pulled on a clean tunic, donned a cheap blond wig, and set off for Porolissum's large public bath.

Bathhouses were always looking for women skilled in the art of massage, especially attractive women. Too attractive, and Brutus knew her face would be remembered; too plain, and no bathhouse would hire her. The trick was to find a look somewhere in the middle. She used the white powder and a bleached wig to diminish her face, and a colorful tunic that clung to her body to attract interest. Nobles of lesser stature who had few personal servants relied on the staff provided by local bathhouses, and they appreciated attractive, well-trained specialists.

Brutus was glad this assignment was ending.

Several times she had sat down to draft a letter to her clients terminating her agreement to eliminate this partner, Vectis Trebellius. She had even calculated how much user fee she would add to the gold they had given her. But in the end, she decided to complete the task. It was a matter of discipline. If she withdrew from this assignment, she should perhaps withdraw altogether from her chosen work and devote her time to overseeing her villas. But she was not yet ready to take up farming.

Through a row of leafless beech trees, Brutus spotted the vaulted roofs of the baths and the plaster walls splashed with vibrant colors to brighten the spirit. They did little for her own this day. She was thinking about her mistakes.

At least she had learned a profitable lesson. Never grow too comfortable in your work, because when you do, calamity follows. At every stage Brutus thought she had made sound judgments, reasonable inferences given the information available. But her work had been shoddy. She had mistaken the bodyguard for the partner. It mattered little that she had matched her victim with the name stamped on the trunk, Vectis Trebellius Quadratus, and had verified it by talking to the driver, the innkeeper, and the men in the carriage. She had forgotten about the trunk. She didn't examine the contents of the trunk. And that was her undoing.

She had made a mistake.

Now her real partner, Trebellius, was on his guard.

Worse, from her perspective, she had spent time talking to the partner … and had found him agreeable. More than agreeable, she had to admit. He was a man she could easily spend her life with. She brushed away the thought. She knew what was happening. Her loneliness was encroaching on her good sense. When she completed this assignment, she promised herself, she would find somebody suitable. Then this aching void in her soul would trouble her no more.

But now she must discipline herself. Emotions must give way. She was in danger. Trebellius knew her real name and already wondered whether she might be the assassin. In the end, it came down to her life or his.

Brutus paused at the bathhouse gates. "Partners are not people," she said to herself. "They are names, objects to blot from a book." If she had never met Trebellius, she would have no hesitation in fulfilling her commitment. She must complete what she started. It was the only way.

The thought gave her focus.

She would go about her business as she always had.

Besides, what did she know about Vectis Trebellius? He was a soldier, after all, a man who undoubtedly had taken many lives himself. Her occupation differed only in the reasons for taking life, she told herself. In all the exteriors Trebellius appeared to be a pleasant man, but no one paid enormous sums of gold to kill pleasant men. He was hiding something … something dark, something sinister. He was by no means guiltless; none of her partners were. The thought soothed her conscience. Soon she would eliminate this partner and put the whole affair behind her.

Brutus entered the bathhouse gates, talked to the freedman in charge of bathhouse services, and in short order convinced him to hire her as a servant. It was an important piece in her plan. She needed to be alone with her partner. She needed to separate him from the soldiers and other officers who constantly surrounded him. And where better to do it than in the bathhouse with its many rooms for rest and relaxation.

She thought about Vectis Trebellius and his love for the hot baths. On the carriage ride across Italia, she remembered how he consistently visited the local baths, even paid forty sesterces for a single night, so the driver had told her. She couldn't blame Trebellius.

In the cold months, what could be more invigorating than to plunge into steaming water, scrub one's body in a hot room and enjoy a vigorous massage? If a Roman were asked to name the one feature about society that pleased him most, he would undoubtedly cite the baths. Only the gladiatorial games rivaled its popularity.

Trebellius was now in barbarian territory, far from Roman amenities, probably already laying siege to a city. After months in such desolate circumstances, she had no doubt the first item on his calendar would be the hot baths. Trebellius would be eager to take his leisure in Porolissum, a town on the edge of the world, but a town that could justly be proud of its magnificent baths. They rivaled anything in the provinces.

Brutus was patient. She would go about her work quietly, waiting for her partner to appear. And when he did, she would perform her duties well. She would be just another thief who murdered someone at the baths. An unfortunate happening, to be sure, but once again her life would have order and clarity.

25

Vectis had been in better moods. His journey to the Roman garrison town of Porolissum, protector of the Dacian frontier, had dragged out to several months. A fever had swept through their legionary escort, affecting everyone, including Julian and himself. Then the rains came, heavy rains that lashed the entire province of Dacia, making travel impossible. Roadways filled with water, bridges washed out, and in mountainous areas whole villages disappeared under mudslides.

"Finally," Julian said, pointing toward the distant town of Porolissum, and the massive wall that ran the length of the horizon. The blue smoke of campfires hung over the town, largely obliterating sections of the wall where the mile castles stood. "I was beginning to despair we would ever make it this far."

"Yes," Vectis said, "but we're here."

"We're here," Julian agreed.

They paused, taking in the sight.

"Frontier barriers," Julian mused. "They still amaze me."

Like the Antonine Wall in Britannia, the German barrier had been constructed from turf blocks and topped with a palisade fence. It had a roadway for military travel, a northern ditch to slow invaders, and stone watchtowers every five hundred feet.

As they neared Porolissum, Vectis could see hundreds of soldiers busily replacing the turf walls of the camp with heavy stone, five feet thick. They were clearly bracing themselves for what they thought was inevitable—a German assault. He saw a refurbished amphitheater and well appointed baths, but he also saw the double walls protecting Porolissum, the newly dug ditches, and the detention areas where soldiers searched travelers crossing the frontier. Procurator Tiberius might have been a political appointee, but he was thorough in his preparations against the German threat.

Vectis spent a day and a night in Porolissum, inspecting defenses, talking with Tiberius, and getting a full sleep. He also went to the baths for a brief but invigorating soak in the hot pool. "I have more respect for the pressures of higher office," Vectis said as they left the baths and joined the afternoon crowds swarming the streets.

Julian frowned. "You're talking about Tiberius?"

"I am. All he wants to do is protect Rome's borders, but he has to deal with the practical aspects of being a governor."

"Which means he has to appoint incompetents like Commodus."

"Well ... he either listens to the Senate or gets himself demoted," Vectis said, his voice trailing off. He was distracted by a group of women rounding the far side of the bathhouse, and one of them looked very familiar.

Julian followed his eyes. "See something of interest?" he asked with a grin.

Vectis shook his head, but his eyes lingered on the spot where he thought he had seen the dye merchant melting into the crowd. He returned to his conversation but couldn't quite clear his mind of his imaginary suspicions.

26

Rome. A tiny dot shimmering in the distant hills was all she saw, but Neeve knew it was the eternal city.

For weeks she and her newly acquired servant, Sammonicus, had traveled across Gallia and into the Italian peninsula. She had kept her eye on him but was pleased with his performance. He actually did know the safest inns and the best roads, as he had claimed. He turned out to be a first-rate bargainer in the marketplace, and reasonably trustworthy when it came to stealing from her. He skimmed some, certainly, but not anything out of the ordinary for a servant. She had spotted him once or twice slipping off to the local army post, but said nothing. She knew he was sending coins to his mother.

The journey to Rome was long and tedious, but uneventful. They continued using the inns, exchanging horses at liveries for moderate fees, and the miles fell away. As they moved farther south into Italia, the extreme cold of Britannia and northern Gallia diminished, and Neeve often removed her heavy cloak during the afternoon hours.

More than once they came to river gorges that normally would have taken an entire day to cross. But Roman engineers had built breathtaking arches across the spans so that travelers could cross easily. In Britannia, Neeve had traveled across Roman bridges, especially in Londinium, but never ones of such height. She ordered Sammonicus to halt at the center of one of the taller bridges, and left the carriage to look over the side. Sammonicus too stepped from the carriage, but a sudden gust caught him, pushing him several steps toward the lip of bricks that marked the edge. He dropped to a crouch to catch his balance.

"Sammonicus?"

"Yes, Mistress." He remained in his crouch, his hands flat on the bricks to steady himself.

Neeve could see he was in no danger, but she enquired about him anyway. "Are you safe?" she asked.

"Did you see that?"

"I saw the wind catch you."

"It felt like Jupiter in the wind, thrusting me toward the abyss," he said.

"You tempt the gods too often," Neeve said. "Fair punishment for your many misdeeds."

He dusted off his hands and stepped back from the edge. "Misdeeds or no, I would not get too close to the side, Mistress."

Neeve swept her eyes across the canyon, taking in the whole scene from one end to the other. "We are so high," she said, stating the obvious. "How could anyone build such a structure?" But she knew the Romans were a special people, different from everyone else.

As they left the arched bridge, she thought about Sammonicus. He was like one of the wolves trappers used in the north country to pull their sleds. Once fed and cared for, the animals provided a certain amount of protection against other wolves, but you could never fully trust them.

Early one morning, when they stopped at a small town, called Antipolis, well within the borders of Italia, Neeve made a stunning discovery. She'd intended simply to fill her water jugs, replenish her meat and bread, and continue on her way. But directly in front of the city courts stood a stone statue of Nemetona, Celtic goddess of war. Neeve approached the statue, hardly daring to breathe as she pushed one foot ahead of the other. The statue looked different but it was definitely Nemetona. She called for Sammonicus to bring the last of their bacon wedges, and whispering a prayer, she laid them respectfully at Nemetona's feet.

When she had finished doing homage, she lifted her head and glanced around, wondering what a Celtic goddess was doing in a thoroughly Roman town. She eyed the people on the street—Romans making their way to shops, cleaning the streets, setting up braziers on the corners—all were tall and blond, and very Celtic in features.

"These people ...." She never completed her thought. She just stared at all the Celts dressed in Roman tunics and talking in Latin. The more important types even paraded by in togas. She remembered Vectis telling her that even in Italia, there were areas populated with Roman Celts. But she never truly believed it.

Curious, Neeve greeted one toga-clad man in the Celtic tongue. He looked her up and down, glanced at Sammonicus, and continued on his way.

Sammonicus said, "They don't speak your island tongue."

"I can see that, but—"

"There are many like you in these parts," Sammonicus said. "They have lived here for hundreds of years."

"But they are Celts," she said.

"They once were, Mistress. Romans now."

It wasn't many days before Neeve realized that scores of towns had the same Celtic-looking people. She marveled that except for a few scattered statues dedicated to Celtic gods, they had forgotten everything about who they were. They were Roman to the core.

They traveled for several days along a stretch of the coastal road where there were few inns and even fewer towns. Neeve had made a point of stopping at the baths in the larger centers to clean herself, or at a river when the baths were unavailable. For two days, they had seen no towns or rivers, but miles of empty, sandy beaches. The sun shone brightly but the wind coming off the sea set Neeve's teeth chattering. In Britannia, no one with any sense bathed in the sea because the frigid waters chilled to the bone. But Neeve felt grimy.

"Stop here," she said.

Sammonicus pulled the horse to a stop and opened the trunk containing Neeve's personal items. He handed her a pot of fuller's soap, a towel, a washcloth, and a clean tunic.

"I'll build a fire over there," Sammonicus said, pointing down the beach.

"Fine," Neeve said, "but attend to your duties."

"Certainly, Mistress, I have much to do."

Neeve waited for him to move the carriage down the beach before undressing. She didn't care if Sammonicus glanced furtively at her while he worked, but she would not have him ten feet away gawking at her

Neeve disrobed in the chilly air, her teeth clenched to stop them from chattering. She looked over at Sammonicus. He was busy collecting wood for the night's fire, and fixing a place above the high seas mark where they could sleep on the sand. The smell of seaweed and the sounds of waves crashing reminded her of the disastrous channel crossing, but she put that out of her mind, and headed down to the sea. Surprisingly, she actually enjoyed the feel of the sand sifting through her toes, and she slowed to plow the loose granules lazily with her feet. Even the sea felt good as she waded up to her waist, the soft roll of the waves unexpectedly warm as she scrubbed her body with a soapy washcloth, and ducked under frequently to seek refuge from the chilly air. She had heard that the seas warmed and cooled slowly, but she had no idea they would retain the summer's warmth this far into the cold season. She filled her mouth with water and swished it around; it had the tangy taste of salt.

"Mistress!"

Neeve turned to see Sammonicus running down the beach toward her.

"Something's in the water!" he hollered. "Come out now."

She whipped her head around, searching for dark shapes in the sea. Then she saw one, floating with the waves toward shore, something large and round. She dropped her washcloth and propelled herself away, half swimming and half thrusting with her feet as she struggled to reach shore.

Sammonicus met her at the water's edge with the towel, his face turned away like a proper servant, but not so proper that his eyes didn't pass over her when he wrapped her in the towel.

"We need to camp somewhere else," he said. "There are dozens of turtles in the water and some have crawled up on the beach."

"Is that what we're running from?" Neeve asked. "Turtles!"

Sammonicus's eyes darted along the shoreline as if he thought he would be attacked at any moment. "I have no idea why they're here. I thought turtles laid eggs in the summer ...."

"Turtles?" She made a face. "I've seen them in the forest. Harmless things—"

"Sea turtles are different," he said. "Some of them are as big as bears, and have bone-crushing beaks! One bite will chomp off a hand or foot."

"Nonsense."

He swallowed, trying to catch his breath. "Mistress, please. We can't stay here."

"All right," she said with a sigh, "we'll camp a mile or two farther down. But I want you to take your spear and find one of the ... ah, less ferocious turtles. I have heard they taste good."

Sammonicus mumbled something about the vicious nature of turtles, but he gathered his spear and sword, and headed across the sand.

They cooked the chunks of turtle meat slowly over the fire. Sammonicus had chosen a grassy spot a hundred yards off the shoreline, protected from the wind by clusters of willow. Neeve rotated the spit while Sammonicus collected wood for the night and cared for the horse. She pulled out a skin of Celtic beer, poured it into a bronze pot and pressed it into the coals at the fire's edge. Her mouth watered. Smoked meat and heated beer. She drew her knife and sliced off a sizable length of dark, steaming meat. Sammonicus did the same and together they drank cups of beer and ate their fill.

"Quite dangerous, turtles are," Sammonicus said. "But you were right, Mistress. It was worth the risk."

Neeve ignored the comment. He was obviously fishing for praise, and she refused to give it to him for so little an effort. "At least the Celtic Romans can still make beer," she said, draining another cup.

The night before they were to enter Rome, Neeve couldn't sleep. She continually fingered her ring and thought about Vectis. Was he dead, as everyone had said? Killed before he reached Londinium?

She refused to believe it. He had to be alive. But now that she had glimpsed the Imperial city sparkling in the hills, she began to fear the truth. "They will know in Rome," the records officer in Londinium had said. She tugged her blanket around her neck and closed her eyes.

PART THREE:
Rome and Dacia

27

Vectis and Julian headed out for the bleak territory above the Dacian Wall, an untamed wilderness where Dacian and German settlements had sprung up like weeds across the land. The lead centurion told him that the previous two winters had been hard, that grain was scarce, and the situation desperate with whole villages starving.

At every settlement, old women and tiny children crowded the roadside begging for bread, their bony faces and sunken eyes like specters from the lower world. They babbled in a strange guttural tongue, holding out empty bowls to the soldiers marching by. The Greeks had a term for babblers that couldn't speak Greek or Latin — barbarians, they called them, because they sounded as if they were chattering: "bar-bar-bar." But if a soldier snickered and mimicked the peculiar sounds, the centurion instantly corrected him with the back of his sword, not because anyone cared about the barbarians, but because talking while marching was a serious breach of discipline. Occasionally, a soldier would slip one of the children a fig or piece of dried meat. That also was a breach of discipline, but the centurion pretended not to notice. The innocent eyes reminded everyone of their own children.

They traveled steadily up the abandoned Roman road built by the great warrior emperor, Trajan, a hundred years earlier. It was old now, with holes and washouts, but still serviceable for the column of marching troops. Vectis was always amazed by the uniformity of scenery on the frontiers of the Empire. It mattered little whether you were in North Africa, Britannia, or here above the Dacian Wall, people lived in miserable conditions.   Their houses, nothing more than shabby piles of twigs bound together with a slathering of muck, were built half under the ground, with floors of trodden earth.   The noblemen had little more to boast about, save their massive wooden doors ornamented with iron pegs.   Vectis could see why the barbarians plundered Roman lands.   Just the thought of walking marble streets, lounging in the hot baths, or kicking up one's feet at the amphitheater for a day of incredible excitement must have presented an irresistible temptation to the savages.

An hour before nightfall, Vectis and Julian arrived at the city under siege, the Costoboci stronghold.   The wind blew warmer in the broad valley where the city had been built, and it was obvious why the Costoboci had originally chosen this site—warm winds and snow melts in the higher elevations, good for a plentiful water supply.

The Roman soldiers had surrounded the entire city, and were already building their fires for the night, making ready for the next day as they cleaned and checked equipment.   They had set up eight camps around the city, the largest opposite the city gates.   Each camp had its own protective moat and stockade, and encircling the city was a timber barricade fronted by a seven-foot deep trench to prevent the tribes from mounting a surprise attack.   The soldiers had also constructed a band of earthworks with hidden pits and sharpened metal hooks to maim intruders who dared venture into the night.

"This is not a camp in chaos," Vectis said to Julian.   "So far I approve of everything Commodus has done."

"He's been here for a whole year," Julian said as a reminder.

Vectis smiled slightly.   Julian would not even concede the obvious, that Commodus had done many things right.   But with such an organized camp, Vectis was shocked at the lack of outer defenses to protect the soldiers' backs against an attack from the surrounding German tribes.

The Costoboci city was situated along a river, as Vectis had expected, but he was surprised to see that the river had dried long ago.   If the city had been under siege for a year, how had they managed to supply the populace with water?   He also heard music and laughter coming from over the stone walls, and when he inquired about it, a soldier told him it was the conclusion to the nightly show. Vectis would have to wait until the next evening to see what he meant. As he rode into the main camp, he became more and more perplexed.

"Tribune Vectis Trebellius to see Prefect Gaius Commodus," Vectis said formally to the aide in an office outside Commodus's excessively large tent. Someone had linked three outsized tents together to form one massive pavilion in the center of camp. Vectis had seen large commanders' tents before, but nothing like this.

The aide looked up, and even in the fading light his face looked malformed with large acne blemishes and pockmarks. "Prefect Gaius Commodus," he said, "prefers the title, Supreme Commander of Rome's Imperial Armies above the Dacian frontier."

"I see." Vectis wondered whether Commodus might allow a shorter version to be used in the event of an emergency, but he held his tongue. He repeated his inquiry using the required title, even though he had no respect for the ridiculous little man.

"Supreme Commander is sufficient," the aide said. "But when opening a conversation with the Supreme Commander, he must be addressed fully and properly."

"I will remember that. Now, may I speak with—" Vectis stopped. He thought he heard a female voice giggling inside the tent. Commodus was with a woman. He tried to rephrase his request: "Will it be possible in an hour or so to speak with—"

The aide shook his head. "The Supreme Commander cannot be disturbed."

"I understand, but perhaps later—"

"Meetings, requests, and anything of similar nature," he said, exhaling, showing his growing impatience, "must be scheduled with the Supreme Commander well in advance."

The giggling increased in volume.

Impervious to embarrassment, the aide scratched a dry patch of skin on his cheek, and said, "Is there anything else?"

Vectis couldn't help glancing at Julian, who stood beside a group of aides near the entrance. Commodus had lost none of his pretentiousness.   Even the spacious outer office with its many hangings depicting glorious battles of famous generals spoke volumes about the man. "When should I return?" Vectis asked.

"It is unlikely the Supreme Commander will have time to see you over the next while," the aide said.

"The next while," Vectis said. "What does that mean?"

"The Supreme Commander has meetings, travel plans, inspections. Perhaps in a few weeks."

"A few weeks!" Vectis felt heat flash across his face. "That's absurd." He pulled out his letter signed by Consul Tertullus and Senator Severus and stamped with the Senate's great seal. "The Roman Senate has ordered me to aid Prefect Commodus ... the Supreme Commander ... in his siege." He stabbed his finger at the document. "I am the assigned military tribune," he said, and then for effect he added, "assigned from Rome!"

The aide swallowed, looking nervous for the first time. "I am following my orders," he said, "and I have specific instructions not to bother the Supreme Commander when he is planning strategy."

"Strategy?"

"That is correct. Stop by at the end of the week and I will schedule an appointment at the first possible opening. Thank you." He turned back to his papers.

Vectis didn't move.

The aide looked up. "Is there something more?" he asked.

"Accommodations," Vectis said bluntly, "unless you plan to deal with it next week." He was angry, and he wanted the aide to know it.

"Someone will conduct you to your accommodations," the aide said, this time trying to sound more civil. "And he will also make certain your aides and escort soldiers are provided with what they need."

Julian gave Vectis an amused look as they left, and murmured, "The great Supreme Commander Commodus hasn't time to see his military tribune for weeks. He must be an amazingly virile man."

They were taken to a tent adjacent to the accommodations set aside for the military tribune. The former military tribune, a man named Ocelum, was still in the process of packing his gear. He would leave at sunup the next morning.

"Happy to talk with you," the tribune said, gesturing for Vectis and Julian to sit on the backless wooden chairs scattered around the room. "Everything you see here, the heating braziers, cots, chairs, table and lamps, I leave for you. You can also have those books over there," he said, pointing to a dozen codex volumes piled on a traveling box. "I have copies. So make yourself comfortable. I suspect you will spend your time in this tent."

"I talked to Legate Rutilius," Vectis said.

"Then you know about this assignment," the tribune said.

"I do."

"Do you know anything about Commodus?"

"He was a fort commander when I was stationed in Britannia." Vectis chose not to say that Commodus was his junior officer at the time. Too much to explain.

"Incompetent?"

Vectis studied the tribune, and then answered, "Very."

"Things haven't changed."

Vectis gestured toward the camp and said, "I was shocked to find the siege so well-organized. The soldiers are positioned reasonably, the ditches clean, the earthwork defenses wisely drawn—even the camp seems to be running smoothly. In Britannia, Commodus had trouble keeping up with the latrine schedule."

The tribune laughed sardonically. "Have you noticed we have ditches to protect us from the city dwellers, but none from the Germans at our backs?"

"I did," Vectis said.

"Commodus says the German tribes are no threat."

"I see."

"Discipline among the troops is poor to none. They grumble about every assignment and train only twice a week."

"Who is the First Centurion?"

"A man named Siccius. He's a solid officer, but his authority has been seriously undermined. When Commodus dislikes his advice, he never hesitates to reprimand Siccius in front of the men."

"Political appointees," Vectis said, shaking his head. Never had he heard of a commander reprimanding his First Centurion in the presence of common soldiers.

"When I arrived," the tribune said, "Commodus had no earthworks, no permanent guard, not even a trench, just a flimsy wall around his camps. If these Costoboci had been Germans, they would have come down in the night and cut everyone's throats. As it is, Commodus has lost over five hundred men in futile attacks using scaling ladders. His battering ram had no shelter over it, no iron tip, inadequate wheels, and he brought only two catapults when a city this size would require twenty." The tribune waved his hand in disgust. "Commodus built his siege tower with too narrow a base so it had to be torn down and rebuilt. It still isn't finished. For the first six months the soldiers rationed food and water because Commodus had no hunters and an insufficient supply system. It never occurred to him that seven thousand men would consume an enormous amount of food and water."

"You organized the camp, I take it," Vectis said.

"I did. But only defenses and supplies. In the next tent you will find a competent staff that can handle the day-to-day operations."

"So I am the logistics officer."

"That's what you are," he said, grimacing. "Commodus runs the siege, and you logistics. He listened to me about the battering ram and tower, but precious little else." The tribune blew out in frustration. "I could go on and talk about the stupidity of the ramp, but the whole situation makes me ill. We look like fools to the Costoboci and, believe me, the Germans have taken notice. I pray Fortuna smiles on you, because you'll need it."

The next morning Vectis approached Commodus's aide and asked about his appointment. He was careful to use the proper designation Commodus demanded.

"Good news," the aide said. "You can meet with the Supreme Commander after he returns from his trip to Porolissum. I will supply details to your aides. Best I can do," he added, anticipating objections.

Vectis couldn't believe a commander in a war situation would refuse to meet with his military tribune for several weeks. Even bitter political enemies accorded fellow officers the respect due their station. He pushed his face toward the aide and said, "Do you know it is more difficult to gain an audience with Supreme Commander Commodus than with Emperor Antoninus?"

"I intend to report that remark to the Supreme Commander," the aide said.

"Excellent idea," Vectis said. "Tell him Vectis Trebellius Quadratus has come back from the dead and he hopes not to die of old age waiting to report." He spun on his heel and strode out of the office.

Julian waited until they were some distance from the tent before speaking. "Have you gone completely mad? Commodus might be a weasel and a buffoon, but he holds our lives in his hands." He shook his head in dismay. "You were the one who lectured me about allowing personal feelings to interfere with responsibility. We are soldiers, you said, and we follow orders without fail."

"I remember," Vectis said quietly.

"Well?"

"Well what?"

"Why would you go out of your way to irritate Commodus?"

"All I did was—"

"All you did was mock the very man who has plenty of reasons to do us harm. You might not want to get back to Rome, but I do."

"You're right," Vectis said, staring off in the distance without seeing anything in particular. He moved his hand weakly in frustration. "I suppose I owe you an apology."

Julian grudgingly allowed a smile to cross his face. "Your apology falls too quickly off your tongue for my liking, but it's welcome nonetheless." Then he turned serious. "I remind you that Commodus has the power of Rome behind him now. He could have us executed. This is a wartime situation."

"That's true, but I might have leverage over Commodus."

Julian looked at him.

"I said, *might*." He rubbed the weariness from his eyes. "But for the moment, I will take extreme care."

"A sensible plan," Julian said.

The two of them left the camp and headed toward the walled city. Commodus was nowhere in sight. They examined the catapults, the siege tower and the battering ram. All were in good working order, though the tower still needed much work before it would be effective, as the military tribune had said. Most of the soldiers were hauling carts filled with earth and stone, constructing a massive ramp against the wall. It was nearly complete. When Vectis asked the centurion in charge how long they had been building the ramp, he said they had been hauling and dumping earth for nearly five months.

"Why build a ramp when the eastern walls are accessible to the battering ram on the flat ground?"

"We tried the eastern side," the centurion said, "but the Costoboci threw timbers from the top of the walls and broke off the ram's heads."

Vectis nodded. "So why didn't you protect it with a shelter?"

The centurion grimaced. "That's what the military tribune told us to do."

"And?"

"The Supreme Commander ordered him off the field." His eyes shifted to the battering ram when he said, "We dragged it back from the eastern side months ago and it's been just sitting here. Most of the shelter is complete, but not enough to protect the head."

"I thought the point was to punch a hole in the wall," Vectis said. "Why waste time building a ramp?"

"My thoughts are unimportant," the centurion said, making it clear he was merely obeying Commodus's orders.

Vectis rephrased his question. "Why has the Supreme Commander chosen to attack here on a steep incline where it's necessary to build a ramp?"

"Because that's where the gates are, and the gates are the weakest part of the city."

"True, but—"

"The Supreme Commander has pointed out on more than one occasion that if we are higher up on a ramp, falling timber won't have the same force to crack the heads."

"Of course," Vectis said, "but on the eastern side you wouldn't need to build this enormous ramp, just extend the shelter to stop the timber from hitting the head."

"I suppose that is another way of looking at it," the centurion said flatly, taking care not to betray his feelings.

Julian caught Vectis's eye and mouthed, "Madness."

Vectis agreed. None of it made sense.

The centurion glanced around to make sure he wasn't overheard. "If I may, Tribune ...."

Vectis nodded his permission to speak.

"The Supreme Commander has always admired Flavius Silva, who sieged the Jewish stronghold of Masada with Legion X. Silva built a massive ramp nearly a hundred years ago, and you can still see it there today. The Supreme Commander says that ramps last a thousand years, and he intends to build one here."

Vectis went away stunned. Commodus was more deranged than he had thought. He was building a monument to himself, and had no idea what his incompetence was costing the Empire. The heart of German lands was no place to conduct an amateurish siege. Any sign of weakness was certain to encourage some barbarian warlord to prove himself in battle against the Romans, especially when Commodus had built no external defenses.

Shortly before sunset a buzz of anticipation swept through the ranks. Everyone in the camp stopped what he was doing and stared up at the walled city. Time for the nightly show.

Suddenly, fifteen of the town's courtesans appeared on the wall, dancing and singing, their hair flowing loosely behind them as they leaped and whirled, their white legs flashing through the slits in the thin tunics they wore.

"Interesting," Julian said.

Vectis nodded.

The courtesans grew louder and more suggestive in their body movements. For twenty minutes they danced and shook their obvious attributes before the enthralled audience of soldiers. Then with great fanfare they set pans of glowing coals along the wall, dumped male goat entrails on top, and howled triumphantly as the sickening stench wafted in clouds toward the Romans. They banged their tambourines and screeched Latin phrases at the soldiers gathered below. "Go home, you Roman dogs!" they shouted. And, "You smell like slimy guts!" Their taunts rose to a crescendo until the screaming blended into a frenzied clamor.

Then by some invisible signal, they fell silent.

They stood in a single line staring down at the waiting soldiers.

The men murmured.

One of the courtesans stepped forward. "Want some of this?" she hollered, lifting her dress, revealing herself.

The soldiers laughed and grunted approvingly.

"All you get is this," she shouted, and the whole line turned around, flipped up their tunics, exposing their bare backsides in contempt.

The soldiers cheered and yelled back at the courtesans. But the women on the wall would not be intimidated. They hurled insults and called the Romans every foul name they could think of. They cursed and spit, they kicked the goat entrails over the wall, and some even filled bowls with their urine and flung them toward the Romans. Then the show was over. They filed off the wall, some singing, some still shouting, and many laughing in full contempt.

"Something's wrong here," Vectis said.

Julian looked at him in the fading light.

"The earth ramp is almost complete and ...." He paused. "These people should fear what we will do to them."

"They should," Julian agreed.

"Then why aren't they afraid?"

"I don't know," Julian said slowly. "It does seem odd, doesn't it?"

"Yes. People about to die do not taunt the enemy."

28

Neeve and Sammonicus arrived in Rome at the worst possible time. It was the third hour after sunrise, a time when every entry street to the capital was clogged with vendors, farm carts, and merchants hauling goods to the city's bazaars.

Neeve gaped at the confusion of people in the streets. Like ants, they filled the cobbleways, moving in every conceivable direction, their faces expressionless as they pushed past others moving too slowly, or stepped in front of carts, ignoring the angry drivers who hurled insults and whipped their mules onward. Slaves bearing important clients on litters cut across the main street, trying to find the best routes to their destinations, and scores of messenger boys darted in and out of the bustling crowds, determined to impress their masters with their industry and speed. All along the way shopkeepers had unlocked their storefronts and were pulling out their wares, and hawkers were lighting their sidewalk braziers for peas and sausages. Even a barber had positioned his chair on the thoroughfare as he sheared a youth's hair.

Seated in the back of her carriage, Neeve exhaled in frustration. She could walk faster.

The confusion of languages stunned her. Latin she understood, but the different accents made it hard to grasp, especially when none sounded like the Latin in Britannia. Once or twice she thought she heard the Celtic tongue, but with the squeaking of wheels, the shouts and calls from shopkeepers, and workers jabbering in their native languages, she couldn't locate the speakers. Greek she heard everywhere, even from an adolescent practicing his rhetorical speech somewhere in an upstairs flat. She didn't speak Greek, but she had heard it enough to recognize the musical sounding tones.

They were nearing the city center with its soaring monuments and obelisks, and its massive theaters and bathhouses. Rising above them all Neeve saw a giant set of buildings. "What are those?" she asked. "Palaces?"

"No, Mistress," Sammonicus said. "They are apartments, the Houses of Felicula, the tallest domiciles ever built."

Neeve stared at the huge buildings that dwarfed the structures around them, towering edifices that soared ten to twelve stories in the air, far beyond the reach of the low-hanging brazier smoke. Never had she seen anything like them.

"Where are the commerce buildings?" she asked, refocusing her mind.

"In the forums," he said, "near the Palatine Hill." He pointed toward the lofty peaks that glistened like jewels in the morning sun.

"The emperor's palace," she said slowly, struck with the thought that she could be so near the ruler of the world. She shuddered. All her life she had feared the emperor and his armor-clad soldiers. Some said the emperor was a god, but Vectis had assured her he was mortal, no different from anyone else. But the emperor *was* different. He spoke, and whole tribes ceased to exist. Neeve's own mother and sister, Nes, were taken captive at his word. Were they now slaves somewhere in his Empire? And at this very minute, Taranis was on his way to Rome to amuse this same emperor, a man whose ravenous thirst for blood knew no limits.

"I had a conversation with the emperor one time," Sammonicus said, turning his head.

"You did?"

"In a manner of speaking. He was riding in his carriage, stopping periodically to scatter coins to the crowds. Everyone was crying out, trying to gain his attention, but with all the noise and clamor ..." he threw up his hands to make the point, "it was impossible. So I tried something different. I started the crowds near me chanting: 'No coins, Lord. Turn your eyes upon us.' We chanted it over and over."

"What happened?"

Sammonicus smiled, as if remembering a triumph. "The emperor stopped, rose in his carriage and said, 'All I have comes from you. Take what is yours.' Then he dumped a bagful of coins over our heads."

"A good day for you."

"Yes, because this is a good emperor." He waited at an intersection for a vegetable cart to pass. "Did you know the Senate has bestowed on Emperor Antoninus the title of Pius?"

Neeve said nothing.

"Unusual," Sammonicus said, "but Antoninus is an unusually good man."

An urban soldier approached them. "No carriages beyond this point," he said to Sammonicus. "Pull into that livery." He jerked his thumb toward a narrow, stone building with scores of stalls, and no less than a dozen carriages waiting to be accommodated.

"You stay with the carriage," Neeve said. "I'll be back when I complete my business."

"Oh, no, Mistress, you should not be unaccompanied on the street."

"I like being unaccompanied," she said. "Stay with the carriage."

"But—"

She gave him a look that told him to hold his tongue. Then with her eye on the tiers of palaces, she headed down the street.

Neeve didn't care what rule of Roman etiquette she supposedly breached by being on the street alone, she had private matters to deal with at the legionary records office, and she wasn't about to have Sammonicus breathing over her shoulder when she made inquiries. But there was more to it than that. The truth was, she didn't want Sammonicus to know she was searching for a Roman soldier. So many women in the provinces had children with soldiers stationed in their area; they lived in the camps that had sprung up around the Roman bases. When the soldiers left, so did their financial support. Desperate, the women showed up at the military headquarters, asking if their men had left them any coins. More often than not, they went away empty-handed. Neeve didn't want Sammonicus to think she was like the hapless camp followers.

Of course, Neeve knew she shouldn't care what Sammonicus thought; he was only a servant. But for some reason she did care, and that bothered her.

The crowds in the street grew thicker as Neeve neared the forums of the Caesars, people constantly bumping into her and continuing on their way as if nothing had happened, shopkeepers grabbing her arm to gain her attention, street workers giving her knowing smiles, and beggars thrusting their bowls in her face. She looked around bewildered, her eyes burning from the smoky cooking fires on every corner. In her brief walk she had passed a hundred shops, at least three baths, a dozen temples, arches, stadiums and countless gardens. Overhead, enormous aqueducts brought water from the mountains to the higher elevations of the city. It was a prime example of Roman engineering genius, she had to admit. Aqueduct water was piped to the myriads of fountains in the streets, to the houses of the rich, and to the baths. Then it flowed through the sewers, into cesspits or rivers, cleansing the city.

Neeve plowed through the mobs thronging the narrow streets that wound through the seven hills. Rome was so different from what she had expected. It was noisy, filled with smoke, and dark at the bases of tall buildings. In the provinces Roman engineers had created straight-line roads that seemed to run forever, and in their towns, all the streets formed a remarkable grid. Here, there seemed to be no organization, just street on street, and alleyways a cart couldn't navigate. Magnificent houses stood side by side with poor tenements, and noblemen rented the ground floors of every building, no doubt paying enormous sums for the privilege. How the less fortunate renters ascended to the upper floors, Neeve had no idea. They must have stored ladders somewhere, but she never saw them.

Neeve continued on her way until she reached an intersection with a thick rope stretching across the road and a placard printed in Latin and Greek: "No animals or carts after the second hour. Severe penalties."

She ducked under the rope and continued toward the forums. She rounded the next corner and stopped. Directly ahead of her was a paved plaza, and at its entryway stood an enormous statue of Julius Caesar. She recognized it from smaller versions she had seen in the provinces. Behind the statue rose majestic buildings of pink and yellow marble, broad walkways and parks. Here the sun shone brightly, glinting off gold-tiled roofs and the wings of goddesses perched atop soaring obelisks. Walls glistened with colors Neeve had seen only in Caledonian sunsets: brilliant orange and flaming red. And the gods ... thousands of them graced the walkways and buildings, some carved in marble, some covered with flesh-like material that made them seem alive and breathing. And she saw Asclepios, in the heart of Rome, towering over images of mortals who were beseeching his favors.

Neeve whispered a prayer, but did not approach the Greek god. She had urgent business to attend to and did not want to be encumbered with duties to the god. She would pay him homage later.

She surveyed the plaza and tried to decide where the records office might be. Hundreds of people flowed in and out of the square, some with a dozen slaves fluttering around them, some carried on litters, and some walking alone, their heads down, moving quickly to meetings or places of business. There were as many women as men, and as often as not, they huddled in groups, laughing, covering their mouths in feigned shock on hearing the day's gossip. A collection of ragged boys scurried through the columns of a temple and around the back of a basilica, chased by two urban soldiers.

Neeve decided to approach two priests coming out of a small temple. "May you have good fortune," she said, hoping she had given a pleasing greeting.

The priests ran their eyes over Neeve and kept moving.

"May I ask where I might find ...." Neeve broke off. They were ignoring her and carrying on a conversation as if she weren't even there.

Neeve felt like pulling out her knife and jabbing one of them in the hind parts to gain his attention, but her saner side prevailed. She glanced over at a group of women. But they were so meticulously dressed in white stolas with jeweled brooches and colorful shawls that she guessed they might not be receptive to a woman clad in leather trousers and a rough tunic. She had already heard women in several Roman towns snicker about trouser-wearing peoples from the frontiers.

She walked the length of the plaza thinking, and for the first time noticed several other forums adjacent to this one. She felt overwhelmed by the sheer size of the area; hundreds of buildings crowded the streets in every direction. She had been told the recording office was located in the Roman Forum, but now she had no idea where to begin.

A thought struck her. Soldiers would know the location of an office dealing with legionary records. She glanced around, looking for urban soldiers. Of course, there was none in sight. Then she spied four soldiers guarding a set of marble stairs that led up a tree-covered hill. Her eyes snapped into focus when she realized she was looking at an entryway to the emperor's palace. Above her were tiers of domes and balconies and marble columns of incredible beauty.

Neeve sucked in a breath to calm herself. She started toward the soldiers. As she neared she could tell they were unlike any she had ever seen. They wore scarlet tunics and gilded armor that flashed with every movement. Though they were Roman in appearance, they were tall and broad across the chest. On their heads they wore dress helmets with scarlet plume-like crests that made them seem even larger.

"May you have good fortune," Neeve said as she approached.

"State your business," one of the soldiers said.

"I would like directions to the legionary records office," she said.

"You have no business with us," he said. "Leave now."

Neeve saw his eyes take in the knife strapped on her hip. His face had no expression and his voice was calm, but she felt she should leave. She backed up, and as she did so, she saw one of the soldiers pick up a throwing spear. She turned and started toward the central part of the plaza, her mind racing. She could almost feel a needle-topped spear plunging into her back. These soldiers, the emperor's guards, she supposed, acted as if they had absolute power. Her mouth felt dry but she managed to put one foot ahead of the other. After twenty paces, she relaxed. The soldier had taken up the spear as a precaution.

Urban soldiers! Two of them were patrolling the far side of the plaza. They would know about the records office. She started toward them but couldn't help sneaking a look over her shoulder at the huge scarlet guards. They were still by the marble stairs, heads constantly moving, watching the forum. That's when Neeve noticed that as crowded as the plaza was, nobody passed within ten feet of the marble staircase.

"The legionary records office?" Neeve said, dispensing with her greeting. Politeness was obviously not helping her so she decided on the direct approach.

"Behind Vespasian," a soldier mumbled.

"Vespasian?"

"The Temple of Vespasian," he said. "Beyond the Rostra."

"No," the other soldier said. "Legionary has been moved to Aemilia."

"That's right, Aemilia," the first said, irritated to have been corrected.

"Where is Aemilia?" Neeve asked.

"Basilica Aemilia!" he said, as if a loud voice made everything clear. Then turning away, he hollered at a vendor who was setting up his wares in the wrong place.

Neeve wandered through the crowds in the direction the soldiers had looked. She grabbed a youth by his arm and shouted, "Aemilia. Where is Basilica Aemilia?"

He stared at her, eyes wide, as if a barbarian had seized him.

"Basilica Aemilia?" she repeated, refusing to release his arm.

"The big building beside the Senate," he said, pointing.

She released him and he scurried off.

She ran her eyes over the two story rectangular building as she walked. It was massive. Endless columns held aloft a gigantic bronze tiled roof, and an elaborate frieze stretched across the entire front of the structure. She ascended a series of broad steps and entered the central hall. She swallowed. The hall must have been three hundred feet long, with a marble floor of alternating colors, a heavy gilded ceiling embroidered with gold and silver thread, inner colonnades of colored marble, porticoes and lounging areas for the fashionable to meet, and hundreds of offices along the sides.

Those who strolled the cavernous hall wore equestrian stripes, and not a few displayed the broad stripe of senatorial purple. City officials, clerks, and messenger boys crisscrossed the hall in rapid succession, and bankers spoke in measured tones as they ambled along with their clients.

Neeve stopped a clerk and asked about the legionary records office. He stared at her rough garb, but directed her to an office at the far end of the building.

Neeve entered the doorway and found herself in a large room with tables and dividers, and endless rows of shelves filled with scrolls and papyrus papers. She had coins ready in case a bribe might encourage a clerk to dig deeper, but realized the futility of a bribe the moment she stepped into the office. The legionary records division was ten times the size of Britannia's dingy room and had more than twenty workers. Bribes worked with individuals, not departments.

"You have a query?" The desk clerk was in his fifties and wore a legionary tunic like everyone else in the office. He never bothered rising from his bench.

"Yes," Neeve said. "I want to enquire about my husband—"

"Papers?"

Neeve furrowed her brow.

He breathed out. "Your papers recording the marriage."

"I don't have …."

Somebody called out from behind a shelf, "Another one Marcus?"

"They never stop," the desk clerk replied, shaking his head.

"That's our boys," the voice behind the shelf said. "Marry every barbarian you get your hands on."

"I married a few myself," an older man with a broken nose and few teeth shouted from across the room.

They laughed. It was coarse laughter like that of the legionaries at the bog, and it irritated her. Neeve gritted her teeth and narrowed her eyes. "This is the legionary records office, is it not?"

"Yes," the clerk said, his eyes barely focusing on her.

"And you keep records on the movements of the various legionaries?"

He breathed out and said, "We do."

"Then I would like to know the posting of—"

"I cannot help you," he said.

"Why? Because I have no papers? They were burned—"

"It doesn't matter why you don't have papers. You-need-papers."

"I understand but—"

"Do you know how many women come in here and say they're married to legionaries? You can't claim money, personal items … you can't claim anything without marriage papers."

"I don't want to claim anything," Neeve said, irritated. "I simply want to know where—"

"You are not listening," he said in a singsong voice. "Without proof of relationship, I cannot tell you anything. Those are my orders." He shuffled some boxes around on his table and then disappeared behind the shelving.

"Mistress," Sammonicus cried, "you must let me accompany you the next time you leave this carriage."

Neeve scowled. "All I said was that my business at the legionary records office did not proceed as I had hoped. That was not an invitation for you to join me." She climbed into the carriage.

Sammonicus puckered his lips. "Forgive me," he said, "but I would be a poor personal servant …." He inclined his head to show his concern that he might offend.

"Speak freely."

"Well … a good servant withholds no truth from his master."

"You have a truth to speak, do you?"

Sammonicus moved closer to the carriage. "Mistress," he said, "the truth is you have charming tunics and capes, but you might want more variety when walking about such a fashion conscious city as Rome."

"You think my clothing inappropriate?"

"Of course not. It's just that Roman sensibilities must be taken into account."

Neeve frowned.

"Your attire is perfectly suitable for the provinces, enviable even, but you cannot expect to do business in Rome dressed in, forgive me, tribal clothing."

Neeve looked down at her tunic and trousers.

"You are such a beautiful woman—I speak with all sincerity—and it is a shame not to dress to advantage."

Neeve tried to divorce herself from her pride. She still found it difficult to listen to Sammonicus's advice, even when he was right. "It's true that I encountered an unusual number of ill-mannered people," she said.

"And that is not to your discredit," Sammonicus said. "Romans are notorious for their arrogance and attitudes of superiority."

"So my dress is causing me problems," Neeve said, thinking.

"In Rome one's dress is of paramount importance." He gestured to her clothes. "Your garments have a certain commonness to them that gives others permission to treat you with incivility."

"You might be right."

Seeing her agreement, Sammonicus grew bolder and said, "You are indeed beautiful, but undeniably a tall woman. So when you wear leather boots and trousers, and carry a knife that could kill a bear, you look more like a barbarian warrior than—"

"Enough! I grant your point. I'll purchase new clothes so as not to offend Roman sensibilities."

"A wise decision."

"But I warn you …."

"Yes, Mistress?"

"You know very well. You enjoyed that conversation too much to suit me. See it doesn't happen again."

"Of course, Mistress," he said as he pulled himself into the driver's seat, and then in barely an audible voice he added, "but I did tell you about your clothes."

Neeve pretended not to hear. She could see only the back of Sammonicus's head, but she was certain he was smiling.

"Oh, Mistress, Mistress, Mistress," Sammonicus bubbled, circling Neeve and waving his hands like an excited camel driver. "You are more incredibly beautiful than I could have imagined!"

Not wanting to be outdone, the shopkeeper gushed, "I have never seen a stola fall so gracefully on a woman before. Everything you drape on your person looks like threads spun by the gods."

Neeve felt foolish standing in the center of the shop and hearing such ridiculous things. She refused to look like the silly Roman women in the forum who spent their lives rearranging folds in their gowns, and piling masses of hair on their heads. But she knew she had to adapt if she wanted to find Vectis. The truth was, she had dressed the part of the lady before, long ago, growing up in Londinium. She could do it again.

She would have to swallow her tongue … yes, she could do it again.

How she hated the wives of provincial administrators in Londinium. They displayed themselves like painted dolls, and took extraordinary care to model proper behavior. They were quiet, but never silent; publicly minded, but never politically intrusive. They fawned over their husbands in public, but left shutters unlatched for midnight paramours. Nothing was more important than a comely appearance: coiffured hair, lavish dress, colored cheeks and lips. What a scandal it was for a woman to wander about the markets, plain-faced and hair blowing in the breeze. Proper women whitened their complexions with chalk and oiled their hair with pomatum. Yes, proper women did all the proper things.

From what Neeve had seen in the forum, she knew Roman women were worse.

She gazed curiously in the shopkeeper's silvered mirror. She wore an ankle length tunic, yellow with red embroidery, a red and blue scarf that draped to her knees, gold earrings and necklace inset with semi-precious stones, and soft leather sandals with open toes that reminded her even Rome had its share of chilly days. She turned slowly, her eyes on the mirror. The shawl was too bright for her liking and her sandals too skimpy. The line of her body seemed too obvious, as if she were flaunting herself. But in the end she was pleased. She was glad she had listened to Sammonicus's advice. There was no doubt that people in Rome would more readily accept her as an equal if she dressed like a Roman matron.

"Will you have your hair done in ringlets? Sammonicus asked. "Or piled—"

"No," Neeve said.

"You have achieved so much," Sammonicus said. "It would be tragic if a minor item were allowed to distract from the whole." He wrung his hands. "To be a proper Roman matron, you must consider your hair."

"I dislike plaits, loops, and any of that Roman grease in my hair," Neeve said, curling her lip. "I oiled and perfumed my hair once, and vowed never again to slather that stuff on."

"Perhaps if you tied it back," the shopkeeper said, collecting her hair with his hand. "I have lovely hair pins."

When they left the shop, Sammonicus stuffed Neeve's travel clothes in a bag, along with her two knives. Neeve felt uneasy without a weapon, but in Roman society, her weapons would be silk, perfume, and a smile.

She had spent more than she had expected, purchasing outfits she probably didn't need. She bought Sammonicus several fashionable tunics for his duties as a servant, and sent him to the haircutters and the baths. There was little point in trying to fit into Roman society when her servant looked like a barbarian gravedigger. That afternoon she again headed for the Old Roman Forum. But this time Sammonicus accompanied her, looking unlike himself in his new attire, and wearing a short, Roman-style haircut.

Neeve thought hard about whether to return so soon to the legionary records office. Her better judgment told her to wait a week, or at least give the desk clerk a few days to forget her face, and particularly her Britannic accent. But the clerk had been notably uninterested in her, and she was eager to find Vectis. With her new attire and a servant speaking for her, she was optimistic.

"The legionary records office?" Sammonicus's face looked puzzled. "Why do we need to call on them?"

His inquiring look irritated her. She knew she would have to supply him some kind of information. "You will say I'm inquiring about my brother, Vectis Trebellius Quadratus, a tribune in Britannia."

"Your brother?" His eyes slithered to her Roman wedding ring.

"Yes, my brother," Neeve said. She felt like clubbing him with the back of her hand. "And my name is Sabina Trebellius Quadratus. Can you remember all that?"

His large brown eyes lit with questions but he inquired no further. He was probably wondering whether she had married this Roman soldier, and she was not about to satisfy his curiosity.

"A proper Roman woman never introduces herself," Sammonicus had said, so Neeve waited as her servant entered the records office. "This is Sabina Trebellius Quadratus," he said, "daughter of the late Gaius Trebellius Quadratus, First Centurion of Rome."

Neeve turned her head slightly and nodded to the clerk.

The clerk jumped to his feet and gave her the kind of smile one gives a superior. Attire definitely mattered, she thought. She was pleased with Sammonicus. He remembered everything she had told him, and he spoke with authority, essential in dealing with soldiers. He was still an awful liar, but today, she was thankful, he came off with an air of authenticity.

"My mistress inquires about her brother, Vectis Trebellius Quadratus, tribune in Britannia."

"We need proof of relationship," the clerk said almost apologetically.

"Proof? Don't be absurd!" Sammonicus said indignantly. "There are a half-dozen statues of my mistress's father set up around Rome. Why not ask proof that Antoninus Pius is emperor? Why not ask—"

"That is enough, Sammonicus," Neeve said, trying to use a Roman city accent. "The clerk is doing his duty, and I admire that in a man." She allowed her eyes to linger on him.

He smiled awkwardly.

Sammonicus bowed and said, "Forgive me, Mistress."

Neeve kept her eyes on the clerk and said, "But if you wouldn't mind … my brother's name is Vectis Trebellius Quadratus, last seen in Britannia."

The clerk hesitated.

Neeve formed a smile at the corners of her mouth. "I would appreciate it," she said.

"Of course," he said, and hurried down a row stacked with boxes. He returned immediately. The older man with broken teeth had been listening and had retrieved the Britannia information. "Which fort?" the clerk asked.

"Outpost Faustina," she said.

"Ah, yes, Faustina," he said. He shuffled through a pile of ledgers and pulled out one from near the bottom, and began reading to himself. "Faustina?" he asked, looking up. "You're sure?"

"Yes," Neeve said.

The clerk showed it to the man with broken teeth. He bent his head down so that his nose almost touched the ledger. "Not good," he mumbled.

"I know Faustina was destroyed," Neeve said, "but I was wondering if you have more information. I would like to know where the army stationed Vectis Trebellius after he left Faustina."

The clerk nodded. His eyes remained on the ledger. "It has two rows of names," he said finally, "thirty to forty men it looks like, all killed by the Brigantes while attempting to reach Fort Trimontium, the headquarters of Legion XX, *Valeria Victrix*."

"Is my brother's name …." She stopped, unable to speak her thoughts.

The clerk glanced at the older man. "I am afraid your brother, Prefect Vectis Trebellius Quadratus, is listed among the dead." He looked up. "I am sorry."

Neeve took two steps backwards, trying to distance herself from the message. She found it difficult to wrap her mind around the awful truth. "Some must have escaped," she managed. "There are always soldiers who escape."

The two men exchanged glances and began talking at the same time.

"Soldiers escape all the time," said one.

"That's true," agreed the other.

"Sometimes the records are wrong."

"Or incomplete."

"Yes, incomplete."

"We see it often."

"Often."

But Neeve saw the pity in their eyes. They knew the records were reliable. She left the office in a fog.

For three days Neeve remained in her room at the inn. She left once a day to clean herself and to eat. Sammonicus tried to rouse her interest in a list of events he promised would cheer her like none other, events never before seen, not even in Rome.

But her mind was lost in thought. She was back in Britannia, holding Vectis, loving him, looking into his intense eyes, and marveling that the gods had allowed her such happiness. She remembered promising Vectis on the brows of the ancient gods, that should the blackest darkness befall them, she would never cease loving him. The blackest darkness had befallen them. The gods had deserted them. And Neeve felt so alone.

The torches were burning again outside the inn. Two nights had come and gone, and now this third was all but spent. Her eyes drifted around the tiny room which was lit by a single candle, and she lay curled on her cot, praying for sleep that never came.

It was raining.

She could hear the steady patter on the roof tiles and the occasional roll of thunder. At the first hints of light she pulled herself out of her cot and opened the shutters. Rain bounced off the ledge, spraying her face. She drew back. Outside, the gray sky melted into the gray buildings, and blended with the hunched figures trudging to work, like slaves bound for the mines. One day is like the next, she thought. It never ends.

And then a sparrow chirped.

Somewhere in the crush of buildings, a sparrow had begun to sing. Neeve scanned the overhangs, looking for birds. Nothing. The nearby trees. Still nothing. Then she saw it. A shabby brown little thing perched on a wooden fence that separated two workhouses. Every minute or so it fluffed its body to shed water and keep warm. And it chirped. It chirped often, turning its head as if it were looking for company. In the miserable rain, the sparrow refused to be discouraged. It kept on chirping.

Neeve closed the shutters. She had wallowed in sorrow long enough. Taranis was on his way to Rome and he needed help. She might not have Vectis anymore, but she would find a way to save her brother. And she had a plan.

Later that morning, when the rain had stopped, Neeve and Sammonicus followed the Appian Way south from Rome to the massive estates that stretched across the forested hills. Along the roadsides stood hundreds of tombs, some with statues, some shaped like houses with doors ajar as if to remind the living that the gates of death always remained open.

"Stop!" Neeve cried. She bounded out of the carriage and hopped over the stone curb. Directly in front of her was an eight-foot marble statue of a centurion holding a silver urn, in which, no doubt, were his ashes. She read the words at the base: Gaius Trebellius Quadratus, First Centurion of Rome.

"He *does* have a statue," Sammonicus said, stunned.

"Not a half-dozen," Neeve said, "but he has a statue, and a magnificent one at that." She searched the marble face staring out at the road, and tried to find Vectis in its features, but she saw nothing. She stared at the ground and wondered if Vectis might have stood on the same piece of soil, but in her heart she knew he never made it to Rome. She set her jaw and climbed back into the carriage.

"Whose estate is this?" Sammonicus asked. They were rolling down a long entrance road that bordered a blue-water lake and farmlands that stretched without end.

"Senator Titus Severus," Neeve replied.

"A senator!" Sammonicus fixed his tunic and assumed an excessively erect posture. "You know a senator?"

"Quiet!" Neeve wanted to think. Senator Severus had invited her, but she was feeling uncertain about the invitation. "Visit me at my estate," he had said. But Romans often invited casual acquaintances to their homes, and they surely didn't expect them to show up on their doorsteps. Still, the senator had given an enormous amount of gold to the priests of Asclepios. Would he have done that if she meant nothing to him?

The thought comforted her and when they arrived at the lavish villa, she stepped out of the carriage with a reasonable amount of confidence, dressed in her most expensive stola and scarf.

A man in an exquisitely tailored tunic approached her. "Welcome," he said, bowing. "Who may I say is calling?"

Sammonicus said, "My mistress wishes to speak." Then he turned toward Neeve, his eyes growing large. He had no idea what to say.

Neeve licked her lips. "This is awkward," she said, "but the senator invited me to visit him while he was touring his holdings in Gallia. My name is Neeve mapmaker, but the senator instructed me to say I drew his likeness on a papyrus square. He said—"

"Yes, yes, of course. You are most welcome." He waved his hand to a servant and said, "Fetch the master!"

Neeve had just started toward the entrance when a man appeared at the door and said, "Welcome! My father has told me much about you."

She felt her mouth fall open. The blind tribune who had tried to steal her horse in Britannia was walking toward her; only he was no longer blind.

29

The courtesans bared their breasts and danced in wild frenzy.

For three days Vectis had watched the nightly entertainment with intense interest. The courtesans carried on much the same as they had before except there were no burning goat entrails, and they spent more time insulting the Roman leaders, calling Commodus a pig brain and Mithras, the god Roman soldiers served, a blind fool adrift in the court of asses.

"What's different these last few days?" Vectis asked Julian.

"They aren't burning goat guts because the wind has been blowing the wrong way," Julian said with a smirk.

Vectis smiled.

"And there are more of them."

"There are more," Vectis agreed. He surveyed the line of courtesans and guessed there were over twenty dancing along the wall. One soldier told him the taunting had begun a few weeks earlier with a single prostitute, and had grown in number ever since.

"They keep shouting about our stupidity," Julian added.

"Yes, they do," Vectis said. "I am wondering why."

Julian shrugged. "They can hardly have missed Commodus's blunders when building the battering ram and siege tower. His continual mistakes are reason enough for the nightly party to grow."

"I have another theory. The number of courtesans is growing because more of them are convinced they have nothing to fear. Our siege ramp is almost complete, but for some reason they think it will fail."

"And what would that reason be?"

Vectis shifted his eyes toward the ramp. "I am hoping to discover that tomorrow," he said.

Early the next morning Vectis and Julian headed out to the ramp, the sounds of men hauling and dumping their carts growing louder as they approached. Hundreds of soldiers under wooden canopies designed to ward away projectiles pulled their carts up the ramp and dumped their loads of mud and stones. The smell of newly ripped earth reminded Vectis of spring planting at his villa outside Rome. He hadn't been to the villa for years, but he had fond memories of servants turning and seeding the rich black earth. Here the earth had a pale yellow hue to it, a sticky mixture of clay and stones.

Vectis eyed the archers manning the walls. They seemed entirely content to allow the soldiers to build their ramp, loosing only the occasional arrow at a worker who wandered too far from the canopy. He was confused. Try as he might, he had no idea why the city dwellers should be so unconcerned about an attack.

The entire situation frustrated him. Something was wrong but he couldn't figure out what it might be. He studied the ramp, the walls in front of it, the weapons assembled for the siege, but not one productive thought entered his head. Even if the defenders had built a container barrier to trap soldiers who scaled the wall, it would hardly delay the inevitable. The same could be said for any resistance they might give, or attempts to burn the Roman siege machines. Commodus might be a fool, and his troops undisciplined, but in the end those same troops would do what they were trained to do— breach the wall, burn the city and devastate the inhabitants.

But something was definitely wrong.

The prospect of dying in a week engenders remarkable humility. Yet these people were anything but humble.

Vectis needed a way to peer over the wall, and the only person that could help him was the chief engineer. He surveyed the work site, ran his eyes along the array of tents flapping in the wind, and headed for the largest open tent across from the ramp. He guessed right. The tent served as a command post for engineers building the earthen ramp against the city wall.

The chief engineer was shuffling around the tent, muttering and gesturing angrily at four of his officers. He was a balding, gray-haired man in his fifties who would not have looked out of place in a tavern with a wine cup resting on his swollen stomach. His sole objective seemed to be to please Commodus.

"No details!" he was saying. "I don't want to hear them. This is my last posting and I won't allow any of you to cause me trouble. Set up your winches and pulleys, work day and night, I don't care. But when the Supreme Commander enters this tent two weeks from now, everything had better be in place."

The engineer suddenly noticed Vectis standing outside the tent. His bloodshot eyes jerked toward Vectis. "Who are you?" he demanded.

Vectis turned toward him, revealing the equestrian stripe on his tunic. "Vectis Trebellius," he said, "military tribune."

"Sorry," the engineer mumbled, swatting at a fly near his face. He glanced around, pushed some scrolls off a couch, and invited Vectis to sit down. Vectis declined civilly. After Commodus, Vectis was the senior officer, but he made a point of speaking respectfully to the engineer. He had learned long ago that a wise commander treated well his cooks and engineers.

"A massive operation," Vectis said, glancing toward the earthen ramp, making small talk.

The engineer grunted.

"At least it hasn't rained … makes the hauling and dumping easier."

"Did the Supreme Commander send you?"

The abruptness of the question shocked Vectis, but he managed to keep a neutral voice when he said, "I'm inspecting the progress of the men."

"So you are here on your own."

The comment angered him, but he said nothing.

The engineer allowed a long, exasperated sigh to escape his lips. "No offense," he said, "but I have been through all this with the other tribune. Whatever you think is wrong, whatever you want, I can't help you … not unless it comes through the Supreme Commander. He becomes enraged if I listen to the military tribune on matters that pertain to the siege. I must clear everything with him personally."

"I understand," Vectis said calmly. "I do need your help, but it has nothing to do with the siege."

The engineer folded his arms. "How can I help you?" he asked, giving the strong impression that he was interested in anything but helping Vectis.

"I want to see over that wall," Vectis said, pointing toward the city.

"Over the wall?"

Vectis felt no need to respond to his incredulous look.

"I can tell you right now," the engineer snorted, "the Supreme Commander will not permit me to build on the ramp."

"If not on the ramp, how about—"

A negative expression formed on the engineer's face and he began shaking his head before Vectis could even formulate his question.

"… a temporary scaffold on the siege tower?" Vectis said, finishing his thought. He was sick of the negative attitudes he had encountered since entering Commodus's camp.

"He would not allow that either. Besides, we don't have the manpower to build a siege tower. The attack is scheduled to begin in mere weeks."

"I need something ready before the attack."

The engineer laughed in derision, his belly shaking under his tunic. "Might as well sprout wings."

"There must be some way," Vectis insisted, refusing to grow angry at the engineer's negative face.

"There is no way," he said emphatically.

"I know a way," a young engineer said behind him.

The chief engineer turned on him. "Absolutely not. You have no time to—"

"I have plenty of time," the younger man said, erupting in high-pitched laughter that sounded like a distressed horse.

"No, no, no. If you make a mistake, I'm the one that deals with the Supreme Commander," the chief engineer said. "I have enough trouble on my hands without—"

"I won't make a mistake!" the man screeched.

Vectis blanched. Rarely had he heard a subordinate interrupt his superior, much less raise his voice. Men had been whipped for less.

The chief engineer glowered at the man, but then shrugged. "Handle this if you want," he said, "but make certain you violate none of the Supreme Commander's orders."

"Certainly, Chief Engineer," the man said in an overly loud voice. He was trying to be respectful, but it came off awkwardly.

Vectis ran his eyes over the young man, guessing his age to be no more than twenty. He wore a specially tailored army tunic adorned with jeweled broaches and elaborate clasps, and even though he had an expensive hand-tooled leather belt and ornate sandals, there was a rumpled look about him. He was tall and thin, and his shoulders slumped badly, making it appear as if he had no chest, and he constantly shifted weight from one foot to the other, his hands playing with the folds of his tunic. He looked at Vectis. "Want to know my idea?" he asked, grinning excitedly, seemingly unaware of how odd his behavior might appear.

Vectis beckoned with his hand. "Follow me," he said. "We can talk at the ramp." Vectis moved quickly, irritated at the whole situation. An incompetent self-designated supreme commander who needed to control everything, a chief engineer afraid to make a decision, and now this juvenile impersonating a Roman officer. The boy was anything but normal, with a half grin permanently pasted on his face, and a nervous horse-laugh spilling out at odd times. Still, the best engineers Vectis had known were unquestionably out of the round. He hoped it was a good sign.

At the ramp Vectis turned on the man and said, "The chief engineer thinks you make mistakes. Do you?"

"I'm the best engineer here," the youth said, offended.

Vectis held his eyes.

"I am! You can ask anyone."

"And the mistakes?"

"He's not talking about engineering mistakes."

"Then what?"

The youth shrugged. "The chief engineer gets upset when I do things that offend Commodus."

"I see," Vectis said. It was the first time he had heard anyone refer to Commodus by anything other than Supreme Commander. "I would think Commodus would punish you himself for offenses," Vectis said, using the name.

The engineer laughed awkwardly again, this time sounding like a child caught stealing honeyed bread. "He's afraid of me," he said, covering his mouth with his hand and opening his eyes in feigned shock.

"And why would that be?"

"Well, it's supposed to be a secret," he said in hushed voice, "but since everyone knows, I suppose I can tell you."

Vectis waited.

"I know people."

Vectis gestured impatiently for him to continue. He was growing tired of the game.

"My father … is the emperor's brother."

Vectis ran his eyes over the youth and said, "Well, that certainly explains it."

"His favorite nephew," he added, chuckling, "so my father says."

Vectis gave him an amused look. "So when you offend Commodus, the chief engineer and not you suffers for the transgression."

"That's the way it's turned out, yes."

"But the chief engineer still becomes angry with you."

"Very angry. My father told him not to spare the discipline … so I have to listen to him." He writhed in his clothes as if ants were crawling up his back. Then in a petulant voice he said, "At least my position allows me to do things no one else will … like this project of looking over the wall. If anyone else tried to help you, Commodus would call it an infringement on his authority … oh, yes, I have seen it many times. But because it's *my* project, he will say nothing." He horse-laughed again. "He might holler at the chief engineer, but he'll never bother us."

Vectis glanced up and down the wall. "Are you saying we can build something on the ramp?"

"No, not on the ramp. The chief engineer would never allow it."

"Then tell me your plan."

"It's dangerous."

"Go on."

"Well, the chief is right," the young man said, pulling at his tunic. "Nothing safe can be built in a few weeks with the manpower we have. To be able to see over the wall requires proper construction, and construction takes time and laborers. We have neither."

"And the dangerous way?"

His high-pitched laughter grated on Vectis's ears. "Well, it occurred to me that I could limb a couple of trees, bind them together and insert the structure into a hole."

"Would that work?" Vectis was wondering whether his strange behavior was not a sign of genius, but of lunacy.

"I think so," he said. "Depends on how much of the city you want to see."

"The section behind the ramp."

"How much of a blind zone behind their wall can you tolerate?"

"How about no blind zone?"

"With no blind zone at any reasonable distance from the wall, your pole would have to be a thousand feet tall." Again, his annoying laugh.

"Explain."

His engineer's eyes blinked rapidly. "When you look down on the wall from an angle," he said, "there will always be a blind zone from the base of the inside wall for a certain number of feet."

Vectis nodded.

"So you need a blind zone."

"Okay, fifty feet."

"A blind zone of fifty feet?"

"Yes."

"How far from the wall do you want to plant the pole?"

Vectis glanced at the broad band of open space surrounding the city wall, thought about their archers trying to pick off someone climbing the pole, and knew he needed no less than two hundred feet distance. "About a hundred feet," he said. Any farther, he guessed, would require an impossibly tall tree. "Figure planting the pole a hundred feet from the wall."

"The wall is forty feet high," the engineer said slowly, his eyes squinting in thought, "the pole a hundred feet distant with a blind zone of fifty … that means the tree pole has to be one hundred and twenty feet tall."

"One hundred and twenty feet? Is that possible?"

"Of course. But it might take some time. Oaks here can reach eighty feet but that only gives us about sixty above the ground because I would need to trim the top some, and then support it with a ten-foot hole and piled stones. To reach one hundred and twenty feet I would use two trees, overlap and bolt them together, and then bind them with rope. It would sway a bit …." He brought his hand to his face, stifling a grin. He could see Vectis's disapproval. "Actually, it might sway a lot," he said. His face turned serious as he tried to reassure Vectis. "But new trees should hold. All this of course assumes little or no wind."

"And with wind like today?"

He rolled his eyes toward the sky as if he were measuring the currents in the air. "The climb would fail. Above a hundred feet anyone climbing would create too much strain on the pole, the arc would increase, and it would snap."

"Suppose the pole is fifty feet from the wall," Vectis said.

"The pole would only have to be eighty feet high," he said instantly, "but at fifty feet the archers would pick him off easily."

Vectis found his eyes on the ground, staring at a lump of clay. He was wondering whether a shield might protect against the archers.

"The land around the city looks level," the engineer volunteered, "but it's not. There's a swelling on the other side of the ramp that relative to the wall is about forty feet higher than here. It's little more than seventy feet from the wall and with the same blind zone, I would need a tree pole of only fifty-five to sixty feet."

"One tree?"

"More stable than bolting two together."

"Good," Vectis said. Find a tree and start cutting."

The engineer gave him a silly grin.

"What's wrong?" Vectis asked.

"Trees that size are a good distance from here. It's going to take some time."

"Then get a crew of men and start moving," Vectis said.

"And even when we find a good tree," he said, clawing at the ants on his back, "we're talking about placing it less than seventy feet from the wall. Their archers will—"

"Let me worry about the archers."

"Of course, you can worry about them. I'll worry about the engineering." He cleared his throat. "But you should know that if someone sixty feet up jerks away from an arrow, he could create a stability problem, especially in high winds."

"Yes, that's why I intend to have you test it first."

The engineer stopped pulling at his clothes. His half smile disappeared, replaced by a frozen look of fear.

Vectis placed his hand on the youth's shoulder. "Have no fear," he said. "Your responsibility will be to build the tower. Someone else will do the climbing."

"And who might that fool be?" the engineer asked, his grin returning.

"You're looking at him," Vectis said.

30

Taranis sat cross-legged on a bed of straw the soldiers had dumped into the cage. The straw came from farmers' barns along the way, and usually it was already dirty or caked in wet clumps when it was thrown through the bars. They never changed the straw, just heaved more in when it suited them. They left it to Taranis and his men to push out the more foul parts. Taranis stared mindlessly at the trees and rocks as the cart rolled along the Roman road. How long had he and his fellow commanders been traveling? Eight weeks? Ten? He didn't know. All he knew was that the scenery everywhere looked the same.

Senior officer Manius Nepos Falco rode at the head of the procession, his pudgy body molded to the saddle like lumpy clay. He never ceased talking about his older brother Mamercus Nepos Falco who was killed at Outpost Faustina. Taranis had no idea who the man might have been, and he didn't care. If he was anything like Manius Nepos, the grave was the perfect place for him.

Taranis often thought about Neeve and Cronn, even prayed to the gods that they would be spared. He had always felt a special bond with his sister, almost from the day she was born. How many times had he heard her little voice calling out, "Wait for me, Taranis, wait for me," and more often than not, he left her behind? Now he would give anything to see her again.

But she was safe—he truly believed it—and it made his journey to Rome bearable. Cronn had found her and together they had headed north, deep into the highland mountains where no Roman would dare to go. Maybe they had even settled on the old Caledonian homestead, maybe planning a life together. And maybe not. Neeve seemed determined to find her Roman officer, a foolish idea to Taranis's way of thinking. How much better would Cronn be for a mate? He was bigger, stronger, and he was a Caledonian.

The cart stopped.

The second in command was arguing again with Nepos. He confronted the senior officer often, but only when he thought no one was watching. Today was different, more urgent. Taranis strained to hear, but his Latin was still poor and he had a difficult time deciphering words spoken quickly. But he had no doubts about the subject: treatment of captives. It was always about treatment of captives.

After the bee incident, Nepos had kept his promise to inflict the cruelest punishments he could short of death. Often he stood outside the cage and jabbed their bodies with sharpened sticks, or beat their backs with rods until they collapsed. When they passed through a gorge, he sometimes stopped the cart so he could climb the rocks to urinate on their heads. Once he withheld water for days and then parked the cart beside a stream. And he regularly rolled their food in dirt or horse dung, and placed the cart downwind from the fire so they would breathe smoke all night. He even threw hot coals at them, causing the straw to burst into flame. Taranis had become used to the layers of grease on his body, but not to the smell that clung to him like a rotting corpse, and he bided his time, waiting for his captors to make a mistake.

"What are they arguing about?" a warrior asked.

Taranis shook his head. "Something about that river ahead," he said.

Nepos dismounted and came striding back to the cart, the translator behind him. "Rome tomorrow," Nepos announced. "But before we enter the eternal city, I have a duty to wash the barbarian stink from your bodies."

The second in command completed his translation and walked away, turning his back on Nepos. He always obeyed the senior officer, but he always made his dissatisfaction clear. Now the soldiers were unhitching the horses and pulling the cart off the road toward a mud slope that led down to the river. Taranis eyed the slope, thinking only dark thoughts.

The cart began to roll. The Caledonians grabbed the iron bars to steady themselves as the cart picked up speed. Taranis breathed in and out rapidly, filling his lungs until he was dizzy. He could see what Nepos had planned. The cart bounced down the slope toward the river, veering this way and that, jerking the warriors off their feet. Near the bottom, a wheel caught on a rock, overturned the cart and propelled the cage into the air

Taranis grasped for the iron bars and braced himself for the collision with the water. The cage hit with a splash, wobbled, and then plummeted to the bottom. The warriors in the cage mashed against the front bars, then scrambled toward the top, trying to shove their faces between the bars to get air as the cage sank. Taranis didn't move. He held his breath and closed his eyes as the icy water covered him. He kept telling himself Nepos needed them alive. He had orders from Julius Verus to deliver the Caledonians alive for his Triumph. This had to be another of his punishments, he reasoned.

The Caledonians thrashed and twitched as their lungs filled with water. More than once a foot or knee caught Taranis in the head, but still he clung to the bars, trying to calm his pounding heart. A minute passed, maybe two. Any second now, he told himself. Any second.

His lungs burned.

He couldn't hold on.

He needed air!

Then he felt a tug. They were dragging the cage out. He was desperate. They had to pull faster! His arms and legs writhed. He clawed at himself. He had to breathe! Now!

His head broke through the surface and he gasped for air. One of the Caledonians also burst through the water, coughing and bringing up his insides. The rest floated like fish in a stagnant pond. Taranis sipped the air and with eyes closed, he allowed his body to rock with the movement of the cage.

Shouts. The Romans were scurrying to rescue the drowned men. They opened the cage and dragged everyone onto the riverbank except the man retching in the center of the cage. Moving quickly, they positioned the bodies so their heads were lower than their feet. Then two Roman soldiers went to work on each Caledonian, pressing on his back, moving his arms. One by one the men disgorged their lungs onto the grass. They were still in spasms when the soldiers hauled them back to the cage and threw them in.

"You see, I told you, everyone alive." It was Nepos's voice.

"Two left still," replied the translator, "and one of them is Taranis."

The soldiers working on Taranis redoubled their efforts, pressing harder and rotating his arms in larger circles.

Taranis remained limp, listening to Nepos talk as he approached.

"Get his feet higher! Press harder than that."

Taranis waited.

Nepos was beside him now.

"Out of the way," Nepos said, thumping a soldier on his back. Nepos dropped to his knees and drove the heel of his palms repeatedly into Taranis's back.

Taranis opened his eyes a crack. The soldiers were standing in a circle, but too far to stop him. He twisted suddenly, swinging his arm behind and knocking Nepos onto his back. Then, springing on top of the chubby officer, he snatched away his dagger. The soldiers jerked out of their shock and started to move, but Taranis already had the dagger under Nepos's chin.

"Translator!" Taranis yelled. "Tell them to hold ground."

The translator said something in Latin and the soldiers stepped back.

Taranis could hear Nepos whimpering, but ignored him. "Translator," Taranis said, "I want your weapons and your horses. If I do not get them I will cut your commander's head off his shoulders."

"Cannot do that," the translator said.

Nepos was having trouble swallowing. He said something rapidly to the translator, which Taranis guessed was an order to surrender because the translator shook his head and spoke harshly to him.

"Make your decision," Taranis said.

"I have already made it," the translator said. "The loss of an officer is regrettable, but I will not surrender this unit. If you kill the commander, these soldiers will kill you, and then all your warriors will die. Do you understand? How many were on those ships? A thousand? Legate Julius Verus promised that after the Triumph, he would conscript them into the auxiliary forces as free men. But if you die ...."

"If I die, Verus will not have his Triumph," Taranis said, but he knew his comment was futile.

"He will have his Triumph," the translator said. He pointed at the chieftains locked in the cage. "He has them and a thousand warriors ... and he will kill every last one. Is that what you want?"

Taranis lowered the dagger. His rage toward Nepos had blinded him. He could not allow his warriors to die, and he knew it.

"Drop the dagger onto the ground," the translator said, "and release the officer."

Nepos pulled away and rose to his feet, grinning.

Taranis glanced at the translator and said, "I will spare his life." Then he jerked Nepos back to the ground, flipped him over, and jammed the dagger through the fleshy part of his buttocks.

31

"Follow me," the formerly blind tribune said, smiling.

Neeve and Sammonicus followed the tribune into the largest atrium she had ever seen. Reception halls in most villas were Spartan affairs with few couches and tables, open roofs, and walls of stone — not a place to linger in the cold months. Neeve couldn't help staring at the centerpiece as she entered the room. The atrium had the usual square opening in the roof to let in rain, but instead of a simple basin to catch the water, a nymph cut from translucent yellow crystal held aloft a golden sphere. It looked as if you could see through the stone. Neeve approached the statue reverently. She reached out to touch the nymph's wings, but drew her hand back, unsure whether the gesture might be inappropriate.

"By all means," the tribune said, motioning her to do as she pleased. "I know little about carving, but I do know that the Greeks breathe a certain life into their statues that the Roman hand could never duplicate. This was sculpted three hundred years ago in Attica, mainland Greece."

"It's beautiful," Neeve murmured, tracing her fingers along its leaf-thin wings. She stepped back and glanced around the atrium. At least a dozen couches graced the edges of the room, and skillfully painted frescoes adorned the walls and outer edges of the ceiling. Through her thin sandals Neeve could feel heat emanating from the mosaic floor, and the walls were warm to the touch.

"The Severus household is honored by your visit," the tribune said.

"Thank you," she said.

Neeve took a breath to summon her strength. Her situation was truly awkward, but she determined to follow through on what she had started. Who but a senator could help save Taranis? Yet, she felt an overwhelming apprehension as she tramped brazenly into the house of Severus. The father had rescued her from the street with no thought of reward, and yet at her hand the son had suffered extortion—the sum of a hundred gold aurei!

She lowered her eyes. This same tribune who was instructing servants to bring food and the best wine would soon discover he was entertaining the barbarian Celt from Caledonia. Then what could she say?

Neeve burned a small amount of incense at the lararium in the corner of the atrium. She had been in Roman homes enough to respect the household spirits when she entered. Oddly, the tribune didn't join her in her veneration but waited until she had finished.

"Please," he said, motioning, "be seated."

Neeve chose a bench-like couch with some firmness to it and handed Sammonicus her shawl. He folded it neatly on a table and then positioned himself a judicious distance away from his mistress, far enough to give the illusion of privacy, but close enough to attend her every need.

She raised her eyes to the tribune across from her. She could still see him sword in hand, his back to her horse, squinting into the dark, trying to focus his damaged eyes. He looked less menacing in a social setting, she thought, especially with a clean tunic, a fresh shave, and his easy smile. With his blindness, Neeve had felt a measure of control over the tribune, but now she could see he had a strong, athletic-looking body, and it was nothing more than the will of the gods that she had escaped with her life. His face had mostly healed, she noted, except for two small burn marks above his right eye.

"My name is Marcellus," he said. "My father has spoken of you so often I had begun to think I knew you intimately."

Neeve smiled and her lips stuck to her teeth. She tried to relax. It was difficult. She had wrenched an enormous amount of gold from the man, and she was wondering what his reaction would be if he were to discover the truth. She shook away her dark thoughts and reminded herself that in the end she had saved his life. That should count for something. Still, the pride of a Roman patrician knew no bounds. She had saved his life, but she had also made a fool of him, stripping him of his gold, and in the process bruising his sense of patrician superiority.

How many times had she heard Romans tell the story of the arrogant Julius Caesar when he was a twenty-two-year-old patrician? Mediterranean pirates captured him and demanded twenty gold talents for ransom. Caesar protested, telling them to increase their demands to fifty talents, which they did. When the pirates received their fifty talents, Caesar befriended them, ate and drank with them, played games with them, even read them poems. He also jokingly told them he would have them all killed. After they spared his life, he hunted them down and crucified the whole band, leaving them writhing naked on stakes in the hot Mediterranean sun.

That's how Roman patricians dealt with barbarians. They smiled, but they avenged their family name.

Neeve eyed her host. How would this patrician react if he discovered she was the Celt from Britannia?

He looked pleasant enough when he said, "I confess I'm at a loss. My father spoke well of you, but unfortunately, he could not recall your name."

"Neeve," she said. "My name is Neeve." She realized she should have given her name after he volunteered his, but her mind was functioning poorly. She did have the sense to avoid designating herself as mapmaker, the way she did to the servant as she entered the compound. That would surely have piqued his interest, and she was not yet ready for that.

"My father described you favorably," he said, handing her a goblet of wine, "but age must be diminishing his sight. He said you had golden hair, were pleasant to look at, and wore barbarian clothing, and that you carried yourself as if you belonged to the gilded circle of Imperial women." He laughed and shook his head. "Without increasing your discomfort … you are so much more than that, and I welcome you to our villa."

Neeve nodded her thanks. "Your father is an exceptional man," she said.

"He keeps your drawing in his library ... on the wall in a special place. I will show you later. It's astonishing how you captured his likeness."

"Thank you," she said. She wondered how long it would be before her speech would betray her. Not long, she guessed, even with her attempt to use a Gallic accent. The safest course would be to speak to the senator directly—away from his son—explain about Taranis, and see if he might be willing to help. It was exceedingly presumptuous to approach the senator when he had already done so much, but she had nowhere to turn. "When do you expect your father?" she asked.

"Tonight, possibly tomorrow," he said. "He's dealing with senatorial business in Rome."

Neeve sipped her wine and sampled the goat cheese on warmed spikes of bread. Senator Severus was away until the next day, and here she was, trapped with a man who could destroy everything for Taranis. She could hardly pop up and announce that she had to leave, not without offending him. Civility demanded she stay for a time and make small talk before she bolted out the door. She smiled and nodded toward the cheese. "Very good," she said.

"You are from Celtic extraction?" he asked.

"Yes, Celtic," she said, trying to keep her answers brief.

"My heritage is Latium," he said. "Not very interesting. My ancestry stretches back a thousand years in this area, and some claim we are from the family of Serranus. Of course, we have detractors who question our Latium roots. They claim we come from Dalmatia, across the Adriatic Sea ... and why am I boring you with such trivia?"

"You were not boring me," she said.

"Yes, I was," he replied, "but you are kind to disagree." He swallowed some wine. "You have a pleasant accent, from Britannia I would guess."

"Yes," she said. Already her attempt to sound like a native from Gallia had failed.

"I was stationed in Britannia as a tribune."

"Oh?"

"I spent time in the northern Caledonian territories."

"Interesting."

"I thought it would never stop raining," he said, laughing.

She laughed too.

"I saw an ancient circle of stones in southern Britannia," he said. "Quite amazing. The locals believe the gods carried the stones to their present location, and I half believe it. They were massive monoliths, greater than anything in the Empire." He paused and looked at her. "Did you ever come across them?"

"No, sorry."

"Where did you live in Britannia?" he asked.

"Londinium," she lied. Her answers were as clipped as she could make them, but she was concerned. She had anticipated small talk. Yet his interest in her background ranged beyond the bounds of simple curiosity. Even Sammonicus had noted his pointed questions. His brown eyes moved restlessly.

Marcellus smiled. "It's strange ... your speech ... seems so familiar to me. I have not had occasion to think about Britannia for some time, but now everything has come flooding back. You sound so much like the native peoples there."

"Yes, Britannia-born peoples sound much alike," she said.

He ran his fingers through his thick hair and shifted his eyes around the atrium, as if he were thinking. "It's odd the way things stick in the mind."

"Yes, like childhood memories," she said, trying to distract him, but taking care not to give a lengthy response. She glanced toward the entryway. She had to leave, and soon. It would be terribly rude to stuff the bread into her mouth and run out the door. But what option had she? If she spoke one more word ....

"You remind me of someone ... it really is uncanny," he said. "You remind me of someone I met in Britannia. She drew pictures as well, called herself a mapmaker."

"A mapmaker?" Neeve said. "An unusual trade." She placed her goblet on a table and said, "I have had a pleasant time. With your permission I will leave and return tomorrow to meet with your father." She glanced at Sammonicus whose swarthy face had turned ashen.

"I suggested she draw my likeness someday," he said, undeterred. "But we parted soon after and I never saw her again." He shrugged. "Actually, I never saw her to begin with because I had been blinded in battle." He motioned to the burn marks above his eye. "She took me to a Roman installation ... saved my eyes ... saved my life."

Her mind raced. "A fascinating story," she said.

"But I wasn't totally blinded," he said. "I could see shadowy images when my bandages were off. The woman was tall and had long flowing hair, much like you."

Neeve leaned back on her couch. She thought about her fine Roman stola, her expensive shawl and sandals. She had even threaded her hair with a gold braid. None of it helped. He knew. He knew from the moment she formed her first words, and no change of accent could fool him. Without sight, she supposed, his other senses were greatly enhanced, and he remembered her voice.

It was time to stop lying; it would only worsen her cause. "I suppose her hair was blond or red like most Celts," she said with a true Britannic accent.

"Blond, I think," he said almost inaudibly. But she could see he was thinking.

"And her voice sounded much like mine."

"It did."

"I'm glad your sight returned," she said. "I knew the gods favored you."

He stared at her, tilting his head slowly, but never taking his eyes off her face. He was having a difficult time believing what he knew to be true.

"You said if we ever met, I would be the only one to know it. That wasn't quite true, was it?"

"It is you!" he said, gripping his couch.

She opened her eyes slightly, but said nothing.

He started to speak, but stopped, looking confused. "You ... you are the Caledonian Celt," he said at last. "You went back ...." His eyes stared at her without comprehending. "How did you … my father found you dying on the street … you were in Gallia."

"I crossed the island channel in a ship," she said.

"After the battle with Julius Verus," he said, understanding.

"Yes," she said. "You were right about your general from Germania. His three legions destroyed our army, made slaves of the rest."

He nodded.

She found herself looking at the mosaic flooring with nothing to say.

"I know why you came to Rome," he said.

She looked up.

"To find your officer from Outpost Faustina … Vectis Trebellius Quadratus. I remembered his name." He motioned to her ring. "Your husband, I take it."

"The Brigantes tribesmen killed him," she said quietly.

"I know," he said. "I thought if he were in Rome, I might meet him, tell him about our little adventure together. I sent a man to the records office … I am sorry."

She couldn't reply. The wound was too fresh. She tried to picture Vectis smiling at her the way he so often did, but all she saw were the somber tombs along the Appian Way. "I must go," she said abruptly. She rose and tried to maintain some sense of dignity as she waited for Sammonicus to place the shawl over her shoulders.

"The afternoon is all but gone," Marcellus said. "Even the Appian Way can be dangerous at night. The evening meal is already in preparation for you."

She managed a smile when she said, "You of all men should know that I am no stranger to a darkened road."

"I grant that," he said, "but I implore you to stay the night. If not for your sake, at least for my father's. He will be distressed to have missed you. And he will worry about you traveling on the road, especially when you might have stayed here."

She paused.

Encouraged, he added, "Believe me, your presence will lift his spirits."

She scolded herself. In her self-pity, she had never even considered how the old senator might feel. And Taranis? Would he not be better served if she followed Roman customs? She would stay, and tomorrow, if all went well, she would pluck up her courage and approach Senator Severus.

Senator Severus arrived as Neeve was preparing for bed. A servant tapped on her door and informed her the senator was delighted to have her taking ease in his home and would greet her in the morning. Apparently, the senator had little fear traveling after dark. Guards, Neeve supposed.

Earlier that day, Neeve had dined with Marcellus and then toured the villa. Their meal was simple but extraordinarily tasteful. Fresh fish with a tangy sauce Neeve had never before tasted, wheat bread baked with cheese, raw cabbage, radishes, beans and marrows, and then warm honey cakes topped with nuts. They also had a dark beer instead of wine. And one other item, they ate sitting up on soft chairs, rather than reclining. Neeve suspected Marcellus had tried to provide a more Celtic-like atmosphere to please her.

The villa, Neeve discovered, was more like a farm than a residence, producing grain, figs, and olives, and an enormous amount of grapes. As far as she could see, the grapevines grew, row after row, mile after mile on the gently sloping hills. But her greatest surprise came when Marcellus took her to a stone building in the middle of a field. Inside were a set of stairs that descended fifteen feet under the ground, to a warren of tunnels where they stored wine in wooden barrels. It was cool and dry, and Marcellus said the temperature never varied on the coldest or hottest days of the year.

The primary residence for the Severus family was in the heart of Rome, where the senator could more easily attend to his senatorial duties. Marcellus managed the family villas, so Neeve had been fortunate to arrive on a day when the senator had planned to visit his son.

The next morning a servant escorted Neeve to an open courtyard where she was wrapped in heated blankets and served steaming herb tea, hot porridge mixed with preserved peaches and grapes. Sammonicus was treated as a guest as well. They gave him his own couch at the edge of the courtyard and servants to attend him. Protocol demanded that with strangers or new acquaintances, Neeve's personal servant should be near to defend her. The thought amused her, as if Sammonicus could defend anyone.

"There you are!"

Neeve turned to see Senator Severus and Marcellus walking arm in arm toward her. The senator's face glowed when he said, "Marcellus complains that my description of you was woefully inadequate, but I can see he was wrong. You are exactly as I remember, bright-eyed and incredibly beautiful."

Neeve smiled. "The last time you saw me, my Lord, I should imagine I was the pallid color of death."

"Yes, I remember."

"But you saved me, Lord, you and the great god, Asclepios, blessed be his name."

"Blessed be his name," the senator agreed. He grasped her hands warmly and beamed into her face. Then he accepted his heated blankets and said, "What is this I hear about you saving my son from certain death in Britannia?"

"Your son exaggerates," she said, "but for whatever small part I played, it was the will of the Fates, as you Romans would say."

"Indeed," the senator said.

Neeve sipped her tea. She avoided mentioning the hundred aurei she had extracted from Marcellus, fearful it might embarrass him. The senator was undoubtedly a quality man, but he was Roman, and when it came to Romans, Neeve had learned to be careful.

"You will stay through the summer," the senator said, nodding as if they had agreed to the arrangement. "Longer if you like," he added.

"Oh, no, my Lord," Neeve said, shocked by the invitation. "I came for but a visit." She found it difficult in Roman society to distinguish between etiquette and a true invitation.

The senator furrowed his brow and said, "Marcellus tells me it required all his skill to dissuade you from setting off on the night road. Can this be so?"

"It is, my Lord."

"Then how can I present my invitation in a way that would induce you to stay? Perhaps if I tell you that you would do us great honor to be our guest."

"I am truly honored by your invitation," she said, "but I cannot impose on your kindness." To accept, she knew, would be to receive yet another kindness from the senator. How could she approach him about Taranis when her debt was so great? It would be better, she reasoned, to have the scales more evenly balanced. The senator had saved her life, and she had saved the son.

"Your presence is no imposition," the senator said. "A cohort of Praetorians could be housed on this villa and go unnoticed."

Neeve smiled, uncertain what she should do.

"Do you have other engagements?" he asked.

"Nothing specific, but—"

"Then it's settled," he said, smiling warmly. "I am a senior senator of Rome, and one advantage of so vaunted a position is that I have my way."

"Then, Lord, I am trapped," Neeve said. "I accept your gracious invitation, but as for the duration, I leave that to the gods."

"Let us drink to the gods," the senator said, holding up his cup of tea.

"To the gods," Neeve said.

"I prefer to drink to our guest," Marcellus said.

32

Balbinus smiled broadly. The day had been proceeding wonderfully. He and Calpurnia had received a note from Brutus saying he had located his partner, had organized a meeting, and would conclude business in due course. For Balbinus, the end of the wretched Trebellius would be like the end of a long day. He was tired of having nothing to report to Senator Coelius, as if he couldn't handle a troublesome situation. But events were drawing to a close, and he was glad.

"You have rented a boat?" Calpurnia said. They were standing on the bank of the Tiber in the shadow of the enormous Theater of Marcellus.

"Three, actually," Balbinus said. "For your maids and my manservants … to minimize our inconvenience."

"Thoughtful, as always," she said.

"This is not just another outing," Balbinus said. "Today I have something special to show you."

"Something special," Calpurnia said. "Hmm, I wonder what it could be?" She eyed the flat-bottom boats. "It's upriver," she said, "or we would have no need of so many rowers."

"True," Balbinus said.

"And there's a large basket … food and wine for the day, I would guess. So we are definitely not stopping at the parks in the Campus Martius. Yes … something north of the city … but not too far because we have promised ourselves to Senator Saufeius Ahala, and we dare not miss one of his gatherings."

"True again," Balbinus said. "You are as alert as ever, but you shall not gain my surprise, because it's something that comes to Rome not once in ten years."

"Not once in ten years," Calpurnia said, her blue eyes locked onto his. She smiled quizzically. "What gossip did I miss at recent celebrations?"

"You missed nothing," Balbinus said proudly, "because what I am privy to, few in Rome know."

"Indeed." She squeezed his arm. "You must give me a hint," she said. "Is it a special garden? A statue? A performance of note?"

"None of those," he said. "It's something alive and breathing."

She furrowed her brow and said, "A colorful bird, or a parrot, yes, a talking parrot from a dark jungle."

He shook his head.

"Then it has to be an exotic animal," she said, "perhaps from beyond the Parthian Empire? Or one of those man-eating fish we've heard about."

"It is exotic, to be sure. You will find none of its kind in Rome."

"Not a fish, not an animal, not a bird, yet it breathes … it must be a human of strange manner."

Balbinus clapped his hands. "You have guessed well. But I must show you my surprise. It's a person of special note for a very special day."

They traveled up the Tiber for over an hour until they reached an abandoned gladiatorial school that seemed to be guarded for no reason. Hundreds of soldiers moved briskly about the grounds, and more were busy renovating the yellow stucco buildings. Balbinus helped Calpurnia from the boat, and together they strolled toward the compound, their crowd of servants following at a discreet distance.

"Your surprise is here?" Calpurnia said.

He nodded, but knew the rundown buildings had left her unenthused. "What I am about to show you," he said, rubbing his hands like a hawker at a bazaar, "will be the talk of Rome in the coming days. I happened on the information in the baths yesterday. Senator Publius Coelius has become quite friendly of late, whether because he sees me as a potentially strong ally, or because he and I have a similar interest in dealing with Trebellius, I don't know. But he told me something known only to the emperor and a few senators." He looked at her, waiting for a response.

"The mighty of this world are seeking you out," Calpurnia said.

He nodded, pleased. He thought the same thing. Increasingly, he was being drawn into the inner ring of power. They were trusting him, relying on him. He licked his lips and couldn't help swelling his chest when he said, "There will be a Triumph this summer."

"A Triumph? How wonderful!"

"Emperor Antoninus has granted Legate Julius Verus a Triumph in the month of Augustus. Julius Verus! He's the emperor's greatest general, and he'll be here in Rome for the summer."

"I've heard of him," Calpurnia said. "He was in Germania for a time."

"He has been everywhere," Balbinus said, "most recently in Britannia. And yet, I have never met the man."

"He has never met *you*," Calpurnia said, correcting him. "I should not undervalue myself if I were you. Gaius Balbinus is a man with unlimited possibilities. He dines with the exalted, and one day he shall be exalted." She patted his arm. "Never forget that some are born to power; others seize it by the throat. The Senate is within your grasp. You must believe that. In the not too distant future, you shall stride through the forums wearing the broad purple stripe and the red sandals weighted with pearls."

Calpurnia's words sent a surge through his body. He kissed her on the cheek. When she was near he felt as if he could climb Tivoli's heights and swim the length of the Tiber. "You must purchase new gowns," he said, "and jewelry ... rings, brooches, necklaces, whatever you need for the Triumph. A woman as attractive as you deserves to be dressed in patrician finery."

"You are generous," she said, pressing into him, "but I have adequate apparel for the summer. I might need a few items ...."

"Of course, whatever you deem necessary," he said. He never wanted to treat her like a mistress on an allowance. "My pleasure increases with your happiness ... and I promise our summer will be like none other, filled with celebrations, dinner parties, processions. It will be a time of great joy."

Her eyes glittered and it gratified him. "I know you have questions," he said.

"Yes," she said. "Who is this special person that compels us to journey up the Tiber? Let me guess. You have the famous general, Julius Verus, tethered like a goat to a pole in one of those shacks?"

"Not Julius Verus," he said, "but somebody almost as intriguing."

Her face crinkled in curiosity.

As they moved closer to the buildings, the number of soldiers grew, and so did her curiosity, Balbinus was delighted to see. "Senator Coelius told me the Triumph will include a thousand Caledonian warriors and many chieftains. The warriors are scheduled to arrive sometime in the next month—that's why the soldiers are rebuilding the enclosures. But the chieftains have already arrived." He ran his eyes over the buildings, found the one he was looking for, and said, "Follow me."

Balbinus showed the guards a note from Senator Coelius, affixed with the heavy Senate seal. They nodded and opened the door. Inside were a dozen or more soldiers and a holding pen with eight gigantic Caledonians. They wore trousers and boots only, and had huge muscled arms with broad chests.

"They look like gladiators," Calpurnia said.

"They are as big as the Germans," Balbinus replied. He bent closer. "I will tell you a secret. Verus intends to dye the darker haired barbarians blond, so they will look more ferocious to the crowds, more like Germans." He laughed. "That's what Julius Caesar did when he paraded Vercingetorix and his warriors through the streets of Rome."

"These are the leaders … tribal chieftains from Britannia?"

"Yes," Balbinus said, finding it hard to quell his excitement.

"And no one else has been here yet?"

"Some have, but few. We will be the center of discussion tonight, I can promise you that."

Calpurnia nodded her approval. "Tonight, you can use our outing to great advantage," she said. "Your reputation can only be enhanced when patricians and equestrians crowd you, begging for morsels of information."

He chuckled, running his eyes over the Caledonian commanders, relishing the prospect.

"I suggest spooning out your gems," she said. "And not too much to any one person. That way you maintain control."

"Sound advice," he said.

"At some point you might want to acknowledge Senator Coelius's role in this adventure. It will make you look strong. Only strong men credit others." She removed a speck from his tunic.

"I should ask a guard about the captives," he said. "They might have fascinating insights."

"An excellent idea," she said.

"I do have some information already," he said. "The centerpiece of General Verus's Triumph, the special person I told you about, is named Taranis, though I'm not at all certain which one he is."

"Taranis?"

"Apparently, his name comes from the ancient Celtic god of the sky. Our soldiers called him the blood god because he attacked without warning and never left anyone alive."

"Taranis," Calpurnia repeated, frowning. "Rare for a Celt to have that name." She squinted at the enormous men in the enclosure and suddenly grasped hold of a support pillar that held the roof aloft.

"Is something wrong?" Balbinus asked.

"No, not at all," she said. Her smile looked forced when she added, "This has truly been a wonderful surprise. But if we want to make our dinner engagement, we might think of heading back."

"But I have not yet—"

"I am so sorry," she said, "but actually I don't feel myself. An illness seems to have befallen me. The sun may have been too much." She put her hand to her forehead.

"We will leave immediately," Balbinus said. "But let me first determine which warrior is Taranis." He hurried over to a guard and spoke briefly to him.

Calpurnia started toward the door.

Balbinus rushed to her side and said, "We'll depart momentarily but look, do you see that tall warrior with the long yellow hair?" He pointed. "He is Taranis, the most feared warrior in Britannia. The guard said he killed everything that breathed—wounded soldiers, women, children, cattle. It didn't matter to him. If it was Roman, it died. Courageous soldiers shook like leaves when they heard that Taranis and his warriors were approaching."

Calpurnia nodded.

"I'm sorry for your illness," he said, "but today we have partaken of the ages." He pointed at the huge warrior again and said, "There stands Taranis, as dire to the Empire as ever were Vercingetorix or Boudicca in their times. And we have seen him for ourselves."

"A wonderful surprise," Calpurnia repeated.

"Tonight, we shall—" Balbinus stopped. Taranis was staring at them. His shoulder-length yellow hair swayed as he moved toward the front of the enclosure.

Calpurnia stepped behind Balbinus.

"You're trembling," he said, concerned. It was the first time she had need of his comfort, and he determined to stand tall in the situation. He put his arm around her to leave.

A Celtic voice rattled the window slats.

Balbinus looked back. The blood god's brilliant blue eyes flashed as he gestured toward them, making Balbinus cringe. Taranis kept repeating the same words, though his voice had softened.

Calpurnia buried her face in Balbinus's tunic and pulled toward the door. Balbinus was not a brave man but he grew angry with the barbarian for creating fear in Calpurnia's heart. She was the only love he had ever had his whole life. "Have no fear," he said to Calpurnia, and then glaring at Taranis, he added, "the fearsome blood god is locked in a cage." The thought fortified his own courage and prompted him to ask a guard, "What's he saying to me?"

"The interpreter is not here," the guard said, "but I think he's talking to the lady, not you."

"Balbinus, please," Calpurnia said, tugging him away.

When they left the building, the barbarian was still talking and gesturing for them to come closer. Balbinus was satisfied with his performance. Faced with a violent warrior who was threatening Calpurnia, he had stood his ground. He had taken control of the situation and had shown his courage.

"The fresh air soothes me like a balm," Calpurnia said.

"You are safe with me," Balbinus said, reminding her of his bravery.

"I truly am," she said.

"What a tale we have for tonight," Balbinus said, "that is, if you feel well enough to attend."

"The air agrees with me."

"Could you have ever imagined it? Taranis, the murderous blood god himself, tries to lure you closer so he can strangle one last Roman before his own demise. A tale worth telling, would you not agree?"

"Indeed."

"But have no fear, I shall dole it out like a nursemaid spooning honey, the whole evening long."

33

As the weeks passed, Neeve had little opportunity to speak with Senator Severus about Taranis. He had been busy in Rome, and on the two or three occasions he did visit the country villa, it never seemed the right moment to bring up her brother's situation.

Neeve spent her mornings learning how to run a villa. The Severus family owned three working villas near Rome and many properties elsewhere, most of them in Gallia. She followed Marcellus as he managed the day-to-day operations of the villas, watched him as he interacted with his workers, haggled over wine prices with local buyers, and dealt with bankers, moving money from one place to another. As a senator, Marcellus said, his father could never deal with vulgar money, so those aspects of the business were left to the overseers and Marcellus.

Neeve enjoyed being busy; it distracted her from thinking about Vectis and taught her about the inner workings of Rome's economy. She soon came to appreciate Marcellus's skills as a businessman. His energy and good judgment had expanded his father's holdings, transforming one mildly profitable villa into three significant enterprises.

She also found Marcellus pleasant company. His easy smile grew on her, and she looked forward to their carriage rides as they traveled from one meeting to another. But for all his affability, he had strange ways, especially when it came to venerating the gods.

Most educated people in Rome, Neeve learned, no longer believed in the gods of the pantheon, at least not in the way she did.

Tales about Jupiter or Venus were nothing more than fables for children and uneducated provincials. Patricians called on the gods publicly for assistance, maintained their temples and sacrificed to their names, but they did not truly believe in them. They preferred philosophies like stoicism, secret mystery religions from the east, or healing cults like Asclepios. But they still reverenced the gods of Rome because these gods were part of the ancient state religion.

Neeve found the Roman attitude confusing. Why honor the gods if they were not real? She concluded they did so because the gods symbolized good fortune. If you treated the gods with respect, good fortune would more likely come your way. Besides, for Roman authorities, reverence of the gods equaled reverence of the state. What Rome demanded more than anything else was unquestioned loyalty to the state.

Marcellus seemed to be an atheist, or at least someone who had little regard for the gods. He never burned incense at the lararium, never gave the expected praise to the gods, and never stopped at any temple they passed. Neeve couldn't remember meeting anyone who completely ignored the gods. She liked Marcellus, but worried some god might take offense at his behavior and punish him with sickness or ill fortune. If you ignore the gods when they can see you, you invite trouble … at least that is what Neeve firmly believed. So at every opportunity when she venerated the gods, she mentioned Marcellus's name so they wouldn't notice his lack of supplication.

The subject of the hundred gold aurei that had so worried Neeve never once came up, and she assumed Marcellus would rather leave it in the past. Then one day while they were tasting wines in the underground cellars, he said, "I have deposited with my banker two hundred gold aurei for you to use as you wish. This account is entirely under your control. You might have need for garments and other personal items."

"I have no needs," she said.

"Everyone has needs."

"I'm managing fine," she said, glancing around the cellar. She felt awkward.

"You're managing fine," he said. "No needs. Why is this not believable?" He handed her a cup of wine from one of the barrels.

She swished a small amount around in her mouth, and then screwed up her face. "Not my favorite," she said.

He tasted it. "Bitter," he said, and marked the barrel with chalk.

"Sammonicus and I have free food and lodging," she said. "How can I possibly have needs?"

"All the same," he said, "the aurei are in your name."

"Really, I cannot accept—"

"It's already done."

"But I—"

"No more discussion. I know how stubborn you can be."

"Stubborn?"

"Stubborn, independent—whatever you call the code you learned in Caledonia. The aurei are now yours, and no longer mine. Send them to your family if you want, but they are yours to do with as you wish."

Neeve stayed silent. She had no family except Taranis. If her mother or Nes were still alive, she had no way of finding them. She did need money; there was no denying it. Her pride told her to reject the gold aurei, but the truth was that her clothing purchases for herself and Sammonicus had drained her finances. With only three outfits, she was constantly scrambling to keep them clean. One thing about the capital—it was expensive. She had to be careful. Her only asset was a horse and carriage, and she knew what it was like to be hawking drawings on the street.

Neeve thanked Marcellus for his generosity, but her face radiated embarrassment. She was glad they were in the darkened cellars lit only by torchlight. How humiliating to act independent when the truth was quite the opposite. She had counted out her coins the day before—twenty-two sesterces—barely enough for the week, if she were frugal.

"You're probably wondering about the amount, two hundred aurei," he said, smiling.

"I rarely beat more than a hundred out of people," she said, uncertain how wise it was to revisit their Caledonian experience.

He laughed, to her relief. "I deposited two hundred aurei to assure you that no one was beating anything out of me. I am delighted to help." He shook his head and said, "I confess your demands in Britannia stunned me. I knew you were no ordinary Caledonian. And when you went back to the war zone despite my warnings … clearly, it worried me. I had never seen your face, but I knew I would not forget you."

She paused.

"And now that I see you …."

"It's too dark down here to see anything," she said, laughing self-consciously, trying to deflect the conversation.

"You bring your own light with you," he said.

She glanced away, down the row of barrels.

He moved closer.

"Marcellus, I don't think—"

"Shhh," he said, as he placed his hands on either side of her face, and held her eyes. Then slowly he leaned forward and kissed her.

It wasn't a long kiss, but long enough for her to feel a tingle flow through her body. She took a breath and stepped back. They had been together for many weeks; he had been just a friend, a tutor perhaps, but never more than that. She felt comfortable with him, so much so that Sammonicus rarely accompanied them on their outings. This was the first time he had ever hinted their relationship could develop into something more, and it left her speechless. She glanced down at her ring, thinking about Vectis. It glinted in the torchlight. Someday she would have to say goodbye to his memory—she knew that—but now was too soon.

"It seems so long ago," she said, "that night outside my barn."

He nodded, and a hint of a smile crinkled the corners of his eyes. He had seen where she had been looking.

"You were waving your sword everywhere, pretending you could see."

"I thought I did rather well," he said, taking her cue to change subjects.

"Stumbling around, walking into doors."

"I confess, you did manage to subdue a blind man."

"A Roman soldier," she said.

"True, and you tied him up with Caledonian new hemp. No chance for him to escape, I take it."

She smiled and opened her mouth to say something.

"Yes, once Neeve mapmaker ties someone, they stay tied."

"You scoundrel!" she said, laughing striking him on the chest. "I did tie you well. How did you escape?"

"Ah, the escape," he said. "It took great skill. I will show you tonight, if you like, at the spring celebration."

She gave him a surprised look.

"Didn't I mention the celebration?" he asked.

"No," she said.

"A small gathering," he said, "fifty to sixty guests. That's what all the activity is about in the gardens. The servants are setting up torches and tables for our guests."

The thought of socializing with Romans made her feel ill. "With respect," she said, "I'll stay in my room tonight. I have items that require attention."

"You declined Senator Ahala's invitation last month," he said.

"I remember."

"Do you also remember your promise to accompany me to the next gathering?"

"I assumed it would be some time from now."

"Romans have many celebrations."

"I feel unready."

"Nonsense," he said. "I don't see how you could be more ready." They tasted another cup and pronounced the wine superb.

She tried again. "Without offending you, I mix poorly with society people and—"

"I mix poorly as well," he said. "Do you know why? Because I dislike many of them, and you will dislike them too. We can compare ledgers as to which ones we dislike the most."

She smiled.

"Please attend, for my sake."

"I will attend," she said, "because you ask. But I may disappear without notice."

After lunch Neeve went to the villa's private bath, as she usually did, and cleaned her body with soap and hot water in the steam room. She thought about the celebration scheduled to begin later in the afternoon. She knew Marcellus and the senator wanted her to enjoy herself, but attending a Roman festivity was not high on her list of enjoyable events. Still, if she could do anything to rescue Taranis, she would, and that included smiling dutifully at a Roman party.

Neeve tied back her hair with a gold braid, put on her gold earrings and necklace of semi-precious stones, and slipped into her soft leather sandals. She had been wearing tunics since her first meeting with Marcellus and the senator, but now she was dressed in her best stola with a pink shawl draped over her shoulders. She looked down at herself and smiled, feeling at least comfortable with how she looked.

"Yes, it is a delight to meet you too," she said, mimicking the words she would soon have to say in the atrium. And, "No, I do not believe I have ever traveled to that part of Italia." She inclined her head politely and cooed, "Ohh, you are too kind—"

"Neeve?" Marcellus's voice came from the other side of the curtained doorway.

She whipped her head around. "Ah ... yes," she said to the curtain, "I'm coming."

"Am I interrupting you?" he asked with a tease in his voice.

"No, not at all," she said, feeling foolish. "I was ... well, if you must know, I was readying my mind."

He laughed. "I hope your mind feels ready, because most of the guests have already arrived."

She pulled back the curtain.

Marcellus started forward, and then stopped. He looked surprised, as if he had expected to see someone else. Neeve smiled awkwardly as his eyes lingered on her body. "You look ... wonderful," he said, "utterly and incredibly wonderful."

"Thank you, my mind feels ready," she said, not knowing what else to say.

"I can see that," he said, glancing her up and down again.

She said nothing.

He held out his hand. "I am proud to attend you." She took his hand, and together they strolled the length of the walkway toward the growing clamor of voices.

Most of the guests were gathered around two long tables heaped with the first course. The men were dressed much the same as Neeve had seen them in the Basilica Aemilia. They wore red sandals trimmed with pearls, and glistening white togas, their purple stripes positioned conspicuously. The women were dressed quite differently from what Neeve had expected. Their stolas shone a brilliant white, as if they were reflecting the sun. Every fold, every exquisite layer was clasped with pearls or emeralds or dazzling jewels Neeve had never before seen. Some wore gowns so sheer that their powdered white bodies shimmered provocatively underneath, to the delight of every man at the gathering. Many had the sole objective of impressing others with their wealth. They sprinkled their hair with gold dust or pearls, they covered their fingers with rings, and they embroidered their purple necklines and hems with thick golden threads.

Neeve laid her scarf aside in the warm rooms and kept her posture erect, trying to appear self-possessed as she mingled with the shorter Roman women. She tried to avoid the petty ones who smiled with their mouths and sliced with their tongues. But she was not always successful.

"You must be Marcellus's latest friend," said a woman with red lips and a stack of hair balanced on her head. The women standing with her looked equally grand.

"Yes," Neeve said, refusing to take any inference from her words.

"You are striking in appearance."

"Thank you."

"Your gown is modest but quite tasteful," she said, smiling.

Neeve smiled back.

"Wool, I take it."

"Yes."

"Lovely. Milesian wool is quite fashionable. To my mind, not everyone can handle silk. Milesian wool is perfectly acceptable." She paused. "It is *Milesian* wool ... isn't it?" Her red lips puckered in concern.

"It definitely comes from a sheep," Neeve said, forcing a smile.

"Well ... it's a sensible gown, and I think it favors you greatly."

"Thank you."

She glanced around at the other women and said, "Marcellus does have a talent for acquiring the brightest flowers."

"Most fade rather quickly," said a short dark woman with an enormous pearl stuffed in her ear.

"They do," agreed the piled hair woman. "But I am certain you do not mean to imply—"

"No, no, of course not," the dark woman said. She looked at Neeve and said, "You are entirely different from the others."

"Oh, yes," said the hair, "entirely different."

"You have a fresh—how should I put it?—a scrubbed look about you that can be attractive to some men."

"How true. So many women suffer the horrors of Batavian caustics to bleach their hair as light as yours." She touched the piled hair on her head and said, "Actually, I would not fret in the least. You are quite fortunate."

"Yes, your hair has that woodsy Celtic appearance," the dark woman said. "You are a Celt, I take it?"

Neeve gestured that she was, but held her tongue. She was a guest of the Severuses, and how she acted would reflect on them. But her anger was simmering.

"Yes, I'm sure you have a little Celt in you," the darker woman said as she studied Neeve's features.

"Northern Italia has its fair share of mixed ones," the piled hair volunteered.

"Actually, I'm a provincial Celt," Neeve said, "not mixed at all. We scrub in the cold mountain streams to maintain that fresh appearance." She turned to go, and simulated a smile as she said, "By the way, my barbarian name is Neeve."

The piled hair clasped her chest. "Oh, my," she said. "I have offended you." She turned to the others and said, "What did I say? Did I say something untoward? Because if I did ...."

Neeve was already across the room when another woman tapped her on the shoulder and said, "Calpurnia?"

Neeve turned.

"I'm surprised to see you here," she said. "You are dressed rather Spartan, I must say … and what have you done to your hair?"

"I think you've mistaken me for someone else," Neeve said.

"You are not Calpurnia?"

"I'm a guest of the Severus household," she said. "My name is Neeve."

"I am sorry," the woman said. Her brow furrowed. She went to a steward to refresh her cup, but looked over her shoulder in Neeve's direction.

It was still early in the evening but Neeve noticed several men who had filled their cups too many times. Most of them sat quietly on couches, calling for more wine, but some talked loudly or stumbled into guests. One man bumped into her and grabbed hold of her for balance. Whether intentional or not, his hand pressed into a sensitive spot on her robe.

"You are a goddess," he mumbled, his eyes glistening, his hands starting to roam.

Neeve pushed his hands away and twisted one of his fingers to make the point. He yipped like a dog and the sound gave her a measure of satisfaction. She left him swaying at the edge of the room.

Tired of drunks and pompous women, Neeve glanced around for Marcellus. She saw him talking to servants near the dinner table and made directly for him. She knew she had to apologize for her unruly tongue. Why couldn't she just have kept silent? Who cared what some old matron thought of her dress? She inhaled through clenched teeth, scolding herself. Every time she opened her mouth, it drove a spike into Taranis. Who else but Senator Severus could help her? She simply had to do better, and in the future she determined she would.

"Sorry I've been so occupied," Marcellus said. "Stay with me and I'll introduce you to some people."

"I'm content just to stay with you," she said.

"Hmm, that suggests you've already met some of our guests," he said.

"One group in particular," Neeve said, motioning with her head to the gaggle of women across the room.

"And you still live?" he said. "A testimony to a readied mind."

"Not ready enough," she said. "I think I owe you an apology."

"You do?"

"I have offended your guests, I'm afraid."

He glanced over at the women. "That bunch needs offending," he said. "I hope you told them they gossip too much."

"I intend to be perfect the rest of the evening," Neeve said.

"You are perfect the way you are."

Neeve smiled. She glanced at the foods laid out on the table. She was used to simpler meals—barley porridge, pork and beer. She decided to ask Marcellus about the more interesting dishes. He gladly complied. Lettuce, he said, was a pre-digestive, as were the bowls of tender shoots cut from leek plants. There were also pickled young tunas garnished with eggs, rue leaves and cheese. In answer to a query from a guest, Marcellus lowered his voice for dramatic effect, and said that the cheeses came from Velabrum Street and the olives from the frosty hills of Picene. The guest nodded his approval and wandered away, satisfied. Neeve confessed she had never heard of Velabrum or Picene. Marcellus laughed and replied that when two cheeses were laid side by side, the one said to be from Velabrum always tasted better. He suspected the same held true for olives hardened in the chilly hills of Picene.

Servants wended their way through the milling guests, replenishing the pitchers of wine on the tables, bringing more heated breads and cheeses,, and attending to the many braziers set up in the gardens where the robust gathered to enjoy the chilly air. More than once Neeve heard someone empty his cup and comment on the merits of one wine over another. Marcellus leaned close to Neeve and said, "Most of them have as much understanding of wine as they do cheese, but take heart, the more they drink, the louder and more authoritative their pronouncements will become."

Neeve looked at him as would a conspirator and asked, "Will you then serve the bitter wine when palates are less discerning?"

"We have no bitter wine," he said, grinning. "But we do have barrels other than these and, yes, the servants have been instructed to make them available later in the evening."

After the main course had been served—sow's paunch, sautéed boar wrapped in slices of antelope and gazelle, pheasant strips, and the succulent breasts of flamingo—the entertainment began. The flutes and lyres encouraged some to dance, some to give poetic readings and some to huddle together sharing the week's gossip. Marcellus chose this time to fulfill his pledge to Neeve; he would show her how he freed himself from his bonds in Caledonia.

"First, you hold your hands like so," he said to a small group of interested guests. "Then you allow your opponent to bind you." A young man stepped forward and bound his wrists. "And then you do this ...." He turned his back and hunched over, twisting his arms into a contorted shape. He turned to the group and held out the rope. They gasped. Several allowed themselves to be bound, but none escaped.

"I still don't understand how you do that," Neeve said.

"Something I've done since childhood," Marcellus said. He bent his thumb across the back of his hand. "My joints are quite loose, you see."

As the evening wore on Neeve had occasion to ask Senator Severus if she might speak to him sometime about an important matter, as she called it. He agreed to talk with her in the coming week. "I hope you know," he said, giving her his warmest smile, "whatever your concern, I am much disposed to your interests."

For the next hour Neeve floated from one conversation to the other. Even the sharp-tongued matrons couldn't affect her buoyant mood. She knew the senator might not be able to free Taranis, but at least she had a powerful ally in the Senate who would speak on behalf of her brother. She took a cup of wine onto a balcony that overlooked the gardens, feeling good to be away from the crowd. The cool air tingled her skin, and Neeve wished she had her scarf to cover her shoulders.

"This where you hiding," a slurred voice said.

Neeve set her cup down and saw the drunken man from earlier in the evening standing in the exit.

"I want to talk," he said, reaching for her.

She side-stepped his grasping hands.

"Nothing wrong with a little talk, is there?"

"Please, I don't—"

He grabbed at the shoulder clasp that secured her dress.

"Stop!" she said as she leaned back.

He caught hold of her dress.

She smacked his hand away.

He reached again and she slapped his hand again.

His face darkened. He balled his fist and struck her in the chest.

Neeve coughed, trying to get air.

He shoved his hand into the top of her gown. She jerked away. He lurched forward. Neeve stepped to the side and slammed both hands into his back. He stumbled toward the balcony rail, folded over it, and tumbled to the garden below.

Neeve heard a woman scream. She peered over the balcony and saw the drunk crumpled on a marble staircase. Two men and a woman were leaning over him. One man listened for the beating of his heart. He rose and said, "Orestes is dead."

"What happened?" It was Marcellus's voice in the garden.

"Somebody pushed Junius Orestes off the balcony," the woman said.

The crowd was growing in the garden, and they were all looking up.

"Neeve? Is that you?" Marcellus asked.

"Yes," Neeve said in a daze.

Marcellus stared up at her, but said nothing.

34

Several weeks passed before Vectis was granted an audience with the Supreme Commander. He found it difficult to think of Commodus as supreme anything, but he knew much depended on his ability to conduct himself properly. The whole process was colossally stupid, but now that Commodus was the senior officer in the field, he had almost unlimited power. So, with a seriousness that befitted the occasion, Vectis presented himself to Commodus's aide shortly before the noon meal. The aide, remembering his last encounter with Vectis, had a decidedly cold look on his face. He rose without speaking, escorted Vectis into a sizable meeting room with an ornate table, brightly colored couches, military wall coverings … and one incredibly large marble bust of Commodus, his eyes bulging, and the corners of his mouth turned down like an irate father.

Vectis thanked the aide, who left without even a nod. Alone, he glanced around the room, and then at the statue. He moved closer. The statue was well done and must have cost a patrician's wage, but it looked nothing like Commodus. He obviously was trying to present an image of a stern soldier, one that enemies trifled with at their peril. Yet, the statue was entirely out of place in a military tent. The combined weight of the bust and pedestal would have required a separate cart, and in hostile territory, every cart was precious. Besides, who would set up a sculpture of himself? Even vain emperors like Caligula and Nero didn't sit in the shadow of their own statues. The whole charade would have been humorous if Vectis's experience with Commodus in Britannia hadn't been so calamitous.

During those days Commodus was terrified of the Caledonians, so much so that he begged to be transferred to a safer post. When Vectis refused his request, Commodus made a deal with Senator Atilius Titianus to abandon his post, leaving Vectis and his soldiers to the mercy of the Caledonian hordes.

The flap to the side door opened.

Six giant Namibian bodyguards stepped through, their eyes raking every inch of the tent. Vectis recognized the elite guards from his time in northern Africa. They wore distinctive headdresses that hung to their shoulders, and each carried more knives than a Caledonian scout. Behind them came a chunky man with short arms whose job it was to announce the presence of Commodus. His mouth opened wide and his jowls shook as he boomed: "Prefect Gaius Jovius Herculius Commodus, the Supreme Commander of Rome's Imperial Armies above the Dacian frontier." That finished, he bobbed respectfully as the diminutive Commodus strode through the tent flap like a conquering general.

Commodus instantly fastened angry eyes on Vectis, as if he wanted to establish at the outset that he had little tolerance when it came to meeting with underlings. He seated himself on a couch without inviting Vectis to do the same.

"Ah, yes, Vectis Trebellius," he said slowly in a high voice. "Your behavior has manifestly disturbed my aide, but I explained we were old friends. That is the case, is it not?"

"Of course, Supreme Commander," Vectis said, using the proper designation.

"And friends overlook mistakes, do they not?"

"They do, Supreme Commander."

"Then we understand each other," he said, stretching out his hands to admire them, then turning up his face, apparently having found something that displeased him. He called for olive oil, and laboriously massaged the golden fluid into the ends of his fingers. He still wore pearl rings on every finger except for the right index, where he had a heavy signet ring embossed with a naked, winged boy carrying a bow and arrow. "I assumed you were killed and reported you as such—you might want to let Rome know you escaped your men's fate." He chortled to himself. "No doubt you thought your arrival would take me by surprise. Hmmm?" He looked up. "Not much surprises me. Oh, yes, I knew you were coming, though I cannot imagine why they would transfer you from Britannia when the province is in such chaos. You could do some good in Britannia. But Rome and her wisdom," he said, throwing up his hands. "We all have to bow to her whims, do we not? In Britannia you were in charge, and here ... well, you can see ... the Fates have selected me as Supreme Commander."

Commodus continued to talk, swelling his narrow chest when referring to his Senate friends who had elevated his station and increased his power.

Vectis stared at Commodus, hardly recognizing him.

The man he had known in Britannia had a scrawny neck and looked like a plucked chicken, his face soft and void of hair—no eyebrows, not even eyelashes. He still had no eyelashes, but now he had blotches above his eyes, tattoos that simulated hair. More oddly, a surgeon had created a long scar on the left side of his neck, giving the impression of a battle wound. His face also had been marked with a hundred pinpricks, which from a distance might have looked like the stubble of a beard, but up close reminded Vectis of the fanatical Cybele priests that wandered the streets shrieking out their apocalyptic visions. Vectis stared at Commodus's head, once hairless and glistening with oil. Now he wore a curly blond wig cut in the style of Augustus Caesar, and he was dressed as an army general with a breastplate, dagger and abnormally thick hobnailed boots. Vectis guessed the boots made him appear taller.

Commodus seemed to sense Vectis's shock at his changed appearance. He scowled, trying hard to duplicate the fierce expression on his marble statue. "Now to your duties," he said, leaning back as if he had reflected deeply on the nature of Vectis's assignment. "I have decided you will handle the logistic side of the siege, and I the assault. Is that clear?"

Vectis nodded. He had expected to be eliminated from the assault.

"Most of the former tribune's staff remains, and they will alert you to rules and procedures."

Vectis said nothing.

"That is all," Commodus said, rising.

"I have a few concerns, if I may, Supreme Commander," Vectis said in a respectful voice.

Commodus blinked several times, betraying apprehension.

"I would like permission to build a defensive perimeter to our backs. We are greatly exposed—"

"Denied," Commodus said brusquely. "The ramp is ready. By sundown tomorrow our business will be finished here." He sucked in some air and folded his spindly arms. "I intend to dispatch the entire population ... as a warning to others. I am no fool, and believe me, I-will-not-be-mocked!"

"The entire population?" Vectis winced.

Commodus's lips twisted into a smile. "Every night they go through their farce, dancing and ridiculing my efforts. Oh, they laugh and call out my name; they taunt me as if I were the village idiot." His smile faded. "We will see if they laugh tomorrow."

Vectis thought about objecting, saying that a Roman client city north of the Dacian barrier could be useful, but he kept his promise to Julian and held his tongue. Arguing with Commodus was useless and probably dangerous. "One last request," he said. "I am as concerned as you about the mocking attitude among the city dwellers. If you could postpone your attack a day or two I would have time to examine the city's defenses to see whether—"

"The attack is not your concern," Commodus said.

"I understand, but an extra day to plan logistics—"

"Your predecessor has planned adequately," Commodus said, annoyed at Vectis's persistence. "The attack will continue as scheduled." He turned abruptly, and with his bevy of bodyguards, disappeared through the open tent flap.

Shortly before sunset, and after the dancing courtesans had vacated the wall, Vectis made a final check on the progress of the tree pole. It turned out to be a bigger project than anticipated. The tree would not be ready to climb until well after dark. Still, once he had found an appropriate tree, the young engineer moved with incredible speed, trimming it, pulling it out of the forest with a score of mules, then dragging it on roller logs across the land until it reached the men working on the hole. At the same time, the engineer constructed a series of wooden blinds around the hole to protect the workers from curious archers watching from the city walls.

"This is a ridiculous idea ... you climbing the tree," Julian said.

"Something odd is going on here," Vectis replied. "You said so yourself."

"I'm not disputing that. But you should assign a soldier to climb this thing." He ran his eyes the length of the tree lying on the ground and shook his head to show his disapproval.

Vectis glanced at the enormous tree, at least ninety feet long and eight across the base, tapering to a foot at the top. The men had left some limbs for hand and footholds, mostly at the top, cropping them at twelve inches. They also hammered ten-inch nails into the rough oak bark to make additional handholds for the climb. Vectis and Julian watched them remove all the rollers from under the tree until only one remained, a thick log twenty feet off the base that made the tree angle upwards and over the hole. This log provided the fulcrum. Then they tied long ropes around the narrow end to help bring the tree upright. Finally, they chained the narrow end to the ground, and piled enormous slabs of rock onto the other end, the base. When the tree bowed from the weight, they released the chains and pulled on the ropes. The top of the tree sprang upright and the heavy base drove forward into the hole.

In seconds the whole operation was over. Gangs of men held the tree in place with the ropes as others tamped mud and rocks into the hole. This done, they heaped eight feet of stone around the base for additional stability.

"Well, they managed to get it up," Julian said, staring at the tree shaft that disappeared into the night sky.

"Amazing, actually," Vectis said.

Julian moved closer to catch his eye. "I am asking you to reconsider the climb," he said.

"I've already made that decision."

"Listen to me, you are the *military tribune,* far too valuable to risk on a climb of this sort. Senator Severus wants you to end this siege before Commodus sets off a German uprising ... and you're no help to Rome if some archer picks you off halfway up the tree."

"I'll have a shield," Vectis said. "Besides, you've seen the glare off those hills at sunrise."

"So you intend to begin your climb at sunrise?"

"As soon as it's light enough to find the climbing spikes," he said. And then he added, "Don't worry. It shouldn't take long to see what there is to see, and then I'll simply slide down the rope. I'll be fine."

"And if it's cloudy tomorrow?"

"It's clear now. It will be clear tomorrow."

"This is ludicrous," Julian said, holding up his hand. "You're the only one with leverage over Commodus. Without you—"

"I don't want to discuss it anymore. I intend to see over the wall, and that's all there is to it."

"Why? What do you expect to see?"

"I said I didn't want to—"

"Just answer one question. What do you expect to see?"

"I don't know."

"You don't know."

"No, but sending a common soldier up the tower is a waste of effort. How can he know what he's looking for if I don't?"

"That makes sense," Julian said. "I'm glad we talked about it."

When Vectis arrived at the tree pole shortly before sunrise, the skies were still clear, but the wind had picked up considerably, causing the pole to sway and groan. His eyes darted to the stakes in the ground where the ropes were fastened, and then unconsciously followed them up toward the top of the tree where they disappeared into the darkness. With every heave of the wind, the ropes grew taut and then slack, giving Vectis a new appreciation for the danger of the assignment he had chosen.

The young engineer left a group of soldiers and approached Vectis. "The wind makes it difficult to climb," he said, "but if it stays at this level, the structure will hold. A new tree has a healthy tolerance."

"I have full confidence in your abilities," Vectis said. "Set up the ladder." He was referring to the ladder needed for the first fifteen feet where the trunk had no nails. They hadn't bothered to use the ten-inch spikes at the bottom because the rolling fulcrum would have crushed most of them when the tree slid into the hole.

"But we've already ...." The engineer half laughed and gestured weakly toward the tree.

"Where's the ladder?"

"On the dirt over there," he said, pointing toward a mound of earth, "but ... the tribune ... ah ... Julian Quintillius, he's already up the tree."

"Julian's what?" He wrenched his head toward the tree.

"He took your shield and climbing boots and ... well, he said you'd be needed on the ground, you know, with Commodus's attack beginning this morning."

"You let him go up in the dark!"

"I assumed you ...." The engineer's voice trailed off as he pulled at the fringes of his tunic.

Vectis squinted up at the tree. "Julian, what are you doing?" he muttered to himself. He could see him now, a murky blob against the sky, straining to find the next handhold, and then pulling himself up carefully toward the heavens. He wore dark clothes so there would be no chance of the enemy seeing him until the last minute when the sun rose.

Vectis was tempted to call up to his friend, but decided against it. It was still dark, and with the pole bending like a reed in the wind, Julian would require all his concentration to keep from slipping. Vectis headed over to the blind where the soldiers were heating a pot of German beer on a small fire. As he sipped his cup and watched the dark outline of Julian nearing the top, he wondered how all this would end.

The first cracks of light appeared abruptly in the eastern sky. At the same time several thousand soldiers in full armor marched in tight blocks toward the work tents near the ramp. Vectis could hear the low sound of voices as the soldiers approached, a clear sign of undisciplined troops. Roman soldiers—particularly the legions—prided themselves in being silent before the enemy. Silence was a powerful weapon. To barbarians who shouted and screamed in a desperate attempt to mask their own terror, silence was like the weight of a huge rock. It crushed them before the battle ever began. It told them their Roman enemies were imbued with god-like characteristics and had absolute surety about the outcome. But these were not legionary forces; they were auxiliaries, and poorly-trained ones at that.

At the head rode Commodus on a white horse surrounded by his six Numidian bodyguards mounted on coal black stallions, a contrast so preposterous that only the Supreme Commander himself could have chosen it.

Trumpets sounded. The soldiers stopped in a broad field and rested their four-foot shields on the ground. They checked their weapons and began talking to each other while their centurions tried to speak over their conversation. Vectis stared in disbelief as soldiers took out water skins and drank their fill in plain view of the centurions. Like barbarians, they talked and slouched and had complete freedom to take in the scenery around them, especially the tree pole. Some even hunched over their shields, leaning on them like tired old men, as if it mattered little whether they stood up straight. Anger flashed through Vectis, and for an instant he almost raced across the field and shook Commodus by the neck.

Sanity prevailed, and Vectis returned his attention to the tree. He was not responsible for Commodus's army, or even for the eventual outcome of the siege, though his duty was clear. He would find out what was going on over the city walls and he would prevent Commodus from stumbling into disaster.

Right now the wind concerned him. It had grown in intensity, swinging the top of the tree in an ever-increasing arc. In the gray light of dawn Vectis saw Julian inching closer to the top, his legs clinging to the pole as his fingers searched for the next handhold.

Vectis called the engineer to his side. "What's all that popping and cracking?" he asked.

"The strain of the wind on the tree," the engineer replied. "I'm concerned, but not about the sounds coming from the tree. It's still quite stable. But the whole structure is leaning." He smiled nervously. "I would bring him down as soon as possible. Even live trees snap in high winds."

A sudden movement on the wall caught Vectis's eye. Archers. They were crowded together and pointing toward the top of the tree. They had discovered Julian.

No longer protected by the night, Julian was plainly visible to the enemy swarming the city's walls, and they eagerly snatched at their arrows. Vectis had thought their archers wouldn't see Julian through the morning glare, and if they did, they would have difficulty targeting him. He was wrong. With slate gray clouds blunting the brilliant Dacian sun, they spotted him instantly and took careful aim.

"Julian! Archers!" Vectis called up to him.

But Julian had already seen them. With one arm wrapped around the pole, he twisted and yanked the disk-shaped cavalry shield off his back and thrust it forward. The tree swayed with his movements and for an instant Vectis thought the top might snap.

The archers loosed their arrows.

Julian scrunched up his body, making as small a target as possible. The arrows ripped through the air, but passed harmlessly to one side, carried by the wind. A second volley sailed out from the wall, and a third, the latter smacking into the tree above and below where Julian clung. Despite the wind and the constant bending of the tree, the men on the wall had found their range.

Vectis whipped his head around, thinking about the catapults. But it was a useless effort. They were near the ramp, being readied for the siege. It would take the good part of an hour to recalibrate the distance.

"What about bringing our archers over here?" Vectis asked the engineer, knowing the answer before he heard it.

The engineer shook his head. "Commodus would never allow it," he said.

Vectis glanced up at the tree. His stomach turned to knots. Julian was on his own.

More archers appeared. They began firing their missiles the instant they arrived, as if there was no greater urgency.

At the ramp, thousands of soldiers began wheeling the huge Roman siege machines up toward the wall, but most of the city's archers, it seemed, were interested only in the man climbing the tree pole. They were hiding something, and that something was what Vectis needed to know. But he would not squander his friend's life on the quest.

"Julian!" Vectis motioned anxiously with his arms for him to come down. Then turning to a soldier, he said quietly, "Fetch a surgeon."

Julian was staring over his shield toward the city. He pulled his head below the metal barrier like a turtle in a shell, and hollered down, "I know …."

But his words were lost in the wind.

"Get out of there!" Vectis screamed.

Julian cupped one hand over his mouth and shouted in slow, distinct words: "I know what they're doing."

In that moment a flood of arrows struck the tree, the shield and Julian's exposed leg. He jerked sideways, instinctively reaching for the arrows protruding from his leg, and then lost his balance. The shield flipped out of his hand and tumbled toward the ground, banging off the rocks piled around the tree pole. He slipped a few feet, but flung his arms around the swaying tree, grasping tightly and shoving his face into the bark. Then, suddenly, he seemed to realize his back was exposed to the archers. He pulled himself around to the opposite side, trying to use the tree as protection.

Vectis knew it was only a matter of time. "Come down the rope," he hollered. "Now!"

The soldiers behind their blinds were gazing up at Julian, watching as he stretched for the rope. They had tied it to a branch near the top an arm's length from the tree so as not to interfere with the climb. But now with the tilt of the tree, it fell just out of reach. Vectis signaled a soldier who mounted the rock pile and took hold of the bottom of the rope. He moved gingerly across the sharp edges, towing the rope behind him.

Abruptly the rope yanked from his hands.

Julian had hold of it and swung his body onto the rope and away from the tree. The top bent under his weight as he started down, moving slowly, hand over hand, his good leg wrapped around the rope to control the descent. Two arrows protruded from his left leg, both in the thigh.

Vectis gulped some air. His breathing had grown so shallow he needed several breaths to catch up. He worried about Julian losing his strength, about the archers on the wall, but mostly he worried about the tree that was now listing a good twenty degrees and bowed at the top.

"Faster!" Vectis shouted up to Julian. But if he heard, it had little effect. The swaying tree dragged the rope back and forth, and with one leg, Julian was struggling just to keep from falling.

"Not good, not good," the young engineer mumbled as he moved closer to Vectis.

"Will it hold?" Vectis asked brusquely.

"The base of the tree will, but ..." he gestured weakly, "the increased wind puts the top in jeopardy."

Julian was halfway down, still moving hand over hand when an arrow slammed into his back. His body sagged and he pressed into the rope. He slid a few feet, and then stopped thirty feet up. For long seconds he hung motionless, as if gathering his strength. Everyone knew his slide would end at the bottom on the rocks.

Crack!

Vectis tilted his head upwards. The top of the tree was bent like a bow at ready, and swaying in the wind, but to Vectis it looked the same as it had before.

"It's going," the engineer said, "on the next big gust." He pointed to a jagged yellow line running up the bark near the bend.

Vectis hollered frantically at Julian to slide, telling him the tree was about to snap.

Julian opened and closed his grip, and managed to slide a few feet before the next big wind.

Craaack!

The top third of the tree folded slowly down toward the ground, taking Julian with it. The rope dropped twenty feet in a few seconds, then stopped with a jerk as the broken piece hung upside down by a sliver of twisted bark.

Julian clung desperately to the rope on the way down, but the sudden stop tore it from his hands. His body flipped into the air, end over end, like a discarded toy, until it skidded into the loose soil less than a foot from the rocks.

Vectis burst across the ground to Julian's side. He lay still, his eyes white and staring, but his mouth moving. "The ramp," he was saying, "they're undermining the ramp."

Craaack!

Vectis didn't even glance up. He grabbed Julian by the arms and dragged him as fast as he could across the muddy clay. The top of the tree slammed into the ground with an explosion of sound, splattering slabs of oak through the air. Not one piece touched them.

"Where's that surgeon?" Vectis yelled as he dropped down beside Julian.

"It's the ramp," Julian mumbled again, almost incoherently.

Vectis glanced toward the ramp. The enormous siege machines were now over halfway up the incline.

Thousands of soldiers were moving steadily upward.

And near the wall, the ramp was hollow.

35

Sammonicus's eyes widened. "An accident?" he said. "How could someone die at a social gathering?"

Neeve shook her head, too depressed to respond. She closed her eyes and tried to breathe slowly. Here she was, a guest of the powerful senator, Titus Severus, and she managed to kill one of his guests. Why didn't she simply walk away, or run from the drunken sot, or at least call someone? That's what she should have done—screamed for help. But no, she was too proud. She insisted on dealing with the problem herself. Now a man was dead, and she could be in serious trouble. She had tried so hard to help Taranis, but now this.

"Mistress?"

"I do not wish to speak of it," Neeve said. "Ready yourself. I will talk to the senator at the morning meal, and then, if he permits it, we will leave."

"Where will we go?" Sammonicus asked.

"Away from here," she whispered.

The next morning Neeve paused at the entrance to the dining room. She had told Sammonicus they would leave after the early meal, but she had deep concerns about how Roman authorities might view the situation. She had, after all, pushed a Roman citizen to his death. She sat down gingerly on a couch and waited.

"A fine day," Marcellus said as he slipped onto the couch beside her.

"You know it's nothing of the sort," Neeve said. She had decided to confront the issue squarely. "I have brought shame on your name and on this house." Her heart beat loudly in her chest. "When the senator arrives, I will tell him the same, and leave directly."

"I don't think you understand the situation," he said.

Neeve swallowed. She was in trouble. In Britannia when a tribesman killed a Roman citizen, the soldiers came and dragged him off to the city courts. The message was clear to all non-citizens: Rome protects its own. "I am prepared to speak to the magistrates," she said. "I will tell them—"

"Neeve—"

"I will tell them it was an accident. That's what I shall say … it was a pure accident. I had no idea he would—"

"Listen to me," Marcellus said. "Several magistrates attended the festivity last night. Do you understand? Orestes—that was the man's name—Orestes was known for his drunken episodes. Last year he accosted a quaestor's daughter … dragged her into the slaves' quarters … created quite a scandal. You have nothing to worry about."

Neeve sipped her apple nectar. She had been prepared for the worst, and now she didn't know what to say. Romans were incredibly protective of their citizens. "Are you certain?" she asked.

"Yes, my father and I talked to three magistrates last night, and they have already dismissed the issue. As far as they were concerned, Orestes received just payment for his debaucherous ways."

Neeve felt the world slowing to normal speed. "What did your father say?" she asked.

"The same. He was embarrassed for having put you in such a position. You were a guest, and he should have been more discriminating with his invitations … entirely his fault, he said. He never should have allowed the man into his home."

"Very gracious of the senator to say so," Neeve said.

"My father never liked the man. On more than one occasion he has complained that Orestes drinks his fill of sour wine before arriving at our villa and then drools into fine wine as if it were sow slop. As for last night, he told the magistrates if he had caught Junius Orestes treating you ill, he would have ordered a guard to run him through on the spot."

"I … I am stunned," she said.

"More than a dozen guests witnessed what happened on that balcony. They all said Orestes lunged at you, so violently they feared for your life."

"And you? You are not upset?"

"Upset? Had I been on that balcony, I would have pitched him off myself, and I told the magistrates so."

"I don't know what to say."

"Say nothing. Eat your morning meal and forget all that nonsense about leaving."

"It might be better if I did leave," she said.

"Not acceptable. If you left, it would suggest the Severus household thought your actions were inappropriate. And we do not. So you see, our integrity is at stake." He grinned. "You cannot leave, at least through the summer. Anything else would do us a disservice."

"Are you certain?" she asked.

"I'm certain," he said. "How could you think otherwise?"

She hesitated, and then said, "I have noticed your busyness these past weeks, and naturally assumed that … well, that you …." Her voice trailed off.

"That I've been purposely busy?" he asked. "Is that what you think?"

"Not purposely busy, more like genuinely busy as you attend to all your duties. I've thought more than once that my presence may have become an intrusion."

"No, no," he said, "you are no intrusion." He sighed. "It's true, I have been busy with certain issues, but please believe me, it has nothing to do with you." His dark eyes held her for a moment to make the point. Then, leaning back he added, "Duties are not to blame for my busyness. I have added items to my schedule because … ah … well, I have been rushing more than usual because of special meetings … here and there. It's hard to explain but I'll just say that these meetings are useful to me … time consuming, but they help me understand who I am, I suppose."

She looked at him, confused.

He shrugged. "Everyone has fundamental questions begging answers, and I am no different. Since my return to Rome I've been searching for answers to my questions. These meetings provide a measure of peace for me."

"I don't understand," she said.

"I'm not sure I do either," he said. "This is a private quest. It takes me away at times and leaves me in contemplative moods at other times." He lifted his hand as if he were trying to find the appropriate words. "I sometimes ask myself why I am so different from other Romans. Why do I have such questions? Others follow the paths of their fathers, and rejoice in their heritage, but I … I find only torment in these things, and an inexorable pull toward something quite hazardous."

"Forgive me," Neeve said, shaking her head. "I'm confused …."

"Of course you are," he said. "I ramble on like a demented oracle." He shifted on his couch, as if to signal a change of conversation. His easy smile returned. "Be assured," he said, "I am exceedingly pleased that Neeve mapmaker—the most interesting person I've ever met, certainly the most beautiful—will remain at our villa."

"And she thanks you for your gracious invitation," Neeve said properly, bowing her head. Speaking in the third person and bowing formally felt appropriate. It distanced her from the conversation, and especially from things she preferred to leave unspoken. She still thought about Vectis constantly, still wore his wedding ring, but there was no doubt her feelings for Marcellus were increasing by the day.

Undeterred by her formal reply, he said, "I have a secret plan. Care to know what it is?" He turned his head slightly, amusement in his eyes.

"Curiosity has been a weakness," she said.

"My plan is to keep Neeve mapmaker around long enough so that I grow on her."

"Hmm … is this your standard operating plan?"

"No, too time consuming," he said. "But in special circumstances I follow this course."

"And this is a special circumstance?"

"Very special," he said.

"You told me that in vineyards some shoots grow favorably, and some require pruning."

"I did."

"Then how can you predict favorable growth?"

"Oh, that's the best part of my plan," he said. "I limit her access to other men. In this way, I compare favorably." He stretched out leisurely on his couch. "From there, healthy growth is predictable."

"A clever plan."

"Yes, I think so."

Neeve smiled. She couldn't help herself. She felt incredibly drawn to Marcellus, but wished she didn't.

36

Vectis left Julian in the hands of a competent surgeon. He was sorry to abandon his friend, but a greater duty called. He remained only long enough to hear the surgeon say, "He's fortunate. The arrow struck the shoulder joint, a painful recovery, but he'll live."

Vectis hurried toward the ramp. The lumbering siege machines were nearing the top of the incline, and long lines of heavily clad soldiers moved steadily upward under the canopies.

"Where's Commodus?" Vectis shouted to an officer at the foot of the incline. He realized he had not used the proper designation, but he didn't care.

The officer pointed toward the engineers' tent.

"Supreme Commander," Vectis said as he entered the tent. "I must speak to you without delay."

Commodus had apparently been giving instructions to his officers, and the interruption displeased him greatly. His eyes locked on Vectis, the corners of his mouth drawing downward. "I thought I made myself clear," he said. "You deal solely with the logistic side of the siege. I handle the assault."

"We must break off the assault immediately. The soldiers are in grave danger."

Commodus smiled coldly. "I will speak with you later. You are dismissed."

"I wish to speak now," Vectis said, stressing the word *now*.

The officers froze. Only their eyes moved slightly.

Commodus's face turned an instant purple, his eyes bulging with rage. Presumably, no one had ever contradicted the Supreme Commander, and Vectis wished he hadn't been the first, but still, even as Commodus opened his mouth to speak, Vectis cut him off, saying, "With respect, Supreme Commander, I would not interrupt but for an extreme emergency."

Commodus recovered enough to say in a pinched voice, "You forget yourself, Tribune."

"I apologize, Supreme Commander, but I have urgent news."

Commodus waved his hand for the officers to clear the tent, and even signaled his Numidian bodyguards to do the same. He waited with arms folded until the last had departed and the tent flaps had been closed. Then he turned toward Vectis and ground his teeth like a rabid dog. "If you ever humiliate me again," he said, "I will have you flogged until you are dead. Do you understand? Dead!"

"Yes, Supreme Commander."

"I'm in charge here, not you." He slammed his open palm on the table and his blond wig bounced on his head. "In Britannia you treated me as if I were a fool, and I said nothing. You ordered me to do this, and ordered me to do that ... you even sent your centurion to inspect my fort, and I had to obey him. A vulgar centurion! Do you know how that offended me?"

Vectis remained mute. He knew Commodus expected silence.

"And now ... after I treated you with great deference, you seek every way to demean me ... setting up a tree tower within sight of my command tent ... barging into my meeting to make demands on me as if you were still the superior officer. You are not! I am!"

Vectis waited, but he was growing concerned about the men on the ramp. "You have been extremely tolerant, Supreme Commander—"

"Don't patronize me! Do you think my small stature makes me a child? Julius Caesar was my size!"

Vectis nodded, though he knew the statement to be untrue.

"Few realize this about Caesar," Commodus continued, as if it were important. He drew in the tattoos above his eyes so they joined in a solid black line. "People see him in bronze and stone, and think those statues represent Caesar's proper height."

"They've dug under the ramp."

"What?"

"I said, the city dwellers have been undermining the ramp. It's hollow."

"Hollow? Preposterous!"

"I'm afraid it's true."

"How do you know this?"

"My military aide, Julian Quintillius—"

"Your aide climbed the tree tower."

"Yes, and he reported—"

"What? What did he report? A tunnel? He saw them digging a tunnel under my ramp?"

"He said—"

"Because I don't believe it. Not for one minute do I believe this report. Is that what you're saying? That they hollowed out my ramp, and no one heard them digging? No, no, that is not possible." He paced the tent. "How could they dig under a ramp of loose earth and stone? It would have collapsed by now. Yes, it would have collapsed. They couldn't undermine loose fill."

"They probably used support timbers with ropes—"

"No, I cannot believe it." Commodus was shaking his head.

"And now they're waiting to dislodge the timbers," Vectis said, completing his thought. "When we have the greatest number of troops on the incline, they will pull the ropes."

"Not possible," Commodus said, shaking his head. "I have never heard of anyone hollowing out a ramp."

"It's been done before, Supreme Commander."

"Not in my experience," Commodus said, thrusting out his neck so that he looked like a chicken.

Vectis clamped his jaw shut. The fool standing before him with the bizarre wig was a political appointee with no military experience, but Vectis dared not remind him of it.

Commodus started to pace again. Then, with his finger wagging in the air he said, "You say your aide observed them digging a tunnel?

Eh? But how could that be? He cannot see under the ground, can he? Of course not. At best he witnessed desperate townspeople moving earth. That's all he saw. Even if they were digging, they likely were doing so to construct an inner earthen wall."

"Julian Quintillius is an experienced soldier. He would know an earthen wall if he saw it."

"Fetch me your aide this instant. I want a talk with him."

"He's in the surgery now—"

"The surgery, you say. Yes, very convenient. I cannot interrogate him. So the story of city dwellers digging under my ramp comes only from your lips." Commodus chuckled without humor. "We're finally getting down to it, are we?"

"I don't understand."

"I think you do. Something smells here. And the foul stench sickens me."

Vectis tried to prevent Commodus from pursuing his line of thought. "Think about it," he said. "Every night the city dwellers dance and laugh at us. Why? Because they know our ramp will fail."

"They dance and laugh," Commodus said, the tiny veins in his neck bulging, "because they understand the destructive nature of jealousy and resentment."

"They know nothing about our situation—"

"They know. Believe me, they know."

"Supreme Commander, listen to me—"

"Oh, I am listening," Commodus said. "And do you know what I'm hearing? I'm hearing the pathetic attempt of a man stripped of his authority, now determined to tarnish my moment of glory." He paused. "It is clear to me, so very clear. You want to stop this siege, to have me pack my tents at the very moment of triumph."

"You cannot believe—"

"Do you understand what I have done here? No, of course not. A man of your limited understanding is blinded to history. You drink the bitter wine of hate and deceit."

"Supreme Commander—"

"A thousand years from now, when people pass this place, they will ask who built this ramp and who laid siege to this city. And they will hear my name. My name! Gaius Commodus built this ramp and laid siege to this city. He obtained a glorious victory in the midst of hostile barbarians. He was like Julius Caesar at Alesia and Flavius Silva at Masada. Yes, Gaius Commodus is one of the immortals!" He fixed his eyes on Vectis. "Do you understand? I will *never* be forgotten."

"Supreme Commander, at least let's clear the ramp and probe it with rods to see if—"

"No! A thousand times no! You want to steal my glory. You want people to say Commodus built this ramp, but ran away, afraid to use it. You want—"

Boooom!

The tent shook as if caught in a gale wind. The table vibrated like a reed instrument. Dust drifted down from the covering overhead.

And outside the air exploded with groans and cries.

Vectis ripped open the flap and dashed toward the ramp.

He stopped. A brown cloud of dust was rising over a massive hole in the ramp. Men were screaming and crying out to the gods they had so long neglected. They pushed and stumbled over the backs of others in their haste to get off the incline, their faces blackened around the mouth and eyes, their bodies bloodied, some with crushed or broken limbs.

The top of the siege tower was still visible in the hole, angled and poking out about ten feet, as if it were a ship's mast going down at sea. Everything else was gone, the ropes, the pulleys, the mules, the soldiers—everything— swallowed by the gaping hole in the ramp. Hundreds of soldiers buried under tons of stone and earth, and hundreds more were limping off the remains of the incline.

Vectis turned to Commodus, who was standing open-mouthed beside him. "Orders, Supreme Commander?" he said.

"Twenty-eight bodies recovered," the centurion said quietly. "Nine hundred and sixty-four failures to report. Three hundred and twenty-two injured." He folded his papyrus record book and looked at Vectis. "Most of the injuries are minor," he said, trying to inject good news. "They should be available for duty in a day or two."

"Thank you, First Centurion," Vectis said. "Double the guard tonight, but all others I want in their tents. They need sleep."

Commodus had fled. Minutes after the ramp had collapsed, Commodus took his Numidian bodyguards and left the field for his tent. He had stayed there the entire day. Vectis assumed command, organizing the rescue and clean up. Unfortunately, few had need of rescue, maybe twenty in all. Nearly a thousand soldiers lay forever under the avalanche of earth and stone.

And then the courtesans appeared on the wall. Less than an hour after the collapse of the ramp, scores of them came out dancing and singing, and taunting the soldiers involved in the rescue.

Vectis beckoned the closest centurion. "Do we have any Scythians among the archers?" he asked.

"Ten, maybe fifteen," the centurion replied.

"Bring them to me," Vectis said. He had long respected Scythian archers. Rome had never been able to produce bowmen anywhere near the skill of the eastern archers. And the best of them all were the Scythians. They could ride and shoot better than standing archers anywhere in the world. Given the chance, they could pick the eye out of an adversary at a three hundred paces.

Minutes later ten thin-boned archers with long black hair and sleek faces approached him.

"Those courtesans," Vectis said. "Can you take down one or two of them?"

The Scythian commander glanced up at the dancing courtesans and his face contorted into a smile. "Which breast?" he asked.

Now the screams were coming from the top of the wall. The Scythians had managed to drop eight or nine courtesans on their first shots; six more died as they rushed for the ramp leading off the wall.

During the day, Vectis felt an overwhelming sense of guilt, as he viewed the suffering around him. Soldiers had every right to expect their officers to lead them to victory and do it in a way that claimed the fewest lives. He had failed them miserably. He had allowed an inexperienced political appointee to dictate strategy, when as the military tribune, he should have found a way to control the situation.

Senator Titus Severus had assumed Vectis's frontier experience in Britannia and North Africa would guard against catastrophe, but the worst happened despite his presence. His duty was clear. He must figure a way to salvage something from the disaster even if it meant confronting Commodus.

Vectis sent for the young engineer. He might be odd, but at least he was competent. And he wasn't afraid of Commodus. Vectis pulled him to the side. "Have you noticed this city rests on a dried riverbed?" he asked.

"Of course," the engineer said. "Every ancient city grew up on a river, and many like this one had the river running straight through the center."

"Where specifically?" Vectis asked.

"The river at this city?"

"Yes, here."

"I don't know specifically," the engineer said. "This town relies on its farms and pigs, and they are outside the walls. That's why the city dwellers are starving." He laughed for no reason. "I mean, you can't see the exact spot where the river entered the walls because it's obscured by years of cultivation."

"I thought as much," Vectis said. "The chief engineer said there was no point asking you." He turned to go.

"I said you can't see the exact spot, but I can figure it out. I just need time."

"You have three hours of light. Take one of those horses." He pointed to a work tent where a dozen horses were tethered. "And don't come back without good information."

With an hour to spare, the engineer returned. For once his half grin had been replaced with a very serious look. He knew why Vectis had him plot the course of the river. "You want to go under the wall, don't you?" he said.

Vectis steadied the engineer's horse as he dismounted. "Did you discover the entry point?" he asked.

"Yes, quite easily, actually. I could see two points where the river might enter, but one had piled stones which told me—"

"We don't have time," Vectis said. The sun was already an orange ball, swollen on the horizon. "Do you know the entry point?"

"Yes, but ... there could be a problem." He struggled in his clothes.

"Let's hear it."

"The entry point is directly below a guard tower," he said, giving Vectis an apologetic look.

"Take me there," Vectis said.

Ten minutes later they arrived across from the tower. Vectis walked along the seven-foot deep trench the Roman soldiers had dug to prevent city dwellers from escaping or mounting a surprise attack. The engineer pointed out the rocks piled along the edge of the wall.

"How long ago did the river change course?" Vectis asked.

The engineer snorted and scratched his face. "Maybe a hundred years, fifty for sure. This is an old city."

"What's their water source now?"

"Springs. This whole area is littered with springs, especially in the hills. Our own supply comes from ...."

Vectis watched his mouth move without listening. He needed to think. Most of the present city dwellers probably had no idea a river originally fed their city. Like all walled cities, the original builders would have dug deeply into the ground when beginning the wall, but where the river entered, they'd have left a gap. To keep out intruders, and yet still allow the river to flow freely, they probably constructed iron bars, which no doubt had rusted away long ago.

By now the sun had completely disappeared, and the city wall loomed black against the starlit sky. Vectis sent for the First Centurion and asked him to bring two of his best soldiers. They crept carefully through a section of defensive hooks and traps and reached the place where the engineer predicted they would find the dry riverbed. The twenty or so soldiers in the tower above exchanged calls as they guarded their respective areas, but Vectis could also hear a good amount of celebration taking place. Evidently, the townspeople were elated at the collapse of the ramp and were toasting their good fortune.

Vectis ran his eye over the stone heaped against the bottom of the wall where the river had once flowed into the city. It was difficult to spot because long ago someone had wisely created a field of stone in front of the blocked riverbed to disguise the ancient gap in the wall. Now the scattered rock worked against them. Vectis could remove stones from the dry riverbed and deposit them in the rock field without fear of being detected, and he could do it safely. The celebrants were creating enough noise to cover a marching army.

They formed a line and lugged rock after rock until they had dug a channel eight feet under the wall. The tunnel smelled like rotting leaves and looked as if it would collapse at any moment, burying them like the unfortunates on the ramp. Halfway through Vectis thought he could identify remnants of an old iron grate, but in the dark he couldn't be certain. He was certain, however, about where the rock fill ended because as he was feeling for the next loose stone, the whole section in front of him tumbled into the city with a crash.

The startled soldier behind Vectis uttered some expletive, then caught himself. Bad enough that the wall had crumbled and resonated through the tower. How much worse to announce their presence with a curse in the Roman tongue?

Vectis poked his head through the hole and gazed into the city, almost surprised at their success. Then, abruptly, he began to repair the last section of the hollowed out wall, hoping to conceal the hole they had made.

He saw legs approaching, clearly one of the guards.

Instinctively, Vectis drew back into the shadows, his fingers slipping out his dagger, waiting. He hoped the man's curiosity would lead him to stick his head into the opening before sounding the alarm. The man sauntered straight up to the hole and then stopped. Vectis readied his dagger, his body coiled, set to spring. The man groaned, and relieved himself, splashing off the rocks and into the hole. When he had finished, he stumbled away, wineskin in hand.

Vectis whispered to the soldier behind him, "Crawl past me and seal the tunnel, and be quick about it." He rubbed the splatter off his face. He had taken enough unpleasant duties for the day.

That night, after scrubbing himself in a bucket of water, Vectis lay awake in his tent, thinking about the breach in the wall. They had created a hole large enough for armed soldiers to crawl through, but not so large that the breach would be easily detected in the morning. Vectis decided to gamble everything on entering the city the next night.

Commodus had seven thousand men at his command, but now with a thousand attack soldiers gone, they had lost a significant part of their ability to mount an offensive. A third of any army had to be kept in reserve for support duties and to guard against counteroffensives. Vectis's plan required a diversion on the opposite side of the city from the riverbed, which meant fewer than a thousand soldiers to enter and control the city. It was a definite gamble, but one that Vectis knew he had to take. The alternative was to slink back to Porolissum, defeated.

The bigger gamble was how Commodus would react to his plans. The man had made it clear that Vectis should keep his nose out of military planning. With Commodus cloistered in his tent, Vectis thought about initiating the attack on his own authority, but he stood to gain a military victory only. He needed more, much more, if he was ever to return to Rome, and from there to Britannia to find Neeve.

PART FOUR:
Schemes and Plots

37

Calpurnia waited for Balbinus by the edge of the Tiber River. She had been shopping in the great porticoes of the Capitoline Hill, buying a few items for the upcoming summer festivities. Behind her at a fitting distance stood a dozen servants bearing packages.

Balbinus arrived full of apologies for his tardiness, but excited with news from the city's gossip mills. He stepped out of his carrying litter and dismissed the slaves with a flick of his hand. Calpurnia smiled. How he loved exercising power, she thought. For so long he had stood in the background, a man of limited authority, but now with his elevated station, he had but to clear his throat and a phalanx of servants would rush to do his bidding. She watched him hurrying down the cobbled path toward her, a gang of attendants trailing him.

"Calpurnia!" he called as he rushed to her side. "You are so forbearing and I so selfish. Can you ever forgive me for my lateness?"

"I confess I cannot," she said. "You will have to be punished. Perhaps I shall lash your bare bottom with wet willows in the private baths."

"A fitting punishment," he said. "I will endure every stroke with courage."

"We shall see," she said, kissing him.

"When you hear the reason for my delay," he said, "you will forgive me."

She took his arm and together they strolled along the broad path that followed the Tiber.

"I was delayed," he said, "because the city is buzzing with fascinating gossip."

"Truly."

"You have heard nothing about the Severus scandal?"

Calpurnia shook her head.

"It seems that the Severuses have taken a Britannic Celt into their home," Balbinus said. "And at their spring festival she killed Junius Orestes ... literally threw him off a balcony."

"You cannot be serious," Calpurnia said.

"Indeed, I am. Apparently, she's some kind of warrior woman from the Britannic Isle ... tall and strong in body ... belonged to one of those throat-slitting tribes beyond the Antonine Wall, they say. Why she's in Rome nobody knows, but she is with Marcellus Severus day and night ... Venus-like beauty, they say." He chuckled. "So who can fault the Severus boy's interest? Everyone's heard about those island women and their sexual appetites."

"It must be the cold weather," Calpurnia said.

"Anything warm excites them," Balbinus said, agreeing. "Well, it seems that Orestes took a fancy to the barbarian woman, tried to touch her or something. Words were exchanged and she slammed his head into the stone rail. Then she hoisted him over her head and hurled him off the balcony. Broke his neck, I'm told, and probably every other bone in his body."

"Amazing," Calpurnia said.

"I should say. When I first heard of it, I had hoped the little episode might divert Senator Severus from pursuing his investigation so ardently. But he and that boy of his were on the situation like flies on meat. I have no idea what they paid ... it must have been a sweet booty because before the guests had time to swallow their wine, the whole issue had been put to bed."

"I am surprised," Calpurnia said. "Senator Severus has powerful enemies, has he not?"

"Certainly," Balbinus said. "Chief among them are Senators Coelius and Tertullus. But as I say, the Severuses headed off any possible embarrassment that same night."

"Unfortunate."

"Indeed. But one thing may be of interest to you." He raised his eyebrows to build suspense.

"What is it?" Calpurnia asked.

"You will swear I have been swilling Sabaium all morning."

"You seem sober. Speak it out."

"Well, apparently this island woman has similarities to someone you know." He licked his thick lips, obviously enjoying the conversation.

"And who might that be?"

"More than similarities," he teased. "They say the two faces are like the die and the coin—the stamp no different from the image."

She sighed, waiting.

"*You*, my love," he said. "It's you! They say your faces are identical."

Calpurnia frowned. "You *have* been drinking Sabaium. Only twins are identical."

"True, she is taller, I'm told, and her hair hangs like a barbarian, but her face is your image. And she has crystal blue eyes, exactly like yours."

"Romans always think foreigners look alike," Calpurnia said. "I agree that Celts from whatever part of the Empire do have strong similarities." She picked up a stone and flicked it into the fast moving waters. The whole conversation disturbed her. A Britannic woman identical to her, Balbinus had said. What was going on? First, she sees a barbarian chieftain with the same name as her brother, and he turns out to be Rome's greatest enemy. And now this woman! Balbinus hadn't been drinking or repeating idle gossip. She had heard the same story earlier that morning when a woman acquaintance came trotting across the forum and breathlessly told her everything about the barbarian woman at the Severus outing.

Calpurnia shuddered.

Could these barbarians be her lost family?

She was from Britannia, the same as these Celts. Her story of being raised by a noble family in Germania was entirely a fabrication. The Roman aristocracy loved their own kind, even if they happened to be from the provinces. She had told Balbinus that wars had devastated her fortune. It made a good story. The truth was she had never even been in Germania, and she had nothing to do with nobility.

A slave since childhood, that's what she had been, first in the army camps, and then passed around from officer to officer. Her beauty and shrewd mind had saved her. Officers sought after her, desired her and showered her with gifts. It was not long before only the highest officers could have her. They spent fortunes to purchase her, and once in their possession, she made certain her affection could not be acquired easily. But when they pleased her, she tripled their pleasure in ways they could never have imagined. They soon learned she was more than a sex slave. She was a woman of substance.

They wanted her approval, her love, she supposed. She gave it sparingly. She demanded tutors in language, in philosophy, in courtly manners. The more sophisticated she became, the more they desired her. Her good fortune came five years ago when an elderly officer freed her. She made it clear her deepest affection could only be given to that person who loved her enough to set her free. On the day he freed her, she left.

Taranis, the island woman ... who were they?

She had dim recollections of two brothers and a sister.

The fragmented memories of childhood swirled around her. She remembered the Romans coming ... her mother picking her up and hurrying across a field, but the soldiers caught them. They dragged her mother by the arms. She struggled. They beat her until she stopped struggling. Calpurnia remembered crying. Then they took turns at her mother, a whole group of them. Her last memory was being thrown into a Roman cart, and seeing her mother in a ditch, lying very still.

Calpurnia knew what she had to do—meet this Britannic woman. Some useful information might come from such an encounter, especially since she was a guest of the Severus household. But Calpurnia would have to be careful. A chance meeting perhaps. Yes, a chance meeting where two women could chat about their households. She would send a runner to wait outside the Severus villa.

"Calpurnia?" Balbinus was staring at her.

"Yes, my love," she said, turning her eyes lazily toward him.

"You seem to be in deep contemplation."

"Yes, I was," she said.

"May I ask your thoughts?"

She took his hand. "I was thinking about you, my love. About you."

"About me?"

"Yes … and how enormously proud I am to be seen with you."

A smile of delight spread across his face.

38

Commodus's clerk jumped from his seat the moment Vectis entered the command tent. "The Supreme Commander cannot be disturbed," he cried, raising his hands in protest.

Vectis pushed past the clerk as if he weren't even there. He continued down the passageway toward Commodus's private rooms with the clerk at his heels. Vectis knew he was casting dice with his life, but the gamble was necessary. Commodus had not been seen since the collapse of the ramp the day before, and if Vectis was to mount an attack, he had to do so immediately. The official word was that Commodus had spent the day with his officers, determining what steps should be taken next. Who those officers might be, Vectis had no idea. But he needed to see Commodus, and he needed to see him now.

Two Numidian bodyguards stepped in front of Vectis as he approached the tent door.

"Vectis Trebellius, military tribune to see the Supreme Commander," he said loudly.

"So you have come to gloat!" Commodus screeched from inside the tent. "Let him enter. I want to pronounce his sentence personally."

The Numidians seized him by the arms and half dragged him before Commodus who was sitting up to his neck in a full-sized bathtub. He had no wig and the crown of his head glistened like the skin of a roasted pig.

"Did you amuse yourself with the other officers?" he asked, propping himself up as high as he could in the tub, his slender shoulders barely visible above the steaming surface of water. "Well? Did you rejoice in my failure?"

"We despaired at the loss of so many good men," Vectis said.

"You think I have no idea what you do behind my back? Oh, I know. Before the gods, I know." His eyes lit up as if he were privy to all mysteries. "I know exactly what you officers of the legionary corps do when someone comes in from the outside. You can't stand to see a political appointee succeed, can you? You act obedient, call me Supreme Commander, but disobey every command I give. That ramp would have been perfectly sound if it had been built in the time I specified. But now I will be blamed for the failure."

"Supreme Commander—"

"Silence!" he shouted. He leapt out of his bathtub, sloshing water over the top and across the thatched floor. He stood before Vectis, crouched like an animal, his body shaking with rage, his pink skin radiating steam as if from a pond in winter. "I will be blamed," he said, "but you will suffer the greater penalty."

Vectis couldn't help noticing that there wasn't a single hair on Commodus's body, not one, from his head to his feet.

"I hope my nakedness satisfies you," he said, curling his lip. Then, turning to his guards he said, "This man has failed to follow orders. Whip him until his skin melts, and then hang him from his broken tree tower so the birds can feed."

"I am protected by Senator Titus Severus," Vectis said. "You should know that."

Commodus turned his back. His pride was determining his judgment, the exact thing Vectis had feared.

"I have found a way to destroy the city," Vectis said.

The Numidians already had Vectis at the door.

"Everyone will say the ramp was a diversion for the real attack," Vectis added.

Commodus signaled with his hand to hold. "What is your plan?" he asked.

Vectis straightened his tunic and said, "In three days you will be dining in the city." Vectis was more interested in exciting Commodus's interest than answering his question. "If I'm wrong," he added, "then I will go willingly to the tree."

Commodus waved away his bodyguards. He suddenly realized he was naked and snatched his robe off a couch to cover himself. "Tell me your plan," he repeated.

"You served with me in Britannia," Vectis said. "You know my abilities. If I say I can take the city in a few days, I can." Vectis realized he had now reached the most dangerous point in his plan. He had to be convincing, but not overly bruise Commodus's ego.

"Proceed," Commodus said.

"I will need assurances from you —"

"I grant no assurances," he said imperiously.

"You are the senior commander, and I the junior … I accept that. But you must understand your position. You have been laying siege to an insignificant Costoboci city for over a year … and you have failed. Yes, you can blame me or some other officer, but when you arrive back at the Senate, they will ask one question: Where are the heads of the city's chief priests and administrators? And you will not have them unless you give me complete freedom to proceed with the attack."

"Complete freedom. What does that mean?" Commodus asked. He looked defeated, but hopeful.

"You will stay in your tent because of a sudden illness, but you will issue orders that I, your military tribune, will direct the attack."

"And when we control the city?"

Vectis knew what he was asking. Senators Tertullus and Coelius had given Commodus this command as a reward for keeping quiet about their link with the rebellious Senator Atilius Titianus. Commanders who sieged cities were allowed to enrich themselves from the city treasury, as long as they brought a respectable amount back to Rome's coffers. "You, of course, will be in complete control once we have the city," Vectis said

"You are confident you can take the city?"

"I am. And I will tell everyone that I merely followed your plan, and achieved a glorious victory for you."

A satisfied look spread over Commodus's face.

"But I will need assurances," Vectis said.

Commodus narrowed his eyes.

"First, you will not kill everyone in the city, only the leaders."

"I don't see why—"

"I intend to give the inhabitants an opportunity to surrender," Vectis said. "I would rather embrace the city dwellers, than wade through their blood—and ours—to claim the prize."

"What else?"

Vectis pulled out a sheet of papyrus. He looked squarely at Commodus and said, "You will sign this paper."

"Let me see that," he said, yanking it out of Vectis's hand.

"It says that while you were in Britannia, former Senator Atilius Titianus ordered you to withdraw from your fort to the Antonine Wall."

"I will never sign such a paper!"

"It's not an admission of failure," Vectis said. "It merely states you had orders to withdraw and that you obeyed them."

"Still, I will not—"

"You are in great trouble here," Vectis said. "You've failed, which means that those who sent you, Senators Tertullus and Coelius, have failed. These are not men who accept disgrace easily, as I think you know. They will turn their backs on you, even hire someone to eliminate you." He leaned closer. "Why have you around when you are a living reminder of their failure?"

"But this letter makes me out a coward," Commodus said.

"Not at all. As far as you knew, every fort commander received the same orders."

A light flickered at the back of Commodus's eyes. "Actually," he said, "that's what I did think." He was starting to reconstruct history in his mind. "I would never have left my post if I thought it put the other forts at risk." He began to pace, thinking. He glanced at Vectis, embarrassed. "The problem is I have already told the Senate ... that is

... they construed my testimony to say you gave the order to retreat to the Wall."

Vectis thought of the men who had died needlessly because of Commodus's cowardice, but he put it aside. "The Senate misunderstood you," he said, providing Commodus a way out. "You wanted to sign this letter to clear up any confusion. A slight revision in testimony will mean nothing to anyone ... especially when you return from the German frontier victorious. Success mutes all criticism."

Commodus wiped his mouth, clearly anticipating his new status as a conquering hero. He swallowed a breath and asked Vectis a second time, "Are you certain you can take this city?"

"I will do it in three days," Vectis said, exuding a confidence he didn't have.

Commodus nodded and reached for his ink jar.

39

Neeve journeyed to the Forum, to the same shop where she had earlier purchased her gowns, choosing several other items, all reasonably priced and well constructed, even if they were not Milesian wool.

She left the shop with Sammonicus trailing behind, a pleasant autumn day with the sun warm on her face and the wind scattering leaves along the pathways. Colder days were coming and she thought it would be nice to take a leisurely walk by the Circus Maximus, maybe see some of the horses housed at the great Circus. She stopped. Directly ahead was an incredibly beautiful woman with an entourage of servants. The woman glanced at Neeve, smiled slightly, and turned back to a conversation she was having with one of her servants.

Neeve found herself gaping at the woman. She was tall, though not as tall as she, had flaxen hair swept up tastefully in ringlets with plaits behind, and brilliant blue eyes.

"Sammonicus," she said, her eyes riveted on the woman, "wait here. I have need to speak with someone."

"Mistress," Sammonicus said, "I should introduce you—"

Neeve ignored him and walked toward the woman, her heart pounding so loudly she felt as if surely one of the servants would be alarmed by the noise. The woman turned her head slightly in Neeve's direction, but continued her conversation, obviously aware of someone approaching, but refusing to acknowledge it. Neeve stopped in front of her and said haltingly, "Please excuse me, but may I speak with you."

The woman glanced around, as if an explanation for the intrusion could be found somewhere on the street. "Do I know you?" she asked.

"No ... no, I'm new to Rome," Neeve said. Then, realizing how witless that must sound, she continued speaking, making things worse: "I was surprised when I saw you because you look so elegant and graceful."

"Thank you," she said, her eyes narrowing.

Neeve couldn't stop staring at the woman's face, and finally blurted out, "You look much like me. Do you realize that?"

The woman stepped back and said, "Yes, perhaps. You have a Celtic background, I take it."

"Yes, from Britannia."

"That is fascinating," she said. "Well, enjoy yourself. It's a delightful day." She turned to go.

"Please," Neeve said. "Could I speak with you privately?"

The woman looked uncertain.

"Not to presume on your time," Neeve said hastily, "but just for a moment."

"Certainly," she said. She whispered something to a servant, and then moved gracefully to a portico for protection from the sun. Neeve noticed that the woman's skin was fair and untouched by the elements, unlike her own robust face and arms.

"I had a sister," Neeve said awkwardly, "but lost her long ago."

"I am so sorry."

"Thank you," Neeve said. "I never thought I would see her again, but today I ... ah, you have such a striking resemblance to me that I ...." Her voice caught in her throat. She realized she had forgotten to breathe.

The woman smiled. "And you think I could be your sister?"

Neeve suddenly felt foolish standing before so sophisticated a Roman lady and asking whether she might be a girl captured by legionaries in far off Britannia. She was about to apologize when she looked into the woman's azure eyes, and a chill swept over her. The woman had Taranis's eyes. "What do you know about your background?" Neeve asked.

"A family in Germania raised me," she said. "They were not my natural parents, but loving nonetheless."

"Not your natural parents?"

"No, my origins were never revealed to me. It was enough to be raised in a noble family, my adoptive parents said."

"Then you could be from Britannia?" Neeve said.

"I honestly doubt it, but I suppose I could be from anywhere," she said.

Neeve stared at her, wondering, not able to fully believe. Could this Roman woman be her sister? Her breath grew shallow once again. Her little sister, Nes. Sweet little Nes. Standing here in the heart of the Empire. She explored her face, looking for a mark from the granite tower by the bog. Nes had fallen from the tower and split her forehead on a jagged rock. She searched for the thin white scar, but the woman had powered her face and nothing could be seen.

"I can see you are a sincere person," the woman said. "I do hope you find your sister. It must be difficult for you."

"Do you have a scar on your forehead?" Neeve asked abruptly.

"A scar?"

"On your forehead."

The woman touched a spot near her hairline and swallowed nervously. "Yes," she said. "I have a small one here. I fell … as a child." She squeezed her eyes closed, trying to think. "I barely remember, but I fell off a rock, I think."

"A rock?"

"Yes, climbing."

"And your sister cried out to the spirits for you," Neeve said, grasping her wrist.

The woman pulled her arm back nervously. One of her guards stepped toward them, but she waved him off. "I really must go," she said.

"Try to remember," Neeve said. "You fell off a rock climbing, and a sister was with you. Can you remember that? She cleaned away the blood and—"

"A sister ... yes ... yes ... I do remember someone, a sister." Her face had a quizzical look.

"I know what's on the sole of your foot," Neeve said, still hardly daring to believe she had found her little sister.

"What?" Her eyes looked frozen.

"A burn mark," Neeve said.

"The burn ... you ... you know about ...."

"It looks like this," Neeve said, slipping her foot out of her sandals and showing the bottom.

The woman's hands jerked to her face.

Neeve replaced her sandal. "Can you remember how you burned yourself?" she asked.

"I ... I remember being under a tree," she said, "and burning my foot on the grass. A strange dream from childhood I have never understood."

"Yes, you were under a tree," Neeve said, "but you stood on a hot coal I had taken from the fire."

"Oh, my! Oh, my!" she cried. "I do remember."

Neeve caught the woman as she stumbled forward. She seemed about to faint.

"I remember now," she said, choking out her words, "the tree, the burning coal, the others ...."

Neeve steadied the woman. "There is a reason we have that burn," she said. "And it has to do with those others you remember."

The woman couldn't reply. She just stared at Neeve.

"Your two brothers, Taranis and Eston, and your sister, Neeve, stood on a hot coal one after the other. They pledged their souls ... that they would never separate. They would always protect each other, search for each other if need be." She looked at the woman and said, "You stood on that coal too, Nes. I am your sister, Neeve."

Neeve could see Nes's lips trembling, her eyes filling with tears. "Nes?" she whispered. "My name is Nes?"

Neeve smiled through her own tears.

Nes stared at Neeve for long seconds, her eyes roaming her face, and then she threw her arms around Neeve, kissing her on the neck. "My sister, Neeve," she whispered repeatedly.

Neeve allowed her tears to flow. Sweet little Nes clung to her and refused to let go. And Neeve felt as if her breast would explode with joy.

Nes squealed with laughter. "I thought you were some deranged woman from the provinces," she said, tapping a finger to her head. They were reclining on couches under a canvas awning in one of the many outdoor eating-houses. Nes kicked off her sandals and called for blankets. Neeve followed her example, and soon they were laughing and sipping hot calda, a diluted wine mixed with spices and aromatic herbs.

Nes continued, "I actually thought you might beat me if I gave a wrong response ... that's why I spoke to my guards, to stay close."

"Did you hear any gossip ... about a Celtic woman?" Neeve left her question hanging.

Nes's eyes widened. "That was you?" she asked.

Neeve nodded.

"All I heard was that Junius Orestes drank too much again and tried to molest a tall Celtic woman at the Severus's country villa." She made a face. "I confess the incident did cross my mind when you approached."

Neeve shook her head and said in a low voice, "It was terrible."

"No one blames you," Nes said. "Everyone knows what Orestes was like. Sooner or later someone would have taken revenge on him. It's just unfortunate you were placed in such an awkward position." Nes reached over and patted her sister's leg. "Let's not talk about him any longer," she said. "Let's talk about you and me ... something far more interesting." She laughed. "I cannot imagine how hard it must have been for you to approach a stranger on the street the way you did."

"It was terrifying," Neeve said. "My manservant has told me a hundred times a Roman lady must be introduced, but when I saw you on the pathway, I had to talk to you."

"I am glad you did."

"But suggesting to someone as elegant as you that we look alike was no easy task. I was afraid you might say you had no goats in your family, and march away."

"Oh, no," Nes said. "Looking at you is like looking into a mirror. Change your hair, your clothes ... a little white powder on your face ... who would know the difference?"

They talked for hours curled up on the outdoor couches. Nes called for stronger drinks, saying that Celtic women needed something with a bite. The innkeeper bowed and made their hot calda progressively stronger until Neeve felt lightheaded, but it was a pleasant feeling, almost euphoric. She told Nes about her lost family, about Caledonia's disappointing wars, and about Taranis being sent to Rome for the Triumph in the summer. Throughout the whole conversation, Nes shook her head in amazement, and more than once gave Neeve a comforting hug.

"You have done well," Neeve said, thinking she should stop talking about herself. "We feared you had been sold into slavery."

"The gods have been good," Nes said.

"And your situation now?" Neeve asked.

"I am the mistress of a rich plebeian named Gaius Balbinus."

"Wonderful," Neeve said. "Are you happy?"

"Oh, yes ... Balbinus is a good man ... a little fat," she said. Then she laughed. "Actually, he's a lot fat, but he is very rich."

Neeve giggled, something she could not recall doing since childhood. It felt good. She drank another cup. That felt good too.

"So if my sister needs anything," Nes said, pushing another drink toward Neeve, "and I mean *anything*, she can come to me ... because I have a rich, fat provider."

They giggled together.

"You must come and stay with us," Nes said.

"I will visit," Neeve said, "but I am situated well where I am."

"And where is that?"

"At the country villa of Senator Titus Severus," Neeve said.

"Senator Titus Severus!" Nes said, impressed. "I had no idea. I knew you attended their spring festival ... but living with them!" Nes blew out in amazement. "We are paupers next to Senator Severus and his handsome son ... what is his name ...?"

"Marcellus," Neeve said.

"Yes, Marcellus. I could be tempted to go for a country ride myself, if I were not so fondly attached to Balbinus."

"Marcellus is attractive," Neeve agreed.

"I have never been to any of the Severus villas," Nes said. "So tell me everything about them."

Neeve told her about the vineyards, the long underground cellars filled with countless wine barrels, the private bathhouses, the many reception and dining rooms. She talked about the senator and his kindly nature, about Marcellus and his business sense, his odd little ways.

"Odd ways? Nes said.

"Nothing important."

But Nes was acutely interested. "Does he eat toads? Or bathe in rhino urine?" she asked.

Neeve started to giggle again. "Nothing like that," she said.

"Then what? You must tell me everything."

"Oh, you are a gossip, little sister," Neeve said, waggling her finger.

"No," she said, smiling. "Gossips repeat what they hear. I merely like to know."

"A brave distinction," Neeve said, "but hardly one that removes the gossip label from your forehead."

"You are right, dear sister. I am a reprobate gossip. Tell me nothing." She paused and smiled slyly at Neeve. "Besides, I already know the secret of Marcellus Severus—he eats children, chops them up in his salad."

"No, no, no," Neeve said. "Marcellus simply attends meetings of some kind, and that's all. Nothing exciting or strange."

"Maybe he's a secret Druid casting spells, or something." She gave Neeve a spooky look.

"A Druid?" Neeve said, laughing. "I grew up with Druids. Believe me, Marcellus is no Druid."

"Well, it doesn't matter," Nes said. "He's a handsome beast, and that covers the deepest sins." She leaned back and said, "I suppose he's like many patricians who barely have time to burn incense to the household gods."

"At the lararium?"

"Yes."

Neeve frowned as she drained her cup. "I don't think Marcellus even knows the lararium exists, the way he rushes by it every day."

"A common thing."

"Perhaps, but I worry when someone ignores the gods." She looked at her sister. "Is it normal for a Roman never to invoke the gods? Because he never does ... not even when his father pronounces household blessings."

"Piety varies," Nes said. "But it all sounds perfectly natural to me. Nothing to worry about. Balbinus hardly refers to the gods either, unless he stubs his toe or something." She leaned closer. "But tell me, what do you and he do when no night meeting is scheduled?" She gave Neeve a leering look and said, "I would bet my jewels he could soon make a woman forget his odd ways."

"We sleep at night," Neeve said, smiling. "And since you are so prying, I will tell you we have consistently slept in our separate beds."

"You are lying to your sister, and that is not nice."

"In truth," Neeve said.

Nes sighed. "What a waste."

Neeve looked at Nes and said, "I am drawn to Marcellus, and perhaps in time we could ... but I have to be purposeful in my actions. Do you understand? What I want or desire is of no import. Taranis needs me. He will arrive in Rome soon, and I must find a way to help him, if that's possible."

"Oh, I am sorry," Nes said. "Of course you have more on your mind than empty flirtation ... and I will talk to Balbinus. Perhaps we might help, though I think such events are beyond our reach."

"There's one other thing ... a sadness in my heart ... a deep sadness for which I can find no consolation."

"You are trembling," Nes said.

"It's the wine," Neeve said. "It has affected my judgment, I fear, and my emotions. I apologize."

Nes moved to Neeve's couch and slipped an arm around her sister. "Sometimes wine merely removes our defenses," Nes said. "I am your sister. You don't need to be strong around me. You can be yourself."

Neeve tried to smile gamely but could not hide the pain. "I once had a love," she said, "a deep love, a genuine love … but now he's gone, and I cannot bear to think he is but dust." She snuggled into Nes's breast and felt unspeakable comfort in her arms.

Nes stroked her hair and kissed her forehead. "Was he from Britannia?" she asked.

"Rome," Neeve said. "Can you believe that? He came from this city. His name was Vectis Trebellius Quadratus, a Roman tribune, and the most beautiful man the gods ever created."

"Trebellius," Nes said slowly. "And you say he died?"

"Killed by Brigantes tribesmen," Neeve said, "over a year ago."

"So sad," Nes said. "So very sad."

40

The entire day before the attack, the Romans made a great show of breaking camp. Vectis ordered them to dismantle their tents along the siege line, hitch the mules to the carts, and haul the catapults to the far end of the city walls, as if readying for departure.

The city dwellers lined the walls, hooting and making merry. They poured skins of wine down their throats and shouted at the defeated Romans until their voices were thin and hoarse. It was a day to celebrate. After a year-long siege, the hated Romans were leaving.

By sunset most of the Roman tents had been taken down. Only the command quarters and the surgery at the center of camp remained standing. The soldiers busily made last minute preparations for their long march back to Porolissum on the Wall, and no one from the city seemed to notice that two cohorts of soldiers had hidden themselves on the opposite side of their city.

Vectis had asked Siccius, the First Centurion, to handpick a thousand men for the surprise attack. From that group Siccius selected fifty to go under the wall, and from the fifty, the ten best were chosen to mount the tower. He also included ten Scythian archers and three soldiers who could speak the Costoboci language.

An hour after dark, Vectis led his fifty soldiers and ten Scythians through the section of Roman defensive hooks and traps, and across the open ground to the tower beside the dry riverbed. They slipped under the wall, one by one, removed the last few remaining stones, and then with shields and full armor, they entered the city. The operation took a good part of the night, and Vectis, concerned about discovery and the lateness of the hour, began operations when only half had made it under the wall. He signaled the men to set up a perimeter, sealing off access to the tower. Then he and his ten soldiers climbed the stairs to the lookout.

Outside the walls, the First Centurion waited with the rest of the cohort for Vectis to storm the lookout tower. The plan was simple. Vectis and his men would take the tower and the tracks along the wall. Then, the centurion's soldiers would climb the secured walls with hooked ladders, and from there the infiltrators would fight their way to the central gatehouse where, outside the walls, the bulk of the Roman soldiers would be waiting.

Everything depended on surprise and a city afloat with wine.

Vectis entered the stairwell leading up to the tower platform, a dark and narrow turret smelling of mold and urine. His soldiers moved softly, but their footfalls made a hollow sound, a kind of echo that Vectis feared would be heard in the lookout chamber above.

When they reached the entrance to the tower platform, Vectis signaled for them to stop, stunned by what he heard. Snoring. Someone was snoring inside the stone turret. He edged toward the arched doorway. The stench of wine. He smiled to himself. He had hoped the image of Romans dismantling their siege camps would lead to festivities, but a lookout tower with snoring soldiers? That was beyond even his hopes. No doubt about it—city officials had opened their stores of wine to celebrate the Roman departure. And chief among the celebrants were these guards.

Vectis craned his head around the doorway and saw five men sprawled on the floor, definitely drunk, and definitely asleep. Their wineskins lay beside them. Another four sat with their backs propped against the stone parapet, their heads drooping on their chests. He stepped into the entrance and saw six or seven more guards, these ones with their backs to him, grasping the stone peaks for support, and staring mindlessly toward Roman lines

Vectis slipped back into the stairwell and held up his dagger. It would be close-quarters combat. A ten-inch blade was quick and deadly. The soldiers in the stairwell silently slid their swords back into their scabbards. They pulled out their daggers and pressed forward.

Suddenly, a guard entered the turret from the wall, shouting and kicking at the others lying on the floor. Vectis signaled with his hand for silence as he pushed his ear to the post. He could hear the soldiers on the floor muttering something that sounded like cursing. Then the guard from the wall laughed and shuffled back to his position. Vectis waited as voices lowered, became murmurs, and slowly drifted away. He glanced back at his soldiers, tightened his grip on his dagger, and charged onto the turret.

They took the guards grasping the stone peaks first, then the ones who staggered to their feet with bewildered eyes. Last were the drunken men on the floor who barely sat up before they slumped back into their own blood. In less than a minute the lookout tower was secure.

Vectis whipped his head around, looking up and down the track. No one had noticed the skirmish on the tower, no one except for one guard who was gazing in their direction through a haze of wine. "Go!" Vectis said, pointing toward the tracks. "Take that guard before he wakes up. Then set up a block as far down the wall as possible. Go!"

Instantly, the soldiers split into two groups, five going one way on the wall, five the other. The guard squinted toward the oncoming soldiers, and then wiped his mouth on his sleeve as if the motion would focus his mind. At the last second, understanding the danger, he let out a cry and staggered backwards. A dagger flashed toward his neck. He clutched the handle of his sword. Too late. His knees buckled, and he collapsed without another sound.

Vectis drew a white cloth from his tunic and signaled the First Centurion outside the walls with his soldiers. He did the same to the men surrounding the tower entrance below. A dozen soldiers and three Scythians raced up the stairs to provide added strength. Across the field came a stampede of Roman soldiers, their rush for the wall creating significantly more noise than Vectis had anticipated. The auxiliary soldiers were poorly trained, and the sound of hundreds of pounding feet and grinding metal reverberated across the open ground. Vectis groaned. The sloppy approach was certain to wake even the drunkest observer.

Shouts came from the towers along the wall.

And horns.

Vectis hopped onto the parapet, whooping and whirling his arms, trying to encourage the soldiers to move faster. No point in stealth when the enemy is blowing horns. "Faster! Faster!" he yelled to the soldiers crossing the open field. "What's the matter with you? Move! Move! Move!" He was standing in full view of the enemy archers on the next tower over, but if his soldiers didn't arrive in short order, it wouldn't matter.

Arrows smacked into the wall directly below his feet. Vectis leapt off the parapet and down to the floor, ducking behind the stone turret. About twenty enemy archers from the far tower had raced along the patrol track to reinforce the next tower over, and their bowmen were launching their arrows into the air in search of a victim. From such distance, they had no hope of accuracy, but whoever was directing them had the right idea. With the number of arrows falling, it was difficult for Vectis or the soldiers approaching the wall to maintain their attack. Arrows had struck more than a dozen Romans, and the ones who had managed to fling their hooks over the top of the wall were hesitating to climb the ladders.

"Centurion!" Vectis called down. "Get them up the ladders!"

Dawn was upon them. The enemy commander now had an idea how many Romans were climbing his walls. Vectis took a quick look over the inner wall at the city streets, still empty, except for a parade ground near the adjacent tower. City soldiers were organizing into units to deal with the invaders. Evidently, the commander in the next tower was neither a fool nor a drunk, and he was determined to stop the Roman invaders. His problem seemed to be rousing others to the call: for over five minutes his buglers had been blowing their horns, but few had responded. The city's defenders had either drunk themselves into oblivion, or had gone into hiding. Romans were known for overwhelming force, not stealth, and the enemy had good reason for thinking that thousands of Roman soldiers had breached their city walls.

It was a good sign for the invaders.

But now Vectis had to get his poorly trained soldiers into the city. They were not used to moving quickly and had no idea how essential speed was in a battle. Vectis ground his teeth. That fool, Commodus. He should have given his First Centurion freedom to train the men. The soldiers were coming over the wall like old men dragging themselves out of a bathtub. A good soldier knew enough to bolt up the ladder and get over the wall. These ones were crawling up with their shields positioned just so against any arrows that might happen their way.

Vectis blew out in frustration. Drunk or not, it wouldn't be long before the city organized and mounted a counterattack.

And then he noticed the empty ladders.

He leaned over the wall, trying to locate the problem.

Soldiers were gathered around fallen comrades rather than climbing ladders. Others were heading to ladders more distant from the archers. "Centurion!" Vectis screamed. "Fill those ladders!"

But Commodus had corrected his centurion so often in front of the soldiers that the men feared the enemy's arrows more than the wrath of their officers. Vectis opened his mouth to yell more commands, but saw the futility of it. He jerked his head around, searching for a Scythian. "You," he called. "Follow me."

With the Scythian in tow, Vectis rushed toward the empty ladders. He hollered down at a group of soldiers bunched together, their shields thrust upward for protection. "Climb now!" he said. They acted as if they couldn't hear him.

He shouted again.

They looked up.

"Now!"

They hesitated.

Vectis turned to the Scythian and pointed toward a man cowering at the edge of the group. "Take that one," he said.

The Scythian's black eyes darted to the man, and back to Vectis.

"Take him," Vectis said. "If you don't we'll all die."

The Scythian swung his bow around and loosed his arrow. It caught the man in the throat. The soldiers gaped at their fallen comrade.

"When this is over," Vectis shouted, "I will behead every one of you ...."

He didn't need to finish his sentence. The entire group scrambled for the ladders.

Moments later Vectis saw his First Centurion pushing men toward the wall, trying to increase the speed of the assault. "Get up that ladder!" he bellowed to one man whose hands had attached to the rungs and refused to move. "There are Romans inside that city!" But the man had frozen in fear. The centurion drew his sword, climbed several steps up the ladder, and thrust the blade into the man's back.

Vectis ran his eyes along the wall. Every ladder was now filled, and the soldiers were actually moving with reasonable speed. He headed down the patrol track, ignoring the arrows that whooshed by his head. Now was not the time for caution. He grabbed as many soldiers as he could and pulled them over the wall. Some he kept on the track to guard against city soldiers who might try to retake the patrol track. The rest he sent below to form a defensive square.

"Tribune, your orders?" The First Centurion had arrived in the tower.

"Organize the men below," Vectis said. "We have to take the central gate quickly."

Vectis paused a moment to study the narrow streets leading to the city gates. The enemy commander had guessed Vectis's objective. His soldiers were clogging the streets with anything they could drag from the buildings. They ripped apart roofs, smashed down walls and doors, and heaped the rubble in massive barricades across the roads. Then they smeared it with tar and set it on fire. Clouds of black soot swirled into the air, making observation impossible.

One street remained open. Vectis squinted into the smoke, but gave up. Why would the commander leave a single street open? An oversight? Or maybe now he was closing it off too. Vectis hurried down the stairs.

The centurion approached him and said, "Scouts report a main road still open to the gatehouse. Do you want to proceed?"

"I saw it before the smoke thickened," Vectis said. "But I don't like it."

"A trap?" the centurion asked.

"That commander knows we're heading for the main gates," Vectis said. "He's inviting us to march up that road."

The centurion grimaced. "If it's a trap, he will move his archers to ground level buildings. Too much smoke to be higher. But wherever they are, they cannot stop a tortoise formation." He glanced at the soldiers lined on the street near the tower. "Even these auxiliaries can link shields."

"I saw something before the smoke closed in," Vectis said. "It looked like men on the roofs along the open street. They can't be archers because, as you say, there's too much smoke."

"Why else would they be there?"

"They were very busy on the roofs," Vectis said.

The centurion nodded his understanding. "Old buildings," he said. "They're loosening stones on the roof, and when we come through, they'll dump them on us. We won't see the enemy or the stones."

"And in the chaos, their archers on the ground could finish us," Vectis said.

"A crafty commander," the centurion said.

"Yes, he knows Roman strategy, that we would like nothing more than to form in tortoise and head down that road."

"You want to clear one of the fires?" the centurion asked.

"No," Vectis said. "Something he will not expect. Barbarian stealth. I will take a third of the men and swing around the fires and approach the gates from the opposite side. It will take time, but I should be able to slip behind that commander's forces."

"Tribune, our troops are unreliable. You've already seen them—"

"I will also take the Scythians and the fifty that came with me under the wall. They're a solid group. The rest will do their duties, I guarantee it."

The centurion nodded. "I'll march the larger group into their trap," he said. "But I urge you to move with all speed. I cannot fool them for long."

Vectis led his men through the smoky streets at double time, a full trot. Their lungs burned from the inhaled grit, and their mouths and nostrils blackened from breathing hard, but they kept moving. Ahead of him Vectis sent runners to find a way around the fires. It proved to be difficult. Once off the main roads, the streets angled away, intersecting with other narrow passageways that led them even farther from the gatehouse. The smoke thinned, but now the streets stunk of garbage and rotting flesh. Vectis guessed the city people had set up houses to store their dead, and the smell was sickening. Choking soot had been better.

Every block or two a flurry of arrows would burst from a building, catching them from the side or rear. Wounded soldiers who could not keep up straggled behind like sick sheep. The rest heard their screams and packed together for safety.

Vectis was growing concerned. They needed to find a way to the gatehouse, and soon. It took a full fifteen minutes before they came across a main artery that led to the gatehouse. But at least they had managed to circle behind the organized resistance.

Increasingly, they came across companies of city soldiers wandering leaderless. On Vectis's instructions, the interpreters who spoke Costoboci called out: "Five thousand Roman soldiers are in your city. Lay your arms on the ground and surrender to the soldiers behind us. Only city leaders will be punished." Everywhere, clusters of Costoboci soldiers threw down their weapons and strained to see the Roman soldiers behind Vectis.

Minutes later the road turned sharply and issued into a huge plaza. Directly ahead on the other side of the plaza was the gatehouse, and in between, blocking the way, stood a thousand fully armed Costoboci soldiers.

The tiny Roman force stopped abruptly.

Vectis had less than three hundred men.

The Costoboci soldiers stared at the Romans.

Vectis drew a long breath. He pointed to the interpreters who shouted: "Five thousand Roman soldiers are in your city. Throw down your arms. Rome will spare all but the leaders."

The city soldiers stood where they were, bewildered.

Somebody in a white robe began shouting from the top of the gatehouse. He was obviously a man of importance, and standing as he was before the entrails of a goat, Vectis guessed he was the high priest. Vectis signaled the Scythians. The dark warriors drew their bows in one smooth motion, and the priest plunged to the ground, his chest bristling with arrows.

"Lay your arms on the ground," Vectis roared, the interpreters repeating his words with equal force, "and surrender to the Roman soldiers behind us. Only leaders will be punished."

Nobody moved.

"Lay your arms on the ground," the interpreters repeated. "Only leaders will be punished."

"Now! Or die!" Vectis screamed and he stepped toward the city soldiers.

One sword fell.

More.

Then the clatter of swords on cobblestone filled the square.

"On your faces," the interpreters boomed as Vectis marched his fifty select men boldly through the Costoboci soldiers. When they reached the gatehouse, Vectis's troops mounted the stairs and lifted the timbers from the gates with surprising speed. No one wanted to be trapped inside a city with a thousand enemy soldiers having second thoughts.

A mighty roar filled the square as thousands of Romans surged into the city. Any of the Costoboci who were not on their faces, instantly dropped to the ground and pushed their knives and swords away from their bodies. Vectis instructed the officers to collect the weapons and secure the city. Then he took two cohorts of soldiers and headed for the crafty commander.

Halfway there the First Centurion joined forces with him.

"The commander withdrew his soldiers to a guard tower," the centurion said. "He knows the gates are open."

When they reached the tower, Vectis could see the commander had sealed the stairwell with stone. The only way to him was along the wall.

"We can approach him on the wings," the centurion said, "but it will cost some blood."

"Get the interpreters," Vectis said.

The interpreters cupped their hands and cried, "The Roman army controls your city. You are trapped. Surrender and only the leaders will be punished."

The defenders in the tower and along the wall screamed back, "We are soldiers. We will fight to the death for our leader."

Vectis stood beside his interpreter and said, "You will all surely die. But I'll waste no Roman lives on you." He glanced around at the wooden buildings. "I will dismantle your houses, heap them against your tower and wall, and burn everything to ash."

The soldiers holding the tower all began shouting at once. It was clear they would not surrender. Their loyalty to their commander was total.

"You have one minute to decide," Vectis said.

The commander appeared on the wall. "If I surrender, you will spare these men?" he asked.

"I will spare them all," Vectis replied, "everyone except you."

The soldiers on the wall gathered round their commander and begged him not to surrender. He ignored them, unstrapped his sword, and threw it over the parapet. It landed with a thud.

The Romans assembled in the huge public square across from the gatehouse. Vectis had kept the looting and raping to a minimum by telling the officers they would be responsible for their soldiers' misdeeds. In one sector of the city the excesses were undeniable. Scores of men had been murdered for no other reason than to clear the way to their women. As a principle of discipline, Vectis had the officer in charge lashed outside the city walls.

The council of twenty was brought before Vectis. These were the city administrators and lawgivers. They were dressed in fine robes, wore jeweled rings and had bloodshot eyes. They had obviously begun their night of revelry too soon. Every one of them had been found hiding in the great houses of the city, some with women, some with boys, some alone. Vectis ordered them stripped and hanged naked from the ramparts.

Then came the captain of the guard and his officers. They had been found in a drunken stupor, all except one, the troublesome tower commander. Vectis was about to pronounce judgment when a procession of horses clattered through the gatehouse. Everybody in the square turned toward the commotion as the Supreme Commander entered the city. He sat imperiously on his white horse, flanked by his Numidian bodyguards on their raven stallions.

Anger surged through Vectis.

Commodus had promised to remain in his tent until the city had been taken and justice dispensed. But here he was, sword drawn, his mouth an angry slash, and his blond wig flopping with every bounce of his mare.

He paused by the ramparts, looked up at the naked bodies, and nodded his approval. "Ah, yes," he said, holding aloft a soft pink hand, "these are they who mocked me. I regret not having seen their faces at the moment of death. But where are their wives and children … their friends and neighbors? I want every last one of them hanging by their necks." He narrowed his eyes and surveyed the crowds of city dwellers. "Translator! Where is a translator? I have much to say."

Vectis stepped forward. "Supreme Commander," he said. "I must speak to you."

"Yes, yes," Commodus said, his eyes searching for a translator.

"Now, Supreme Commander. It is of the utmost urgency."

"Everything is urgent with you," Commodus snapped.

Vectis motioned to one of the Numidians and said, "Help the Supreme Commander off his horse."

"I can dismount myself," Commodus said angrily.

The instant Commodus's feet touched the ground, Vectis turned and started toward the gatehouse. "We can talk in the guard room," he said over his shoulder. It was an old ploy, but it worked. If you start moving, people invariably follow.

Vectis waited inside the guard room.

Commodus came through the door spewing out invectives in his irritatingly high voice. "… and now you interrupt me when I was about to—"

Vectis slammed the door behind Commodus and shoved his face an inch from the Supreme Commander's tattooed countenance. "You are supposed to be in your tent," he said through clenched teeth. "I have made commitments to these people, and I intend to keep them."

Commodus pulled away and said, "You forget yourself, Tribune. I will have you thrown off a cliff—"

"That day is over," Vectis said. "Every soldier out there knows I took this city in one night while you dithered for a year deciding what to do. The army will see it as pure jealousy and punish you as a murderer … you will likely be beaten with rods until dead."

"I … I am the commander of—"

"You have a choice," Vectis said. "Hold your tongue when we go out there, in which case I will praise you for your brilliant planning, and everyone from here to Rome will treat you as a conquering general … or vent your spleen and kill half the city." Vectis fixed his eyes on Commodus. "But if you go on a killing spree, I will make certain everyone in Rome knows you were cowering in your tent while I cleaned up your mess."

"These people mocked me," he said. "Why should you care what I do?"

"I care because I gave my word as a Roman officer that I would spare all but the leaders," Vectis said.

"But I'm—"

"Make a decision," Vectis said, walking out the door.

Minutes later the Supreme Commander strode out the door and across the square to his horse. He stepped on the back of one of his Numidian guards, held his wig, and mounted his horse. "The tribune was … ah … concerned with a report about German tribal movements north of here," Commodus said, striving to sound thoughtful. "But in my command tent I receive couriers daily … and I assured him, and now you, that there is no crisis, and no fear of German attack." His head swiveled toward Vectis and he said, "Tribune, you may proceed."

Vectis thanked the pompous ass for his assurances and signaled for the captain of the guard and his officers to be taken to the wall and slain with a sword. They had abandoned their posts and had been found drunk, but they were soldiers and deserved to die with honor.

"Well done, well done," Commodus was saying as they dragged the slain soldiers away. He locked eyes with Vectis, turned the corners of his mouth down, and nodded his approval.

Vectis bit his tongue. The men who had died were the enemy, and sloppy soldiers, but they had gone to their deaths bravely. But Commodus, sitting on his horse with a pretend battle wound on his neck, was an insult to all soldiers, enemy or not. Vectis wondered how Commodus would react if he were thrust into the fray. He knew the answer, of course, and turned away.

"Bring the tower commander," Vectis said.

Two soldiers pulled a man, hands bound, before him. He was a solid-looking man, taller than Vectis, with short hair and a heavy-boned face. He had the dispassionate look of a soldier about to die.

"What is your name and rank? Vectis asked through an interpreter.

"Borislav Olejnik," he said. "Sector commander."

"You caused me a great deal of trouble," Vectis said.

"Not nearly enough," he replied.

"Do you know why I saved you for last?"

He snorted.

"Do you?"

"An example," he said. "Romans love to make examples of people who resist. So do your worst. I am not afraid." He turned to the crowd and shouted, "Do you hear me? I am not afraid."

"Are you afraid to live?" Vectis asked when the murmurs subsided.

He looked at the interpreter, uncertain what Vectis meant.

"You are a worthy opponent," Vectis said, "an officer of quality. I know this because your soldiers would have willingly died for you."

"My soldiers?" he said, a trace of bitterness in his voice. "I failed my soldiers."

"You had no chance," Vectis said. "Your superiors failed you. That's the tragedy of war. The bravest always die."

The commander waited.

"You say you are not afraid to die, but do you want to die?"

"Life is preferable to death," he said. Then he added, "Unless it is life without honor."

"We need client cities above our northeast barriers," Vectis said, "cities that pay tribute and welcome Romans. But we also need strong men to run them."

"Puppet cities."

"Neutral cities," Vectis said. "We make no claim to this territory, nor to your area of influence. But we cannot have cities on our borders hostile to the Roman Empire. So I ask you, are you afraid to live?"

"I am not afraid to live if this city has true freedom," he said.

"Rome wants the raiding of our outposts to cease. Do you pledge to rid marauders from your city?"

"No raids will be launched from this city," he said. "This I pledge."

Vectis pulled out his dagger and cut the bonds off his wrists. A great cheer rose from the people.

Commodus shifted uncomfortably on his horse, but he said nothing.

The First Centurion approached Vectis. "We've rounded up the prostitutes who were dancing on the wall," he said. "As many as we could find."

"Bring them," Vectis said.

Nine women with tattered dresses, heads bowed, shuffled toward him. They continually mumbled something in the Costoboci language, but never once raised their eyes to Vectis.

"What are they saying?" Vectis asked.

"They are repeating the phrase, 'Lord, have mercy on us,'" the interpreter said.

Vectis glanced at Commodus, whose face darkened as he beheld the courtesans. Then to the translator Vectis said, "Repeat what I say loudly and clearly. I want all to hear."

The translator nodded.

"The great Gaius Commodus," Vectis shouted, "Supreme Commander of Rome's Imperial Armies above the Dacian frontier ... is terrible and merciful." He paused for the translator. "He it was who devised the plan to conquer your city. I was merely the instrument of his hand."

Commodus pushed back his shoulders and raked the inhabitants with his eyes. He was trying to look as terrible as possible.

"As tribute, the Supreme Commander will take custody of the city treasury and collect half of all the possessions of the rich."

The crowd remained silent. They had expected to lose more.

"But our great leader is generous. You are now a friend of Rome. To seal our friendship, the Supreme Commander had decreed that your sacred temples should remain intact. Not one item of value shall be touched."

Wild cheers filled the square.

Commodus whipped his head around. His wig slipped to one side.

Vectis turned to the courtesans. Their heads were still bowed, but they, along with the crowds, were stunned by the benevolent treatment of their conquerors, and they felt a glimmer of hope. The courtesans murmured louder, "Lord, have mercy on us, Lord, have mercy on us."

"The Supreme Commander has little tolerance of those that mock Rome," Vectis said grimly. "But being a strong man, he respects strong people, even if they are only women. He grants you mercy."

For an instant the courtesans stood like frozen figures, hardly believing their good fortune. Some cried, some clasped their hands and groaned, and some threw themselves at Vectis's feet in thankful adoration.

"No, no," Vectis said. "Thank the Supreme Commander. He is your benefactor."

The courtesans obeyed at once, charging Commodus as he sat on his horse, and covering his feet with kisses. Watching Commodus trying to push the women away was the most enjoyable moment Vectis had since leaving Italia. He wished Julian could have witnessed the scene.

As an afterthought, and mostly to sting Commodus, Vectis turned to the centurion and said, "The council members will no longer need their robes. Give one to each woman, and leave a few jeweled clasps on each. Tell them the Supreme Commander is generous in his mercy."

Hours later, as the sun hung low in the sky, Vectis thought about Neeve. All that remained of her was a memory. War had so ravaged Britannia that he despaired for her life, but he would return to Rome and convince the Senate to reassign him to Britannia. Yes, he would search for her in Britannia.

He well knew that Neeve had never quite reconciled herself to being married to a Roman officer, nor to the conquering nature of the Empire. "I am a soldier," he had told her long ago. "But always I temper duty with mercy. I am no butcher."

He glanced up at the men hanging on the ramparts and wondered what she would think of him now. "Cut them down," he told the centurion. "Return their bodies to their wives and families."

41

Brutus glanced around her room for the last time. Weeks had passed since her encounter with the rat, and not one of the rascals had entered her room. She took that as a favorable portent.

She donned her blond hairpiece, powdered her face, and strapped two needle blades on her back. She pulled a tunic over her head and practiced drawing the daggers several times. Satisfied, she started for the bathhouse. The wait was over. She had received a note from her informant: Trebellius was hours from Porolissum. By the afternoon she would meet with him—her partner—complete her assignment and head home. Already she had sent a courier to the exchange liveries on the road to Apulum to prepare Fell Ponies for her journey. At the close of every assignment she took the same precaution. If something went wrong, she intended to outdistance any would-be pursuers.

Brutus arrived at baths the same hour she usually did, but this time she handed the bathhouse overseer five sesterces to usher the tribune, Vectis Trebellius, into her room when it came time for his massage. Attendants often tried to get special clients into their rooms, so her request raised no particular concern. She then checked to make certain the livery had delivered her Fell Ponies to the rear of the baths. She followed the route she would take after finishing with Trebellius, along the hall and across the exercise yard to a gated exit. She touched the key in her belt as she peered out the gate. The ponies were there, one tethered to a post, the other tied to the lead pony. She could see a cavalry spear and bow lashed to the lead animal. Never had she been forced to use the military weapons, but she carried them nonetheless. Brutus believed in being prepared.

She also had hired a local blacksmith to guard her ponies, providing him with a story to satisfy any curiosity he might have. She had learned long ago that there was nothing like having a local to guard your property. They knew the people to watch, and when strangers made inquiries, their answers had the ring of truth.

Brutus quieted her mind, and visualized the coming drama. Gone were the feelings of ambivalence about killing a good man. She was a professional, and he was a partner, nothing else. She pictured a host of possible ways events might unfold, and followed each through until she was safely beyond the city gates. It would be an excellent day … a triumph of the will when determination would rule emotions. With eyes still shut tight, she whispered: "Come, Vectis Trebellius, my partner. Come, let us dance."

Vectis watched as the soldiers carried Julian to the wagon, covered him with blankets and readied him for the journey to Porolissum.

"Did you say goodbye to Commodus for me?" Julian asked, his eyes fluttering open.

Vectis laughed and said, "The Supreme Commander was too busy sending dispatches about his recent victory to bother with the likes of you."

Julian smiled weakly, shifted on his thick cushions, and fell asleep almost immediately.

For the next four weeks Vectis and his column of soldiers traveled slowly, stopping frequently at the inns to aid Julian in his recovery. When they finally reached Porolissum, Vectis was tired and cold, but happy to be back inside the Empire's borders. Soon he would be heading for Rome, and there he would talk to Senator Severus about reassignment to Britannia. He was eager to search the island province for his precious Neeve.

"I saw Porolissum on that last rise," Julian said. He had pushed himself to a sitting position in the back of the wagon Vectis was driving.

"Lie back," Vectis said. "The surgeons said you should be sleeping."

"I'm tired of sleeping," Julian said.

"Then rest on your side."

"Tired of that too," he said. "Besides, these cushions do nothing to soften the ride. I need to relieve myself."

"Want me to stop?"

"No, hurts too much to move." He groaned. "My shoulder is throbbing. My leg aches. I'm freezing in this damned wilderness they call a province. And you are a terrible driver."

"If you're starting to complain, you must be getting better," Vectis said. "Drink more wine. It will numb the pain."

Julian mumbled something and rolled over onto his side. Vectis motioned to one of the escort soldiers who reached into the wagon and pulled a blanket over Julian. Vectis was glad to be nearing Porolissum. The frontier town had about the best baths in the provinces. Hot steam was what Julian needed, more wine and a gentle massage to rub away the aches.

Vectis thought about Commodus sitting high on his white mare, surveying the defeated city dwellers as if he were Alexander the Conqueror. Calling the little fool Supreme Commander was the most ridiculous thing Vectis had ever done. Commodus had the wrong temperament for battle. He took everything personally, especially the enemy's mockery of him. Any reasonable commander would understand that the enemy was simply trying to summon courage. But Commodus wanted the streets flowing with Costoboci blood. Who would ever capitulate to the Roman army if their reward was wholesale slaughter? A soldier had to punish rebels harshly to prevent further rebellion, but he also should grant mercy. Non-Romans had to believe that cooperation with the Empire would benefit them and bring a stable future.

Vectis glanced at his escort soldiers. They would be with him until he reached the Adriatic Sea, which was a good thing. He had come to respect the assassin with the needle-thin dagger. The man was like a phantom, blending with locals, leaving no trace of his presence, except for bodies huddled on the floor. Vectis had all but accused the dye merchant, Tiberia Baebius Merula, of being the assassin. But he had received letters confirming her identity as a purveyor of dyes. How foolish he must have sounded to her. He could imagine her telling the story at every gathering, how a frightened tribune thought she was a secret Empire assassin of princes and soldiers. Even thinking about the situation heated his face with embarrassment. She had been quite open about her feelings for him, and he returned her agreeable demeanor with suspicion and mistrust. And it didn't help that she was attractive. He was thankful he would never see the dye merchant again.

Vectis sent the soldiers on ahead to arrange accommodations with Procurator Tiberius. Then, taking half a dozen men for protection against the phantom killer—he had learned his lesson—he and Julian set off for the baths. A soldier helped the wounded tribune out the wagon at the bathhouse entrance, and supported him as he hobbled up the stairs.

"I'll be in the exercise yard lifting stone balls," Julian said.

"I thought you might challenge some local wrestlers."

Julian smiled and disappeared inside the doors.

Vectis took the cart around to the rear of the mammoth building. He dumped his slicker on the seat and helped a guard secure the mule to a post already in use by two ponies. Vectis eyed the ponies. One was tied to the other, as if the owner was preparing for a long journey and wanted to switch mounts as he traveled. The only riders who used that method were army couriers delivering urgent messages of enemy movements. Vectis moved closer. One small bag. Strange, he thought, someone leaving bows and spears, and even a clothing bag strapped to a horse. Thieves were everywhere. Leaving a few cushions and a beaten up slicker was one thing, but weapons and a travel bag .... He opened the tie and looked inside the bag. A woman's dark tunic, leather breeches and boots.

He stared at the ponies, thinking.

"Tribune, is something wrong?" one of his escort soldiers asked.

"Everything is fine," Vectis said. But he was thinking about the dye merchant.

He ran his eyes over the vaulted roofs of the baths, the cheerful paint brightening the plaster walls, and the evenly spaced narrow windows. He glanced up and down the streets. If he was expecting something to spark in his mind, it never happened.

"Master?"

Vectis turned to see a huge blacksmith standing behind him, hammer in hand.

"A boy has been watching these ponies for me," he said respectfully. "I can see you are a man of honor, but I have been paid to make certain no one interferes with them."

"Who paid you?" Vectis asked.

"A woman of means in our town," he said.

"A dark haired woman?"

"Blond," he said.

"Two ponies," Vectis said. "Is she planning a long journey?"

The smithy laughed. "Across town," he said. "Her little girl rides behind her. Safer with the ponies tied together, she says."

Vectis thanked him and left slightly embarrassed.

The possibility of a female assassin intrigued him, ever since the murder of the Egyptian prince, but now he was thinking assassin every time something odd appeared, especially if it involved a woman. He had to get beyond his fixation. But no matter how hard he tried, he couldn't put the thoughts behind him.

He entered the bathhouse.

"Do you have many women patrons today?" Vectis asked the freedman in charge of bathhouse services. He knew he was obsessed, but he needed to ask.

"None," he said. "These hours are reserved for men only."

"There are no women in the building?"

"There are women, certainly," he said, confused. "We have cleaners, massagers, food servants and ... oh, I understand, Master. You want a young lady delivered to your room. That will present no problem—"

"No, I ... I was merely wondering if you might have recently hired women to work at the bathhouse. I was ... ah ... looking for my sister."

"Of course, Master," the freedman said, obviously not believing the reason given. "All our workers have been with us for some time now," he said.

"Thank you." Vectis hurried away feeling like a bigger fool than he had with the smithy. But at least his mind felt settled.

Ten minutes later he found Julian in a steam-filled room.

"Where are your guards?" Julian asked.

"Outside the room," Vectis said. "I told them to enjoy the baths themselves. They will rotate and keep a couple of guards nearby."

Vectis plopped down across from Julian and sighed. The heat felt incredibly pleasant, especially after so long in the northern wilderness. He leaned against a cedar post and soon the sweat poured off his body. "Is there anything better than this?" he asked as he scraped his legs with a metal strigil to remove the weeks of dirt.

"I can barely see you," Julian said. "If someone enters the hot room with a towel in his hand, we probably should inspect it."

"All this is embarrassing," Vectis said. "I have guards out there who probably think I'm some trembling villa dweller who imagines enemies behind every bush."

"Cheer up," Julian said. "More likely they think you're like Commodus."

"Commodus?"

"Yes—a man so vain he hires guards to increase his sense of worth."

"Thank you," Vectis said. "I feel enormously cheered."

Julian laughed. "A perfect place for a murder," he said as he passed a hand in front of his face, disturbing the steam. "If our assassin slips past the guards—"

"If he does," Vectis said, "he'll find a cruel surprise." He opened a bundled towel and revealed a gleaming dagger.

Julian laughed, and then groaned with pain. "I swear," he said, "one arrow in the back is easily worse than ten in the leg."

"You've never had ten in the leg," Vectis said. "We might want to experiment sometime."

"A fine idea, but you can volunteer for the experiment."

Vectis smiled and covered the dagger with his towel again.

Julian shifted position and asked, "Do you think our assassin friend might have given up trying to eliminate you?"

"I don't think so," Vectis said. "He likes challenges. He killed the Egyptian prince in public."

Julian grunted. "Do we have to worry this far out in Dacia?"

"Probably not," Vectis replied. "But he found me high in Samnium territory in that foul inn. He is quite persistent, that much is certain."

"Persistent and skilled," Julian said. "A lethal combination."

They headed to the hot pool, and then to the cold room for a plunge.

Brutus smiled pleasantly and pressed a coin into her assistant's palm. "These are important men," she said. "And they are generous, so follow my instructions exactly."

The assistant nodded eagerly.

"When the bathhouse overseer brings the tribunes for a massage," Brutus said, "place them in separate rooms and wrap them in heated towels. They will be thirsty, so offer them wine to relax."

"Yes, Mistress."

"The wine is strong," Brutus said, motioning to a pitcher sitting on a stone pedestal, "so don't be alarmed if they look sleepy. Simply help them onto the table and cover them in heated towels. I will arrive shortly after that, and you will leave. Do you understand?"

"Yes, Mistress."

"They will be thirsty," Brutus repeated, "so remember to offer them wine."

"I will remember, Mistress," she said.

"Boy!" Julian called, waving away the steam. "Fetch me another wine." He looked at Vectis and asked, "Aren't you thirsty?"

"Yes," Vectis said, "but I'll wait until the dry rooms."

Julian gulped his fourth wine. "It's diluted," he said, "but I need everything I can get for the pain."

"You need one of those grain drinks, like Sabaium," Vectis said.

"Precisely," Julian said.

They followed the bathhouse overseer to the massage rooms. The guards waited outside the suite as a young girl escorted Vectis and Julian into separate rooms and covered them in hot towels.

"Would you like wine?" the girl asked.

"I think I'll wait," Vectis said.

"It is delicious wine," the girl said.

Vectis glanced at the pitcher, shrugged, and said, "I am thirsty."

She handed him a cup of wine. He sipped it and found it quite tasty. He drank all of it and asked for another. She poured a second cup and helped him onto the broad massage table. He drank part of the cup and placed it on the edge of the table. Then feeling very tired, he flopped back and she covered him in heated towels. Somewhere deep in his mind he realized he had left his dagger on the bench.

Vectis fell asleep ... or dreamt he had fallen asleep. He opened his eyes. His world was rotating in large swirls. He tried to focus on the woman leaning over him. She was beautiful, like a celestial being, and her blond hair hung loosely to her shoulders.

"Neeve?" he said, flinging his hand out and knocking his wine cup onto the floor.

She pulled back the thick towels, exposing his chest.

He squinted his eyes and concentrated on her face. It wasn't Neeve. It was someone else. She had a long reed in her hand. Not a reed.

A knife.

A long thin knife.

A needle knife.

He tried to sit up, but could only prop himself up on his elbows. The room swirled around him, but the woman's face remained constant in the center. It was the dye merchant. She had blond hair now. A wig, maybe. And she was holding a needle knife.

"You are very good," he managed to say.

Brutus looked down at her partner. He was struggling against the drug, trying to make sense of what was happening.

"I was right," he said in barely coherent speech, "I was right."

She fingered her slender dagger.

He managed to focus his eyes briefly. Then he smiled. "The dashing ... Empire assassin," he murmured.

She smiled wistfully.

He collapsed onto his back, no longer able to support himself.

Brutus moved into a striking position.

His eyes fluttered. He knew what was happening, but could do nothing. He lay still, waiting.

She took a breath.

And another.

What was wrong with her?

She squeezed the bone hilt of her dagger. Her mind raced. She remembered him helping the mother with two small children ... remembered him protecting the magician from the drunken mountain men ... pulling off his miserable oil slicker so she could be warm. And she remembered his touch, the warm touch of his hands.

She looked into his face. The corners of his mouth were still turned up with the remnants of his smile. It reminded her of how he had laughed at his own foolishness for trusting a woman who had betrayed him.

Her breathing grew shallow. She reached out and touched his dark hair, ran her fingers along his cheek. A deep sadness gripped her, and miserable despair, because she knew she had utterly lost all connection with her wretched soul. Whatever compassion she had once possessed was gone, snuffed out by years of ruthless discipline.

Brutus grew calm.

Her hand relaxed.

Her eyes fixed on her partner's chest, and she drew her arm back ever so slightly, and plunged the needle blade down toward him.

In that instant a white flash exploded in her head. She crashed to the floor and lay there groaning. Shards of pottery covered her body and the floor around her. Her white tunic was soaked with wine. She rubbed her face, trying to gather her wits. Somebody had struck her with a wine pitcher. She looked up. The injured tribune was standing over her with his fingers wrapped around a broken handle. He was dazed from the drug, leaning against the massage table.

Clomping in the outer hall.

Guards, Brutus realized. She whipped her head around. Her needle dagger lay near the door. She rolled over, snatched up the dagger, and rose to a crouch. The curtain drew back and a guard peered inside. She stepped toward him and slammed the dagger into his stomach, twisting upwards. He groaned, and collapsed on her shoulder. Brutus pushed him to the side and ripped her dagger out of his body. The second soldier stared at her, wide-eyed. He reached for his sword. She lunged forward arcing her blade upward, trying to strike something, anything. It pierced his right arm. He cursed. The dagger spun out of her hand. He dropped his sword.

They eyed each other.

Then realizing she had no weapon, he drew his soldier's dagger. Brutus raised her hands, palms outward, to signify her compliance. He curled his lip, grabbed her hair, and yanked her toward the floor. The wig pulled free from its weave. He looked down at the blond wig in his fingers. A mistake. By now her second needle-blade flashed in her hand and she was moving forward. He thrust his dagger at her, but she was already inside his arms and driving the needle under his ribs. He crumpled over her, his knife slicing into her back.

Brutus crawled from under his bulk, her tunic sticking to her skin. She reached behind. Her hand returned wet with blood. She took a deep breath to see if her lungs were clear. They were. The dagger had struck the leather scabbard on her back and sliced across her skin. It wasn't serious, but she would have to replace her wine-stained and now bloodied tunic.

"Stay … where you are."

Brutus turned toward the injured tribune.

"Don't move," he said as he pushed himself off the table, trying to protect the sleeping Trebellius. The tribune's eyelids were half-closed, and he stood only with the support of the table. For some reason the drug hadn't worked as well on him as it had on Trebellius. But well enough. Almost immediately, he lost his balance, stumbled backwards and dropped onto the bench, his hands fumbling with a towel. She ignored him, and swiftly changed her tunic.

That done, she glanced at Trebellius, and sighed. She knew what she had to do. "Tribune," she said, "are you awake?"

He nodded, but his head still drooped.

"Tell Trebellius to enjoy his life," she said. "He deserves it."

The tribune didn't respond.

Brutus stepped over a body and sat on the bench beside the man. "Are you listening?" she asked, giving his arm a shake. "Tell Trebellius I'm sorry for—"

Brutus saw the towel slide off his lap, the dagger shimmer, and felt a thick piece of metal push deep into her stomach.

"Oh, no," she managed. "No, no, no ...."

She staggered to her feet, the dagger sticking out of her. It burned like a heated poker. She looked down at the tribune, but he was slumped over asleep. She snorted, almost a laugh, trying to comprehend. He had enough in him to do this, she thought, and now ... and now .... She steadied herself at the end of the table. She had to think ... be calm ... remove the dagger. Yes, she would remove it. She touched the handle. A bolt of pain flashed through her body.

She had to do it.

She took a breath, gritted her teeth and yanked out the blade. A gush of blood flowed down her stomach, soaking her tunic and legs. She stood crouched for long seconds, not daring to move.

A surgeon, she thought. An army surgeon. He could cleanse the wound, sew her stomach. Brutus's face dripped with icy sweat. She mopped her brow but only managed to smear her face with blood. She could taste the coppery tang in her mouth. Trebellius moaned. She glanced over at his sleeping form. All because of you, she thought.

Brutus stumbled out the curtained doorway and down the hall, leaving a trail of blood. Her assistant saw her and shrieked. Brutus lurched across the exercise yard, one hand holding her stomach, the other waving the dagger in warning. Men scattered like villagers before a leper.

She staggered up the stairs to the gated exit, a series of chills sweeping over her. At the top of the stairs she tripped. She picked herself up and grasped at the iron bars to keep herself from falling again. Control, she told herself … control … you can do it. But she was losing her vision. Her head felt light and colors sparkled before her eyes. She fumbled with the leather ties on her belt and pulled out the key. Her breathing was ragged, her fingers slick with blood.

"Control," she whispered.

She ground her teeth and focused on opening the lock, but her hand trembled. She pressed her fingers against her breast to calm the shaking. Then, sucking in some air, she shoved the brass key into the opening, and turned. Her fingers slipped. She dragged her hand across her tunic to dry it, and then squeezed the key as tightly as she could, but her hand slipped again. The blood slithered like oil. Brutus closed her eyes to focus her energy. Then she gathered up the bottom of her tunic and wrapped it around the key. She squeezed as hard as she could and wrenched the key to the side. The gate clunked open.

Brutus grabbed the iron doorframe for balance. Then, taking a breath, she started through the gate. Her legs didn't respond. It was as if they were clay. She tried to lift them over the stone sill but the effort almost took her consciousness. Dark patches swirled around her head, threatening to overwhelm her.

"No!" she shouted to herself, and the anger surged through her body, giving her one last spurt to hobble over the sill and across the cobblestone to where she had tied her ponies. But Brutus was spent. She bumped blindly into the lead pony, her hands groping for the saddle horns in a hopeless attempt to pull herself up. Her arms had no life. She tried again, this time throwing her body onto the saddle. The explosion of pain pulled her into darkness, but she willed herself back.

Control ....

Brutus slid off the pony, clutching at its mane for support, her head flopping, her breathing coming in gasps. She squinted through the haze around her. A wagon ... a wagon behind her ponies ... the seat was lower ... she could drive the mule to the surgeons ....

She listed toward the wagon, unhitched the mule from the post, and crawled up into the driver's seat.

An overwhelming tiredness settled on her. She groped with her fingers for the reins, but couldn't find them in the fog. She felt her determination slipping. She slumped on her side. It felt pleasant. She wanted sleep to take her. Her body was hunched against an old oil slicker. She tried to focus on it, then laughed in disbelief. Trebellius's coat. She was lying on Trebellius's coat. She pressed deeper into the slicker and closed her eyes.

"Vectis Trebellius," she breathed. "I have exchanged my life for yours ... and you will never know it."

She looked into his eyes and touched his dark hair again, trailing her fingers along his cheek.

Wisps of fog blew across his face, blurring his image.

She reached out to him, but he was gone.

The fog deepened.

The darkness thickened.

She felt herself sinking and the shadows covering her.

42

When Calpurnia arrived at the majestic Basilica of Julius Caesar, Balbinus was already waiting for her at the curb.

She scrutinized him out of the corners of her eyes and said, "Hmm … tell you I have a surprise and you get here on time."

"Nonsense," he said, his pink cheeks glowing. "You said your surprise would change my life—that's what hastened my heels."

She took his arm and together they ambled through the basilica's enormous central hall, crossed the marble paving, and ascended the broad stairs that led to the second floor. At the top he paused for breath and said, "Death by exhaustion, that would certainly change my life."

"You shall not die, my love," she said, "at least, not until you discover my surprise. You are too inquisitive to let it happen."

"Let's move quickly," he said, starting toward a room where two of his servants waited. "I grow faint."

The servants bowed and opened the doors.

Balbinus squinted into the darkness. He looked at Calpurnia, his face filled with questions. The room was shuttered closed, dark, and empty except for two candles flickering on the floor. "What is … there is nothing in the room," he said finally.

"Ah, but there is," she said. "Look more closely."

They stepped inside and the servants closed the doors, making it even darker. He waited for his eyes to adjust. "I see nothing," he said.

"Be patient," she said. "It's worth the effort."

"Wait!" he cried. "I see something between the candles, "lying on the floor."

"What do you see?"

"A cloth, a black cloth," he said.

"My surprise is under that cloth," she said. "But first you must solve a riddle."

"I am poor at solving riddles."

"I will help you," she said. "Listen carefully. What hides in the dark, drinks in the dark, and is eaten in the light?"

"A mouse," he said.

"No."

"A rabbit?

"No."

"An animal that lives underground?" he asked hopefully.

"It's not an animal," she said.

"Oh, Calpurnia, you know I cannot guess. You must tell me."

She kissed him and said, "I will give you a clue, but you must guess."

He nodded.

She spoke in a conspiratorial tone when she asked: "What attends secret meetings in the dark, drinks a sacred liquid in the dark, and is eaten by beasts at the Circus Maximus in the full light of day?"

He chewed on his ample cheeks. "You don't mean the wretched blood-drinkers, do you?"

"I do, my sweets, the wretched, despicable blood-drinkers."

His face wrinkled in questions. "This is your surprise?" he asked.

"No, not my surprise," she said. "But it makes my surprise possible."

He stood in the middle of the darkened room, dumbfounded.

"Would you like to see my surprise?" she asked.

"Cause me to wait no longer," he said.

"Then you shall see it," Calpurnia said, throwing open the shutters.

The brilliant morning light filled the room. Balbinus shaded his eyes as he gazed onto the Old Forum. The window looked directly across at the huge bronze doors of the Senate.

"You once called me a dreamer of dreams," she said, "when I promised to make you a senator someday." She stared at the Senate building. "Do you recall that, my Lord?" she asked, her voice low and husky.

His eyes darted to hers. "What are you saying? Tell me plainly. I can no longer abide the game. Please tell me now."

Calpurnia returned to the center of the room where the candles still burned. He was desperate to understand, but she knew, as with physical sensations, the waiting increased the pleasure. She knelt, pursed her lips, and blew out the candles. Then she slipped her fingers under the black cloth and slowly folded it back.

"Calpurnia!" he exclaimed. "What ... what is this?"

"It's a tunic," she said quietly. "The broad stripe signifies the rank of senator."

"I know that but I ... I cannot wear such a tunic," he said.

"Not now," she said, "but come the summer festivities, you will surely don this very tunic."

"But how ... how can this be possible?"

She sidled up to him and draped an arm over his shoulder. "You have dreamed of being a senator," she said. "Today I shall tell you how dreams can come true." Then dropping her voice to a whisper, she spoke her next words directly into his ear: "What would you give me, dear Balbinus, if this dreamer gave you your dream?"

"If you gave me my dream," he said with his eyes fixed hungrily on the Senate doors, "I would buy you whatever you demanded ... I would give you jewels until you bent under their weight ... I would fall at your feet and worship you."

She touched his ear with her lips. "I want none of that," she said.

"What then?" he asked, his breath short and clipped. "Name your desires and you shall have them."

"I simply want you," she said, nipping his earlobe.

"But you have me," he said.

"I am a mistress," she said. "I want a permanent share in the wealth of Rome. My price is marriage—without husband control of my affairs."

"Most marriages today are without husband control," he said.

"Yes, but I desire a written agreement saying I possess half of your wealth."

For a moment he stared at her, confused. Then he said, "What I have is yours. For some time now I have considered you not a mistress, but a partner in life."

Calpurnia knew that the phrase, partner in life, spoke well for her, but she also knew the word "wife" was better. She looked Balbinus squarely in the eyes and said, "Then we are agreed."

"Yes ... yes, certainly," he said.

She kissed his lips and parted them with her tongue. "Do you think I would make a passable wife?" she asked.

"You will make other men sick from envy," he said, "and me from exhaustion." Then he turned serious. "I will give you your prize," he said, "if you can truly make me senator."

"I believe Fortuna has smiled upon us," she said. She talked about Senator Severus and the power he wielded in the Senate, his investigation of Atilius Titianus's attempt to overthrow the emperor, and the possible connection between the rebellious Titianus and Senators Tertullus and Coelius.

"Yes, yes, I know all this," Balbinus said.

"Then let me ask you, who dislikes Senator Severus more than Senators Tertullus and Coelius?"

"Possibly me," Balbinus said.

"True," she said, "because you have much to lose if Severus continues on his quest. But then, so do Tertullus and Coelius."

"They do."

"So would it not be beneficial to disrupt Severus's mission before he finds those responsible for the rebellion?"

"Extremely beneficial."

"And what would Senators Tertullus and Coelius give to see such a disruption take place."

"Their first born," Balbinus said.

"And how about an elevation to senator for the loyal Gaius Balbinus?"

Balbinus began chewing on his cheek again. "Senator Severus is a determined man," he said. "I cannot think of anything that might disrupt his investigation."

Calpurnia smiled and asked, "Would he be so single-minded if his only son were about to be executed for belonging to a forbidden cult?"

"A forbidden cult? What cult?"

She continued to smile.

"No ... no, it cannot be. The blood-drinkers? He's a blood-drinker? I don't believe it."

"It's true," she said. Then she told Balbinus about how she met with the barbarian woman from the Severus household. "She told me the servants think Marcellus Severus is an atheist ... that he never mentions the gods."

"An atheist," Balbinus said, shaking his head.

"He never burns incense to the household gods either," she said.

"Never?"

"Apparently not. Even more curious, he sneaks out to secret nightly meetings. What could these meetings be, but the despicable rituals of blood-drinkers sacrificing children?"

Balbinus licked his lips. "Could it be possible?" His eyes darted everywhere, thinking. "A blood-drinker ... Marcellus Severus ... who would have believed it?"

"I don't think the elder Severus knows," she said, "so it should come as quite a shock when Tertullus and Coelius accuse his son of belonging to the subversive cult."

Balbinus rubbed his hands together jubilantly. "Severus paralyzed," he said, "and Tertullus and Coelius eager to make me a senator." He grabbed Calpurnia and kissed her. Then he threw back his head and howled. Like a wolf he howled and hooted with joy. "For this news," he said, "I would make you my wife ten times over. You are truly a gift from the gods, the finest woman a man could ever have."

Calpurnia smiled triumphantly. She had reason to be proud. She had risen from the filth of slavery to the pinnacle of civilization. Men had bought and sold her, used her for every imaginable pleasure, paraded her around their private parties, humiliated her ... and on occasion dropped a few bobbles into her outstretched hand. They little realized the determination that burned in her soul. She smiled and laughed, and worked hard to please them, but all the while she was using them to pull herself—rung by rung—out of the miry pit.

And now she would be a senator's wife.

It was no easy task worming information from the barbarian woman, Neeve. She was a strong and wary type. Calpurnia had to make the barbarian seek after her. Yes, Calpurnia had reason to be proud. Within the space of a few hours she had convinced a complete stranger to trust her with information so devastating that it had potential to shake the foundations of the Empire.

As it turned out, the woman was probably a blood sister—who could deny the striking similarity and physical evidence such as burns and cuts? But what did blood mean? This woman and her brother were nothing to her. Still, it was a great stroke of fortune. For all her strength, Neeve was a simple island girl with silly notions of family and trust. She had even called her Nes, an absurd name that suited a pet chicken more than a human.

Calpurnia had seen Marcellus Severus on several occasions. He was an attractive man with a quick wit and ready smile. It was unfortunate he would become grist for her advancement. But his fate mattered little to her. If the beasts took him, it was his own doing. Was it her fault Marcellus entangled himself with a sick cult like the blood-drinkers? She had no sympathy for him. And Neeve would not be protecting him if she knew what they did in their darkened chambers.

It was unfortunate that Neeve had fallen in love with Vectis Trebellius, someone that Brutus would soon eliminate. Actually, since Neeve assumed he was dead anyway, it mattered little. As for Balbinus, she would tell him nothing about Neeve and Trebellius. He had enough to think about.

Calpurnia understood the world; it was a brutal place where only the strong survived. Her sister was kindly, but gullible, and would soon learn not to trust strangers. Still, the meeting had left Calpurnia quite unprepared to deal with emotions long suppressed. Holding her sister to her breast and stroking her hair and kissing her forehead—simple things—but they caught her off guard. In the future she would have to steel her mind against feelings that served only to diminish her.

43

Senator Titus Severus sat on a straight-backed couch outside the meeting hall where Emperor Antoninus Pius customarily met with dignitaries from other lands. Severus had been waiting over an hour for the emperor, and he was growing more uncomfortable by the minute. He fiddled with his cane. His leg ached when the weather changed, a souvenir from a war wound as a youth. But suffering a bit of leg pain was not the problem. Never once in his long acquaintance with the emperor had he waited on a visitor's bench like a foreigner. Titus Severus was worried.

The ornate doors opened. A page approached the senator and said, "The emperor will see you now."

Severus rose and limped past six Praetorian guards. He entered an arched hall lit by skylights of colored glass, the huge room entirely empty except for Emperor Antoninus, who sat on a couch. When he saw the senator he rose and walked toward him. "Titus," he said informally. "I'm so glad you were able to come."

"Emperor Antoninus the Pius," Severus said, smiling.

"Do not embarrass me," the emperor said. "Antoninus will suffice. We are alone ... two old friends who have seen better days."

Severus rubbed his leg. "Acts up at the wrong time," he said. "Soon I will be carried by litter everywhere like my grandfather."

"Ceionius Severus," Antoninus said. "I remember him well. A great man. I never knew whether he would smack my hind parts or give me honey treats."

"You were not alone," Severus said, laughing. "How quickly time eats away at us all."

Antoninus gestured toward a wide couch. "Please, rest yourself, old friend." He offered him wine and bread filled with various kinds of meats and cheeses.

Severus took the wine but thought better about the rich foods.

"How long have we been friends?" Antoninus asked. "Fifty years? I don't know ... but a lifetime for certain."

"A lifetime," Severus agreed.

His brow furrowed. "I never wanted to be emperor. The divine Hadrian begged me, beat on me, cajoled me ... in the end I accepted with reluctance. Do you know why I was so reluctant? Because I knew affairs of state would prevent me from pursuing my heart. In the Imperial chair, I cannot act with freedom." He gave a great sigh. "I knew I would hurt my dearest friends because greater responsibilities called me to make decisions against their interests."

Severus stared at him but said nothing. He was not eager to discover what decisions might be made against his interests.

"I kept you waiting ... unforgivable, but the truth is, I could not face you. How could I look you in the eye and tell you about the decisions I have made?"

"Please," Severus said, "say what you must. The gods raise up the great and give them power, some to rule as tyrants, some to do their will. You have always followed the will of heaven. You are a rare jewel, Antoninus, and I trust you without reservation. What you decree, I accept."

"I know that," Antoninus said, "which is why of all men I am most miserable."

Severus felt his stomach sicken.

"You know why the Senate insisted on designating me Pius? Some think it had to do with my treatment of my aged father-in-law, or my inclination to choose the more merciful judgment, or because I make loans at four percent ... none of these. They designated me Pius because I reversed Hadrian's execution orders. In the last months of his rule, Hadrian had decreed that scores of people, including senators, should be put to death. I set aside that order and freed those under the sentence of death."

"I remember," Severus said. "A noble deed."

"Noble or not, it was just," Antoninus said. "But I also promised the Senate not to interfere in their collective judgments. If they made a ruling, and I were to approve it, I would not later change it because I had counter desires."

"I have heard you speak of it many times," Severus said.

"Yes, but now I find myself skewered by my own decrees." He looked at the senator. "You know I have always been interested in orphanages ... the suffering of children ... probably because my own father died when I was young."

"Yes, I remember."

"And you know I have little tolerance of cults that brutalize children, sacrifice them, drink their blood in a quest for immortality." He paused. "You have long supported my efforts to rid society of these people."

Severus knew he had, but in the present circumstances, he was hesitant to say so. "I have," he said, "but I have often been concerned that some might be wrongly identified with a forbidden group."

The emperor smiled and patted Severus's arm. "Have no fear, old friend. I would not entrap you with your words. I agree with you ... some have been falsely accused, and I would go further—not all banned groups are as wretched as generally thought. To be sure, the Druids sacrifice humans. We've seen them do it. But others such as the blood-drinkers ... who knows the truth? Some good men were said to have been blood-drinkers ... even a consul of Rome, as I recall."

"Flavius Clemens," Severus said.

"Yes, Clemens and his wife, Domitilla, during Domitian's reign."

"Clemens was one of Rome's best consuls," Severus said. "I cannot imagine him drinking the blood of children, even if he belonged to the so-called blood-drinking cult."

"I agree," Antoninus said.

"Another member of the drinkers was Sergius Paulus," Severus said. "He was governor of Cypress during Nero's reign, and a fine man, I've been told."

"I have heard the same ... but Nero!" Antoninus curled his lip in distaste. "He started all this hatred of the drinkers when he blamed them for the central fire."

"He needed land to build his extravagant Golden House," Severus said.

"He did. And emperors have been hated for his excesses ever since."

"Some emperors," Severus corrected.

"True," Antoninus said. He shook his head. "Nero was the worst kind of emperor."

"Indeed."

Antoninus took a length of cheese bread and leaned back on his couch. "I will confess to you, Titus," he said, "For all the talk of drinkers consuming the blood of children, I cannot say for certain that the charge is true. Who knows ... they may drink bulls' blood like many cults, or sprinkle themselves with pigs' blood like the Eleusians."

"Was not Hadrian a member of Eleusis?"

"He was, and also Augustus. That's my point. These secret religions invite distortion. Hadrian once told me people thought he and other members of the Eleusian cult drank pigs' blood every full moon."

"A reason to hope for clouds," Severus said.

"Truly," Antoninus said, laughing. His face grew serious. "My thoughts are unsettled on these secret cults. I really have no idea what they do when the sun goes down, and since I cannot trust the rumors, I have followed the wisdom of Hadrian and Trajan—give the blood-drinkers, and the practitioners of the black arts an opportunity to turn their backs on such practices. If they refuse, then, and only then should they suffer the extreme penalty." He looked at Severus. "We cannot allow fanatical priests to sacrifice children and innocents, if that is truly what is happening."

Severus agreed, but was concerned with the direction of the conversation. "I have often spoken against human sacrifice," he said. "But aside from the Druids, we know little about what these groups do."

"Yes, rumors are not the best way to make judgments," Antoninus acknowledged. "But cults that deny the ancient gods are dangerous, even if their individual members pose no threat." He poured some wine, as if he needed to brace himself. "Take the blood-drinkers, for example. They refuse to pay homage to the gods of our fathers—we know that. This in turn weakens our collective belief in the power of Roman gods over our enemies. Soldiers lose confidence, and with the frontiers in perpetual chaos, our survival is at risk."

Severus nodded, but said nothing.

"Now, if we were to extract one individual blood-drinker," Antoninus said, "a good one say, a loyal Roman in many respects, he would cause us no ill effects. We might not care what his private beliefs were. But collectively," he raised a finger, "ah, collectively, he and his fellow cultists are like a dagger pointed at the heart of Roman civilization."

"Dear Antoninus, you are describing an individual without naming him. If you have reservations about me—"

"No," Antoninus said sadly, "it's not you. If it were, I would not be so distraught. We could talk, solve the problem—"

"Not my son, Marcellus."

The emperor sipped more wine. "Do you remember when I lost my daughter?" he asked. "My world shattered. I would have gladly given my own life ... but sometimes we cannot protect the ones dearest to us."

"What has Marcellus done?"

Antoninus looked at his friend and said softly, "He has been accused of belonging to the blood-drinking cult."

"That is fabricated nonsense!"

"I dearly hope so," Antoninus said, "because if he has involved himself in the proscribed cult, I cannot help you."

"It's Coelius and Tertullus, isn't it? They'll do anything to halt your investigation of the Senate chamber."

"I wondered whether the investigation might have made you a target ... I have decided to remove you from—"

"No," Severus said. "I will not be bullied off a proper—"

The emperor held up his hand. "For the time being," he said. "I will announce you have taken leave for family matters. They might drop their pursuit of Marcellus."

"But blackmail of this sort—"

"Yes, yes, I quite agree," Antoninus said. "But this painful situation would not have surfaced, but for my investigation, and your willingness to head it. Let me salve my conscience. I know the pain you suffer."

"But caving in to Coelius and Tertullus ...."

"If it were only Coelius and Tertullus," Antoninus said, "I could handle it. But they have conscripted a goodly number of senators to their cause. Many, like you, are on record about their loathing of the blood-drinkers—as am I—and I simply cannot now say this or that drinker is exempted from prohibition."

"I understand," Severus said, "but Marcellus is no blood-drinker. He would never harm a child, much less drink its blood."

"I know that," Antoninus said.

"And if he has associated himself with them—and I do not believe he has—then we have totally misunderstood the cult."

"That may well be," Antoninus said. "But remember, even for you I cannot change what Roman citizens believe and what the Senate has proscribed ... so talk to him."

"I will," Severus said, rising. "But I would like to know how Coelius and Tertullus came across this supposed information about Marcellus?"

"They said a guest of yours from the provinces ... a woman called, Neeve, I believe—"

"Neeve?"

The emperor nodded. "Apparently she informed them that Marcellus was heavily involved with the proscribed cult. As evidence they say he refuses to pay homage to the gods and attends secret nightly rituals in underground tombs."

Severus felt a dull pain at the base of his neck. His mind swirled with fragmented pictures of Marcellus striding past the lararium ... but he pushed them away. He refused to believe his son could have involved himself with the wretched blood-drinkers. It was simply not possible. But in his heart the senator was concerned.

The emperor rose. "Let us not despair too soon," he said. "Forbidden fruit often tempts the young. Many go through stages of curiosity." He embraced Severus. "One thing I can do is delay those in the Senate who are eager to arrest the cultists. Bring me word of his loyalty to the ancient gods, and we can lay this to rest."

As the senator left the hall, he rubbed his leg. It ached more than usual.

The next afternoon Senator Severus arrived at the family villa outside Rome. He went straight to the villa overseer. "Where is Marcellus?" he asked.

"In the west fields, Master," came the reply. "The olive groves, I think."

"Fetch me a carriage," Severus said. "I will drive it myself."

"Yourself?" The overseer hesitated on hearing the strange request, but only for an instant. Within a few minutes the senator was lashing the carriage horse toward the west fields. A half-mile from the fields he stopped. He needed to calm himself. He would do no one any good, especially Marcellus, if he came racing across the fields, making demands. Marcellus was a grown man now, fully capable of deciding things for himself. The senator had long given him freedom to chart his own course, and now would be a foolish time to start being the overbearing father.

A sensible approach. That's what the situation required. He would explain the dangers of the present course his son was taking, being careful not to assign blame, and his son would respond as he always had, with intelligence and good judgment. He took several deep breaths to calm himself, straightened his tunic, and flicked the reins.

"Father?" Marcellus stepped away from Neeve and the head olive grower, a man named Labienus. He had been discussing with Labienus what they always discussed in the lower fields—how to drain the runoff water. It was a perennial problem in the late spring. "Is anything wrong?" Marcellus asked.

"Of course not," the senator answered, smiling calmly. "Am I too old to drive a carriage myself?"

"You are not too old, Father," Marcellus said.

The wind was blowing briskly off the wet fields, giving the air a damp smell. "Still having a problem with standing water?" he asked as he stepped from the carriage and kissed his son.

"Another drainage ditch will do it," Marcellus said, laughing. "Isn't that what I promised last year?"

"I think so," the elder said. A small lake had formed at one end of the field. "Less of a problem than in the past," he said with an encouraging voice. He returned his eyes to his son and said, "If you have time, I would like to speak with you."

"Certainly," Marcellus said. He glanced at Neeve and then to his father. "Is this private? Or …."

"Not private, but it's one of those family things," the senator said, trying to sound off-handed in his speech. His words hung awkwardly.

"Labienus can take me to the villa," Neeve said cheerfully.

"Excellent," replied the senator. He looked at Labienus and said, "Give us a few minutes, and then return with the carriage."

Labienus bobbed his head and helped Neeve into the carriage seat.

When they had left, Marcellus eyed his father and said, "Something serious?"

"I hope not," the senator said. "You know I have my enemies in the Senate, and they will seize on anything to do me damage."

Marcellus waited.

"They cannot attack me directly, so they are spreading rumors about you, hoping to unsettle me."

"And what would these rumors be?" Marcellus asked.

"Senators Coelius, Tertullus and others are accusing you of belonging to the blood-drinking cult." He raised his eyes to his son and said, "Please tell me this is not so."

Marcellus took a breath and then said, "I'm not a member of the cult—"

"Praise be to the gods," the senator said.

"But ...." Marcellus hesitated. "In the past months I've attended a number of their meetings."

"I see."

"They meet mostly at night, and I was curious."

"I understand," the senator said, holding up his hand. "When I was young, I was curious about many things. For a time I even tried to find members of the Mysteries of Dionysus because I had heard about their wild sexual activities." He smiled to himself, remembering his foolishness. "I guess I wondered what a priestess trained in the Greek secret arts would be like in her chambers." He felt his face redden. Talking to a son about such things was proving uncomfortable. He cleared his throat. "Anyway, that's what youth is all about—curiosity, experimentation, folly."

Marcellus didn't reply.

"Experimentation is fine," the senator continued, trying to make a transition. "Nothing wrong with curiosity, as long as you obey the law of the land."

No response.

The senator hoped the silence meant his son was considering his words. "Now, let me see," he said, "you have ... ah ... attended a few of these meetings because ... ah ... because you have been curious about such people." He shrugged. "Understandable. I think it more interesting to consort with a priestess than people who drink blood." He smiled. "But, if you have satisfied your curiosity and are willing to put these things behind you, I think we can avoid problems with the Senate."

"Father, I don't think you understand," Marcellus said. "My interest in what these people teach is not a passing curiosity."

"I don't care what your interest is," the senator said firmly. "You will declare the blood-drinkers to be a false cult, no longer associate with them, and never again attend a meeting for any reason. Are my wishes clear?"

"They are clear, but with respect, Father, I cannot obey."

"You ... what? You cannot obey?"

"I am sorry, Father."

"You choose strangers over your own father?"

"I'm not choosing them over you. But you are asking me to deny what I believe to be true."

"So you refuse to obey me?"

"It's not a matter of obeying you—"

"That's exactly what it is," the senator said. "I am telling you now, Marcellus. You will obey or ... or I will take from you your inheritance." He fixed his eyes on his son. "Are you listening? Everything we have is mine to do with as I please."

Marcellus nodded. "You may take my inheritance," he said, "but know that when you do, I shall still love and respect you. Yet, I cannot do what you are asking."

The senator closed his eyes. "I do not wish to take your inheritance," he said quietly. "What I have is yours. It always has been ... always shall be. But you cannot seriously defend this disgusting group of people. Not after the way I raised you to respect innocent life."

"These people respect innocent life," Marcellus said, "and they are not disgusting. They are quite the opposite."

"I cannot believe this is my son talking," the senator said, losing the calmness he had been carefully cultivating. "If your mother were alive—"

"Why would you bring Mother into this?"

The senator clamped his teeth in anger. He knew he shouldn't have mentioned his departed wife but it slipped easily off his tongue. He turned his back, wanting space from the conflict. The whole situation was too much for him.

"Father, you misunderstand—"

The senator kept his back to his son when he said, "I refuse to believe you have become an atheist and a hater of Roman society.

Would my own flesh sacrifice children and lap their blood to satisfy his thirst for immortality?"

"Nobody kills children," Marcellus said in raised voice.

"Don't even speak to me," the father replied. "I feel ill talking about such practices. Have I taught you nothing?"

Marcellus remained silent for long seconds that seemed like minutes to the old senator. Then he spoke in a measured voice. "I have attended meetings, as I said, but never have I seen anyone sacrifice humans, much less children." He paused. "They don't even sacrifice animals."

"Then where does all the talk of blood-drinking come from?" the senator demanded, looking at his son. "Rumors do not arise from pond vapors. They have some basis in fact."

"All I know is that when the people of the Way meet—that's what they call themselves, people of the Way, they do not like the term, blood-drinkers—when they meet, they have a communal meal and drink sacred wine to remember the death of their leader, Chrestus. They call the wine the blood of Chrestus, but it's nothing more than the wine we store in our underground chambers. I even brought a barrel one evening for the Way to use. Believe me, they drink no blood and never even perform a simple sacrifice."

"They might not have performed their gruesome ceremonies when you were there," the senator said, "but I tell you, they do it in secret. These cults always do their evil in secret."

"This is not true," Marcellus said.

"It is true. They are deviants. Killing children … drinking blood … indulging in sexual perversions." The senator gave a knowing look. "Oh, I have heard all about it," he said. "These blood-drinkers dig tunnels under the tombs, and when night falls, they gather near the bones of former members to perform their dark rituals."

"Not true," Marcellus repeated.

"They hold up bones and sing about the dead," the senator said. "Sometimes with the newly deceased, they eat their rotting flesh and—"

"No—"

"Then the brides of this charlatan Chrestus come … and these women give themselves to his priests as love slaves, doing whatever it is they do in the filthy blackness of underground tunnels. Later they light lamps and chant songs about living forever. They slit the throat of a child without blemish and drink its blood, calling the red liquid the medicine of immortality. In the final moments, they snuff out the light by throwing scraps of meat beyond reach of dogs chained to the lamps. And in the blackness, brothers and sisters, family members of all ages, drink and copulate in random unions." He shook his head in disgust. "The excesses of the Cybele cult are tame compared to these degenerates."

"These rumors are worthless lies," Marcellus said.

"So the whole of Rome is wrong, and you are right?"

"I've attended the meetings."

"They are deceiving you," the senator said. "These cults … they never reveal everything to novices. Give them time, and you will discover their foul practices."

"I don't believe it."

"Everyone knows what these people are like. They are diabolical geniuses of hate. Can you deny they hate Rome's ancient gods?"

"Of course I deny it," Marcellus said. "They don't hate the gods. They teach that the stories about the gods are just that—stories. You know as well as I that most educated people in Rome hold the same view. They might pay lip-service to the pantheon of gods, but they don't actually think Jupiter or Mars are running around the skies intervening for us."

"Atheists," the senator said. "Blood-drinkers reject the gods of Rome … which makes them atheists."

"Not atheists. They believe in one God, like the Jews."

"The Jews! Jews are no different from astrologers or magicians. Every fifty years we have to purge Rome of them. You don't want to link yourself with that bunch of troublemakers."

"All I am saying is that the Jews believe in a supreme god, denying all the rest, and so do the people of the Way. They are not atheists."

"Marcellus, please," the senator said, lifting his hand. "We can discuss philosophy all day, but it will hardly change what the Roman people think of these blood-drinkers. Nor will it change the penalty of death for anyone belonging to this cult. Now, once again, I implore you to stop attending these meetings."

"I cannot do that," Marcellus said.

"Do you know what you're saying?"

"I think I do."

"The Senate already has your name ... sooner or later they'll arrest you and feed you to the beasts. That's what happens to blood-drinkers. I cannot protect you. Do you understand? This is not a childhood game."

"I understand," Marcellus said. "But I believe these people have found the true way to God. Never have I felt such peace about—"

"Be sensible," the senator said. "If you want peace, take a year to wander the Greek isles, or walk the endless beaches of Gallia—I care not—but to continue with these blood-drinkers is to dance with skulls and bones. In a few months there will be no drinkers left. These people of the Way, as you call them, will be plowed under like weeds at planting."

"Truth can never be destroyed," Marcellus said.

"Don't speak foolishness—"

"Chrestus is the truth."

The senator sighed, and then said as patiently as he could, "Marcellus, listen to me. Every conquering empire destroys religions and their so-called truths. We've done it, and before us the Greeks, and before them the Persians. Some religions are banned, like Druids and blood-drinkers, some wither in the face of superior beliefs, and some blend with others and lose their identity. But nothing remains constant. Come back in a thousand years, and the Druids and drinkers will be gone. But Rome will endure because we have built our Empire on solid foundations. We might not be eternal as people say, but we are the nearest thing to it. And these blood-drinkers? They are builders on sand, and within your lifetime they'll disappear." The senator paused. "Attach yourself to permanence," he said, "not to fanciful beliefs headed for oblivion."

"These beliefs *are* eternal," Marcellus said.

"Do you know that for certain?" the senator asked. "Do you really know they teach the truth?"

"I believe it is truth," Marcellus said. "As much as I believe my mother loved me, I believe this to be true."

"Well and good," the senator said, his mind racing, trying to think of the right words to make clear his son's folly. "I am not asking you to deny this god. No, no, not deny your god. I am simply asking you to pay homage to the other gods as well ... so you ... ah ... won't offend the state deities, and in turn the Senate. But in your mind, you understand, secretly in your heart, you can pay the greater homage to your special god. Any reasonable god would understand what you are trying to do." He looked at his son. "Is this not a practical solution?" he asked.

"It is but—"

"A great purge is coming," the senator said. "Planning is well on its way. During the festivities for Legate Julius Verus's Triumph, the blood-drinkers will be killed in the Circus Maximus. By summer's end, like so many other cults, they'll be nothing but a memory. All I am asking you to do is nod your head toward the state gods. Surely you can do that."

Marcellus stared at the ground, thinking. Then he said, "The people of the Way teach that to acknowledge other gods is to deny the one true God. They say we are called to be witnesses to this truth, even if it means death."

"And what do you believe?"

"I don't know."

"A simple nod is all I'm asking," the senator repeated.

Marcellus glanced at his father. He was still thinking.

The senator had no idea what else he could say that might break through to his son, and he didn't want to say too much. Better to seed Marcellus's mind and trust his good judgment would lead him to the right decision. He tried to straighten his back, knowing how dejected he must look, but he couldn't summon the strength. His life force had drained from him and he felt nothing but despair. His eyes wandered over the hills and the hundreds of twisted olive trees. "My great grandfather planted many of these trees," he said. "Olives, figs, grapes—they have always been important to me. But they are like brown grass without you."

He placed his hand on his son's shoulder, hoping the contact would mean something.

Marcellus breathed heavily.

The senator continued. "That big tree on the left," he said, "you fell from it and scraped your knee when you were six. Can you remember what I told you?"

Marcellus nodded. "You said you loved me so much you would happily take the pain on yourself ... if it would spare me."

"And do you remember what you said?"

"I cried," Marcellus said, "because I realized I would never take the pain for you."

The senator smiled. "But that's the way it should be. Fathers should find a way to take the pain for their children, not the other way around." He scraped the dirt with his sandals. "I am so sorry, Marcellus. I cannot take the pain for you. And the pain is coming. Believe me, it is coming if you continue on this same path ... and my life will be an empty room with you and your mother gone."

Marcellus stared at him.

"I am certain this god of yours is kindly," the senator said, "not a jealous, vindictive god. Surely he would understand if you held your father's hand and nodded toward the city gods." He paused to make solid eye contact. "Will you do that for me? Will you pay a small homage, just enough to satisfy our enemies?"

Marcellus opened his mouth to speak.

The senator held up his hand. "Delay your answer," he said. "For now, I ask only that you think on my words. Will you grant me that much?"

"Of course," Marcellus said.

"You are all I have," the senator said, kissing his son. "All I have." He turned, and with his cane, started toward the villa.

44

As Neeve rode back to the villa complex with Labienus, she had that old feeling of discomfort that she often had around Romans. Senator Severus was a kindly man, of that she had no doubt. His kindness usually made it easy to set aside her natural caution about Romans, but these people, she reminded herself, were the masters of the world. And one thing about Roman masters, they never shied from asserting authority, especially when events were not to their liking.

Something had gone wrong, dreadfully wrong. Neeve could tell by the tension in the senator's voice. He smiled and kissed his son, he asked about water in the fields, but his manner screamed calamity. Not once did he make eye contact with her. For a man who had always greeted her with a hug or a squeeze of her arm, today's behavior was unusual in the extreme.

Neeve tried to assess the situation calmly. Maybe a relative had died, or a financial problem needed attention, or something else had arisen on the villa. A thousand possibilities crossed her mind, but still she had the nagging feeling something had gone wrong, and the senator was blaming her.

When they arrived at the house, Neeve sent a servant to find Sammonicus, and then went directly to her room. Her mind was reeling with images of Marcellus and the senator talking in the olive grove, and she thought she knew what might have gone wrong. The senator had discovered her secret. Somehow he had learned about Taranis. He had discovered that the Caledonian chieftain coming for the Triumph was her brother. She wished she had said something to the senator, but the time never seemed right to tell him about her brother, and now it was too late.

"We're leaving?" Sammonicus said. His face showed disappointment. "Why must we leave?"

Neeve glared at him. "I didn't say we were leaving for certain," she said. "I simply asked you to water and feed the horse, ready the carriage and your belongings. We might be leaving, and if we are I want to do so in the minimum amount of time."

"I thought we were staying through the summer," he said, his face contorted in pain.

"Do as I say," she snapped. "You've been living like a land baron here, getting the Severus servants to do your duties. You think I don't know about what you've been doing? I know. And I know about the times you've signed out carriages for rides with your lady friends in the country … the female servants you lounge around with in the hot baths when the master retires to his dining rooms."

"Mistress, never once did I—"

"Don't insult me with your denials," Neeve said. "I said nothing because it harmed no one, and because, free or under orders, everyone needs social company." She moved toward him. "But now … when I ask you to do my bidding, I expect you to be moving before I conclude my sentence."

"Yes, Mistress, of course," Sammonicus said, his dark eyes trying to escape hers. "I will complete your tasks within the hour." He bowed and disappeared.

Neeve glanced around the room. She had started to gather her things when a servant tapped on her doorpost.

"The senator requests your presence in the library," the servant said.

"I will come directly," she said. She closed the curtain and paused, steeling her mind. The senator had to know about Taranis. What else could it be? But how would he know? Taranis wasn't even near Rome yet. She had checked several times at the Imperial offices in the forum. Everyone said the warriors from Britannia were still en route and that General Verus would not arrive for weeks. Neeve sighed. Senators were doubtless privy to more information. She should have talked to him earlier. Now it seemed as if she had been deceiving him.

Neeve washed her face and put on her best tunic. Minutes later she presented herself to the servants outside the library. They opened the doors and ushered her into a rectangular room filled with codex books. The far end had panels inlaid with fabrics and embossed wood depicting a walled city with farmers digging in the fields outside the gates. In the center of the middle panel, a diamond-shaped section of black walnut protruded out six inches like a shield, and there at the focal point of the room, hung her drawing of the senator.

"I will not detain you," the senator said. He was standing beside a full statue of someone who looked much like him, but Neeve guessed it was an ancestor. The library contained ten such statues and a half dozen busts, many of them women. "Today, as we speak," he said, "my enemies in the Senate are plotting ways to destroy my son, Marcellus. Do you know anything about this?"

Neeve frowned. "No," she said. "I know nothing."

"You haven't talked to any senators or senatorial aides?"

She shook her head.

"I have been a senator for nearly forty years," he said. "Do you think I cannot tell when someone is lying to me? Celts are born liars— I understand that. It's a way of life for you people. But I foolishly thought you were different. I treated you well, never like a servant or a hireling."

"Senator, I—"

"What did they give you? Silver? You betrayed my only son for silver?"

"I don't understand."

"Yes, you do," the senator said, his voice lifeless. "Someone approached and offered you a sum of money to spy on me and Marcellus. You refused. They offered more, significantly more, and you perhaps still refused, maybe even told them to leave you alone. But before long they were talking about vast sums of silver, almost beyond comprehension, and it proved irresistible, didn't it? All they wanted was a little information, they said. It wouldn't harm anyone.

So you scuttled around like the shabby guest you are, and you discovered that Marcellus had attended a few meetings with these blood-drinkers."

"No, I spoke to no one."

"You ran off to your odious friends and collected your bags of silver. No doubt you have already deposited them with a banker. But did you calculate what would happen to my son?" He looked at her with tired eyes. "No, I suppose not. Greed thinks only of itself."

Neeve felt her breathing grow shallow as he unhooked her drawing from the wall. He had framed it in light walnut to contrast with the dark background. "I have been preoccupied or I would have shown you this earlier," he said. "There was a time when I would come in here, sit down, and gaze at the picture, and I would imagine that one day you would find your way to my door. You would kiss me as a father and I would delight in your company and your refreshing ways. I would even dare to think that you and Marcellus might ...." He shifted his eyes away. "Now it all seems so useless." He smashed his hand through the center of the drawing and crushed the parchment fragments in his fingers.

"Senator Severus," she said, "you must believe me—"

"I do not," he said.

"Please ... you must—"

"The emperor himself pronounced your name as the one who betrayed Marcellus."

"The emperor?" She was stunned.

"What is done in secret," he said, "is often heralded at the city gates.

Please take your drawing and leave. I find your presence intensely painful." He dropped the scraps of parchment onto the mosaic floor and left through a side door.

Neeve glanced around the empty library. It seemed darker and colder now that she was alone. She bent over and collected the larger pieces, and set off to find Sammonicus.

Neeve spent several days trying to locate her sister. She knew Nes would be paying a visit to the Severus villa, and soon, so she needed to explain the situation. Neeve went first to the courthouse to see if they could direct her to the Balbinus estate. They did, but when she arrived, the servants informed her Balbinus was doing business in southern Italia for the week, and Nes had retired to her private villa on the Esquiline Hill.

As they traveled from one place to another, Neeve quizzed Sammonicus about the blood-drinkers. He knew little. He had heard they were an eastern cult that drank human blood, but was uncertain why. Someone had told him the cult believed fresh blood was the milk of eternity, and drinking regularly preserved life forever on the earth. No one knew much about them, he said, because they met secretly in graveyards at the blackest hour. Like most eastern mystery religions, they kept their practices to themselves. One odd thing about blood-drinkers, Sammonicus said, was their unwillingness to acknowledge the gods. That's how the state caught them—it forced suspects to burn incense to images. If they refused, they were put to death.

Neeve had never heard of the blood-drinkers before she came to Rome, but it was clear the Romans hated the outlaw group as much as they hated Druids. They had all but exterminated the robed priests from Gallia and Germania, and were well on their way to doing the same in Britannia. Apparently, they intended to rid the world of blood-drinkers as well.

Romans were tolerant of religions in conquered kingdoms, but they stood like a wall against human sacrifice. At least that was their public objection to Druids and blood-drinkers. Neeve suspected there was more to it. She knew in Britannia the Romans wanted to destroy the Druid priesthood because they were the unifying force among the tribes. The blood-drinkers were probably a threat because they turned their backs on the state gods and refused to bend a knee to the emperor. With Rome, Neeve had learned, it all came down to control and preserving world domination.

Neeve thought about the terrible mess she had created at the Severus household. The only person she had ever spoken to about

Marcellus and his odd ways was Nes ... and certainly her sister could be trusted. Being a Roman, Nes must have wondered whether Marcellus could be a blood-drinker, but Nes would never tell others about so devastating a possibility. She would know the consequences and keep it secret. Yes, she would definitely keep it secret.

But the emperor had named Neeve as the person who betrayed Marcellus. How could that be ... unless Nes had spoken to Balbinus and someone overheard the conversation? Is that what happened? Neeve didn't know, but she was relieved when her carriage arrived at Nes's villa. Her spirit was low. She needed to talk to her sister. Somehow Neeve had seriously injured the Severus household, and Nes would be able to cheer her, and together they might even find a solution to this awful mess.

"Who shall I say is calling?" a gate servant asked.

"Neeve mapmaker. I am sister of your mistress."

Minutes later Neeve was ushered into an exquisitely decorated dining room, smaller than the Severus's, but equally beautiful in wall coverings and marble mosaics on the floor. Neeve took the couch offered to her, while Sammonicus waited in the atrium.

"I am surprised to see you," Nes said as she entered. "I trust you are in good health."

"Events these past days have greatly distressed me," Neeve said awkwardly.

"I am so sorry," Nes said. "Nothing serious, I hope."

"Terribly serious," Neeve said. Then she told Nes the whole miserable tale about Marcellus, Senator Severus's accusation, and the Senate's hatred of blood-drinkers.

"Of course they hate blood-drinkers," Nes said. "Such people deserve to die."

Neeve frowned. Nes's words seemed cold. "You have no compassion for Marcellus?" she asked.

"I'm more sorry for you than him," she said.

"Me?"

"You are suffering because of Marcellus's foolish decisions," Nes said. "He should have known better. Secrets cannot be kept forever, especially when others might profit by making them public."

Neeve accepted a cup of herb tea, but she was feeling uncomfortable with Nes's comments, and her matter-of-fact way of speaking. The last time they were together, Nes was warm and caring, but now she seemed distant, as if Neeve's visit was an intrusion. "Secrets do get out," Neeve acknowledged, "but I still feel responsible."

Nes waved away the comment. "Did you tell lies about Marcellus? Did you force him to attend secret meetings banned by the state? No. You told the truth, and he chose to do what he did. So why should you feel responsible? What Marcellus has done is on his own head."

"I should have kept it private," Neeve said.

Nes shrugged. She seemed not to care.

"Senator Severus was deeply upset," Neeve said, almost to herself.

"Of course. He's father to a traitor."

Neeve frowned. "How could you say that? Marcellus is not a traitor."

"Use whatever word you wish," Nes said. "He's a Roman who aligns himself with Rome's enemies and refuses to pay homage to the state. What would you call him? Misguided? I call him a traitor."

"You are harsh in your judgments," Neeve said.

"No harsher than the state," Nes replied.

"You are surely right," Neeve said. "That's why this whole affair so troubles me. Senator Severus had given me his trust, and now he sees me as a greedy spy who betrayed him for silver." She looked at Nes and said, "It wasn't the senator's anger that shamed me. Not his anger ... no, it was the desperate look in his eyes. He was frightened. He's afraid for his son, and he has no idea how to protect him."

"Why should you be concerned?" Nes asked, sneering.

Neeve looked at her sister. "You seem so—"

"I am merely curious why you would be so concerned."

"I care about them," Neeve said.

"About the Severuses? They brought this on themselves."

"You seem almost glad that—"

"I am glad," Nes said. "It's about time Senator Severus experienced first-hand the suffering he has inflicted on others."

"Suffering?"

"Senator Severus is always involved in one investigation or another," Nes said. "He cares little whether he hurts innocent people in his misguided quests. I wish no one ill will, but I cannot feel remorse for such a man."

"I know little about Senate investigations," Neeve said, "but I have found him to be a thoughtful, gracious man."

Nes said nothing.

"He's been especially kind to me."

Nes nodded.

"Now I'm unsure what to do."

"A difficult situation."

"It truly is."

"I suppose we can talk about this another time," Nes said, smiling artificially.

"Yes, I suppose so."

Nes glanced around the room as if she was waiting for Neeve to leave.

The gesture shocked Neeve, and irritated her. "I have a question for you," she said.

Nes returned her eyes to Neeve.

"I told only *you* about Marcellus," Neeve said. "You must have spoken to somebody ...." She left her words hanging.

"I cannot think of anyone," Nes said.

"You didn't tell Balbinus?"

Nes took a biscuit from a tray and said, "Balbinus and I have seen little of each other these past days," she said. "We certainly had no conversation about Marcellus Severus."

"So you told no one?"

Nes shook her head slowly, her brow furrowed, as if she were trying to recall a situation contrary to her recollection. "I spoke to no one," she said, dabbing her biscuit into her tea.

Neeve didn't believe her.

"Actually," Nes said with the same thoughtful look on her face, "it never even occurred to me that Marcellus might belong to the blood-drinkers. They are such a contemptible lot, and he has always impressed me favorably."

Neeve eyed her sister. "I told no one about Marcellus, except you," she repeated.

Nes sipped her tea. "Secrets will get out," she said. "I suppose a dozen people could have noticed Marcellus's strange behavior. Romans are attentive to such things."

"Yes, they seem to be," Neeve said. "You said yourself, people profit by making secrets public."

"Sad, but true," Nes said.

Neeve pushed her tea away. She tried to recall her conversation with Nes at the outdoor eating-house when they had wrapped themselves in blankets. Nes kept calling for stronger drinks, saying that Celtic women needed something robust. She had laughed and teased and made Neeve feel as if she were talking to a trusted friend. But Nes could not be trusted. She had manipulated the discussion from first to last, and when she left that afternoon, she undoubtedly went to someone who exposed Marcellus to the Senate.

"Well, this has been a lovely visit," Nes said, rising.

Neeve remained seated and said, "I'm troubled because I told no one about Marcellus except you, and you say you told no one—"

Nes blew out in exasperation. "I have explained that people in Roman society spend a great deal of time scrutinizing each other. They use every means to gain advantage. As powerful men, the Severuses have many who wish them ill. Obviously, someone observed Marcellus engaged in unusual behavior and reported him. It happens all the time."

"Does it happen all the time that the emperor names the accuser?"

"I don't understand," Nes said.

"The emperor has named me as the person who witnessed Marcellus engaged in unusual behavior."

"I see."

"Do you?" Neeve set her jaw and said, "Somehow the emperor knows what I told you, and only you, about Marcellus."

"Gossip spreads in many ways," Nes said.

"Why are you lying to me?"

Nes's face hardened. "I am not lying," she said.

"Yes you are, and we both know it."

Nes walked to the entrance of the dining room. "Sisters sometimes have disagreements," she said. "Perhaps we should talk another day."

"I'm not leaving until I have my answers."

"Well, I have no answers to give," Nes said, smiling with her mouth.

"Do you realize what you've done?" Neeve shouted. "Senator Severus was the only person I could go to about Taranis. Now because of you, the senator will have nothing to do with me. Do you understand? Taranis will arrive soon and—"

"You are so provincial," Nes said. "Taranis has been here for weeks."

Neeve stared at her in stunned silence.

"That's right. Your precious barbarian brother is in a compound north of Rome as we speak. I talked to him the first day he arrived."

"You talked to Taranis?" Neeve was speechless. "What … I mean, how is he …?"

"He's perfectly fine," Nes said. "He wants to be left alone … to rest in the hands of the gods, as he put it. He said you should return to Britannia."

"You lie!" Neeve was standing now.

"I tell the truth," Nes said. "He knows nothing can be done about his situation, and he wants you to leave."

"Why didn't you tell me you had met Taranis?"

"I attached no importance to it," Nes said.

"You attach no importance to Taranis, your own brother?" Neeve could hardly choke down the anger welling up in her.

"Taranis is just a name to me," she said. "I have recollections of him … and you, for that matter, but they are quite dim and of little consequence. Why should either of you concern me?"

"Is that the way you feel?"

"Exactly the way I feel."

"Then you are nothing but a selfish person—"

"Who are you to judge me?" Nes said in raised voice.

"Tell me why you betrayed my confidence and exposed Marcellus. For silver? Or gold? Why? Tell me why."

"I won't tell you anything."

"You won't because you are ashamed," Neeve said.

"I am ashamed of nothing."

"Then tell me."

"You are such a provincial fool," Nes said, curling her lip. "You have no idea of how anything works."

"So you will not tell me," Neeve said, determined to stick to the subject. "For a few coins you would betray your own family."

"You want to know? You really want to know?" Nes's eyes flashed with rage. Then she paused, and her cool eyes returned. "If I ever used the information you so childishly gave me—which I did not—but if I did, I would have used it wisely. I would have exchanged it not for a handful of coins, as you seem to think, but for something great, like a seat in the Senate for Balbinus." Her eyes burned into Neeve. "Did you hear me? Something great, like a seat in the Roman Senate!"

"You are contemptible," Neeve said, "as bad as the blood-drinkers everyone hates."

"Your superior attitude sickens me," Nes said. "Do you know what I have been through? Do you? I was captured and you escaped. Have you forgotten that? I watched Mother while they raped and beat her to death—"

"Mother?"

"That's right … Mother," Nes said. She bit her lip as if she were trying to keep her composure.

"I'm sorry—"

"I'm sure you are," Nes said coldly. "After Mother died, I was taken to the camps. You know about the camps? You know how many survive? Can you even imagine what it's like to service twenty or thirty soldiers every day? Every-single-day!" She smashed the back of her hand on a urn, knocking it flying. "No, you wouldn't know anything about it because you have had a good life, pampered, never wanting for anything, a family around you. You come riding high into Rome with one of the most powerful senators as your benefactor. And now, when something finally goes awry in your pleasant little life, you strut in here complaining that I've been selfish."

"You've had a difficult life," Neeve said, "and if I could change it I would. But that gives you no right to destroy others for your own selfish gain."

"It gives me every right," Nes said.

"No, it does not. Your selfishness destroyed Marcellus—"

"Nonsense," Nes said. "I deny everything you say."

"Deny if you want, but you couldn't have done worse had you murdered Marcellus yourself ... and I tell you this ... you ruined any chance Taranis might have had to escape his death sentence."

"I am tired of talking," Nes said. "It's plain to me—you have had it too easy for too long. One day you'll discover that the only person you can depend on is yourself. Then you will make the most of what's around you, or like chaff on a summer threshing floor, the wind will carry you away."

"Then let the wind carry me away," Neeve said. "Better that than living a life of deceit and betrayal."

"Guards!" Nes called. Two fully armed men entered the dining room. "My sister needs assistance to her carriage," she said.

"At least tell me where they're keeping Taranis," Neeve said.

"Why should I bother?"

"Because your mother would have wished it."

Nes dropped her eyes to the floor. Then, forcing a smile, she said, "Why not? You can tell your brother how your irresponsible, trusting nature cost him his life." She walked to the door, shrugged and said, "You will find him an hour north of Rome at an abandoned gladiatorial school on the Tiber. Pay the guards some coins and you can chat all day." With that, she turned and walked back into her villa.

45

Marcellus waited patiently near the back entrance to Rome's largest livery on the Aventine Hill. Workers had scattered fresh straw over the mud-packed floor, but after standing on the damp ground for the better part of the morning, his legs felt like lumps of ice. He was watching a carriage, hoping the owner would return.

Few paid attention to him, dressed as he was in the rough garb of a peasant, just another servant waiting for his master. Hours passed. Scores of horses and mules were taken up and down the runway, but no one approached the carriage in the fourth stall. The afternoon light was fading; it grew colder. Marcellus was beginning to wonder if the owner would use his carriage that day, when a slave leading a Libyan dappled-gray stopped beside the stall. He hitched the gray to the carriage and moved down the runway into the street.

Marcellus followed. With afternoon crowds filling the cobbleways, it was easy to keep pace with the carriage as it wended its way toward the villas on the north side of the Aventine. Fifteen minutes later the slave pulled the carriage to a stop in front of a wooden gate. He opened a small speaking portal and called inside. The gate creaked open and he drove the carriage into the compound.

Marcellus walked behind the carriage as if he were an attending servant. He managed to get halfway to the peristyle house before a steward challenged him.

"I wish to see your master," Marcellus said.

The steward frowned. He glanced around the yard to make certain no one else had entered the compound.

"He's expecting me," Marcellus added.

The new information gave the steward little comfort. Marcellus had entered the villa compound without an invitation and without using the master's name, certainly unusual, and it put the steward on guard. His eyes took in the intruder's rough clothing and he immediately called for support.

"Your master has asked me to visit him today," Marcellus said in raised voice, trying to overcome his lowborn appearance.

"Stay where you are," the steward said, now flanked by four other men. He signaled someone to fetch the master.

The door opened. "Who are you?" the master of the house demanded.

Marcellus ran his eyes over the man who had appeared in the doorway. He had a fringe of hair that boiled up around his head, chunky arms, a round stomach, and cherry blemishes dotting his neck. From his stunned eyes, Marcellus guessed he had been sleeping. "I'm sorry to have disturbed you," Marcellus said. "I was wondering if—"

"Who-are-you?" the master repeated.

"A friend," Marcellus said, trying to keep the conversation civil. He was shocked at the man's angry demeanor. "We have met several times," he said. "Perhaps if you would give me a few minutes ...."

The man smoothed his hair and strode out toward Marcellus, his heavy eyebrows knitted in irritation. "If I were you," he said in a threatening voice, "I should answer my query."

Marcellus glanced around at the unfriendly looking servants and said, "Could I possibly speak to you alone?"

"I have no time for this," the master shot back. He turned to the servants who were looking on, open eyed, and said, "Ten stripes, and then throw him into the street. This scoundrel needs to be taught a lesson."

"I attend meetings at night," Marcellus said in lowered voice, unhappy with the treatment he was receiving. "I think you should provide me with a few minutes."

The master licked his lips. His eyes swept the faces of the slaves now gathering at the edges of his compound and then came to rest on

Marcellus. "Back to your labors," he snapped. "I will speak to our visitor."

Marcellus followed the master through a garden entrance and into the inner courtyard. The master seated himself imperiously on a cushioned bench, his eyes burning into Marcellus, whom he left conspicuously standing. "Now," he said, pointing a finger like a court magistrate, "who are you, and why are you here?"

"We have never spoken," Marcellus said, "but I know you from the meetings."

"You know me?"

"You are Rubellius Anicus Faustus," Marcellus said, "cell leader at our meetings."

Faustus scratched the pimples on his neck. He seemed to be assessing Marcellus's response. "How did you find me?" he asked.

"I marked the wheel of your carriage," Marcellus said, "and checked the liveries for the mark. Then I followed your carriage here."

"My name?" he said tersely. "How did you know my name?"

Marcellus gazed at the man, and for a moment was tempted not to answer. At the meetings Faustus acted with a certain self-importance, especially when he expressed his opinions, but his impatience and outright surliness had taken Marcellus by surprise. Faustus was treating him as if he were one of his slaves. It was the clothing. He couldn't consider Marcellus as a brother from the meetings because the pair seemed to be at different stations in Roman society. Marcellus took a breath and ignored Faustus's haughtiness. "Your name is chiseled on the entrance pillars to the garden," he said.

Faustus turned his head slowly toward the pillars, processing the information. "So you think you made a grand and profitable discovery," he said, snorting.

"No, I—"

"And now what?" Faustus's eyes narrowed. "You want gold or you turn me in?"

"You misunderstand. I came here to—"

"Let me round out your education. I am protected by important noblemen—magistrates, equestrians—many of whom have spoken to senators on my behalf."

"No, no," Marcellus protested. "I'm not here to cause you trouble. I am a believer like you. I simply have questions … and since you are the cell leader, I thought I should talk to you."

Faustus slumped back into his cushions, breathing easier. "You know," he said, "you are violating the agreements we made in our cell. We use no names and never acknowledge each other in public life. And most importantly, we never, ever, visit someone at his private residence." He raised his voice on the last sentence.

"I understand, but—"

"You understand nothing," Faustus said, his florid face trembling with rage. "You speak of secret meetings, and do so in front of my slaves? How dare you come here?"

"I apologize," Marcellus said. "I had no wish to put you in danger."

"Danger? You think I'm concerned about danger? I care nothing for myself. My times are in God's hands. I care only about the sheep in my charge. What will happen to them if I am carted off to the beasts? Who will teach them the truth of the kingdom? You?" He sneered and waved his hand dismissively. "How could anyone replace me with my training and knowledge? You didn't think of that, did you? You come marching in here—into my private home—confusing my servants with your mumblings about secret meetings, and not once did you think of anyone other than yourself."

"I am sorry," Marcellus said, "but I have tried to talk to you several times. You leave so quickly at the close of the meetings—"

"I do," Faustus said. "I have little care for my own life, but as a cell leader I have a responsibility to preserve myself for the good of others." He popped a pimple on the back of his neck and said, "Now, what is so important that you would disturb me in my private villa."

"A great purge is coming," Marcellus said, "scheduled for the Circus Maximus during the Triumph for Julius Verus."

"Purges come and go," Faustus said in a solemn voice. "We are the wheat of God to be ground by the teeth of beasts that we might emerge spotless in his kingdom."

Marcellus paused, surprised Faustus should reply in such an aloof way. He sounded as if he were delivering one of his nighttime homilies. "Should we not warn others of the danger?" Marcellus asked.

"The blood of martyrs establishes believers," Faustus said. "We wish not to die, but we die willingly for the sake of those that come after us."

"So the more that die, the better it is for the people of the Way?"

"A hard truth, but one that must be borne with grace and courage," Faustus said.

"It is a hard truth."

"Baptized in fire, ushered into glory," Faustus intoned. "Our shattered bones become the seeds of the church."

Marcellus nodded. "I first came to faith after seeing believers die with such courage," he said.

"One flower crushed, another arises," Faustus crooned, as if he were reciting verse. "Planted in sorrow, watered in blood."

Marcellus thought about his father, and the sadness that awaited him if he were to lose his only son.

"Yes, to follow the Way is difficult," Faustus continued. "Each of us has his own calling, some to teach, some to administrate, and some to be the gristle that breaks the damn devil's teeth before the howling mobs of Rome. I myself have been called to leadership ... but how glorious to be called to the martyr's den." He wagged his head. "To seal one's testimony with blood ... what a privilege." He locked eyes with Marcellus and said, "Would that the God of heaven might choose me for such an honor!"

Still standing, Marcellus gazed down at the cell leader, his balding head, his soft body, and his smug-looking face. He had serious doubts whether Faustus wished he had been called to martyrdom. Even a brave man would shrink from such a horrific death.

"You have fears," Faustus said. "I can see it. But you must seal those fears away in a closet. That's what I do. Remember the faithful who have gone on before, and be strong. Those who persevere to the end will experience eternal Sabbaths."

Marcellus nodded. He didn't like this man. Faustus might be a believer, but he was pompous and insincere. Still, since Marcellus had been attending the meetings, he had become convinced that Chrestus, as the Romans called him, had risen from the dead and was truly alive in their community. Marcellus had tried to deny it many times, had turned his back and shut his ears, but in quieter moments when he was alone, it seemed as if Chrestus were calling out to him. Strange that he should have such inner urgings. No one he knew, apart from those in the meetings, had this irresistible pull toward Chrestus and the Way. When he listened to the testimonials of other believers, he discovered that many had similar experiences. They could not explain why this religion of Chrestus satisfied their inner longings, but they knew it did. It answered the deep questions about the purpose of existence, what happens after death, and it gave peace amid the tumult of life. Why should it matter if a few like Faustus were hypocritical? His hope was not in Faustus, but in Chrestus.

"I trust my words have given you strength," Faustus said, intending to conclude the conversation.

"I have a question," Marcellus said.

Faustus gestured his consent to speak.

"My father is growing old and would be grievously wounded were I to die in the purge. He has asked me to pay a small homage to Rome, perhaps light some incense to the Roman pantheon of gods. I would be doing it for my father, not to preserve my life or to deny the God of heaven. I'm wondering if—"

"You would be a stench in the nostrils of God," Faustus said. "He would spew you out of his mouth like filthy water."

"Do all cell leaders agree with your view?" Marcellus asked.

"All agree," Faustus said. "If you deny Chrestus before men, he will deny you before God in heaven."

"Even if I lit the incense privately before the emperor or certain members of the Senate?"

"Privately … publicly—it's all the same. What matters is what God in heaven sees."

Marcellus stood quietly for a few moments, thinking about his father.

"Control your fear," Faustus said. "Not everyone will be dragged onto the sands of the Circus. Antoninus the Pius might be a pagan, but he has great respect for life. He would not permit a large purge like in the time of Nero. Yes, a few will give their lives, and if in the time of testing they compel you to bow to pagan gods, you must steadfastly refuse. But in the end, I think it likely the purge will pass you by."

"I think not," Marcellus said to himself.

"When you walk through the fire, you shall not be burned," Faustus recited, "and the flame shall not consume you." He smiled to himself, satisfied with his quotations. Then he repeated, "The purge will likely pass you by. Have courage."

Marcellus didn't reply. He was still thinking of his father.

"You disagree?"

"In this case, I think I do."

"Come, come," Faustus said, appearing curious. "You act as if you will be central in the purge. Someone of your station cannot have that inflated an opinion of himself, can he?"

"I have no inflated opinion of myself," Marcellus said, wishing not to prolong the conversation. He had warned Faustus about the coming purge and had received his answer about burning incense privately. Now he wanted to leave. "I thank you for your time," he said.

"You are low-born, are you not?"

"As you have pointed out many times," Marcellus said, "all are equal in God's sight." He wanted to avoid answering the question.

"You speak unusually well for a low-born."

"I suppose so," Marcellus said.

"Your pattern of speech is curious, now that I think about it. I am vexed. How could you, a low-born, be of any concern to the state?"

Marcellus hesitated, tired of the persistent questions.

"I demand an answer," Faustus said. "Why should you be a concern to the state?"

"For the same reason I would be given the opportunity to burn incense privately before the emperor," Marcellus said with a sigh.

Faustus shifted on his cushions. "I don't understand."

Marcellus waved his hand. "It matters little," he said.

Faustus leaned forward, fascinated. "Who are you?" he asked.

"I'm a believer ... who happens to be a senator's son."

"A senator! But ... your dress ...."

"I wore common garb ... as I do at the night meetings ... for anonymity."

"You came here alone, with no servants or guards?"

Marcellus nodded.

"I thought you might be a higher station than you appeared," Faustus said, "but a senator's son!" He looked ridiculous leaning forward with his mouth open. Then, suddenly, he seemed to realize he was sitting while a patrician stood. He jumped to his feet. "Please," he said, pulling out a couch, "take your leisure."

"Thank you," Marcellus said, "but I must be going."

"Your father ... he is concerned?" Faustus asked, fishing for a name.

"He is," Marcellus said. "His enemies in the Senate are eager to do him harm, and now they have something to exploit—my allegiance to the people of the Way."

"A senator's son," Faustus said, mulling over the thought. "I had no idea. You could help our movement."

"I will be gone in the purge," Marcellus said.

Faustus tapped his chin in thought. "I might be able to help you."

"How?"

"I told you I have many noble friends ... not senators or patricians of your status," he said, "but important people nonetheless. If I talked to them, maybe we could reach an accommodation. It would cost some gold ...."

"I'm sure my father will be spreading gold and silver around in the coming weeks, but I doubt it will deter his enemies from demanding that I pay homage to the Roman gods."

"Yes ... I see ... there is one other item of which you might not be aware. Purges of late have taken into account the leadership of our community. The emperor and senators often ignore leaders that cause no problem because Rome wants stability, even in outlawed groups like us. If they send me to the beasts, for example, who knows what radical leader might arise in my place? You understand? Roman officials crave predictability and I try to give it to them. I faithfully teach my cell members the truth of Chrestus. I encourage them when I can, but I keep my shadow low on the wall."

"You avoid needless exposure."

"Yes, by God's grace, I do. I take care not to incur the wrath of the state. They have concerns about those who proselytize so I avoid such activities. It is the right thing to do."

"But we are called to spread the good news of Chrestus, not to hide our lights under a bucket."

"True, but there are different callings, as I said. Believe me, we have no shortage of proselytizers. The Way is replete with them. If a proselytizer is taken to the Circus Maximus, little is lost. But teachers ... now that's entirely different. Teachers such as me are scarce. It takes years to become proficient in the sacred books. The key is to determine your calling. As I said, some are called to teach, some to preach, and some to make proselytes. I teach."

Marcellus said nothing.

"I also go out of my way to praise Roman officials, and I always stress that the Way presents no danger to the Empire, exactly what Luke the Physician did in his two letters to the Way. Have you ever read those letters?"

Marcellus shook his head.

"They were written a century ago in a complicated style of Greek, not everyday Latin, so only scholars like me, or educated, well-born Romans like yourself, could understand them." He frowned. "You do have a deeper understanding of Greek than simple marketplace mutterings?"

"I do," Marcellus said, but he was growing weary of Faustus. "I take it you have read the letters through?"

"Oh, yes, many times, and they make excellent reading. Interestingly, Luke goes out of his way to praise every Roman official he can. He was trying to calm Roman fears, you see." He gestured with his hand and said, "That is exactly what I try to do. Many in our number have a different view. They think we should push hard in our preaching and teaching, regardless of the consequences."

"And you disagree," Marcellus said.

"Look where it gets them," Faustus said. "The sands of the Circus. Of course, in the day of testing we should never deny Chrestus, but it's foolish to squander our lives when we can better serve the community alive."

"I think I understand you," Marcellus said.

"My point is that many Roman officials are sympathetic to leaders like me who take care not to stir up trouble. And since you are patrician-born, and educated, I could say you are a valued assistant to me. They might see you as less of a threat and decide not to pursue you."

"And how might I be able to repay the favor?" Marcellus asked.

"I have need of nothing," Faustus said, "but we do have widows and orphans among us that have genuine needs. I try to help where I can, but my funds are limited. Some have deposited moneys with the bankers and have designated me as steward over those accounts. You might wish to do the same."

"Let me think about it," Marcellus said, starting toward the compound gate.

"Yes, of course," Faustus said, smiling broadly, unable to contain his excitement.

A servant opened the wooden gate.

"Shall I contact you?" Faustus asked.

"No, I will contact you."

"At the cell meeting?"

"I plan to change cells."

"But how shall I—?"

Marcellus stepped through the gate and was gone.

PART FIVE:
A Great Sadness

Two Months Later

46

Vectis was tired of traveling. It had been a long journey from Dacia and already the hot summer months were upon them when he and Julian arrived in Rome. Julian had fully recovered from his injuries and was eager to visit old friends in the capital. For his part, Vectis intended to seek out Senator Titus Severus and try to gain a posting in Britannia. He had not given up on the idea of finding Neeve.

It felt good to be back in Rome. The events in Dacia had an unreal quality to them, as if somehow they belonged to a faraway dream. The assassin turned out to be the dark-haired woman after all, and Vectis had little doubt she was the same woman who had killed the Egyptian prince. Julian had been affected less by the drug because of the volumes of diluted wine he had consumed during the day. Yet, Julian's memories were patchy. He recalled coming to Vectis's aid when he heard a goblet crash to the floor, and he thought he might have struck the assailant with a wine pitcher, but beyond that he had no memory.

The soldiers in his detail believed they had saved Vectis and Julian's lives. Two of their number were found dead on the floor, but before they died, they appeared to have mortally wounded the assassin and driven her off.

Vectis' recollections were different. They were fragmented and confused, but he believed she might have spared him at the last minute. He remembered someone in a blond wig leaning over him with a needle dagger in her hand, and time enough to finish him.

They found her outside the bathhouse in Vectis's cart, wrapped in his oil slicker. The first reports said she had been killed, but now Vectis couldn't be certain. A second account said that the blacksmith had taken her to the army surgeons in Porolissum where she survived. Whatever was true, Vectis had no doubt the soldiers at Porolissum would execute her for the murders at the bathhouse.

After spending several days at his villa outside Rome, Vectis set off for the Senate House. He had arranged a meeting with Senator Severus to discuss reassignment to Britannia. He had no idea whether any of the outpost archives might turn up letters helpful to the senator's investigation, but he was willing to try, especially when it meant returning to Britannia.

Vectis wended his way through the early morning crowds in the Old Forum. The business day had not yet begun, but already the walkways bustled with people—sightseers, most of them visitors from the provinces. No one, it seemed, wanted to miss any part of the summer festivities. Even the gangs of slaves were singing as they gathered their tools after a night of scrubbing walls, burnishing bronze doors, and setting up placards for the great Triumph of Legate Julius Verus. Yes, the festive season was upon them.

"Tribune?"

Vectis turned and saw a young aide standing at the base of the steps leading to the Senate.

"Are you Vectis Trebellius Quadratus?"

Vectis said he was and followed the aide into the cavernous Basilica Aemilia next to the Senate House. Vectis was taken to a reception room where Senator Severus awaited him. The senator rose when Vectis entered the room, a gracious gesture because he was Vectis's superior in every respect. "Ah, Vectis Trebellius," he said. "I am delighted to see you again."

"Thank you for making room in your schedule," Vectis said.

The senator nodded pleasantly, but he looked exhausted, his body thin, face haggard, posture stooped. He moved slowly to his couch and all but dropped onto the cushions. He motioned for Vectis to sit.

"The Senate is impressed with your accomplishments," Severus said, "and as your sponsor, I am bursting with pride. Not only did you clean up a mess, but you did it while preserving a senior officer's dignity. Remarkable."

"Thank you, Senator," Vectis said, surprised he would know anything beyond Commodus's boastful reports.

The senator smiled wearily. "Oh, yes, we know what you had to deal with in Gaius Commodus. We've had many dispatches beyond regular channels—from Rutilius of Legion XIII, Tiberius from Porolissum, and even from the Imperial family. All glowing reports."

The senator said nothing more about his Imperial family comment, but Vectis guessed the young engineer had sent private letters as well.

"Your Dacian service has brought great honor to Rome and to me personally," Severus said.

"I am proud to have served," Vectis said properly.

"You will excuse my abruptness," Severus said, his face changing, "but I have a difficult day ahead of me. I presume you have a request."

"I do," Vectis said. "It concerns your Senate investigation—"

"That has been discontinued," Severus said.

"Discontinued?"

"I have reached a compromise with two of the senators involved," he said. "We negotiate all the time on matters of interest. I've agreed not to pursue the investigation if they ... how shall I say, ignore certain matters of importance to me."

"I see." Vectis handed him the papyrus sheet with Commodus's signature stating that former Senator Atilius Titianus had ordered him to withdraw from his fort to the Antonine Wall.

"Ah," Severus said. "This document exonerates you. I knew it all the time." He glanced up. "I will make certain the appropriate senators read it." Then, pausing, he asked, "Besides clearing your good name, is there another reason you should be interested in this investigation?"

Vectis hesitated, then decided to speak his mind. "I'm embarrassed to say my reasons are purely personal."

Severus drew a long breath and exhaled. "We all have personal issues," he said. "Nothing wrong with that. I take it you would you like a posting in Britannia?"

"I would, but—"

"No, no," Severus said, ignoring his objection, "you have earned the right to ask. But it will be an Imperial posting, not a Senate assignment. Recent events have made it difficult to do business in the Senate, and since I have an appointment with Emperor Antoninus this afternoon, I will ask him to assign you as a military tribune in Londinium."

Vectis thanked him and left the basilica elated. He would be heading for Britannia soon, and with an Imperial appointment. Much better than he could have expected. With the emperor his sponsor, he would have greater freedom to search the province for Neeve.

Neeve and Marcellus moved steadily through the morning crowds, she clasping tightly to his arm, he staring at the paving stones as they walked, neither of them speaking a word. Since leaving the Severus villa, Neeve had taken a set of small rooms in the heart of the city. She had not seen Senator Severus since that day in the library, only Marcellus, but he visited her often.

All around Neeve and Marcellus, the Old Forum bustled with activity, as throngs of people flowed in and out, their voices blending in a constant drone. When they neared the Basilica Aemilia, Neeve pulled Marcellus toward the marble balustrade of the Rostra, the famous platform where notables gave their speeches.

"You cannot go through with this," she said.

Marcellus glanced toward Neeve's body servant, Sammonicus, who moved a reasonable distance away to give them privacy. He turned back to Neeve and said, "You shouldn't have come."

"Two little words! That's all you have to say. Two words! What is so difficult about saying, *Anathema Chrestus*?"

"Because it means, 'I curse Chrestus,' and I will never say that."

"They're only words," she said, "mere words. You light a few incense bowls and say, *Anathema Chrestus*, and it's finished. You go home. Your father is happy ... and you can continue with what you've always done. Even go to your meetings, if you choose."

"I cannot deny what I truly believe—"

"Don't you understand? Nobody cares what you truly believe. But this issue has gone too far. Now the whole Senate knows about your ties to the followers of the Way." Neeve looked at him, confused. "You simply need to satisfy them ... say a few words, light a few bowls ... you can do it ... make a public showing in front of the senators, and this nightmare is over." She pressed close to him and held his eyes. "You need to do this for your father," she said, "... and for me."

"For you?"

"Yes, for me. You have been patient when all I could think about was Vectis. And I am sorry, so very sorry for making you wait. I have been such a fool. But now I have decided. Vectis is only a memory. I know that. He is never coming back ... and I ... I think I love you, Marcellus. No, I *do* love you, very much." She pressed into him and whispered, "I want you to live not only for your father's sake, but for mine. I love you, Marcellus. Please don't leave me. I need you." She knew she could never love him the way she did Vectis, but from her heart she had spoken the truth.

He reached for her, tilted her head up, and kissed her. "I've waited so long to hear you say those words," he said. "I only wish that circumstances were different."

"They could be different," she said, kissing him almost in desperation, her hands stroking his face as she began to sense the horror of their situation. "Oh, Marcellus, please," she said as she planted kisses on his cheek. "Everything could be so different if you would—"

"My world has changed this past year," he said. "The God of heaven has set my feet on a new path, one that leads directly to him."

Neeve pulled away. "No, no," she said. "This is not true. There is no single path leading anywhere. All you need to do is—"

"Neeve—"

"No! Listen to me!" She grasped hold of his arm and shook it as if she were trying to wake him from a deep sleep. "You had doubts in the past," she said. "You told me so. How can you now be so certain? How can you say the Way is the only path to truth?"

"I sense it at the core of my being," Marcellus said. "It's as if the truth has seized me." He pointed to a statue of Julius Caesar at the corner of the Rostra and said, "The great Caesar walked these tiles a thousand times. Try to imagine he never entered this forum … never spoke from the Rostra. You cannot. Neither can I. Caesar was here, he was even in Britannia, and we both know it. When we believe something, we cannot simply close our eyes and say, 'I no longer believe.' No, what we believe is woven into our being." He paused. "I believe Chrestus is the Way to eternal life. I believe it, and I cannot deny it."

"But you had doubts," Neeve insisted, her voice betraying a thread of defeat.

"Yes, in the beginning I did have doubts … I wrestled with myself … but now, even if I tried not to believe, I would still find myself believing. Can you understand that?"

"What about us?" Neeve asked, wiping away a tear. "Will you throw everything away because you believe in Chrestus? Is that what this god wants? Does he desire you to die? Does he want your father in mourning, your enemies strutting about in triumph, and me once again weeping at the loss of a beloved?" She tugged at a strand of her hair until it hurt. She needed control. She had lost Cronn and Vectis, was denied even a single visit with Taranis—"We don't want your coins," the soldiers had said. "You can see him at the Triumph." And now, Marcellus.

"I cannot deny what I believe," he repeated quietly.

Neeve groaned, suddenly feeling as if her world were sliding into a dark pit, a place where nightmares had become reality, and where there were no handholds to pull herself up to the surface. She covered her face with her hands, knowing she had no words to speak, nothing to say that would move his resolute heart. He had chosen a path away from her, and there was nothing she could do. "All I've ever known in my life is death and sorrow," she said, her voice barely audible, "… please, Marcellus, if not for yourself, then for me … I beg you, have mercy on my pitiful soul. I cannot bear to lose you."

"I am so very sorry," he said, his hand caressing her shoulder, comforting her.

She lifted her eyes, searching his when she asked, "Could this Chrestus be so unloving ... so callous?"

"Chrestus is not callous," Marcellus said. "But I confess, I have no idea why he has placed before me such a bitter cup. I only know that his ways are higher than my ways, and his thoughts greater than my thoughts."

"Do you love me?" Neeve asked.

"You know that I do," he said. "I have told you many times, and I tell you again ... I love you more than anything in this world."

"And you want for us to be together?"

"I do, truly I do ... and I love life dearly, oh, how I love life!" And then he added, his face in anguish, "But I cannot utter the curse."

"You *can*, Marcellus, you can."

"I am sorry, but I cannot. I will not."

Neeve glanced toward the Senate House. "We have so little time," she said.

He nodded.

No one spoke. She could hear him breathing, hear her own irregular breaths, but neither could think of something to say. She turned away and found her eyes wandering the faceless men and women crisscrossing the forum. The people seemed to move in a blur, their garments an indistinguishable smudge of color, and Neeve realized her eyes were filled with tears.

"Master," a servant called. "The senators are asking for you."

Neeve grasped Marcellus's hand and began to speak quickly. Her voice was choked with emotion ... and desperation. "If you cannot utter those words," she said, "let's leave this place. Let's leave now."

"Neeve—"

"We'll go to Britannia ... or the other side of the world if you like ... to Parthia. I don't care. But let's go together, and live our lives. Can you not do this for me?" She threw her arms around him and clung to his neck. "For me," she whispered urgently into his ear, "do this for me, and I will serve your god the rest of my days."

He said nothing.

She pulled back to look him in the eyes. But they were shut tight.

"No!" she shouted. "Marcellus, you listen to me ...."

He started to turn.

She clutched at him. "Please, oh, please ...." The tears flowed down her cheeks.

He unhooked her arms and touched his lips to her forehead. "I love you," he said, and then he turned and walked toward the Senate House without glancing back.

Neeve pressed her face into the cold marble of the balustrade, and watched him mount the Senate steps, and disappear into the darkened entrance.

47

Vectis descended the steps of the Basilica Aemilia to the floor of the Old Forum, hardly able to contain his excitement. Senator Severus had agreed to post him in Britannia. The old senator had much on his mind—personal problems, he said—but always the man of integrity, he managed to deal fairly with Vectis's requests. Soon Vectis would have permission to travel to Britannia and begin his search.

Julian was probably right that Neeve had been killed in the uprising, but Vectis could never rest until he was certain. He remembered the last time he saw her, when the Caledonians had overwhelmed his outpost in northern Britannia, and she sat on her horse alongside the Caledonian chieftains, her hair tied up like a submissive Roman wife, trying to tell him she would forever be his Neeve. Now she was somewhere in the untamed province of Britannia ... or lying cold in the ground. But whatever her fate, he was determined to find out.

Vectis had heard all the rumors about General Verus—that he had captured Taranis, and would parade him before the crowds at his Triumph. He hoped Verus would dispatch Taranis quickly and with dignity. The Caledonian commander had once spared Vectis's life, and for him to be humiliated in Rome would be a gross injustice. A brave adversary like Taranis deserved a clean death.

Vectis started across the forum, his eyes on the marble tiles as he contemplated his journey to Rome's most distant province. He stopped. He had been thinking so much about Neeve he imagined her standing by the Rostra. He ran his eyes over the historic platform with its many statues and prows of ships from Rome's sea battles. The throngs milled about, flowing this way and that, moving in chaotic patterns, at first swarming past the Rostra, then melting away. Vectis lifted his eyes to the marble balustrade of the great dais. A woman was standing near the bottom, staring at him. He swallowed. Neeve? He struggled to get air. Could it be Neeve? He stepped around someone to get a better angle.

Four large Gallic slaves bearing a litter moved slowly into Vectis's line of vision and then stopped; the man inside the litter seemed to think this would be a good time for a chat because he was beckoning to a friend. Frustrated, Vectis pushed past several people until he had a clear view. Neeve was gone. He whipped his head around. He had lost her! He ran his eyes frantically across the faces where he had last seen her. Nothing. Could he have been mistaken? Then he saw a flash of flaxen hair. He moved slightly, squinting his eyes. It was Neeve! Standing in front of the Rostra was his beautiful Neeve. She was dressed in exquisite Roman garments and talking to a stranger, but there was no mistaking her tall, strong body, her golden hair and crystal blue eyes. Neeve was in Rome!

Vectis stumbled toward her, elbowing shocked people out of his path. He flung his hand in the air to get her attention, but she had turned away. She was now staring in another direction. "Neeve!" he called. "Neeve!" But his voice was swallowed in the din of the crowd. He kept her in sight as he moved closer. He slowed. Something was wrong. She was wiping her eyes. Tears. Her eyes were glassy with tears. Vectis shifted his gaze to the man beside her. He had a patrician look about him, but was young and muscular, like a soldier. At that moment the man bent over and kissed Neeve, and she pressed herself tightly into him, kissing him back, almost frantically.

A servant was beckoning the patrician, who acknowledged the request with a wave. Neeve was grasping his hand now, and talking very fast. She tugged at his arm. He was protesting, but she continued, imploring him. Vectis blinked once or twice when Neeve threw her arms around the man and clung to his neck. She was kissing him, rapid kisses across his cheek. Now she was whispering into his ear … and the man said something in return. He pulled away and moved briskly toward the Senate House.

Vectis gaped at Neeve through the milling crowds. He couldn't move. He tried to focus his thoughts, but all he could see was his lovely Neeve clinging to the strange young man. She was crying softly now, her face pressed against the marble of the Rostra. What was happening? His precious Neeve in Rome, and crying for another man. Vectis started toward her, but then stopped. As much as he wanted to talk to her, to hold her, to touch her, he knew he could not. Something was dreadfully wrong.

An hour later, Neeve was still standing in the shadow of the Rostra, her eyes fastened on the Senate House. Vectis had positioned himself among the stalls between the Senate and the Basilica Aemilia where he was just another bargain hunter along with hundreds of others that wandered the forum, haggling over prices.

The Senate doors opened and a contingent of Praetorians strode out with the patrician in their midst, his hands bound. Neeve never moved. She watched the procession march briskly across the forum and up the road that led toward the holding cells near the Circus Maximus.

The senators soon appeared, talking among themselves, some in heated conversations. Senator Severus was among them, but even in the press of senators, Vectis could see he was alone. Other senators glanced furtively in his direction, but no one approached him. It was clear he wanted privacy. He shuffled slowly down the Senate stairs, leaning heavily on his cane. At the forum floor, he stopped and surveyed the ancient marketplace as if he were searching for someone. Whoever he was looking for, he didn't find. He gestured to a fleet of servants who rushed into the crowds, scouring faces. He seemed determined to find the elusive person.

Vectis glanced at Neeve, who had secreted herself in one of the Rostra's many niches. He shifted his eyes back to the senator, to Neeve, and then to the servants who were closing in on her position. Senator Severus seemed to be looking for Neeve. Minutes later a servant found her and brought her to the waiting senator.

Vectis burned with curiosity. Neeve had journeyed to Rome and was standing less than fifty paces from him ... and she had greeted Senator Titus Severus with tears and a hug, as if they shared something deeply personal. Vectis moved to the outer ring of stalls, closest to the Senate steps. He still couldn't hear them, but if he could see their expressions, he might put the puzzle together. He peered around a stall selling leather goods. Neeve was explaining something to the senator and the old man was nodding, but he had an anguished look on his face, as if he were suffering bereavement. Vectis wondered if his personal problems had something to do with the young patrician the Praetorians led away.

A carriage pulled up in front of the Senate House. A flutter of servants helped Neeve and the senator into the covered vehicle, and soon they were out of sight at the other end of the forum.

Vectis approached one of the servants still in the street and said, "Senator Severus has had a difficult day."

"You know the master?" the servant asked.

"Tribune Vectis Trebellius ... your master's first appointment this morning," Vectis said in way of explanation. "The senator told me the whole difficult story." He was fishing for information.

"Heartbreaking," the servant said.

"Yes," Vectis said. "What will happen now?"

"Master Marcellus Severus has been ordered to the Circus tomorrow," he said, "and the senator can do nothing to stop it."

"The Senate has rendered its final judgment?" Vectis asked.

He nodded. "They have no tolerance for blood-drinkers."

"A blood-drinker? Marcellus Severus a blood-drinker?"

"I cannot believe it either," he said. "But the young master refused to pay homage to the city gods. A tragic day."

"Indeed," Vectis said. He glanced in the direction the carriage had gone. "Will the mistress be joining the senator at his villa?" he asked.

"Yes, the master's city villa," the servant said.

Senator Severus stopped the carriage at the Palatine Hill. He prided himself on facing events squarely, regardless how overwhelming they might seem. But now his lips trembled as he tried to speak. "Thank you for forgiving an old man," he said. "I have wronged you deeply. I should have known you would never betray me."

"The fault is mine," Neeve said. "I was foolish to trust my sister. But I would never do anything to hurt you or Marcellus."

"I know that," he said. He accepted help out of the carriage and called for a litter to carry him up the Palatine Hill. "These months have proved difficult," he said. "Marcellus is my only son and I ... I am afraid that ...." He turned away to recover his courage. He cleared his throat. "If he had been killed in battle," he said, "or died of a fever ... I could accept it better ... but throwing his life away on this ... this foolishness ...." He pressed his hand to his mouth. It helped. He turned to Neeve and said in a steady voice, "You are welcome to sit with me tomorrow, but I strongly advise against it."

"I intend to be there," Neeve said. "Until the last minute, I will be there."

He hadn't the strength to contest her decision.

"Perhaps the emperor can find a solution," she said hopefully.

He patted her hand. "Yes, perhaps," he said. "But I sense a darkness in the Fates. I will try ...." He could speak no longer. He felt his eyes burning. "I must go," he said. He climbed into the litter and turned his face away.

"I heard it went badly this morning," Emperor Antoninus said.

"Badly? Yes ... yes, it went badly," Severus said, looking straight at the emperor. He had determined to present a strong image. "I have no right to be here," he said, "but I was hoping you might have thought of something I missed."

"You have every right, old friend," Antoninus said, "but, I confess, this is a difficult situation." He breathed out in frustration. "I thought Senators Tertullus and Coelius had agreed not to pursue the matter."

"They kept to their bargain," Severus said, "but stories like this cannot be contained. They spread like tenement fires ... and in due course other senators were demanding a full investigation."

"They accused your son when they knew I supported—"

"No, no, they were careful. They claimed to be upset that anyone should utter scurrilous things about a senator's son. They sent for Marcellus because, as they said, they desired only to clear my good name." Severus spoke quietly, his voice matter-of-fact. "It was all quite proper."

"And Marcellus refused to honor the city gods."

"Yes, and now he sits in the Circus stockade."

The emperor stared at Severus. "I don't see what I can do," he said. "The Senate has made its judgment under my rules. I cannot even banish him."

"I know," Severus said in a defeated voice. "Believe me, I know." He turned to go. "I came only because of your invitation, and because I held out hope that something might still ... but I see how the Fates are moving."

"The Fates are harsh at times," Antoninus said.

"One item of business," Severus said, glad to change the subject. "Vectis Trebellius, military tribune at the Dacian siege—"

"Yes, a fine officer," Antoninus said, "son of the great First Centurion, Gaius Trebellius."

"The same. He requests an Imperial appointment to Britannia—"

"Request granted," the emperor said. "I will send an aide to discuss with him how and when he wishes to fill the appointment."

Severus nodded his thanks.

"Will you be there?" Antoninus asked.

"At the Circus? How can I not?"

"Then I want you to use my Imperial box. I refuse to attend this event out of respect for you, and to show my disapproval to those senators who went on this blood-drinking excursion. When they see you in my chair, they will understand my anger."

"You grant me too much," Severus said. "I cannot accept."

"I am ashamed of how little I have granted you," Antoninus replied, "and I encourage you to reconsider my offer. I want you in my box for reasons other than lending you support. I have an idea ... a flimsy one, to be sure, but it may prove beneficial."

Severus waited.

"Sometimes when death grasps us by the throat, we are overwhelmed by the sweet breath of life, and our minds concentrate marvelously." He tugged at his beard. "In the Imperial box Marcellus can more easily see you. A father's bond with his son is strong. At the last moment he might change his mind ... and if he does ... if he lights one small bowl—"

"You will set up a shrine on the sands of the Circus?"

"I will ... and I will send my aides to tell him if he even moves toward the shrine, a hundred soldiers will rescue him from the jaws of the beasts."

Severus hardly recognized the sound of a sigh when it escaped his lips.

"But he must lay hold of the altar," Antoninus warned. "Without that, he will die."

48

The underground chamber at the Circus Maximus was small and dark, a rectangular space used to house animals with shafts of light slanting through the bars at one end. The soldiers had packed more than thirty bodies into the tiny enclosure, making it difficult, though not impossible, to squeeze past others in the cell. Five or six children were also among the adults, and they were crying from hunger. The group agreed to use one corner of the cell to relieve themselves, but it mattered little since the floor was already sticky with urine and animal excrement.

Marcellus stood with his back against a stone wall, his eyes resting from time to time on the faces of others in the cell, most of them complete strangers, but now willing partners in the festival of death. The great purge of blood-drinkers his father had talked about never happened. Emperor Antoninus allowed only a few to be gathered into the Senate's net, a representative number to satisfy those who hated Chrestus and the Way. Faustus was right: Antoninus refused to take the path of the bloody Nero, who had slaughtered members of the Way as if they were senseless beasts, even used them as torches to light his gardens.

In the end there was no great purge, just a small number of unfortunates gathered as a warning to others, and Marcellus was one of them.

Above, he could hear the roars and laughter of the gathering crowd. They had come for the afternoon chariot races, all wearing the colors of their respective racing stables: red, white, blue, green, purple or gold. Meanwhile, they were being entertained with humorous fare, jesters spearing flapping ducks, African pygmies wrestling enormously fat women, and of course, executions. Some were simple beheadings of Roman citizens who had violated the law; some were more elaborate dramas with foreigners being cooked in ovens for daring to steal from citizens. A favorite in Rome was the hatchet contest: two blindfolded men with hatchets searching the sands for criminals bound hand and foot. Whoever killed the most won a prize.

At one end of the cell, where the light slanted in, an iron-barred gate led to the Circus sands, and provided a good view for anyone who chose to look. Most averted their eyes.

Faustus was also locked in the cell. He seemed not to have noticed Marcellus, so absorbed was he in talking to the bored guards on the inner side of the holding pen. "You need to contact Magistrate Oppius Pipinna," Faustus said through the metal grating in the oak door. "My name is Rubellius Anicus Faustus—"

A bowl of soup or slop—Marcellus didn't know—smashed into the grating, splattering Faustus in the face.

"Shut up in there!" a guard hollered.

"Contact Magistrate Pipinna," Faustus repeated. "That is all I'm asking."

Marcellus watched Faustus wipe the slop off his face and balding head. A man beside him whispered words of encouragement, and Marcellus heard Faustus insist he was not wavering in his faith. "To the contrary," he said in full voice. "I am eager to be the wine that stains the consciences of Rome."

"Then, please," a woman said, "stop trying to contact your magistrate friend. We are all afraid, but to look for escape defeats the very purpose of our deaths."

"It's true," said a thin man in the back. "We need to die calmly, bravely, so others may see and believe in Chrestus. Let the Druids screech their curses. We will be at peace, knowing that when our eyes close in death, they will open in eternity."

Others murmured their approval.

"You misunderstand," Faustus protested. "Like you, I had my chance to deny Chrestus, but I would not. I asked for the magistrate because ... because he assured me only Druids would be sacrificed before the Circus mobs. I am concerned about all of us, especially the children. If there has been a mistake ... you see ... I thought maybe ... if someone made a mistake ...." He wiped the smooth skin on the top of his head again, as if the action made his rambling comprehensible.

Several men squeezed Faustus's arm in encouragement, but Marcellus knew they saw through his weak denials.

The children were crying again. They'd probably had no water or food for more than a day. Marcellus pushed toward the grating and said, "I have valuables to give away."

The head guard was instantly at the window. "Shove them through the door," he said, referring to the cutaway at the bottom.

"I want wine and soup for the children," Marcellus said.

"What do you have of value?"

"Cilician sandals," Marcellus said, "calf leather, very soft, very expensive. Worth more than you make in a month." He pulled them off and waved them in front of the grating. The floor felt cold and slippery.

"Shove them through."

"Wine and soup," Marcellus said.

"What's the point? You'll all be dead before noon."

Marcellus said nothing.

"I might just take your sandals," the guard said.

"I know your orders," Marcellus replied. He motioned over his shoulder to the iron-barred gate on the opposite side that led to the Circus sands. "That's the only door guards have authority to open."

"Soup's all gone," he said. "I got wine and a little bread." He clomped over to his station and back again. Seconds later a handful of broken bread rolled under the door, and then two bowls of diluted wine. "Sandals," he said.

Marcellus waited as the women collected the bread and wine, and then he shoved the sandals through.

An hour later Marcellus heard a commotion at the guard station outside the cell. Somebody of importance had arrived. Faustus pushed his way to the window grating and shouted in a relieved voice, "Magistrate Oppius Pipinna! How glad I am to see you!"

The door clunked open.

Half a dozen soldiers stood with swords drawn at the entrance, with the magistrate beyond.

Faustus started toward the door.

"Marcellus Equitius Severus," a guard shouted. "Come forward."

"Magistrate?" Faustus stretched out his arms the way one would greet a friend. "Please take a moment and—"

"Silence him," the magistrate said.

A soldier instantly smashed Faustus across the head with the flat of his sword. Faustus fell back into two men and would have tumbled to the floor had there been more room.

"Marcellus Equitius Severus," the guard repeated. "Identify yourself."

"I am Severus," Marcellus said.

The magistrate motioned for him to step forward, and when he did, the official whispered to Marcellus that he was being afforded an additional opportunity to sacrifice to the city gods. A private room with two senatorial witnesses had been readied for him to pay homage, after which he would be released. When Marcellus declined the offer, the magistrate sighed, and gave him a message from Emperor Antoninus that a shrine would be set up on the sands of the Circus. All he need do is light one incense bowl to the Roman pantheon, and his ordeal would be over. He would be freed.

Marcellus nodded.

He also informed Marcellus that his father would be seated in the Imperial box at the pre-race entertainment.

Marcellus smiled. Even at this dire moment, it struck him as humorous that anyone could so casually call the murderous events entertainment.

When he returned to the cell, Faustus slid in beside him. "You know Magistrate Pipinna?" he asked.

"No," Marcellus said.

Faustus rubbed the ugly bump on his head where the soldier had struck him. "Did the magistrate say anything about me?" he asked.

"I'm sorry," Marcellus said. And he truly was. Faustus had a desperate look in his eyes, something Marcellus had seen before—on the battlefield. At the last second, when the enemy were so close you could smell them, some men simply collapsed. They could no longer hold their pretense of bravery, and a paralyzing fear overwhelmed them. Faustus had probably spent most of his life pretending to others, maybe even to himself, and now his façade was crumbling. To his credit, he had remained steadfast when he might have turned his back on Chrestus. He was certainly a believer, a true follower of the Way, but he had debilitating weaknesses.

"I don't understand," Faustus mumbled. "I was told ... they assured me someone would come and ...." He never completed his thought, but stood quietly staring at his feet.

Marcellus felt no condemnation for Faustus. In less than an hour, everyone in the room would be huddled on the Circus sands, waiting for the beasts. Who among them would boast of his strength then? It was easy to boast of courage when there was no test. But outside that barred door ... there was plenty of test for everyone.

The leaders in the group were praying now, asking Chrestus to give them courage for the trial before them. Everyone gripped someone's arm, and the touch of another provided unusual comfort. A few of the women hummed spiritual songs, mostly to themselves. Afterwards, the thin man gave instructions on how to behave on the sands. They would stand together, quietly, and wait for the beasts to come. It was permissible to cry out when the animals took them. Even the brave feel pain, he said, and it was normal to scream. Similarly, the women should feel no shame if their robes were ripped from their bodies. The only shame on this day, he said, would fall on the Roman mobs themselves when they saw what they had done.

The thin man smiled slightly and looked from face to face. "I know this is difficult," he said. "It's difficult for me. But the important thing to remember is our trial will be short." He shifted on his feet and looked apologetic. "I pass this on for what it's worth ... I have been told the less a person struggles, the quicker death comes. I wish I could give you more comfort, but I can think of nothing to say.

What I do know is for the rest of eternity, we will rejoice that we have been chosen to die this day."

No sooner had he finished when about fifteen Druids were dragged procession style onto the sands. A great clamor burst from the crowds as the dark-robed priests shrieked curses at the taunting mobs. Two guards accompanied each Druid, who kicked and screamed every step to the torture stakes. Some even broke free and had to be tackled by the pursuing guards, and then dragged back in dramatic fashion. The Druids could easily have been bound, but the sight of the evil priests cursing and twisting and shaking their fists at the crowd made for good entertainment. Marcellus even suspected the dark robes had been supplied to heighten the effect. Druid adherents in Rome were rarely caught wearing ceremonial robes. More likely, someone discovered a Druid magical egg or charm in their possession.

Two Druids were chained to each stake, their arms left free so the crowds could see them thrashing about in anger. Then a bucket of tar mixed with resin was sloshed over each of them. As they tried to wipe their faces, the sticky mess clung to them, giving the crowd a good laugh. A gate opened. Out came a mule pulling a cart filled with loose straw, and a single drummer leading the way. A dozen children played on top of the straw pile, giggling and throwing handfuls of straw at each other. The mob roared its approval.

The drummer led the cart to the first stake. The children drew back in mock horror when they saw the Druids.

The crowd whistled.

Frightened, the children flung clumps of straw in the Druids' faces to cover their ugliness.

The crowd cheered.

Despite all their efforts, the Druids could not ward away the straw. From a distance each looked like a small haystack with four flailing tentacles. The cart moved on to the next pair, and the next, until all bristled with yellow straw.

An announcer's voice boomed: "The Druids like fire, so let us indulge their taste."

Three dwarfs wearing hideous masks and Druid robes burst across the sand, brandishing torches in both hands. They sprinted three times around the Druids, screeching and howling, jumping and twisting, a parody of Druid priests before a battle. When the bound Druids responded with their own snarls and shrieks, the crowd exploded in laughter. Suddenly the dwarfs stopped. They moved toward one of the stacks of hay and tried to discover what was hidden inside, repeatedly leaping into the air, trying to see the oily faces. But no success. They were too short. Then they had an idea. One dwarf clambered up the backs of the other two, and together they inched closer to the bound Druids. The top dwarf thrust his face toward one of the Druids, and predictably, the Druid swatted the dwarf off his perch.

The crowd howled in delight.

The dwarf picked himself off the ground, enraged. He dusted sand off his dark robe. He snatched up his torches. He marched to the straw pile and set it ablaze. Then all three sprinted down the line, lighting everything.

The mobs cheered and stamped their feet, drowning out the screams of the Druids.

Marcellus turned away. Already the smell of burned oil and resin, and cooked flesh, filled the air.

In short order, soldiers dumped the Druids' smoking remains into a cart and hauled the mess away. Their carcasses would be used to feed the many animals housed around the Circus Maximus. Romans were an efficient people.

Rap! Rap! Rap!

"You're next," a guard shouted through the inner grating.

Marcellus's eyes drifted around the room, and then to the outer iron gate. Workers had cleared away the oil-stained sand and were now scattering the section with new sand. Young boys brushed the area with wooden rakes to give it a fresh, new appearance. Finished, the workers piled their tools into carts and disappeared from Marcellus's view.

Guards with spears marched toward them.

The iron gate opened.

Marcellus's heart began to pound.

"Out!" the guards shouted.

The people of the Way trudged up a short gangway and through the door. Marcellus said a prayer, and stepped onto the Circus sands.

The crowd roared to life.

49

Neeve and Senator Severus entered the Circus Maximus as the Druids were being lighted on fire.

Neeve could never understand the Roman fascination with death. They had built their amphitheaters the world over, and passed their days watching men struggle for life. Even in their chariot racing stadiums, like the great Circus Maximus, they supplemented events with executions, cruel games, and revolting life-death confrontations, like the one about to unfold.

Sammonicus followed the lead of the senator's servants and seated himself several rows back. Neeve could see he was trying to act the part of an important aide, but he couldn't hide the look of awe in his face … seated as he was in the emperor's section at the great Circus of Rome. Neeve felt dirty sitting in her place of honor, as if she approved of Roman death sports. She could see the howling mobs beyond the Senate quarter, jumping to their feet, holding up coins, arguing with each other as they gambled fortunes on which Druid pair would die first, or scream the loudest, or some other sick question that intrigued them. The whole situation filled her with anger. She knew they would soon be wagering on Marcellus and his suffering.

Neeve ran her eyes over the huge hippodrome, 2000 feet long, 600 wide, and easily holding 300,000 spectators. It seemed as if all Rome were here. She and the senator were seated comfortably in the luxurious Imperial box at the north end of the stadium. Directly below, the Druids were shrieking in the fires, their bodies twisting, their arms flailing in useless movement. At the far eastern end, some kind of gladiatorial contest was taking place, but Neeve had no interest in either event. She was searching the many gates along the inner wall of the Circus, wondering which one contained Marcellus and the people of the Way.

A series of doors opened, and gangs of men trotted out pulling carts behind them. They ripped the smoking Druids off their stakes and threw them into a single cart. One Druid seemed to be still alive, so a worker signaled with his arm. A grotesque figure suddenly appeared, carrying a hammer, and wearing the mask of Charon, ferryman of the dead. He raised his hammer over the Druid's head and struck down several times. Then he slammed a hook into the body and dragged it across the sand and through an open door. The crowd cheered. That done, the workers heaped the charred posts and still smoldering straw into another cart, and scraped the grimy sand into piles. Then they loaded the refuse sand into yet another cart and headed for the doors. Others spread fresh sand, and behind them ten-year-old boys smoothed the surface. The whole area was clear in a remarkably short time.

Marcellus started across the sands.

In the shadow of the Circus Maximus, the sprinkled mixtures of sand felt cool on his bare feet, but as he moved into the light, it had the feel of sun-baked ocean sand, warm and dry between his toes, and it reminded him of trips to the Greek isles when he was a child.

"Move!"

A spear jabbed a half inch into Marcellus's back, and he instinctively jerked forward to lessen the injury. The others in the group quickened their pace toward the central area of the Circus, but their pace was not quick enough to satisfy the guards who began poking their spears into the hind parts of those not trotting rapidly enough.

"Faster!" the guards hollered, making a sport of it.

The sight of blood-drinkers being chased across the sands like nervous chickens brought gales of laughter from the crowds. Roman mobs had no liking for the blood-drinkers. Poor entertainment, everyone said, because they died like farm animals. They simply huddled in a group and waited for the beasts to come. They didn't run away, or fight, but acted as if their suffering was their ticket to eternal joy once the ordeal was over.

Marcellus had watched blood-drinkers die before, many times. In fact, he had come to the Circus Maximus long months ago specifically to see them, shortly after he had heard someone talking about Chrestus. That was why he had determined to die bravely today. What greater stage would he have to proclaim the truth of Chrestus? And how could he make that truth more memorable than to seal it with his own blood? But he had to be strong, and already his palms were sweating, and his breath short.

They stopped midway between the northern end of the stadium and the central spine around which the chariots raced. The soldiers forced them to face the Imperial box. "Bow!" an officer cried. "Show your respect for Rome."

Nobody bowed. They kept their eyes on the sand.

The officer ran his eyes over the group and shook his head, disgusted. A guard handed him a bag of cheap swords. "Who wants to defend himself?" the officer asked, holding up the bag.

Silence.

"If you slay a lion," the officer said, "you win your freedom."

Still silence.

"Are you all sheep?" He glared at the huddled group. "Maybe the women among you have courage," he said with a sneer. "Any of you women want a sword?"

No one spoke. Then the thin man said, "We have come here to die for Chrestus."

The officer eyed him briefly, sucked his teeth, then looped some spittle toward the ground. "Die if you want," he said. "I feel nothing for any of you. If you think you're dying for some noble cause, you're wrong. Nobody cares. Not them ...." He motioned with his head to the crowd. "And not me. You drink human blood, and now the beasts will lap yours from the sand." With that he stalked off, taking his bag of swords and guards with him.

The mobs grew still, waiting for the coming of the beasts.

Marcellus could hear cheers for some other event at the far end of the stadium, but he never turned to look.

"Try to be calm," the thin man said. "Chrestus is waiting for us at the gates of heaven."

Marcellus raised his eyes to the crowd. It was an amazing thing to see the galleries of people from the vantage of the Circus sands. No wonder gladiators and chariot drivers became intoxicated with the cheering; it was as if all Rome were looking down on them. He glanced at the lofty Imperial box with its broad terrace overlooking the Circus. He hoped to spot his father, and wondered vaguely whether Emperor Antoninus might be present. Sending a delegation to the holding cell had been a gracious gesture by the emperor, but Marcellus knew his father had played a role.

Marcellus froze. "Father!" he said, without even realizing he had spoken. He could see him now, sitting in the emperor's chair, and pointing toward the shrine set up under the Imperial balcony. Marcellus bit his lip, so hard he could taste the salt from his blood. He stared at his father who kept gesturing toward the shrine. Marcellus could never make him understand ... no matter what he said or did. "Why not include Chrestus as one of your gods?" his father had asked repeatedly. But to include pagan gods would exclude Chrestus, and his father could not understand.

Marcellus patted his shoulder several times, something he had learned from his father when he was an infant. It meant, "I love you."

His father clasped his arms across his chest in despair.

Marcellus patted his shoulder again, and turned away.

"Have courage," the thin man was saying. "It will not be long now."

A foul smell drifted across the Circus. Already five or six lions had been hoisted up from their cages below. More appeared, from all sides of the hippodrome, until over forty bounded along the edges of the enclosure, blinking in the bright light and lashing their tails as they moved ever closer to the group huddled in the center.

Suddenly, someone broke from the group, racing for the shrine under the Imperial box. Marcellus groaned. It was Faustus.

Neeve helped Senator Severus up the steps of the Imperial box toward the exit. "I cannot watch," he said, collapsing. "I cannot watch." Two servants took over Neeve's duties and carried the old man to his waiting litter. Neeve started back toward her seat, but not without a nauseating feeling in her stomach. She had decided to be with Marcellus at the end, but what purpose did it serve, she wondered, if he had no knowledge of her presence? She moved closer to the prominent chair where the senator had been sitting, but paused as several senators rose to greet each other.

Below, on the sands, something caught her eye. A man was racing toward the shrine, but Neeve couldn't see who it was because of the knot of senators blocking her view. A surge of hope shot through her body and she jerked her head around to see if Marcellus's father might still be in sight. He was gone. She turned back, trying to see past the men, hardly daring to believe that Marcellus had finally come to his senses. But it was only a balding man of middle age with his arms hugging the shrine.

"*Anathema Chrestus!*" he screamed, looking up at the Imperial box. "*Anathema Chrestus.* I curse Chrestus! I curse him to the ground! I curse the day I heard his name! *Anathema Chrestus!*" His eyes darted around, looking for someone to rescue him.

Neeve glanced at the soldiers emerging from their enclosures. The City Prefect sitting at the edge of the Imperial box rose and waved the soldiers back to their positions. Mercy would be granted only to a senator's son today, and only if he approached the shrine.

The man wiped the sweat off his balding head and snatched up the incense sticks from their bowls. He thrust them into the torch flame and held the smoking sticks in the air. "I serve only Jupiter and the gods of Rome," he cried. "Blessed be Antoninus Pius, god of Rome, god of the universe. *Anathema Chrestus!* I curse Chrestus! May he rot forever in the grave."

In that instant a lioness hit him from behind, sending the man and the shrine flying through the air. Another beast streaked across the sands, slamming her body into his and clamping her jaws around his neck, shaking and twisting in savage fury. The first locked her jaws onto a leg, hoping to secure something for herself. A third arrived, a male. He immediately claimed the soft belly for himself, ripping out great quantities of meat.

The mobs leapt to their feet, straining to view every tug and shudder of the beasts.

Shaken, Neeve turned her eyes back to Marcellus.

Marcellus gaped in horror as three lions ripped at Faustus's body. The poor wretch's leg still twitched, but he was dead, his ordeal of fear over. No doubt he was standing before Chrestus at this very moment, Marcellus thought, and wondering why he had not stemmed the tide of fear bare minutes longer. But the God of heaven was merciful. He understood the failings of his people. Faustus had surrendered to his weak nature, but he was not beyond God's mercy. At least he had made it to the blood-soaked sands of the hippodrome, when others claiming faith had chosen different roads.

Marcellus glanced up, searching for his father, but he had left. Marcellus's eyes strayed across the faces near the Imperial box, and then paused. He squinted. Neeve! Neeve was sitting in the seat next to the emperor's chair. And she was staring at him. Without thinking, he smiled. She smiled back, weakly, but it was a smile.

Someone grabbed his arm.

"Please," the woman beside him said. "My husband cannot ... he cannot help ...." She motioned toward her son, about eight years old, and instantly Marcellus understood. The men had agreed to spare the children from a horrendous death by ending their lives at the last moment. No one could predict who would be taken first, and the thought of a child, alone, being pursued by beasts, was too much. Already the lions were growing bolder, moving in an increasingly tighter circle. Soon the more aggressive would begin picking off the outside people.

Marcellus rested his hands on the boy's shoulders and looked at the father. The man's face was the pallid color of death, but he managed to nod. Marcellus turned back to the boy, kissed the top of his head, and snapped his neck. The child dropped to the sand, lifeless. The mother wept. Marcellus picked up the boy and placed him gently in the father's outstretched arms. Not once did he look at the mother. He couldn't bear to see her face.

From the quiet sobs everywhere, Marcellus knew other men had performed the same merciful act. The children were gone.

The smell of the beasts grew stronger as they neared, and their bodies had the stench of rotting flesh. Their backs were covered with ulcers and open sores, their hair layered with brown muck, probably from being kept in damp holes underground. From their hollow faces and protruding ribs, Marcellus guessed they hadn't eaten for weeks.

"I see the angels," a voice said. "Let us go out to meet them." It was the thin man. "I will show you how." He moved slowly toward a knot of lions, his hands hanging loosely at his sides. The skittish animals made a hasty retreat. The thin man continued toward them. Twenty feet out he stopped. The beasts closed around him, but their fear of humans made them wary. The man swayed gently from side to side, humming quietly to himself.

One of the males growled. Hunger was beginning to overcome fear.

Several more growls.

A ragged looking male took two hesitant steps toward the thin man, seemed to freeze, and then flashed toward him, leaping onto his back and clamping down on his neck. The man's legs buckled and he crumpled to the sand without making a sound. The crowd roared. The other lions burst toward the fallen prey, ripping off chunks and darting away to gulp down their prize.

Another man started toward the lions. But having tasted meat, the beasts were eager for more. They bounded toward their victim and tore him in pieces before he even hit the ground. Lions everywhere were growling and snapping at each other, vying for scraps of meat.

The island of victims pressed closer to each other. They would all suffer the same fate, but instinct told them to stay in a tight group.

The lions circled slowly now, moving in a crouch.

Marcellus licked his lips. His heart pounded.

He tried to think about Chrestus, but all he could see was blood soaked sand and crushed bones everywhere. The bodies were gone. Amazing how fast lions could eat.

Suddenly, a huge lioness bolted from the pack and snatched a woman from the edge of the group. In that instant a dozen others attacked, their powerful legs ripping up the sand as they raced toward their victims. Marcellus felt their hard bodies brush past him, so forcefully he almost lost his balance. On every side the beasts were pulling people to the ground. He could hear the clamor of the crowd, and the victims' cries as they were dragged across the sand.

Dust floated through the air and Marcellus wiped grit from his mouth. Four or five individuals were still standing, including the woman beside him. She grasped his arm and shouted, "I'm so frightened!" But before he could turn, he felt her jerked away. He saw her terrified face as she plunged toward the ground. Another beast pounced on her, and another, until she was covered with animals eagerly devouring her slim body.

Marcellus sucked in air through clenched teeth and glanced around. Two others remained, a man and a woman. They were hunched over in the settling swirls of dust, legs apart, as if standing on a rolling surface. Marcellus realized he too had bent his legs the same way. He tried to relax and stand erect like the thin man. Dying bravely wasn't easy.

He suddenly remembered Neeve in the Imperial chair and looked over his shoulder in that direction. He thought he saw her, but couldn't be certain. His mind felt ragged and unfocused, and he started to smile, but then stopped, thinking how foolish the gesture would appear. He wanted her to know he had been strong to the end, and that the Way was the true road to heaven. It was worth dying for.

Something heavy crashed into his back. Marcellus staggered sideways, trying to catch his breath. He felt a shredding pain in his leg. A lioness had seized him below the knee and was shaking violently. Marcellus toppled to the sand. The shaking stopped. His leg was gone. Nausea swept over him and his stomach reacted, but nothing came out; he hadn't eaten for two days.

He saw the male coming. It sprang from more than ten feet out and slammed its huge paws down into his body. Marcellus felt his ribs snap. He could no longer breathe. He lay there, still. The lion clamped down on his head and hoisted him into the air. The pain in his leg disappeared, replaced with intense pressure on the front and back of his head. He wanted to scream but he had no air. He could no longer see. His eyes bulged. The crushing pressure increased, and exploded in a profusion of lights. His whole body warmed, and he felt as if he were floating … as if he were being carried in someone's arms.

Neeve sat rock still in the Imperial box, her hands covering her mouth, her eyes never blinking as she watched a lion drag Marcellus by the head across the sand. Another had ripped off his leg. She closed her eyes. She would see no more. She had been with him to the end as she had promised the senator, but she would see no more.

Neeve took a deep breath and exhaled slowly. The crowd had grown quiet. They were waiting for the next entertainment filler. She left the Circus Maximus stunned by what she had seen, especially the thin man strolling into the jaws of the lions. These people of the Way … how could they believe so strongly in the afterlife? Who but deranged people would willingly give their bodies to the beasts?

Yet, she knew Marcellus, and he was anything but deranged. He loved life, and had once believed in the Roman gods like everyone else. Then he changed. She partially understood. In Gallia, after Asclepios had healed her, she paid homage to him as the greatest of the gods. The difference was that the people of the Way believed Chrestus was the only way to the god of heaven, and except for the balding man, they willingly died for him. She would never die for Asclepios.

The whole event left her with a deep sadness. Marcellus was gone. He could have lived, but he chose death rather than deny his god, Chrestus. Could Chrestus be the true god, the door, as Marcellus said, to eternal life? Mucia, the high priest, claimed Asclepios was the greatest of the gods, and he was very convincing. But these people ….

Neeve stumbled out onto the plaza and collapsed on a stone bench under a portico. She felt very tired. Later, at a less emotional time, she would try to discover the meaning of what she had seen. But not now. Not now.

PART SIX:
Blossoms of Hope

50

Vectis stared down at the carcass that had been Marcellus Severus. The larger lions had cleaned out most of the meat, leaving the tougher scraps for the sick that were now approaching in a subservient crouch. A dozen soldiers, spears glinting, moved quickly across the sand toward the Severus body, shooing away the lions. They had been sent to preserve the body for a funeral, or at least as much of the body as they could. Relatives sometimes paid for the extra service, but it was costly.

Vectis watched them jam a hook under Severus's exposed ribs and drag his body toward an open gate. He grimaced. He had met Marcellus on several occasions and had a good impression of him, but he would never have recognized him on the street. He also would never have imagined a senator's son belonging to the perverted blood-drinking cult. From what he had heard, the cult met secretly in the tombs to drink human blood, believing that blood was the liquid of immortality.

He surveyed the scattered bones of the cult members and the lions still fighting over their prizes. Women ... children ... all torn to pieces. He shook his head. What a useless end. The blood-drinkers were brave—he had to give them that—but fools in choosing a god. Only a fool would serve so cruel and demanding a god. Of all the gods of the pantheon, Vectis couldn't think of one that would demand this of his followers. Was Chrestus so uncaring he would rather have beasts devour his followers than see them pay a small homage to another god? Could he be that jealous?

More soldiers appeared. They rapidly drove the lions back to their cages, jabbing them with spears and thrusting torches in their gaunt faces. Workers from under the stadium emerged, along with a dozen cart drivers. They hurried across the stadium, throwing remains over the cart rails. Roman crowds were impatient and eager for the next event. As with the Druid remains, the half-eaten bodies of the blood-drinkers would be chopped up and fed to the animals during the coming week. Vectis saw them throw pieces of a young boy into the cart and then the shredded remains of a slim woman, her pretty face oddly intact. Vectis took a deep breath. Never had he seen people die so willingly—peacefully—if you could call it that, eager to prove to the Roman mobs that Chrestus waited for them in the next world. He wondered about their beliefs, and their hope beyond the grave, and he wondered how many in the crowd were thinking the same thoughts.

Not many, he guessed, as he glanced around the hippodrome. Most in the tiers of people were beginning to get restless. They had been standing for five or ten minutes now, stretching, collecting bets, eating from their lunches, and Vectis could hear them talking about the blood-drinkers—a boring lot, they said—died too submissively. But at least they had the excitement of seeing a man renounce Chrestus, cursing him even, and then being torn apart by the beasts. A hilarious event, they concluded.

Earlier, Vectis had followed Neeve and Senator Severus to the Circus, but lost them in the sea of spectators. He had hoped to locate them in the cordoned area for senators, but his own seat was so distant from the better seats on the northern side, he could hardly make out individual faces in the swaying crowds. Then by chance he had spotted Senator Severus in the Imperial box and what looked like Neeve sitting beside him. Now, with a break in the entertainment, Vectis was pushing his way through the throngs of people crowding the gangways, trying to get a better look at the Imperial box, but even from the opposite side of the Circus, Vectis could tell that the Imperial seats were empty. Neeve, the senator, even the servants were gone. He swept his eyes across the adjoining areas cordoned off for Rome's nobility, hoping that maybe the senator and Neeve were visiting with someone. But it was a futile hope. Neeve and the senator were in no mood to socialize.

The crowd suddenly quieted and many took their seats. A man in a crimson wig and a deep voice was announcing the chariots scheduled to race that day. Vectis glanced once more at the empty Imperial box and then headed for the exit.

Outside the stadium, the wind blew crisply across the plaza, fresh and clean smelling, as if Vectis had suddenly wandered into another world. Crowds were sparse, a few groups here and there, but mostly people were already in the Circus Maximus or were racing up the entrances trying not to miss any amusements. Vectis crossed the square, his eyes on the stables where the nobility housed their carriages. He hoped to catch Neeve before she drove off with Senator Severus.

He stopped. In the center of the plaza under a long portico built to provide refuge from the afternoon sun, Neeve sat by herself, her hunched body drained of life as she gazed at the granite paving. An olive-skinned servant with thick, black hair waited discreetly behind her on a stone bench, trying to give her privacy.

Vectis moved into the shadow of a chariot-racing statue, one of the many that had been set up around the Circus Maximus to honor famous past drivers. He needed time to think. He couldn't just barge into Neeve's life, especially when she was obviously grieving for Marcellus Severus. The problem was that he had no idea what her relationship to Marcellus had been, but he suspected it was substantial. The thought of Neeve in someone else's arms unsettled him, but he did his best to be realistic. How could he blame her for trying to start a new life after two years? Had he not been drawn to the dye merchant and, but for his concern that she might be an assassin, would have stayed with her? Neeve thought he had been killed, and with good reason. Commodus had reported him dead.

He now understood why Neeve had been crying by the Rostra, why she had clung to Marcellus so frantically, clutching at him, kissing him. She was begging him to choose life over what turned out to be his horrific end on the sands of the Circus. Vectis could only imagine her state of mind, and in that moment he knew what he should do. He would give her the privacy she needed, how long he didn't know, but time enough to sort out her feelings. Only then would he approach her.

He started to leave but found it difficult, almost as if he were abandoning her. He indulged himself, watching her for a few more seconds. She was smoothing her hair now, absentmindedly, her eyes still on the paving stones. That's when he saw the ring. She was still wearing his family wedding ring on her left hand. Vectis swallowed. That had to mean something, he thought.

"Mistress!" The servant was addressing her.

"Not now," Neeve said.

Vectis eyed the servant and was shocked to see his hand on his dagger. He suddenly realized he had been staring so intently at Neeve that the servant had become nervous. Vectis looked away, chastising himself for his foolishness. He should have left sooner. He turned to go.

Abruptly the servant departed his bench and began speaking rapidly to his mistress.

Neeve raised her eyes, looking at him.

Vectis stared at her, not knowing what to do.

She jerked to her feet and opened her mouth as if to speak, but no sound escaped her lips. Then, ever so slightly, her brow furrowed.

Vectis started toward her.

She smiled, and took several halting steps toward him as well, ignoring the servant who was tugging at her arm, trying to hold her back. As she neared, she suddenly stopped. Her smile disappeared, replaced with a bewildered look. She glanced around the plaza and then returned her gaze to him. A wave of emotion seemed to catch her by surprise, and her eyes moistened. She gulped some air and regained her composure. Her smile came back, and she shook her head in disbelief. Then she moved quickly toward him, crushing her body into his and pressing her lips to his ear.

"I thought you were … oh, Vectis, they told me you were dead," she said.

"I feared for you too," he said, closing his eyes and drinking in the sensation of being close to Neeve at last.

Her hands clutched at his arms and shoulders, as if she were trying to prove to herself he was not a spirit. Then she pulled back and ran her eyes over his face

Vectis smiled. It was the one thing about Neeve he could never forget—the incredible blue of her eyes, like a sunlit ocean. He bent his face toward hers until he could see nothing but her eyes and feel her soft breath on his lips. Then they kissed, a long slow kiss so intoxicating that Vectis forgot he was standing in the center of the plaza at the Circus Maximus.

Late that afternoon Neeve and Vectis arrived at his family villa on the outskirts of Rome. For most of the carriage ride Neeve could think of nothing to say, so stunned was she at finding Vectis outside the Circus, and so dispirited to have witnessed Marcellus's last moments. Vectis seemed to understand that something was bothering her, but he never asked what it was or why she had been sitting outside the Circus. He did express surprise at finding her in Rome, and she managed a cheerful face when she said that no Roman officer in Britannia would marry her and so she was forced to leave the province.

Vectis carried the conversation. His accounts of Commodus and the siege in Dacia made her laugh, but the sound of her laughter was like a spike in her heart. Marcellus had died for his ardent beliefs, and here she was, hours later, carefree and enjoying frivolous stories. How shallow could she be? The guilt was almost unbearable. When Vectis turned to the more serious situations of Julian's near death and the assassin who had almost succeeded in her mission, a bolt of fear flashed through Neeve. She realized how close Vectis had come to dying and how empty her life would have been without him. But somehow, the upsetting story made her feel more comfortable. At least she didn't have to bear the guilt of hollow laughter.

Sammonicus sat up front driving the carriage, which made discussion awkward for Neeve. She knew he was straining to hear every tidbit. He undoubtedly had noticed she was avoiding all mention of the Severus household, and of course her warm relationship with Marcellus. Neeve struggled with her conscience over whether to tell Vectis about Marcellus, but in the end decided to remain silent. What good would it do, she reasoned, to talk about a ghost? She had cared deeply for Marcellus, but her love for Vectis had never diminished. If at some time he asked her directly why she had been at the Circus Maximus, or why she had seemed so downcast, she might tell him the truth. But for now, she decided to spare them both the pain.

"Well, here it is," Vectis said as the carriage entered the gates to his villa.

Neeve stepped out of the carriage and ran her eyes over the grounds. "It's perfect," she said, "exactly as I imagined it would be." She had seen the tension in his face as they neared the villa. He was no doubt wondering whether she would be pleased, and she determined to put him at ease.

"It's small," he said, "but it has a fountain, workable farmlands, and a bathhouse behind the west wing of the villa." He pointed to the distant trees and said proudly, "You can't see it, but an aqueduct runs underground over there … it feeds the Esquiline Hill in Rome ... and a shunt pipe feeds this villa."

"I am so pleased," she said, glancing at the flowers and sculptured bushes that lined the perimeter walls. The compound was tiny in comparison to Nes's villa on the Esquiline, and certainly dwarfed by the sprawling Severus estates, but she didn't care. Vectis was a soldier, not a landowner, and she was honored to be standing in the compound where he had been raised. She squeezed close to him and said, "This is our home."

An old man shuffled toward them, his back bent, his hair white, and a broad grin on his face. "Master Vectis," he said, but his eyes were on Neeve.

Vectis hugged the servant and said, "My father's freedman, Pudens. He looks kindly, but he has used the switch on my backside many times."

"And see what a fine man he grew into," Pudens said, his eyes still on Neeve.

"He is also very curious," Vectis said. Then turning, he said, "Pudens ... my wife, Neeve."

"Honored, Mistress," Pudens said, bowing, and his eyes inspected every inch of her.

"Well?" Vectis asked, smiling.

"Too pretty for you," Pudens said as he shuffled back toward the villa.

"I've told him all about you," Vectis said in way of explanation, "but I never thought you two would meet."

"I'm glad we did," Neeve said.

"We have only four servants," Vectis said, "all freedmen. Pudens was given his freedom the day I was born, as a gift to the gods. The others I freed when my father died. None of them are body servants, but I suppose you can make do with—"

"Caledonians do things themselves," Neeve said, putting Vectis at ease. She motioned toward the carriage and said, "Sammonicus is highly skilled at many duties. I can think of no finer a body servant than what I already have."

Vectis glanced over at the servant, who was now a whirl of activity.

Neeve smiled to herself. Sammonicus had been listening. He had been listening to every word.

Darkness had fallen. Neeve and Vectis had taken their baths, eaten their evening meal, and sipped a few cups of wine. Neeve was pleasantly surprised that even after a separation of two years, she felt entirely comfortable with Vectis. But try as she might she couldn't shut out the crude laughter of the Circus crowds, the screams of the dying, and the images of lions streaking toward Marcellus. It was his last seconds that bothered her most, when he straightened his body and glanced over his shoulder, trying to smile her way. He had wanted to tell her that he had found the truth, that she should not feel sorry for him. But her heart ached, and all she could see were those starved lions ripping at Marcellus's body.

They were in the bedroom now, and she barely remembered entering the room. Vectis had lit several lamps, some in the corners, some at the foot of the bed. He was doing everything right, and yet she was still seated in the howling Circus Maximus, entirely consumed with thoughts of Marcellus.

"I can wait," he said.

She stared at him in the flickering light.

"I can," he said. "You're my wife, not some—"

"Hush," she said, touching her fingers to his lips, and her love flowed out of her into his silent face. She struggled with the pain-filled images still streaming through her mind, and she grieved for how she had retreated into herself and wrested away the enthusiasm from her beloved's eyes. "I have followed a winding course," she said, "a raging river, at times ... but always I have thought of you."

"I have thought about you too," he said, "every single day."

She wished she could laugh and tease, throw off the burdens of the day and soar through the skies like a wild falcon. But her dark memories bound her to the ground. Like a lost soul, she could find no release.

"Do you want to talk about anything?" he asked.

Neeve shook her head, but strived for a pleasant look. She groaned inwardly. What was the use? She wasn't fooling anyone with her act. Vectis was looking at her now, expecting her to say something. But she couldn't talk about Marcellus, not tonight, maybe not ever.

"Today, I went to the great Circus," she said quietly, "to see the chariots run but ... instead I saw Druids burned and blood-drinkers eaten by beasts." She breathed deliberately, afraid that if she didn't, she would forget altogether and be gasping for air. "I was not prepared for such cruelty," she said, "and ... well, I was not prepared."

He wrapped his arms around her.

She pushed into his warmth, happy to be near him, and thankful she had spoken the truth, if only partial. She loved Vectis deeply, but her heart was broken for Marcellus.

Vectis kissed her on the cheek and then several more times until he reached her lips. She turned her head slightly to accommodate him and felt his mouth moving on hers. She responded, opening her lips and pressing into him. She could feel his hard body against hers and pressed even closer. She closed her eyes to concentrate on the movement of their mouths and on the heat that was gathering in her.

It was good to be alive.

So very good.

All her thoughts had been about Marcellus, and hardly had she noticed the miracle of this day. Vectis had been dead to her, but now he had been given life. The spirits of the world took away so often, but they also gave, and Neeve was determined to enjoy their gifts while she had them.

His hands caressed her shoulders, her back, her stomach, her secret places. Her heart pounded. She tried to speak, but it sounded more like a moan.

A new sensation surged through her body, one so overwhelming that it blunted the tragic events of the day. No longer was she trying to please a husband; she was greedily pleasing herself. She grasped at him, clutched him, thrust her tongue deep into his mouth. Her breath was ragged and her legs seemed about to crumple.

She pulled her head back and looked directly into his eyes. "You might be able to wait," she said, "but I cannot, not for one minute longer."

Later, when he was inside her, Neeve felt her world fall away. His body covered hers, and she felt protected as they rocked back and forth, back and forth. Only once did she see Marcellus, but he gave her that easy smile she liked so much and then faded away.

51

Neeve woke in the pale light of dawn to the sound of birds singing. A crisp breeze blew through the open window and across their feathered bed. She turned toward Vectis. He was still asleep. She kissed him and massaged his body gently.

His eyes half-opened. "I'm awake," he said groggily, and rolled over.

She pushed closer to him, wrapping her arms around his chest, and kissing his neck. "Can you hear the birds?" she asked, still snuggled in close.

He lifted his head, eyes blinking. "The sun's up?"

"Yes," she said, "a new day."

He sighed and started out of the bed, but she pulled him back.

He smiled. "I would like to accommodate you, Mistress Trebellius," he said, "but now that I'm awake, I realize that I have duties—"

"Tell me about your duties," she said, moving her hands in more interesting places.

"Well," he said, "I promised to meet Pudens at sunup to … ah … we were supposed to examine …."

"Is something wrong?" she asked.

"Yes, I am having trouble concentrating," he said.

"You cannot concentrate?" she asked as she rolled on top of him.

"It is difficult," he said.

"How could that be?" she asked, rubbing her hips into him.

"I'm not sure," he replied. "Continue what you're doing, and I will think of an answer."

She continued, and he pulled her night tunic over her head, and the two of them seemed to melt together in perfect rhythm.

Vectis completed his duties with Pudens by mid-morning and found Neeve's servant feeding the horses in the stable.

"Sammonicus, isn't it?" Vectis asked casually.

"Yes, Master," Sammonicus said, stepping out of the pinewood stall.

"You have attended the mistress since Gallia, have you not?"

"Yes, Master, since Gallia."

"Then you will know how she met Senator Titus Severus," he said.

Sammonicus nodded, and told him how the senator had taken Neeve to the Asclepion temple and how he had provided finances for her journey to Rome.

Vectis then asked about the misunderstanding between the senator and Neeve that led to her leaving the Severus villa.

Sammonicus shifted his eyes nervously around the stable. "Perhaps if you asked the mistress—"

"I am asking you," Vectis said.

"Yes, certainly, Master, but I have given an oath to the mistress not to talk about what I might inadvertently see or hear."

"Commendable, indeed," Vectis said. "I know about her brother, Taranis, and about Marcellus," Vectis said, pressing two denarii coins into his palm. "So you would not be violating your oath when I already know most of the story."

"That is true, Master," Sammonicus said, his dark eyes fixed on the coins. "But the mistress has a terrible, severe temper when angry. If she discovered—"

"She'll never know," Vectis said. "And certainly, I would respect your confidence."

"I do know some things, Master," Sammonicus said as he slipped the coins into his belted purse, "but I make it a practice to close my ears to private conversations—"

"Of course you do," Vectis said. "Now ... why did the mistress leave the Severus villa?"

Sammonicus hesitated.

"As I said, I will never reveal to the mistress what you tell me this day, but if you refuse to fill in the missing pieces ...."

Sammonicus jammed his fingers into his thick hair, his eyes darting everywhere.

Vectis moved closer. "What do you think your mistress would do if she learned you had told me about her involvement with Marcellus Severus, about her visit to the Circus with the senator, about Marcellus's tragic death—"

"I said nothing to you about—"

"The mistress has a terrible, severe temper," Vectis said.

Sammonicus shifted his eyes to the straw bedding and said, "I am sworn to secrecy ... but since you already know .... The mistress has a sister in Rome named Calpurnia, mistress to Gaius Balbinus, a nobleman."

"A sister?"

"Yes, Master. She sometimes uses the Celtic name, Nes. Apparently, my mistress told Mistress Calpurnia that Marcellus had connection to the blood-drinkers."

"I see."

"Purely innocent, my mistress was," Sammonicus added. "She saw no significance in her observations, but ... ah ... Mistress Calpurnia understood the political advantage against Senator Titus Severus—"

"And used the information," Vectis said.

Sammonicus nodded.

"So the senator was angry and asked you to leave," Vectis said to himself, "but now he knows the truth ...."

"He knows my mistress would never have spoken against Master Marcellus Severus. She loved him deeply and ... ah ... of course she loved the senator even more deeply," he added awkwardly, "and would never have done them harm."

Vectis eyed Sammonicus. The servant was rubbing the back of his neck, obviously hoping his words had gone unnoticed. "The friendship between Marcellus and the mistress does not interest me," Vectis said. He used the word friendship to put Sammonicus at ease. Neeve had thought him dead, and if she had fallen in love with Marcellus ... well, he could put that aside and pretend it was only a friendship. He preferred not to inquire further. She was still wearing his ring outside the Circus, and that gave him great comfort.

"You are a wise man, Master," Sammonicus said, "and if you will permit me ... you are without doubt a man in whom Fortuna delights. The mistress has risked everything to journey from the northern reaches of Britannia to find you." He paused and shook his head in amazement. "Rome's most distant province, and still she came looking for you."

Vectis patted Sammonicus on the shoulder. The servant was transparent in his support of Neeve, but he was right. Neeve had risked much. And now she was despairing, not only over Marcellus, but over the prospect of her brother dying in Legate Julius Verus's Triumph. Vectis couldn't imagine how he might help the Caledonian chieftain, but he wanted to learn what he could about Neeve and the powerful Senator Titus Severus in case something might spark upon his mind. When he heard the name Balbinus, he thought that maybe, just maybe, something could be done.

"It really is extraordinary, Master ...." Sammonicus was still talking, trying to underscore his point.

"What is?"

"How much the mistress has gone through to find you ... wars, shipwreck, hunger, sickness—"

"Sammonicus—"

"Attacked by thieves—"

"Sammonicus."

"Yes, Master."

"Your mistress is right ... there is no finer a body servant than you."

"Thank you, Master."

The following week Neeve remained at the villa while Vectis did business in Rome. She was not yet ready to enter the life of a Roman matron, especially if it required her to smile sweetly at other Roman matrons and listen to their empty-headed chatter. Every day she thought about Marcellus, and every day she fought back waves of sadness, but she had determined to enjoy the gift of life.

Neeve also thought about Taranis, constantly, and in the days after her visit with Nes, she had tried to visit him twice. She offered the soldiers handfuls of coins, but they had strict orders from General Verus to keep everyone away, unless specifically authorized by him.

Marcellus's death had shattered Senator Severus, and even in her desperation, Neeve knew she could no longer impose on him. The Triumph was upon them, and no amount of persuasion—even by Senator Severus—could save Taranis. Her brother would be paraded through the streets of Rome and then executed before the howling mobs. Such was the nature of Roman justice.

THE HOURS OF
DECISION

52

"He knows!" Balbinus cried. "Vectis Trebellius knows everything!"

Calpurnia stared out the atrium window and swallowed some wine.

"He's been snooping around, talking to people .... you can imagine what he's learned!"

Calpurnia sipped her wine again.

"This Brutus was supposed to be the best," Balbinus said, pacing the floor. "He was supposed to eliminate Trebellius before he could cross the Adriatic, and then he was supposed to finish Trebellius in Dacia. Remember his letter: 'All is well, proceeding as planned.' That's what our wonderful assassin said." Balbinus stopped pacing and said, "Well, I ask you ... what did I get for my gold?"

"Plans sometimes go wrong," Calpurnia said.

"Oh, I would agree they went wrong," Balbinus said, laughing crazily. "Brutus dead and Trebellius alive ... Trebellius who should be rotting in his grave!" He shouted his last words straight at Calpurnia.

Calpurnia didn't respond.

"Silence. When I need you, I find silence."

"I'm thinking," Calpurnia said.

"Thinking ... I see ... well, since you are thinking, you might want to think about what we should do when Trebellius arrives. His note said he would pay his respects at the sixth hour, and that time is almost here."

Calpurnia turned away from the window. "The first thing you need to do is send your guards back to their quarters. They will only create suspicion."

"Suspicion! Trebellius knows, I tell you. He is coming to take my life."

Calpurnia shook her head. "He cannot know anything about Brutus. Even we know little beyond that the assassin Brutus might have been a woman—"

"I don't believe those reports for one minute," Balbinus said.

"Reports are sometimes garbled in transmission," Calpurnia agreed, "but this makes my point. We know little about Brutus, and Trebellius undoubtedly knows less. Believe me, you have nothing to fear. All Trebellius knows is that someone hired an assassin to eliminate him, and that person could have been anybody, including Senator Coelius."

"Then why is Trebellius coming?"

"First, the guards," Calpurnia said.

Balbinus turned on his heel and marched out the atrium door. At the end of the broad hall he shouted new orders to the captain of his guard. He groaned to himself. With the guards in their quarters, he would be at the mercy of Trebellius. By the close of the day, he knew he would be lying on the floor with a dagger in his throat. He could feel the moving of the Fates, and their movement was not favorable.

Balbinus hurried back to the atrium in time to see Calpurnia slipping a knife into her stola. "You *do* fear Trebellius!" he cried, his lips trembling. "You think he has come to pay a blood debt."

"Nothing of the sort," Calpurnia said. "People intent on murder do not send notes announcing their visits." She secured the knife under her waistband. "But the prudent safeguard the future. One can never see all eventualities."

"Oh, why did I ever listen to Coelius and hire an assassin?" Balbinus flopped onto a couch beside the wine table. He wrapped his chubby fingers around the wine pitcher and poured himself a large cup. He choked it down and filled another. "Now Trebellius is coming to kill me."

Calpurnia plucked a cloth from the table and cleaned wine splashes from Balbinus's tunic. "We must be calm," she said. "Trebellius has other reasons for his visit—"

"What reasons? What possible reasons could Trebellius have for calling?"

"That, my love, I confess I do not know," Calpurnia said.

Balbinus drank more wine. "Could he be trying to discover who hired the assassin?"

"Possibly," Calpurnia said, "but I think not. Trebellius is a soldier. He deals with death every day. Once a threat is eliminated his kind rarely hunts for the political source. He deals with threats as they come."

A servant appeared in the door. "A carriage," he said.

Calpurnia glanced out the shutters. "Three carriages," she said. "Business people—bankers, I would guess."

"Bankers? Trebellius has bankers with him?"

"You can rest easy," Calpurnia said. "Whatever is on Trebellius's mind, it certainly is not murder."

Balbinus rose, wiped his mouth clear of wine, and waited for his guest to arrive.

"Vectis Trebellius," Balbinus said, smiling. "How good of you to visit."

"Gaius Balbinus," Vectis said in acknowledgement, but he spoke quietly and kept his eyes level to make it clear he was not paying a social call. He turned to the woman by the window and felt his mouth drop slightly. He tried to cover his astonishment, but did a poor job.

She smiled briefly and nodded a greeting. "Yes," she said. "I do look like my sister."

In another situation Vectis would surely have commented on the amazing similarity. He could never have imagined anyone even remotely like Neeve, but here, standing before him, was a woman with the same incredible beauty, the same penetrating eyes—though infinitely more calculating—and it seemed, with the same inner strength.

"Care for wine?" Balbinus asked.

Vectis shook his head. It was all he could do to wrench his eyes away from the scheming Calpurnia.

"Please," Balbinus said, gesturing toward a couch. "We can discuss even serious issues seated like civilized—"

"I would rather stand," Vectis said.

Balbinus reached for his cup.

"I am a soldier," Vectis said, "not a diplomat. So let me get straight to the point."

"Yes, certainly," Balbinus said.

"Marcellus Severus is dead because you chose to inform certain Senate members of his association with the blood-drinkers. Senator Titus Severus is filled with rage, and he has sent me to exact retribution."

Balbinus gave Vectis a bewildered look and said, "I ... I don't understand what you—"

"Save your denials for someone who is gullible enough to believe them," Vectis said. "The senator has enormous wealth, and therefore enormous power to see you two wriggling on gibbets in his gardens ... but for the sake of Mistress Calpurnia who is sister to my wife, I have prevailed on him to exact a lesser retribution."

"We have done nothing ... I really am at a loss...."

Vectis ignored Balbinus's babblings.

Calpurnia spoke: "What would this retribution be?" she asked.

"Everything you possess," Vectis said. "You have taken everything from the senator, and he will now take everything from you—your villa here, the property on the Esquiline Hill, your gold at the bank ... everything."

"That is ridiculous," Calpurnia said.

"Ridiculous or not," Vectis said, "those are Senator Severus's terms."

"And if we send you away empty-handed?" Calpurnia asked.

"Then you will suffer the senator's wrath. He will hire a thousand assassins if need be, until your screams rend the farthest corners of the heavens. He has no other use for his wealth—his son has been taken from him."

"I am sorry for the senator," Calpurnia said. "It is a tragic thing to lose a son, but Balbinus is right, we had nothing to do with—"

"Make your denials, but Senator Severus cares not," Vectis said.

Calpurnia moved closer. "Balbinus has many friends in the Senate," she said, "including First Consul, Servius Sulpicius Tertullus, Senator Publius Coelius and—"

"Have you noticed how silent they are of late?" Vectis asked. "They know the emperor is on the verge of breaking his promise not to execute senators. Even a kindly man like Antoninus has his limits. That's why he allowed Senator Severus to sit in the Imperial box, to show his anger."

"You cannot do this to me," Balbinus said in a pleading voice. "I have served others all my life, and now that I finally have acquired modest possessions, you want to take it all away—"

"This whole charade is outrageous!" Calpurnia said in raised voice, interrupting Balbinus. But Vectis knew she was bluffing.

"I will take that wine now," Vectis said. He splashed a swallow or two into a cup. "You have only the time it takes me to finish this drink. Make your decision."

Calpurnia and Balbinus exchanged words out of his hearing, but their urgent whispers told Vectis they were taking his threats seriously. He hadn't actually talked to Senator Severus, but he reasoned it didn't matter. Balbinus and Calpurnia were not about to contact the senator.

"We have decided," Calpurnia said. "We have done nothing wrong and will grant you a handful of hay."

Vectis set his wine down, and without a word, headed for the door. Outside, as he climbed into his carriage, a voice stopped him.

"Let me speak privately to you," Calpurnia said. She moved close to him, closer than appropriate for a woman in Roman society. Vectis could smell the soft perfume on her body as she bent near to whisper her comments. For a moment, her eyes held him captive as she said, "I know you take no pleasure in harming me. You are not that kind of man. But I realize I have trusted the wrong people." She played with the sleeve of his tunic. "All I'm asking is for your mercy ... to leave my villa on the Esquiline, and perhaps a few coins. I would be grateful." She caressed his arm and said, "We are strangers, you and I, but we could become friends ... I truly believe that."

Vectis pulled his arm away. "Senator Severus demands you sign over everything," he said. He looked directly into her eyes to show that he understood her manipulative ways.

Undaunted, she continued: "Vectis," she said, using his name, "surely you would not want—"

"Driver!" Vectis called.

"You win," Calpurnia said abruptly. "Come in and we will talk."

"We have nothing more to talk about," Vectis said. "When I leave, your opportunity leaves with me."

Calpurnia hesitated.

Vectis signaled the driver.

"Bring the senator's bankers," Calpurnia said, as she trudged back to the house.

In the presence of Severus's bankers, Balbinus and Calpurnia signed over everything they owned—their properties, the contents of their residences, their slaves, and every last gold piece in the bank. The bankers affixed their seals and informed the pair they must vacate the villa in three hours. And then, leaving two court officials to ensure their orders were carried out, they left.

"We have nothing," Balbinus moaned. "Absolutely nothing."

"You have your lives," Vectis said, "more than Marcellus has."

"I cannot believe my sister would do this to me," Calpurnia said quietly. "She must have told the senator I betrayed Marcellus to the Senate, when I did nothing of the kind. And now, while I go destitute, she greedily picks over my bones like a vulture." Her eyes burned into Vectis when she asked, "What profit will my sweet sister, Neeve, take from this day?"

"Profit?"

"Yes, profit," Calpurnia said, irritated. "Surely the senator will give her something for carrying out this vile plot against us."

"Actually," Vectis said, half-smiling, "Senator Severus has nothing to do with this."

Calpurnia stared at him.

"Didn't you notice you signed over your holdings to a Severus bank account controlled by your sister?"

Balbinus and Calpurnia exchanged shocked looks.

"Yes, it's true," Vectis said. "Neeve owns everything now."

"My sister ... she ... she ...."

"The Fates," Vectis said, "they continually surprise us, do they not?"

Calpurnia's face turned ashen, and she moved shakily toward a couch. "Neeve owns my villa," she said, "... Balbinus's villa ... she owns it all?"

"Yes, Neeve is now mistress of all that you had," Vectis said. "But have no fear, she is a generous mistress. You may take a horse and a carriage ... no, two horses if you like ... and as much goods as the carriage will allow. No jewelry, of course."

Vectis noticed Calpurnia fingering something in her waistband. He guessed she had concealed a small knife and was now thinking irrational thoughts. He rested his hand on the top of his ten-inch legionary dagger and said, "You haven't much time. You might want to pack."

Calpurnia withdrew her hand. She understood Vectis's gesture. Then dropping her eyes to the floor, she said bitterly, "Now I know why that whore came to my villa on the Esquiline ... she wanted to inspect my property because she had already planned to steal it from me—"

"It's sad when sisters fight," Vectis said, "but if it consoles you any, let me tell you that Neeve has no idea I'm even here." He paused, and then raised his eyebrows. "That's right, she has no idea. But when she hears of her good fortune, she will undoubtedly put it toward a noble cause."

"What noble cause?" Calpurnia asked, her lips curling in a sneer.

"One day you will discover the answer," Vectis said. "But for now you may find comfort in knowing your evil has produced good."

53

The great day of the Triumph had arrived.

Legate General Julius Verus came riding through the crowds, standing in a gilded chariot and crowned with a laurel wreath like a god. He was flanked by hundreds of dancing minstrels, flute-players, and children who flung saffron and flower petals into the air. Before him stretched a thousand Caledonian warriors in chains, the darker-haired ones dyed blond to simulate their ferocious counterparts on Rome's eastern frontier. Behind him rode his officers, and behind them marched three thousand hardened legionaries, the best of Legions II, VI, and XX, who had conquered Britannia's Celtic tribes.

Tethered by his neck, the blood god, Taranis, chief of the Caledonian nation, walked behind General Verus's chariot. Verus had taken care not to bind the giant warrior in a way that would diminish his ferocious appearance. Simple chains around his wrists and a rope on his neck showed him to best advantage. Verus had made a wise decision. At every turn the crowds gasped at the huge, well-muscled warrior, whose long yellow hair flowed to his shoulders, and whose piercing blue eyes raked the onlookers.

The procession had begun at the Aventine Hill, gave a full circuit at the Circus Maximus, passed around the Palatine and through the Arch of Titus, and then entered the Sacred Way that led into the Old Forum. Thousands of toga-clad citizens jostled for position in the streets, craning their heads to catch every movement of the procession. The minstrels played and danced with abandon, and the crowd responded with cheers and whistles. Overhead, on the tiers of balconies, more citizens waved and cast handfuls of flowers onto the unhurried procession below. The countless colonnades that lined the parade route were decked in colorful garlands of wild flowers, and smoke from hundreds of incense stations drifted softly into the air, bestowing blessings on all who inhaled the sacred fragrance.

Neeve and Vectis waited in the boisterous throngs near the Rostra, restrained by a double row of urban soldiers. In the center plaza before the Rostra, a full cohort of the scarlet Praetorians stood, their plumes rising above their helmets, their silvered armor flashing in the sun.

As the general's chariot neared the Rostra, the city's magistrates and equites surged out of the Basilica Aemilia wearing festive robes and waving palms. Then the immense bronze doors to the Senate opened and the great patricians emerged and gathered on the steps to await the conqueror. An enormous roar shook the Old Forum as Legate General Julius Verus's chariot approached the Rostra. And another roar when Antoninus Pius, Pontifex Maximus, Imperator of Rome, suddenly appeared on the ancient podium.

The crowd grew louder.

Praetorian officers escorted General Verus to the Rostra.

The crowd pressed forward.

Neeve felt the crush of hundreds of bodies, citizens packing in tightly, trying to gain a better vantage. They were cheering and straining to hear every word from the various dignitaries who praised the emperor and his favorite general, Julius Verus, but all Neeve could think about was Taranis. At times she would catch glimpses of him through the sea of heads, and she fought back images of her brother being slain on the Rostra—no matter what deal Vectis had made with General Verus.

"Last night I had hope," she shouted in Vectis's ear, "but today I have nothing but dread."

"I confess I feel the same," Vectis replied. "But we did what we could. Verus has long desired land and wealth—it's his one real vice. That's why I went to him. I knew when given the choice between enormous wealth and the momentary satisfaction of killing a barbarian chieftain, he would choose the wealth."

"We have signed everything over to him," Neeve said, "everything Balbinus and Nes owned. He can do as he wishes."

"Yes," Vectis said, "a gamble on our part, but our only option."

"Will he keep his side of the bargain?"

"I don't know," Vectis said. "I wish I did, but I don't. In the time I served with him in Britannia, he had a reputation for vanity, sometimes a temper, but always he was an honorable man."

Neeve was having difficulty hearing Vectis over the cheers and cries of the people. She wondered how they would possibly hear anything from the Rostra. "Sooner or later Roman mobs call for blood," she said.

"They do," Vectis said, "but I'm hoping Verus will satisfy them with something else."

"Satisfy them how?"

"I gave General Verus a reason for releasing Taranis. I told him your brother had spared the lives of the Romans at Outpost Faustina and deserved mercy. I suggested the crowds would respond favorably if he sent Taranis to the auxiliaries for ten years."

"What did General Verus say?"

"He liked the idea. He knew what Taranis had done at Faustina and agreed that ten years in the auxiliaries would be fair treatment. He said that legions always need aggressive warriors to lead their auxiliaries, and who better to attack Rome's enemies than the great blood god himself?"

Neeve hated it when the Romans called Taranis a blood god, but she said nothing. If General Verus wanted to call him a blood god or anything else, she didn't care. The only thing that mattered now was Taranis's life.

A sudden blast of horns dropped the volume of the crowd considerably. Four Praetorians led Taranis toward the Rostra. He no longer had the rope around his neck, but they had bound his hands behind his back, readying him for execution. They stopped at the bottom of the steps that led up to the Rostra, and waited.

A heavy man with a booming voice began to speak, a professional orator, a man well capable of telling the dramatic story of Legate General Julius Verus and his arrival in Britannia. The general found the province in chaos, the forts overrun by ferocious Celtic tribes, and Roman soldiers scattered and fleeing for their lives. At that dire moment, the booming voice intoned, the great General Verus gathered vestiges of Rome's legions and went out to meet the vast numbers of Brigantes tribesmen, tribal warriors that had been killing and looting their way through the province. Within weeks the brilliant general had defeated the Brigantes and restored order to central Britannia, as far north as Emperor Antoninus' Wall.

The orator paused, and in the silence, he swept his hands dramatically through the air as if he were painting a picture, saying in full voice, "But General Verus had yet to cross the northern barrier."

The crowd pressed closer, listening.

With that he described the Caledonian hordes waiting beyond the Wall, how they had destroyed every army the Empire had sent against them, and how they had left the Roman outposts and forts along the Wall in smoking ruins ….

All alone, ignoring the danger, the general marched his legions beyond the Wall. He knew that many soldiers were terrified of the Caledonians, not because they stood a head taller, or because their heavy swords could split a legionary shield in two. They feared the Caledonians, the orator boomed, because of their leader … Taranis, the blood god.

That was the cue for the Praetorians to start up the stairs, bringing with them the tall, yellow-haired barbarian.

The orator continued, telling the story of General Verus rescuing Legion XX, his brilliance in battle, and his capture of the celebrated blood god. Then he paused dramatically, gestured behind him and cried: "I give you Rome's greatest living soldier: Legate General Gnaeus Julius Verus!"

The Old Forum exploded as General Verus strode toward the marble balustrade. He thanked the emperor, the senators, his matchless legionaries, the gods, and everyone else he could think of … and lastly he thanked the people of Rome whose strength he always took into battle. Then he likened his war with "Taranis the Blood God" to the divine Julius Caesar's war against "Vercingetorix the Invincible."

Neeve was having difficulty focusing on Verus's self-serving speech, but the people in the forum hung on every word. Rome's greatest living general had saved their Empire from the barbarians.

Finally, with two Praetorians on either arm, Taranis was brought forward. He looked even larger on the Rostra, his huge body dwarfing the general walking toward him. Even the Praetorian Guardsmen seemed like miniature soldiers.

A hush fell on the ancient plaza as General Verus unsheathed his sword, the blade sliding out of its scabbard with a metallic sound, cold and deadly. The Praetorians pulled back Taranis's arms to expose his chest.

"No, no ..." Neeve moaned, her words barely a whisper.

Vectis put his arm around Neeve, but his eyes never moved from the scene unfolding on the Rostra.

General Verus raised his sword for the downward plunge.

Neeve closed her eyes.

The general paused.

He turned to the crowd and said loudly, "I am the arm of Rome, a servant of the people of Rome. I do not slay this man for my own pleasure, but for the pleasure of the people of Rome."

The crowds cheered.

"If I slay him now, the people's pleasure is fleeting. But if I bind him over to the amphitheater—which many have begged me to do—the people may delight in him for months, until at last he tumbles headlong into the bloody sands, where he deserves to be."

A cacophony of sound rose from the Old Forum. Men were shouting, trying to influence those around them.

"Which will you choose? The Rostra or the sands?"

"The sands," the people chanted. "The sands."

Neeve turned to Vectis. "What does this mean?"

Vectis blew out in relief. "Your brother will not die. Verus is binding him over to a gladiatorial school."

"Taranis ... a gladiator? But General Verus promised to send him to the auxiliaries. He ... he's breaking his word!"

"He is," Vectis said. "But at least he's sparing his life."

"Sparing his life! Gladiators rarely last a month."

"I know," Vectis said, squeezing her closer. "I know."

54

The next day Neeve and Vectis visited Taranis at a holding pen across from the Flavian amphitheater. General Verus had not yet transferred the Caledonian commanders to the gladiatorial school but would do so by that evening.

Neeve screwed up her nose as they entered the cramped, low-roofed building—a chain of holding pens for goats. The smell was overpowering. She followed Vectis down the narrow passageways which had only occasional slits in the roof to allow in light. Except for the goats, the building seemed empty.

"Over here," Vectis said, pointing down a corridor to a more brightly lit area. Twenty guards had crowded into one of the pens and were casting bets.

"I want to hear you say my brother's name," a voice shouted. "You will crawl to me and beg my forgiveness. Only then will the whipping stop."

Neeve could hear other voices—laughing and grunting—guards calling out their wagers. They were betting on the number of lashes it would take before the man broke and begged for forgiveness. As she neared, she could see it was her brother Taranis, and her breath caught in her throat. She shot a glance at an officer standing alongside Taranis's pen, and she made straight for him, her anger boiling. He was gazing through one of the windows that overlooked a courtyard, the opposite direction from the rowdy soldiers inside the holding cell.

"Are you in charge?" Neeve demanded.

The soldier eyed her as he turned, then shook his head. "I am second officer and translator," he said. "The ranking officer is in the holding pen, exerting his authority." His voice had an edge to it, as if the whole process infuriated him.

Neeve heard a lash.

And then a nasty voice. "Mamercus Nepos Falco," the voice cried. "I want to hear you say my brother's name."

Another lash.

"Mamercus Nepos Falco," the voice shrieked. "Say it!"

Neeve took several steps toward the pen, but felt a hand restraining her. It was Vectis. "Don't say a word," he said, and from the seriousness in his eyes, she knew he was worried that the situation could spin out of control if she barged forward angrily. And she was definitely angry, seeing her brother bent over a rail with blood running off his back. She tried to breathe deeply and slowly. Better to let Vectis handle things. He definitely had the cooler head. She ran her eyes over the pathetic, little man with the whip. He looked exactly like that weasel Nepos she had known at Outpost Faustina in Britannia, only younger.

"Are you Officer Nepos?" Vectis was now inside the holding pen.

"*Senior* Officer, Manius Nepos Falco," the man said, mopping his brow. Evidently, whipping was hard work.

"Vectis Trebellius Quadratus," Vectis said formally, "past military tribune for Legate Julius Verus in Londinium."

Nepos bobbed his head, impressed. "Your arrival is timely," he said. "This is the blood god himself, Taranis—"

"Yes, I can see that," Vectis said.

"This barbarian murdered my brother in Britannia, and I am exacting my revenge before he passes from my custody."

"And well you should," Vectis said. "This barbarian has murdered countless Romans in their beds." He glanced across at the other Caledonian commanders who had been placed in an adjoining cell, and then returned his eyes to Taranis. "But you need to exercise care with this one."

"I am," Nepos said.

"That's wise. Because Legate Julius Verus has invested much in Taranis."

"I understand completely."

"Good," Vectis said. "Legate Verus can be quite exacting. Men who have mistreated his greatest trophy from Britannia have lost rank, been put under the whip, and even suffered dragging."

Nepos's face changed.

"Verus desperately wants the blood god healthy and strong when he performs in the amphitheater, and he would not take kindly if someone accidentally damaged his prize." Vectis grinned and said, "A terrifying Taranis in the amphitheater will not lessen the general's reputation, if you take my meaning."

"I do," Nepos said, "and I thank you for your caution." He motioned to his whip and said, "No iron tips, just leather. Produces the desired pain, but will not seriously injure the general's prize."

"Wise," Vectis said, nodding. He turned to leave, and then stopped. "You say your brother served in Britannia? I think I knew him when I was prefect of the five outposts above the Antonine Wall."

"You were the prefect?"

"Yes, headquartered at Faustina."

"Faustina!" Nepos's face registered shock. "That is the exact place my brother was posted ... his name was *Mamercus* Nepos Falco ... did you—"

"Ah, yes ... Mamercus Nepos ... yes, I remember him well. He was my supply officer. Unfortunate death. I watched him die."

"You watched—"

"A tragic thing," Vectis said, dropping his voice. "I am certain you've seen it as well ... men who run in the face of the enemy ... not uncommon. Your brother fled the outpost with thirty others in hopes of saving his life, but the Caledonians gobbled up their little band."

"No!" Nepos shouted. "This is not true! My brother died a courageous—"

"I am sorry," Vectis said. "Plenty of officers witnessed his ... well, I will not call it a cowardly end. As soldiers, you and I know how difficult it can be at times. Faustina was minutes from destruction, and every soldier out there thought his life was over … I confess I too had little hope."

"No," Nepos said, his eyes darting around the faces of the soldiers. "My brother was … I refuse to believe this is true."

"Mamercus Nepos was an honorable man," Vectis said. "One cowardly event does not tarnish an entire lifetime."

"No, this cannot be," Nepos said almost to himself.

"Plenty of witnesses," Vectis repeated.

Nepos stared at the rough wooden flooring of the cell for long seconds, and then his shoulders sagged and the whip dropped from his hand. Without a word, and without looking up, Senior Officer Manius Nepos Falco headed for the door.

In the hour before the guards arrived from the gladiatorial school, Neeve was allowed to talk with her brother. The second officer placed Taranis in a cell by himself, and Neeve spoke to him through the bars. She was pleased that the officer had stepped away, giving them privacy.

"The gods are with us," Neeve said, formally, almost awkwardly.

"Even here," her brother replied, taking her hand. He glanced over at Vectis who was standing on the other side of the cell. "Every time I see that Roman," he said, "he surpasses my expectations. A husband worthy of you."

It was a comment she hardly expected Taranis to say, especially when he used the word, husband, and it melted her heart.

They talked about the battle, about her fears of Taranis's death, and about Cronn. It had been so long since she had mentioned Cronn's name that her eyes turned glassy when she thought about her giant protector. She told Taranis about the shipwreck and about Sammonicus—his feeble robbery attempt on the shoreline and his encounter with the Asclepion priests. It felt good to hear her brother laugh. Nes had survived, he knew, but he was surprised to hear about her scheming ways.

"I'm sorry about the arena," Neeve said, as the soldiers came to take him away. "Vectis tried to have you assigned to the Roman auxiliaries, but it seems—"

"The common warriors are being sent there," Taranis said. "They will live a decent life, and that is sufficient for me and the other commanders."

"But you and the commanders are all being sent to a gladiator school," she said. "You will be gladiatorial slaves,"

"I am what I choose to be," Taranis said, "and I do not choose to be a slave of Rome."

Neeve looked at her brother, not certain he understood. "They will force you to fight trained gladiators," she said. "These men fight to the death."

"Grasshoppers," he said.

"No," Neeve said in an earnest voice, "they are powerful men, trained to kill."

Taranis patted her hand. "I have watched Rome's premier gladiators training north of the city," he said. "Believe me, they are grasshoppers."

As they led him away, he said, "They make money for every victory. A superior gladiator can win his freedom. And you need not worry; I will be what I choose to be."

Neeve signaled Sammonicus, who was waiting with the carriage at the end of the street.

"Your brother seemed in good spirits," Vectis said as they stepped into the carriage.

"He doesn't understand," Neeve said. "His warriors are being released to the auxiliaries and that's all he cares about."

"What about the gladiator school?"

"He's not worried. Grasshoppers, he calls them."

"But you fear for him."

"Yes, I do, greatly. Don't you?"

"In truth, when I look at your brother, I do fear. I fear for the poor gladiators that will face him."

Later, as they neared their villa, Neeve said, "Maybe it's time we attended to our own lives."

Vectis gazed at her with a question in his face.

She returned his look.

"Mistress Trebellius," Vectis said, smiling. "Could you be talking about children?"

Sammonicus turned but immediately looked away when his mistress caught his eye.

Neeve pushed closer to Vectis. "The sleeping rooms at the villa are always a good place to talk," she said.

55

Senator Titus Severus sat before the shrine to the god, Asclepios, making supplications. It was a small shrine he had set up in his villa, but he attended it regularly. He glanced at the door. His personal servant had entered bearing a dispatch message.

Severus frowned, wondering why his senior aide would interrupt him with a letter of condolence. He already had a pile of them in his library.

"Is this something important?" Severus asked, motioning for his servant to approach.

"I believe you will find it so," the servant said.

Severus nodded his consent to remove the cloth covering. Inside was a parchment square made of treated goatskin and framed in light walnut.

"From Mistress Neeve mapmaker," he said, handing it to the senator.

The old man gazed down at a drawing of himself, and of Marcellus hovering over his shoulder like a spirit, only his son had an easy smile, full of life. The senator didn't know how long he stared at the drawing, but eventually he rose and made his way to the library. There he placed the drawing in the empty space on the wall, and he offered up a prayer to Chrestus.

56

Balbinus lashed the mules, but the stupid brutes had minds of their own. "Trebellius said we could have horses," he complained, "and what did the court officials allow us? Two miserable mules!"

"We can exchange them at the next station," Calpurnia said.

"We have lost everything," Balbinus moaned. "We have enough finances for a week, maybe two. Whatever shall we do?"

"You keep lamenting our condition," Calpurnia said. "I too felt that way, but now we must look forward. Setbacks are the landscape of the great. Do you think Alexander bewailed his situation when his father died? No, he saw it as an opportunity to do greater things than his father ever dreamed."

"Alexander had his father's army," Balbinus said. "I have nothing but this carriage."

"You have me," Calpurnia said.

Balbinus looked at her and shook his head. "Why should you want me when I have nothing? I'm not an utter fool. In a day, a week, perhaps, I shall never see you again."

"You underestimate yourself," she said, brushing a stray hair out of his eyes. "There is something about a senator I cannot resist."

Balbinus glanced behind him at his senator's toga and snorted. "I once had a dream," he said, "but now I have two mules and a carriage."

Calpurnia moved closer. "I intended to tell you later," she said, "but I can see that now might be a good time."

"Tell me what?"

"You think I'm a spendthrift," she said, "but there is a villa in North Africa, a rather large villa, with servants and vineyards and rolling farmlands, and it is owned by one Gaius Balbinus."

"I own a villa?"

"Technically, the owner is *Senator* Gaius Balbinus," she said. "Sellers grant credit to senators more easily, so I enhanced your station. I purchased the villa some months ago and have few payments remaining." She smiled. "When we arrive in North Africa we will be accepted in the highest circles. You can imagine how easy it will be for a former senator to gain credits from provincial bankers for whatever needs he might have. North Africa is a distant province, but in time, I think, we shall build enormous wealth."

"But I am not a senator."

"How do they know?" She kissed him softly on the lips.

His brow furrowed. "If you managed all this, why would you not simply leave me and take possession of the villa yourself?"

"Because, my love, I told you long ago, in the stars we find our destinies and the stars have led me to you." She kissed him again, this time more sensually. "And besides," she said, "the bankers never allowed me to put your assets in my name."

ABOUT THE AUTHOR

William V. Crockett is a writer, scholar, and professor in New York. A graduate of University of Winnipeg, Princeton Theological Seminary, and University of Glasgow (Ph.D.), he has lectured and written extensively on theological issues. With his expertise in classical antiquity, Crockett is making his mark as a novelist. His two novels, *Worlds Apart* and *A Celt in Rome* are set in the second century Roman Empire. He lives with his wife, Karen, in rustic Sussex County, New Jersey, where he is hard at work on a modern thriller, *The Apocalypse Gene*, set at Yale University.

Made in the USA
Lexington, KY
03 October 2012

17855491R00296